THE
YEAR'S BEST
MILITARY SF &
SPACE OPERA

★

THE YEAR'S BEST MILITARY SF & SPACE OPERA

★

Edited By

DAVID AFSHARIRAD

THE YEAR'S BEST MILITARY SF AND SPACE OPERA

Baen Publishing Enterprises
P.O. Box 1403
Riverdale, NY 10471
www.baen.com

ISBN: 978-1-4767-8058-0

Cover art by Sam Kennedy

First Baen printing, June 2015

Distributed by Simon & Schuster
1230 Avenue of the Americas
New York, NY 10020

Library of Congress Cataloging-in-Publication Data

The year's best military SF and space opera / edited by David Afsharirad.
     pages cm.
   ISBN 978-1-4767-8058-0 (paperback)
1. Science fiction, American. 2. Imaginary wars and battles--Fiction. 3. Space warfare--Fiction. 4. American fiction--21st century I. Afsharirad, David, editor.
 PS648.S3Y36 2015
 813'.0876208--dc23
                                        2015009359

Printed in the United States of America

10 9 8 7 6 5 4 3 2 1

TABLE OF CONTENTS

★

STORY COPYRIGHTS

YEAR'S BEST MILITARY SCIENCE FICTION AND SPACE OPERA

YOU DECIDE WHO WINS!

Other anthologies tell you which stories were the year's best—*we're letting you decide which of these you liked best.* Baen Books is pleased to announce the inaugural Year's Best Military Science Fiction and Space Opera Award. The award honors the best of the best in this grand storytelling tradition, and its winner will receive a plaque and an additional $500.00.

To vote, go to
http://baen.com/yearsbestaward2014

Registration with Baen Ebooks is required. You may also send a postcard or letter with the name of your favorite story from this volume and its author to Baen Books Year's Best Award, P.O. Box 1188, Wake Forest, NC 27587. Voting closes August 31, 2015. Entries received after voting closes will not be counted.

So hurry, hurry, hurry! The winner will be announced at Dragoncon in Atlanta, held over Labor Day Weekend 2015.

Acknowledgements

My thanks fist and foremonst to all the contributors,
and to the editors of the publications in which these stories first
appeared. Also to David Drake for a fine introduction.
And to Tony Daniel, Hank Davis, and Toni Weisskopf, for their
expert guidance in bringing this anthology to publication.

THE YEAR'S BEST MILITARY SF & SPACE OPERA

★

PREFACE

★

by David Afsharirad

EVERY FEW YEARS some arts reporter or Respected Author™ comes along and writes an opinion piece declaring the short story either dead or dying. And we fall for it every time. News outlets around the country and on the Web bemoan the decline (and eventual death) of that once-lauded American form. You'd think that the regularity with which this particular article (and it *is* the same article, no matter who writes it) circulates would tip us to the dubious nature of these claims. But each time at least some of us are certain that *this* will be the time. That, sure, we were wrong before, but *now?* Now the short story really is on its last legs.

Perhaps this is true in literary fiction, though last I checked Tobias Wolff was still in top form and publishing regularly. And it may well be that that rarest of birds, the mainstream short story, is on the endangered species list, though George Saunders' *Tenth of December* debuted at #3 on *The New York Times* hardcover bestseller list in 2013, and if that's not mainstream, I don't know what is. It's an indisputable fact that there's not much short fiction being published in the Western genre these days . . . but that can't be what they're talking about, right?

Regardless, one place that the rumors of the short story's death have always been *wildly* exaggerated is in the field of science fiction. True, we may no longer live in the times when science fiction pulps clogged the corner newsstand, but any arts reporter or Respected Author™, no

3

matter how jaded, would be hard pressed to look around at the various print magazines, online outlets, and original anthologies published every year and declare that the science fiction short story is in anything but excellent health. A hale and hearty beast it is!

Science fiction was born in the pulps, and existed in short story (or novelette or novella) form for years before moving to the novel. Yes, there were exceptions to this (*Frankenstein* and the works of Jules Verne and the scientific romances of H.G. Wells—please do not write me letters listing science fiction novels to prove me wrong). And true, science fiction novels were being serialized in those same pulps almost from the get-go. But even still, the history of science fiction as we know it today is largely a history of its best short stories. More than any other genre, SF is defined by its greatest short fiction.

Golden Age writers like Asimov, Clarke, and Heinlein paved the way for excellence in short SF in the pages of John W. Campbell's *Astounding*. And it was Heinlein and Bradbury who brought science fiction (some would say kicking and screaming) into the mainstream by selling their short stories to "slick" magazines like *The Saturday Evening Post*, *Mademoiselle*, and *Collier's*.

By the 1960s, the Golden Age was over—but not so the era of top quality short science fiction. The New Wave continued the short story tradition, with authors such as Samuel R. Delany, Ursula K. Le Guin, and James Tiptree, Jr. bringing new perspectives to the genre. The New Wave, like the Golden Age before it, grew out of a short story tradition, with most tracing the beginning of the movement to the British magazine *New Worlds*, edited by Michael Moorcock. Today, when seminal works of the New Wave are discussed, it is not a novel that is most often first mentioned, but Harlan Ellison's groundbreaking anthology *Dangerous Visions*. (This then leads to mentioning *Again Dangerous Visions*, which leads to complaints about *The Last Dangerous Visions*, the most famous unreleased short story anthology of all time, I think it's fair to say.)

But during this same era, publishing was changing. The paperback was outpacing the magazines, and science fiction writers turned to the novel format to explore the stories they wanted to tell. (If I had to put money on it, I'd wager that this is when the first of those "The Short Story is Dying" articles started circulating.) But the SF magazines held on while so many other fiction periodicals fizzled. (The big three,

Asimov's, *Analog*, and *The Magazine of Fantasy and Science Fiction*, are still going strong today; you'll find stories from each between the covers of this book.) And new anthologies edited by the likes of Groff Conklin helped short SF transition to the new paperback format.

But what about today?

"I just read an article saying that the short story is dying," you say because you have not been paying attention to what I've written. Or perhaps you have been paying attention but don't believe me because the article you read was by a Respected Author™ and I am just a lowly editor.

Well, ignore him, I say! The science fiction short story is not dead, is not dying, and—dare I say it?—will never die. If anything, sitting in the second decade of the 21st century, we're spoiled for choice. Look around the internet and you'll find dozens of outlets for science fiction short stories. Numerous original anthologies are brought out every year, by both small presses and big publishing houses. And, as mentioned, the venerable digests are still around and putting out quality stories, month after month. They are joined by other print magazines that are younger but of no less quality.

In fact, with so much short science fiction being published every week/month/year, it can be hard to sort the good from the bad, the excellent from the not-for-me-thanks. Sadly, Sturgeon's Law still applies in the science-fictional-sounding 21st century. I fear, like the cockroach, it shall always be with us. For those of you unfamiliar with the term, Sturgeon's Law states, "ninety percent of science fiction is crap." (The corollary, "but so is ninety percent of everything" is useful to remember.)

And in that ten percent of quality (or at least non-crap) science fiction, there are going to be stories that don't appeal to certain readers. A story that changes one person's life causes another to fling the book across the room. Sometimes you want an obscure, mind-bending piece of flash fiction with an ambiguous ending (or at least I do; maybe I'm weird), but other times you want some good old-fashioned space opera. You want a story of military derring-do. You want a tale that makes you feel like a kid again, reading Edgar Rice Burroughs under the covers after you were supposed to be asleep. A well-written story that makes you think, yes—but that also lets its hair down and has some fun. A story with a beginning, middle, and end, by God!

For example: How about a private eye on the trail of a conspiracy on the lush jungle Venus we wanted, not the poisonous uninhabitable Venus we got? Or a man bent on beating a robot to the last untouched hunk of rock in the solar system? Or how about an ice miner determined to throw off the shackles of a repressive corporation and write his own destiny? Or a young Warrant Officer tasked with defending a planet from an insectoid alien menace?

"Do these stories, and stories like them, still exist?" you ask. "And if so, where can I find them?"

I'm glad you asked.

They do still exist, and in great number. Where can you find them? All over. I don't think that there was a single anthology or magazine, whether online or in print, that I read last year that didn't include at least some of this type of story.

So, you could go out, like I did, and read (or at least skim) everything you can get your hands on—*Asimov's, Lightspeed, Clarkesworld, Analog,* every themed and tribute anthology out there, every single-author collection, every ebook exclusive, et cetera—separating the wheat from the chaff and finding the stories that speak to you.

Or, you could do what you've already done and buy *Year's Best Military Science Fiction and Space Opera.* (If you are reading this in the bookstore, please don't crease the spine until you do buy the book—and you *will* want to buy the book.) Herein, submitted for your approval and for your reading pleasure, are the most thrilling, pulse-pounding, and thought-provoking stories of the past year. Stories of future military men and women, space opera on a grand scale, and edge-of-your-seat adventure tales in the pulp tradition. Stories that prove that the short story isn't dead, isn't dying, and that the Golden Age of the science fiction short story is the ever-present now.

Excelsior!

—David Afsharirad
Austin, TX
February, 2015

Oh, just one more thing:

I can't promise that you'll love every story in this book. Some will strike you as better than others. Such is the subjective nature of taste.

I've got my favorites (and wouldn't you like to know what they are!), and you'll have yours. And I'm curious, after you put the book down, what story did *you* consider worthy of the superlative of this volume's title? Which of these fifteen tales really was the year's best?

Luckily, I won't have to wonder for long; you're going to tell me. Baen Books is giving you the opportunity to get in on the action. That's right: *you* pick The Year's Best Military Science Fiction and Space Opera Story.

To find out how you can cast your vote, go to http://www.baen.com /yearsbestaward2014. But don't hesitate! Voting closes August 31, 2015. (If you are reading this in some distant future, I apologize that it's too late for you to weigh in on this year's award. Also, are flying cars and personal jetpacks a thing yet, or are we still waiting?)

The winner will be announced at DragonCon in September and will receive a cash prize and a plaque.

Pleasant reading and happy voting.

—DA

EXCITEMENT! ADVENTURE! SCIENCE FICTION!
My Personal Look at Space Opera and Military SF
★
by David Drake

1.

FIRST THE GROUND RULES: it's a lot of work to edit an anthology, as I know from having edited many of them myself. It's therefore important to me to say that I did *not* do the work on this one. David Afsharirad is the editor, and I believe his (our) publisher, Toni Weisskopf, was looking over his shoulder. My only involvement is to write this introduction and to read the stories as a fan.

I'm writing the introduction *as* a fan. I haven't studied SF as an academic would: I'm simply an antiquarian who's read quite a lot of science fiction over the years. This is an overview from an informed layman, and you may well decide that the layman's viewpoint is very quirky.

The main point I'd like readers—you—to consider is this: Military SF and space opera are often grouped together, as they are here. Edges blur, and many writers work in both genres (I do myself).

At core, however, the categories are quite different in tone, and they came from different directions. Icthyosaurs were not early porpoises.

Now, on to the work.

2.

BEFORE THE ADVENT of dedicated SF magazines (the traditional date is April, 1926, the first issue of *Amazing Stories*) most SF stories were economic/political. (Please add 'in the opinion of David Drake' to any similar statement hereafter.) There was little or no SF adventure, except (sometimes) in the case of Lost World stories.

A typical SF story from *Argosy* in 1910, say, might involve someone discovering how to transmute lesser materials into gold and what that does to the world's economic system. Another form of SF story (generally at book length) involved a traveller who found a Utopia and described how it differed from current political systems.

Stories of these sorts go back a very long time. We have Lucian of Samosata's *True History*, describing among other things a voyage to the Moon, but people tend to forget that Lucian (in the 2nd century AD) was satirizing earlier—and in some cases *much* earlier—travellers' tales.

There was quite a lot of future war fiction also, but I would call it basically political fiction. The writers were trying to swing the public toward appreciation of a new weapon (the tank in Wells' *The Land Ironclads*; the submarine in Doyle's *The Danger*) or a revised military system (Chesney's *The Battle of Dorking* or Kipling's *The Army of a Dream*, one of the few stories of genuinely militaristic—not military— science fiction).

I'm tempted to make an exception for Griffith's 1901 *A Honeymoon in Space* in which the British hero's spaceship routs the armed forces of other planets with quickfirers and Maxim guns. He also swoops across the United States in aid of a contemporary political party, however, which appears to me to better display Griffith's real interest.

3.

FOR ME, space opera started with E.E. Smith's *The Skylark of Space*, published in *Amazing Stories* in 1928 but written a good decade earlier. The heroes invent a space ship and zoom about the galaxy, meeting and interacting with alien races. There are wars and battles, but the focus isn't on what war does to individuals or society itself. (Except that if you're fighting an alien race bent on genocide, it's better to win. I don't think Smith considered that a question for debate, any more than I do.)

Further, the only economic point I remember involves the hero bringing back a platinum asteroid—to destroy the market for platinum jewelry. That will free scientists who need non-reactive crucibles from having to bid against wealthy women who want the metal for its scarcity value.

Smith focused on fun and adventure. He was extremely popular in his day, and he created the genre of space opera: adventure on far planets. When I was 13 I loved *Skylark* and Smith's later space opera series. The line-by-line writing causes me problems when I reread the books as an adult, but they remain exciting fun.

4.

EARLY SPACE OPERA tended to be multi-cultural and multi-racial. No, it wouldn't be politically correct today (if only for gender portrayals), but it was written by people who were trying to say something positive about how intelligent people (from Earth, Mars, or wherever) ought to behave toward one another.

Real Military SF appeared in the 1920s also. Here the tone was often quite different—and quite unpleasant, even to a reader as non-PC as I am. One strand of this MSF grows from Turn-of-the-Century Yellow Peril novels; now the Yellow Hordes had airships, and they were frequently led by Bolshevik super-scientists.

At its best, this genre was racist and xenophobic. The stories in which the villains have enlisted Africans as cannon-fodder are like nothing else I've seen, apart from some American Nazi publications which I filed when I was a book page at the University of Iowa Library in the 1960s.

5.

THE 1940s brought Military SF stories which focused on how battles were fought, what sort of men became soldiers (pretty universally men, I think), and how soldiers interacted with civilian society. These stories were about war and battle, not about race and ideology. Their appearance was presumably a result of World War II itself.

In part this was because *everybody* had become interested in war: professional writers choose subjects which interest potential readers. Bluefish chase sardines, and porpoises chase bluefish. 1943's *Clash by Night* (by the married couple of Henry Kuttner and C.L. Moore) is such a story. Neither writer had any military experience at the time (Kuttner was later drafted), but they created a masterpiece of battle and warriors.

A few stories, though, came from the writers' own experience. I strongly suspect that was the case in 1949 with *The Rocketeers Have Shaggy Ears* by Keith Bennett, though I never met him to ask. In form *Rocketeers* is a standard pulp adventure (a band of soldiers fights its way through murderous jungle and hostile natives) but tiny details and the whole *feel* of the story convince me that Bennett had been an artilleryman on the jungle islands of the Southwest Pacific.

I can't think of a story which better shows (not tells) the exhaustion of a long exposure at the sharp end. Notice how the soldiers start out talking about women, but later talk about food. By the end they don't talk about anything, just scan the terrain with tired eyes as they trudge forward, their guns ready.

The Last Objective by Paul Carter appeared in 1946, but Carter wrote the story while he was still in the Navy; his commanding officer had to approve it before it could be sent to *Astounding*. It's just as good as *Rocketeers*, but it's different in every other fashion.

Carter describes wholly militarized societies and a war which won't end until every human being is dead. Rather than viewing this world clinically from the outside, Carter focuses on a single ship and the varied personalities who make up its crew. (The vessel is tunnelling through the continental plate rather than floating on the sea, but in story terms that's a distinction without a difference.)

Carter is pretty sure that his CO didn't actually read the story before approving it. My experience with military officers leads me to believe that he's right, though it's also possible that his CO simply didn't understand the story's horrific implications.

6.

I LOOK ON the immediate Post-World-War-II period as the Golden Age of space opera, but at least in part that may be because I cut my teeth on the SF appearing then. Poul Anderson started out writing 'lead novels' for the pulps which were the right length to be reprinted as one half of an Ace Double book; he went on to write serials for the top digest magazines, which then came out as full-length books, sometimes in hardcover. Poul's later work was more thoughtful and complex than his pulp adventure, but it was still fun.

Keith Laumer, Anderson's younger contemporary, wrote a different kind of space opera: sometimes broadly humorous, often political (bureaucratic) satire—but occasionally giving the reader an unexpected emotional kick. Keith was less concerned with science and engineering than Poul, but he was more skilled (and enthusiastic) at writing action scenes.

A wide range of people wrote space opera in the '50s and '60s; Anderson and Laumer weren't even the ends of the continuum. That said, between them they do illustrate how rich the space opera of the period was.

And to my taste, they were the best of a very good lot.

7.

A PAIR OF EXCELLENT and very influential Military SF novels came out within a few months of one another in 1959: *Dorsai!* by Gordon R. Dickson, and *Starship Troopers* by Robert A. Heinlein. Both men were skilled, successful writers. (Heinlein had helped editor John W. Campbell to create the Golden Age of SF.) In these novels they were at the top of their game.

Dorsai and *Troopers* defined the Military SF field when they appeared, and they summed up the thirty-odd years of MSF development that had come before.

8.

THE MOST IMPORTANT THING that's happened to space opera in the '70s and later is that non-print media have overwhelmed the field. Even a writer as good and as successful as Dave Weber hasn't had the impact that *Star Wars* did in 1977, and earlier yet, *Star Trek* tie-in novels had begun to glut the market for adventure SF. (Tie-ins to the *Dungeons and Dragons* game had a huge impact on adventure fantasy at the same time, but that's outside my present scope.)

Star Wars and *Star Trek* were both classic space opera milieus. Jack Williamson or Edmond Hamilton could have written either series in the '30s, and in fact Hamilton's wife, Leigh Brackett—who wrote some of the best space opera of the '40s—scripted *The Empire Strikes Back*. The plots weren't new, but the format was.

9.

IN THE EARLY '70s Joe Haldeman, Jerry Pournelle, and I began writing Military SF. We weren't better than Heinlein and Dickson, but we were combat veterans, something which had been very rare in MSF until we appeared. (The only exception I can think of was Keith Bennett, and that's my deduction from his story . . . which constitutes circular reasoning.)

Note that there were many SF writers who were combat veterans— C.M. Kornbluth, one of the best SF writers ever, fought in the of the b Battle of the Bulge—but they didn't write *Military* SF. Gordy spent his military service mowing lawns in California, and Heinlein's brief service as a naval officer ended in 1930. (The Navy refused to grant him a security clearance when he wished to return at the beginning of World War II.)

The new thing which I think the three of us brought to Military SF (I'm speaking from the inside now, and that's harder than you might think) is a view of the pointless brutality of war. Nowadays everybody knows that, but at the time *Analog's* reviewer called me a pornographer of violence (to my face as well as in print), and I heard Jerry called worse things. I suspect the same happened to Joe when he was in the Iowa Writers' Workshop, but I wasn't there to hear it.

Joe, Jerry and I changed the field so completely that most people today don't realize there was a change. (When I took Introduction to Geology in 1966, Continental Drift was a hypothesis; a decade earlier it had been an *absurd* hypothesis invented by a meteorologist.) Now you don't have to be a combat veteran to describe the pointless brutality of war, any more than you have to experience combat to describe its horror or to show cynical contempt for politicians and war aims.

It's unusual for people who haven't seen combat to understand what that brutality does to the soldier, however. A few Military SF writers did describe this in their fiction without having been there themselves. Paul Carter, whom I've mentioned above, was one. Two other exceptions are Richard C. Meredith and Barry Malzberg. Barry wrote the novella *Final War* and as editor bought Meredith's *We All Died at Breakaway Station*. Though all three had seen military service, nobody had been shooting at them at the time.

10.

YOU DON'T HAVE TO be a swashbuckling adventurer to write exciting space opera. You don't need to be a combat veteran (or even a veteran) to write excellent Military SF. (I haven't written a better story than *Clash by Night*.)

As a reader, all you can demand of either genre is that it tell a good story, the same thing you would ask of any other type of fiction. Every once in a while, though, you may stumble over a real truth here, one that you wouldn't have found in other genres.

I hope that you find that to be case in this anthology, or perhaps in some of the stories and authors I've mentioned above.

—Dave Drake
david-drake.com

CODENAME: DELPHI

★

by Linda Nagata

Karin Larsen is a handler. For eight hours a day, she sits in front of a bank of monitors, overseeing battlefield activity remotely with a series of drones, and directs military personnel half a world away. At times, it feels like a video game. Only when she makes a mistake, people die— and there's no reset button on reality.

"**VALDEZ,** you need to slow down," Karin Larsen warned, each syllable crisply pronounced into a mic. "Stay behind the seekers. If you overrun them, you're going to walk into a booby trap."

Five thousand miles away from Karin's control station, Second Lieutenant Valdez was jacked up on adrenaline and in a defiant mood. *"Negative!"* she said, her voice arriving over Karin's headphones. *"Delphi, we've got personnel down and need to move fast. This route scans clear. I am not waiting for the seekers to clear it again."*

The battleground was an ancient desert city. Beginning at sunset, firefights had flared up all across its tangled neighborhoods and Valdez was right that her squad needed to advance—but not so fast that they ran into a trap.

"The route is *not* clear," Karin insisted. "The last overflight to scan this alley was forty minutes ago. Anything could have happened since then."

Karin's worksite was an elevated chair within a little room inside a

17

secure building. She faced a curved monitor a meter-and-a-half high, set an easy reach away. Windows checkered its screen, grouped by color-codes representing different clients. The windows could slide, change sequence, and overlap, but they could never completely hide one another; the system wouldn't allow it. This was Karin's interface to the war.

Presently centered onscreen were two gold-rimmed windows, each displaying a video feed captured by an aerial seeker: palm-sized drones equipped with camera eyes, audio pickups, and chemical sensors. The seekers flew ahead of Valdez and her urban infantry squad, one at eye level and the other at an elevation of six meters, scouting a route between brick-and-stucco tenements. They flew too slowly for Valdez.

The lieutenant was out of sight of the seekers' camera eyes, but Karin could hear the soft patter of her boot plates as she advanced at a hurried trot, and the tread of the rest of the squad trailing behind her. Echoing off the buildings, there came the pepper of distant rifle fire and a heavier caliber weapon answering.

Onscreen, positioned above the two video feeds, was a third window that held the squad map—a display actively tracking the position and status of each soldier.

Outfitted in bulletproof vests and rigged in the titanium struts of light-infantry exoskeletons—"armor and bones"—the squad advanced through the alley at a mandated ten-meter interval, a regulation that reduced the odds of multiple casualties if they encountered an IED or a grenade. Only Lieutenant Valdez failed to maintain the proper distance, crowding within two meters of the seekers in her rush to answer the call for backup.

"Valdez, this is not a simple firefight. It's a widespread, well-planned insurgent offensive. Every kid with a grudge—"

"No lectures, Delphi. Just get these seekers moving faster."

Any faster, and the little drones could miss something critical.

Local time was past midnight and no lights shone in the alley, but in night vision the walls of the buildings and the trash-strewn brick pavement gleamed in crisp, green detail. Karin wasn't the only one monitoring the seekers' feeds; a battle AI watched them too. It generated an ongoing report, displayed alongside the windows. She glanced at it and saw an alert for trace scents of explosives—but with a battle in progress that didn't mean anything. Otherwise the report was good: no suspicious heat signatures or whispering voices or inexplicable motion within the apartments.

Her gaze shifted back to the video feed. A faint gleam caught her attention; a hair-thin line close to the ground that justified her caution. "Tripwire," she announced. She reached out to the screen; dragged her finger across the line. The gesture created a fleeting highlight on the display screen of Valdez's visor, clearly marking the tripwire's position. "Six meters ahead."

"Shit." Valdez pulled up sharply. A faint background tone sounded as she switched her audio to gen-com. *"Tripwire,"* she said, addressing her squad. *"Move back."*

The tone dropped out, and Valdez was talking again solely to Karin. *"Ambush?"*

"Searching." It was a good bet someone was monitoring the tripwire.

A set of windows bordered in blue glided to the center of Karin's screen: Lieutenant Deng's color code. The insurgent offensive had erupted all along the northern border, striking hard at Deng's rural district. At approximately 2200 she'd been lured into an ambush. The resulting firefight had left one of her soldiers seriously wounded.

Distance did not mute the impatience—or the frustration—in Deng's voice as she spoke over the headphones, *"Delphi, where's my medevac helicopter?"*

On nights like this, a big part of Karin's job was triage. Deng's situation was no longer "hot." The insurgents had fled, and the helicopter had already been requested. Determining an ETA would not get it there faster. So she told Deng, "Stand by."

Then she swiped the blue windows out of the way and returned her attention to the feeds from the seekers, directing one to fly higher. The angle of view shifted, and Karin spied a figure crouched on the sloping, clay-tiled roof of a low building not far ahead. She drew a highlight around it. "Valdez, see that?"

A glance at the squad map showed that Valdez had retreated a few meters from the tripwire. One specialist remained with her, while the rest of the squad had dropped back under the supervision of a sergeant.

"I see him," Valdez said. *"Target confirmed?"*

"Negative. Twenty seconds."

Karin sent a seeker buzzing toward the figure on the rooftop and then she switched her focus back to Deng's blue-coded windows, fanning them open so she could see the one that tracked the status of the medevac helicopter. The offensive was unprecedented and air support was in high demand. Deng's wounded soldier was third on the list for pickup. "Deng, ETA on the medevac is forty-plus minutes," Karin warned; that was assuming the helicopter stayed in the air. She slid the blue windows away again, switching back to Valdez.

Wind soughing between the buildings veiled the soft buzz of the seeker so that the figure on the roof didn't hear it coming. Details emerged as the little drone got closer. One of those details was a rifle— aimed at Valdez. "Target confirmed," Karin said without hesitation. "Shoot to kill."

Valdez was watching the same feed. *"That's a kid!"*

It *was* a kid. The battle AI estimated a male, fourteen years old. It didn't matter. The boy was targeting Valdez and that made him the enemy.

"Take the shot."

The boy fired first. He missed, but he squeezed the trigger again. His second shot caught Valdez in the shoulder, spinning her into the wall. *"Fuck."*

"Valdez, get down!"

The lieutenant dropped to a crouch. The specialist was already hunkered down behind her. He aimed over her shoulder and shot— but too late. The kid had opened a roof-access door, retreating inside the building.

Karin checked Valdez's biometrics: high stress, but no indication that the slug had penetrated. Her armor had protected her.

"A biometric ID on the shooter is in the system," Karin told her. "You can hunt him down later."

"Right. I'm going to drop back, rejoin the squad, and go around."

While Valdez reorganized, Karin switched to her third client, Lieutenant Holder. The set of windows monitoring his squad was coded orange. Holder was assigned to a district just outside the city. Tonight his squad waited in ambush for a suspected small-arms shipment coming in from the west. She checked his status: nominal. Checked the squad: noted all seven soldiers in position on either side of an asphalt road. Checked the wide-field view from the infrared camera on the squad's surveillance drone and noted the suspect truck, still at almost five kilometers away.

There was time.

Karin sighed, took a sip of chilled water from a bottle stashed in a pouch at the side of her chair, and for just a moment she squeezed her dry eyes shut. She'd already been six hours on-shift, with only one ten-minute break, and that was two hours ago. There would be hours more before she could rest. Most shifts went on until her clients were out of harm's way—that's just how it was, how it needed to be. She'd learned that early.

Karin had trained as a handler for the usual reason: money. She'd needed to pay off a student loan. Two years so far, with a fat savings account to show for it. The money was good, no argument, but the lifestyle? Some handlers joked that the job was like a video game—one so intense it left you shaking and exhausted at the end of every shift—but for her it had never been a game. The lives she handled were real. Slip up, and she could put a soldier in the grave. That was her nightmare. She'd had soldiers grievously wounded, but so far none had died on her shift. Lately, she'd started thinking that maybe she should quit before it happened. On a night like tonight, that thought was close to the surface.

The blue windows slid to center again. Karin popped the bottle back into its pouch as an irate Deng spoke through her headphones. *"Delphi, I can't wait forty minutes for the medevac. I've got six enemy at-large. They have their own wounded to worry about, but once they get organized, they're going to move on the settlement. If we don't get there first, there are going to be reprisals. I need approval from Command to split the squad."*

"Stand by."

Karin captured a voice clip of Deng's request and sent it to the Command queue, flagged highest priority. But before she could slide the blue windows aside, someone opened an emergency channel, an act that overrode the communications of every handler on-shift. *"I need support!"* a shrill voice yelled through Karin's headphones. She flinched, even as she recognized Sarno, another handler. The panic in his voice told her that he had made a mistake. A critical mistake, maybe a fatal one. *"I need support! Now. I just can't—"*

His transmission cut out. The shift supervisor's voice came on—calm, crisp, alert: the way handlers were trained to speak. *"I'm on it."*

Karin's hands shook. Sarno worked a chair just a few doors down from her. He was new, and new handlers sometimes got overwhelmed, but panic was always the wrong response. At the end of the shift, every handler got to go home, smoke a joint, collapse in a bed with soft sheets, get laid if they wanted to. Their clients didn't have that option. Sarno needed to remember that. Sarno needed to remember that however rough it got in the control room, no one was trying to end *his* life.

Right now the supervisor would be assisting him, coaching him, getting him back on track. Karin refocused, striving to put the incident out of her mind.

Dragging the gold-rimmed windows to center, she checked on Valdez, confirming the lieutenant had safely exited the alley. There were no alerts from the battle AI, so Karin switched to Deng's window-set. Rigged in armor and bones, the squad had formed a perimeter to protect their wounded soldier. Around them, dry grass rustled beneath spindly trees, and the stars glowed green in night vision. Karin switched to Holder. He was still hunkered down with his squad alongside the road. An infrared feed from Holder's surveillance drone showed the target vehicle only a klick-and-a-half away, approaching fast without headlights.

Just as Karin brought her attention back to Valdez, the shift supervisor spoke.

"Karin, we've got an emergency situation. I need to transfer another client to you."

"No way, Michael."

"Karin—"

"No. I've got three active operations and I can barely stay on top of them. If you give me one more client, I'm going to resign."

"Fine, Karin! Resign. But just finish this shift first. I need you. Sarno walked. He fucking walked out and left his clients."

Sarno walked? Karin lost track of her windows as she tried to make sense of it. How could he walk out? What they did here was not a video game. There was no pause button on this war. Every handler was responsible for the lives of real people.

Michael took her hesitation as agreement. *"I'm splitting the load. You only have to take one. Incoming now."*

Her throat aching, she took another sip of water, a three-second interval when her mind could rove . . . this time back to the kickboxing session that started her day, every day: a fierce routine that involved every muscle—*strike, strike, strike*—defiantly physical, because a handler had to be in top form to do this kind of work, and Karin hated to make mistakes.

As she looked up again, a glowing green dot expanded into a new set of windows, with the client's bio floating to the top. Shelley, James. A lieutenant with a stellar field rating. *Good,* Karin thought. *Less work for me.*

As she fanned the windows, the live feed opened with the triple concussion of three grenades going off one after another. She bit down on her lip, anxious to engage, but she needed an overview of the situation first. Locating the squad map, she scanned the terrain and the positions of each soldier. There were five personnel besides Shelley: a sergeant, two specialists, and two privates. The map also showed the enemy's positions and their weaponry—field intelligence automatically compiled from helmet cams and the squad's surveillance drone.

The map showed that Shelley's squad was outnumbered and outgunned.

With little shelter in a flat rural landscape of dusty red-dirt pastures and drought-stricken tree farms, they protected themselves by continuously shifting position in a fight to hold a defensive line north of the village that was surely the target of this raid. The insurgents' ATVs had already been eliminated, but two pickup trucks remained, one rigged with a heavy machine gun and the other with a rocket-launcher pod, probably stripped off a downed helicopter. The rockets it used would have a range to four kilometers. Shelley needed to take the rocket-launcher out before it targeted the village and before his squad burned through their inventory of grenades.

The sound of the firefight dropped out as her get-acquainted session was overridden by Deng's windows sliding to the center. A communication had come in from Command. Deng's request to split the squad had been approved. Karin forwarded the order, following up with a verbal link. "Deng, your request has been approved. Orders specify two personnel remain with the wounded; four proceed to the settlement."

"Thanks, Delphi."

Karin switched to Holder. His ambush would go off in seconds. She did a quick scan of the terrain around him, located no additional threats, and then switched focus to Valdez. Cities were the worst. Too many places for snipers to hide. Too many alleys to booby trap. Karin requested an extra surveillance drone to watch the surrounding buildings as Valdez trotted with her squad through the dark streets. She'd feel more secure if she could study the feed from the seekers, but there was no time—because it was her new client who faced the most immediate hazard.

Lieutenant Shelley was on the move, weaving between enemy positions, letting two of his soldiers draw the enemy's attention while he closed on the rocket launcher. The truck that carried the weapon was being backed into the ruins of a still-smoldering, blown-out farmhouse. The roof of the house was gone along with the southern wall, but three stout brick walls remained, thick enough to shelter the rocket crew from enemy fire. Once they had the truck in place, it would be only a minute or two before the bombardment started.

Not a great time to switch handlers.

Karin mentally braced herself, and then she opened a link to Shelley. The sounds of the firefight hammered through her headphones: staccato bursts from assault rifles and then the bone-shaking boom of another grenade launched by the insurgents. A distant, keening scream of agony made her hair stand on end, but a status check showed green so she knew it wasn't one of hers. "Lieutenant Shelley," she said, speaking quickly before he could protest her intrusion. "My codename is Delphi. You've been transferred to my oversight. I'll be your handler tonight."

His biometrics, already juiced from the ongoing operation, surged even higher. *"What the hell?"* he whispered. *"Did you people get rid of Hawkeye in the middle of an action?"*

"Hawkeye took himself out, Lieutenant."

Karin remembered her earlier assessment of Sarno's breakdown. *He had made a mistake.* What that mistake was, she didn't know and there was no time to work it out. "I've got an overview of the situation and I will stay with you."

"What'd you say your name was?"

"Delphi."

"Delphi, you see where I'm going?"

"Yes."

He scuttled, hunched over to lower his profile, crossing bare ground between leafless thickets. Shooting was almost constant, from one side or another, but so far he'd gone unnoticed and none of it was directed at him.

Karin studied the terrain that remained to be crossed. "You're going to run out of cover."

"Understood."

A wide swath of open ground that probably served as a pasture in the rainy season lay between Shelley and the shattered farmhouse. He needed to advance a hundred meters across it to be within the effective range of his grenade launcher. There were no defenders in that no-man's-land, but there were at least eight insurgents sheltering within the remains of the farmhouse—and the second truck, the one with the machine gun, was just out of sight on the other side of the ruins.

She fanned the windows just as the lieutenant dropped to his belly at the edge of the brush. Bringing Shelley's details to the top, she checked his supplies. "You have two programmable grenades confirmed inside your weapon. Ten percent of your ammo load remaining. Lieutenant, that's not enough."

"It's enough."

Karin shook her head. Shelley couldn't see it; it was a gesture meant only for herself. There weren't enough soldiers in his squad to keep him out of trouble once the enemy knew where he was.

Would it be tonight then? she wondered. Would this be the night she lost someone?

"I advise you to retreat."

"Can't do it, Delphi."

It was the expected answer, but she'd had to try.

Nervous tension reduced her to repeating the basics. "Expect them to underestimate how fast you can move and maneuver in your exoskeleton. You can take advantage of that."

The shooting subsided. In the respite, audio pickups caught and enhanced the sound of a tense argument taking place at the distant farmhouse. Then a revving engine overrode the voices.

Karin said, "The other truck, with the machine gun, it's on the move."

"I see it."

Linda Nagata

A check of his setup confirmed he had the feed from the surveillance drone posted on the periphery of his visor display.

He used gen-com to speak to his squad. *"It's now. Don't let me get killed, okay?"*

They answered, their voices tense, intermingled: *"We got you . . . watch over you . . ."*

Valdez's window-set centered, cutting off their replies. *"Delphi, you there?"*

Her voice was calm, so Karin said, "Stand by," and swiped her window-set aside.

". . . kick ass, L T"

Shelley's window-set was still fanned, with the live feed from the surveillance drone on one end of the array. Motion in that window caught Karin's eye, even before the battle AI highlighted it. "Shelley, the machine-gun truck is coming around the north side of the ruins. Everybody on those walls is going to be looking at it."

"Got it. I'm going."

"Negative! Hold your position. On my mark . . ." She identified the soldier positioned a hundred-fifty meters away on Shelley's west flank. Overriding protocol, she opened a link to him, and popped a still image of the truck onto the periphery of his visor. "Hammer it as soon as you have it in sight." The truck fishtailed around the brick walls and Karin told Shelley, "Now."

He took off in giant strides powered by his exoskeleton, zigzagging across the bare ground. There was a shout from the truck, just as the requested assault rifle opened up. The truck's windshield shattered. More covering fire came from the northwest. From the farmhouse voices cried out in fury and alarm. Karin held her breath while Shelley covered another twenty meters and then she told him, "Drop and target!"

He accepted her judgment and slammed to the ground, taking the impact on the arm struts of his exoskeleton as the racing pickup braked in a cloud of dust. Shelley didn't turn to look. The feed from his helmet cams remained fixed on the truck parked between the ruined walls as he set up his shot. The battle AI calculated the angle, and when his weapon was properly aligned, the AI pulled the trigger.

A grenade launched on a low trajectory, transiting the open ground and disappearing under the truck, where it exploded with a deep *whump!*, enfolding the vehicle in a fireball that initiated a thunderous roar of secondary explosions as the rocket propellant ignited. The farmhouse became an incandescent inferno. Night vision switched off on all devices as white light washed across the open ground.

Karin shifted screens. The feed from the surveillance drone showed a figure still moving in the bed of the surviving truck. An enemy soldier—wounded maybe, but still determined—clawing his way up to the mounted machine gun. "Target to the northwest," she said.

The audio in Shelley's helmet enhanced her voice so that he heard her even over the roar of burning munitions. He rolled and fired. The figure in the truck went over backward, hitting the dusty ground with an ugly bounce.

Karin scanned the squad map. "No indication of surviving enemy, but shrapnel from those rockets—"

"Fall back!" Shelley ordered on gen-com. Powered by his exoskeleton, he sprang to his feet and took off. *"Fall back! All speed!"*

Karin watched until he put a hundred meters behind him; then she switched to Holder, confirmed his ambush had gone off as planned; switched to Deng, who was driving an ATV, racing to cut off her own insurgent incursion; switched to Valdez, who had finally joined up with another squad to quell a street battle in an ancient desert city.

"Delphi, you there?" Shelley asked.

"I'm here." Her voice hoarse, worn by use.

Dawn had come. All along the northern border the surviving enemy were in retreat, stopping their exodus only when hunting gunships passed nearby. Then they would huddle out of sight beneath camouflage blankets until the threat moved on. The incursion had gained no territory, but the insurgents had won all the same by instilling fear among the villages and the towns.

Karin had already seen Valdez and Holder and Deng back to their shelters. Now Shelley's squad was finally returning to their little fort.

"Is Hawkeye done?" he asked her.

She sighed, too tired to really think about it. "I don't know. Maybe."

"I never liked him much."

Karin didn't answer. It wasn't appropriate to discuss another handler.

"You still there?"

"I'm here."

"You want to tell me if this was a one-night stand? Or are you going to be back tonight?"

Exhaustion clawed at her and she wanted to tell him *no*. No, I will not be back. There wasn't enough money in the world to make this a good way to spend her life.

Then she wondered: When had it ceased to be about the money?

The war was five thousand miles away, but it was inside her head too; it was inside her dreams and her nightmares.

"Delphi?"

"I'm here."

In her worst nightmares, she lost voice contact. That's when she could see the enemy waiting in ambush, when she knew his position, his weaponry, his range . . . when she knew her clients were in trouble, but she couldn't warn them.

"You want me to put in a formal request for your services?" Shelley pressed. *"I can do that, if you need me to."*

It wasn't money that kept Karin at her control station. As the nightmare of the war played on before her eyes, it was knowing that the advice and the warnings that she spoke could save her soldiers' lives.

"It's best if you make a formal request," Karin agreed. "But don't worry—I'll be here."

PERSEPHONE DESCENDING

★

by Derek Künsken

Sabotaged, tossed down through the toxic atmosphere of Venus, Marie-Claude, armed only with her spacesuit and her wits, must outsmart a political faction that wants her dead—and a planet bent on destroying her.

SIXTY-EIGHT KILOMETERS above the surface, in the thin yellowed haze of the photochemical zone of Venus' atmosphere, Marie-Claude emerged onto the roof of the floating factory. Yellow-brown cloud curved away below her in all directions, while the stars poked through a sky whitened by a big sun, inviting an artistic soul to make something of it. A dumb maintenance drone, one of many on the factory, floated by, wiping the glass of the roof.

Her suit battery status blinked from green to yellow. She jiggled the pack. Yellow to green again. An environment laced with acid bred all sorts of shorts and power leaks. The *colonistes* called all these irritating maintenance problems *bebbits*, after the little biting flies of Québec's wilderness.

She leaned on the wing of her plane, just for a quick break from the life of cramped factory to cramped habitat. The fast, empty wind caressing her suit was a doubtful thing, an experience at a remove, a ghostly touch that froze the bones. The *colonistes* did not touch Venus. They experienced the idea of her through their suits. Venus wrapped herself in clouds deeper and heavier than an ocean. Marie-Claude could only stand on the shores they'd built and watch Venus, as she might watch a movie, something to be left behind when she returned to the floating habitats. Venus isolated them from everything except the violence with which she touched them, bathing them in hotly cancerous solar radiation, suffocating them with thin, anoxic air, reaching up for them with tongues of sulfuric acid, delighting in marking them with acid scars where she gnawed through environmental suits and protective films.

Her battery toggled from green to yellow again. She whacked the *bebbit*. Back to green. She opened her plane and climbed in.

"Renaud," she radioed her supervisor, "Marie-Claude here. I'm taking off from plant six."

Take-off from a factory was a bit like the short and long seconds at the peak of a roller coaster. A ramp simply led off a lip and into the yawning atmosphere. She started her engine, taxied to the top of the ramp and rolled down, faster and faster.

At the edge, a loud snap shook the plane, and a shrieking hole opened in the side. The plane spun. A glimpse of the factory spun by, showing, at the edge of the ramp, a cleaning drone, with a part of Marie-Claude's wing in its grabbing claw.

It shouldn't have been there. It shouldn't have grabbed at her plane.

She spun away. Dashboard darkened. She plunged toward the yellowed cloud deck. Marie-Claude's heart thumped too loudly. Thoughts loud, useless. Pilot training dragged her fingers to scrabble under her seat for the ejection switch, but the cockpit floor had bent, jamming itself against her seat. She couldn't reach it.

"*Merde, merde, merde*," she whispered.

"Marie-Claude! What's going on?" Renaud's voice crackled in her helmet. "You're losing altitude!"

No ejection seat. Busted plane. Flat spin. Sulfuric acid clouds. "*Câlisse!*" she swore.

"Marie-Claude! Do you read me?"

Terror froze her lungs with cold fingers. Jerk harness free. Plane shuddering. Move to gaping hole in the cockpit. Too loud. Fingers gripping seat. Jump. Thin air whipped. Clouds below, racing up. Scream. Tumble away. Small parachute yanked lightly at her. Voice in her ears. Hands searching for parachute cords. Parachute above her. Parachute above her. Breathe. Breathe. Answer.

"Plane blown. I'm on my secondary chute." The small parachute barely slowed her. Only a fraction of an atmosphere resisted her descent. The air would not thicken to a full atmosphere for about ten kilometers. By then, it might be too late for rescue.

"I'm coming your way," Renaud said.

He radioed orders to the rest of the team, to the habitat platform five kilometers higher.

Marie-Claude tasted black on her tongue. She gritted her teeth, willing herself not to puke in her helmet. Shock. Probably shock. Her stomach churned harder. Do something.

She patted her suit. Adrenaline might mask leaks or injuries. Seals and fabric and coatings okay. Heater and heat exchanger running. Oxygen pressure a bit low, but green. Main battery still green. Sealed pockets on the arms and legs of her suit contained bits of her tool kit. Breathe. Renaud was on his way. Be calm.

The plane dragged a trail of smoke through the haze. About five kilometers below, the smoke column bent sharply. In that moment, in the vast clouds, relative movement was born. She and the habitats and factories lived in the super-rotating layer of the upper atmosphere, in winds that circled Venus every four days. Her plane had dropped into the slower-moving cloud deck beneath and was slowly falling behind her.

"*Merde!* Renaud, the transition layer is higher today! I'm going to fall out of the super-rotating winds." She did not add, *and out of your reach until you've circled the planet.*

"How soon?"

"A few minutes."

Where the bottom of the super-rotating winds touched the top of the lower clouds, the smoke column had been torn into a string of eddies, dark berries on the stretched lines of yellow clouds beneath. She rode nothing more than a bit of resined fabric on thin carbon cables. "The turbulence will shred my chute."

"I'm on full throttle, Marie-Claude. We'll get there."

She looked up into the yellow-white sky. She couldn't see any planes. Sixty-one kilometers separated her from the surface of Venus. She had a few minutes before it would become very dangerous for Renaud or any of the other crews to rescue her.

The factory shrank to a toy-like gray stub far above her, but another shape was growing, resolving into a repair drone, descending on two propellers whirring behind it. Coming toward her. It wasn't programmed to do that. It was not programmed to do anything but clean and fix simple leaks, unless engineers gave it more specific repair tasks.

"Renaud! Did you program one of the repair drones to come get me?"

The radio crackled, echoing lightning from the deep deck of the lower clouds. "No. I didn't think we'd have enough time to do that. I'll see if I can have someone on it."

"That's not why I'm asking. On take-off, I collided with a repair drone. It shouldn't have been anywhere near the launch ramp. I think it grabbed part of my wing."

"Are you sure?"

She hesitated to tell him over the radio. Drones wouldn't grab her plane unless they were programmed to. Sabotage. Whoever had done this would be as likely to hear. "I think someone tried to kill me, Renaud. I think they reprogrammed the drone. Plant six was added to the inspection route late and my name was put on it. And now this drone is following me down."

"What? Hang on. I'll access it from here."

Marie-Claude waited, time ticking below her as the smog thickened and the drone approached.

"I can't get in. Its antenna is offline."

"I can't get away," Marie-Claude said.

"I'm almost there."

The drone neared, only three hundred meters from her. Its grasping claws were open, capable of tearing her parachute. Only a half kilometer below her, the smoke of her plane was a thinning gray streak. She took a deep breath.

"It's not going to happen, Renaud. The suit can keep me alive in the upper cloud deck, but without a chute, I'm just going to drop until I cook. I've got to save the chute."

"Marie-Claude! What are you doing?"

Instead of pulling on the brake loops of her parachute, she pulled all the suspension wires on one side until the canopy spilled. She fell. Her stomach leapt. Arm over arm, she pulled her parachute close until she hugged it, and only its edges slapped frantically at her arms in the wind. She tucked her legs and tumbled.

Thinly glowing clouds above. Darkness below. Spinning. Two sides.

"Marie-Claude!" Renaud yelled.

Turbulence hit like a fist. She was spinning dust. If she blacked out she was dead. Yelling in her radio. Droplets of sulfuric acid rain streaked the glass of her helmet. The world darkened. The buffeting and spinning wanted to tear her apart, but finally the bumping stopped and she fell again. She let her chute go. The canopy flapped and bloomed and yanked her upright.

A voice spoke in her radio, nearly overwhelmed by static.

"I'm through the transition," she said. "My parachute is okay. The pressure is a tenth of an atmosphere. Temperature is about minus twenty Celsius. I'm not dead."

Yet.

The planes now had a relative wind speed difference to her of about one hundred and fifty kilometers per hour. And the planes were only rated for up to two atmospheres of pressure and about eighty degrees. After that, the sulfuric acid chemistry became too hostile. The *Laurentide*, the main habitat, had a few probes to study the deep atmosphere and its life forms, but none of them would be nearby. They could probably refit something with which to rescue her in a day or two, but by the time the *Laurentide* was back overhead, she would have descended well past finding.

Duvieusart Inquiry Transcript, page 772

> 3:30 P.M., CHLOÉ RIVERIN, CHAIR: We now have Monsieur Renaud Lanoix, who leads the *Nouvelle Voie* party, but who was also the engineering foreman on April sixth. Could you describe for the Inquiry your view of the events of April sixth?

> 3:30, RENAUD LANOIX, ENGINEERING SUPERVISOR: Thank you, Madame Chairman. At approximately 2 P.M., Mademoiselle Duvieusart radioed, as per procedure, that she had arrived at Plant Six and started her normal inspections and work planning for later technical crews.

3:30, SANDRINE GROGUHÉ, INQUIRY MEMBER: A question, Madame Chair?

3:30, CHLOE RIVERIN, CHAIR: Go ahead.

3:30, SANDRINE GROGUHÉ, INQUIRY MEMBER: Monsieur Lanoix, in a number of reports, the press contends that Mademoiselle Duvieusart was not even supposed to be at Plant Six that day, and that the shifts were changed to draw her there.

3:35, RENAUD LANOIX, ENGINEERING SUPERVISOR: The schedule had been changed a few days earlier. Mademoiselle Duvieusart was put on Plant Six for April sixth.

3:35, SANDRINE GROGUHÉ, INQUIRY MEMBER: Who had access to the schedule—to change it, that is?

3:35, RENAUD LANOIX, ENGINEERING SUPERVISOR: A number of people have access to the schedule. Changing it is a normal part of any week's work, Madame Groguhé. I have access, as do most of the engineers, including Mademoiselle Duvieusart.

3:35, SANDRINE GROGUHÉ, INQUIRY MEMBER: You don't have . . .

3:35, FRANÇOIS BEAULIEU, INQUIRY MEMBER: Madame Chair, Monsieur Lanoix is not able to tell his story.

3:35, SANDRINE GROGUHÉ, INQUIRY MEMBER: Monsieur Lanoix has neglected to bring up important details.

3:35, CHLOE RIVERIN, CHAIR: Go ahead, Madame Groguhé, but please be brief.

3:35, SANDRINE GROGUHÉ, INQUIRY MEMBER: Monsieur Lanoix, fine, many people have access to the schedules, but through accounts that identify those making the changes. Who made the changes to the schedule to set up Mademoiselle Duvieusart for the sabotage of her plane?

3:35, RENAUD LANOIX, ENGINEERING SUPERVISOR: We know who accessed the schedule, Madame Groguhé. My lawyers have suggested that I should not reveal what I know here, so as not to interfere with criminal investigations.

3:40, CHLOE RIVERIN, CHAIR: This Inquiry has the authority to compel witnesses, Monsieur, and our legal counsel suggest that the danger to criminal proceedings is minimal as the cat is already out of the bag, and on the top of blog feeds over most of the Solar System.

(REPORTER'S NOTE: In camera consultation between Inquiry counsel and witness counsel.)

3:45, RENAUD LANOIX, ENGINEERING SUPERVISOR: The schedule was changed by an override code from the *Bureau du Gouverneur*, masked behind a dummy admin account.

3:45, CHLOE RIVERIN, CHAIR: The press, especially the *nationaliste* press, has made much of this being a *séparatiste* plot to frame the *nationaliste* cause. What are your thoughts on that?

3:45, RENAUD LANOIX, ENGINEERING SUPERVISOR: I don't think that theory holds water. The sabotage was amateurish, that is certain, but Mademoiselle Duvieusart was not supposed to have survived those first few instants to tell us that the repair drone was acting strangely, which allowed us to pull the curtain back on the plot.

Marie-Claude wiped the drizzle of acid from her faceplate. Her oxygen display had yellowed. Only a few hours of oxygen left. And she continued descending. She hung in a rain of sulfuric acid, fifty-eight kilometers above the surface of Venus. Nowhere to refuel or recharge or repair or even stop.

In the distance below, a flock of spherical, gas-filled photo-synthesizers blew with the wind like pollen. Blastulae. Sometimes storms brought them as high as the photochemical zone, where they quickly died from the changes in pressure. They were small and neutrally buoyant at this altitude. They were not buoyant enough to stop her descent. Maybe if she could put enough of them together?

Perhaps a kilometer below, in the brown-yellow gloom, a cluster of dark spots moved, backward relative to the wind that carried her. They were much bigger than the blastulae. She tugged at her control lines, turning to get a better view, and hard enough to spill some of the air from her parachute. Her horizontal speed picked up, and she dropped faster. And only because she had turned did she see that the repair drone had followed her.

Repair drones had not been designed specifically to survive in the cloud deck, but they were hardy. In the photochemical zone, it might have run forever on solar power, but it also cracked sulfuric acid into hydrogen and solid sulfur, which could be recombined later to work in shadow. It could follow her a long time if it could take on enough ballast to sink as fast as she, and if it could survive the heat and acid.

Marie-Claude gritted her teeth and spilled her parachute. She plummeted. Two hundred meters. Four hundred. Six hundred. She finally let the wires go, and the parachute unfurled. The murk of the burnt yellow clouds hid her from the repair drone.

And two hundred meters below floated a pod of thirty rosettes, large Venusian plants. Their bulbous ochre heads were composed of six radially symmetric gas-filled chambers, each one a meter across. Sulfuric acid and organic materials collected in the cup formed by the tops of the six chambers. From the center of this cup grew a large triangular frond, a fine black net with which to filter the photosynthesizing microbes from the atmosphere. Beneath the six chambers hung short, heavy trunks which stored nutrients and provided ballast. They hung like weird, rootless trees, orphaned in the vastness of an ocean of cloud.

Carefully, Marie-Claude matched her horizontal speed and descended, until with uncertain hands and unsteady feet, she landed on one of the rosettes, scrambling to grab its frond before she slipped. The round, woody platform was slimy with decomposing microbes slowly being absorbed by the skin of the rosette.

The rosette began to sink under her weight, although slower than she'd been descending in her parachute. But, as the pressure increased, so would the buoyancy of the rosette, until she finally stopped descending. And in the meantime, she could hide here from the repair drone. She shook acid rain from her parachute and laid it over herself like a tarp against the drizzling acid.

She sank into the somber clouds for a long time, as the rain stopped. In the enforced quiet, her arms tingled, as if she wanted to hit something, for a long time. She was going to die. She was sinking into the toxic atmosphere of Venus because someone had decided to kill her. Nervous, angry, baffled tears tickled hot lines onto her cheeks. She cursed the acid. She cursed the world and politics. And she cursed herself for coming to Venus.

The Americans, Australians, and British still raced against the Chinese for the industrial and economic dominance of Mars. Egypt and Saudi Arabia had taken Vesta and Ceres, and had staked claims on dozens of other asteroids with robotic prospectors. The Russians, perhaps for having lost the Moon to the Americans a century earlier, took it for their inheritance. The first wave of Solar System colonization was complete by the time Québec separated from Canada.

L'Assemblée nationale decided to make their mark as an advanced nation by colonizing Venus. There was no money to be made on Venus, no resource it could provide to Earth or the rest of the Solar System that could not be gotten for cheaper from the Egyptians or the Saudis, but her clouds were of scientific value. Strange microbial extremophiles had been found, feeding a deep, inaccessible ecology. Basic scientific research would not finance the effort and colonization was not cheap, but the president had wanted *un grand geste*, a starward look for her new nation.

And it was a *grand geste*, approached with an earnest, prideful, counterproductive fervor. Little matter that the new republic had to launch Anglo hardware on Egyptian rockets, and that it trained its engineers in Houston. *La République du Québec* was colonizing Venus.

They ought to have started with robotic stations in the atmosphere, to prepare the way for astronauts, but *la République* had the romantic eagerness of a teenager, throwing waves of engineers, chemists, meteorologists, and doctors into space with cramped habitats, optimistic assumptions, and fickle support. They were part of *la grande histoire*, and dreams thrive in fields of willful blindness.

—From *Commentaries
on the Foundation of the Venusian State*

The clouds thinned and broke beneath her, and a frisson of awe was born in Marie-Claude. She rode the rosette near the top of a kilometer of clear air between the yellow-brown upper cloud deck and the angry dark clouds of the middle deck. The cavernous space was empty, carved into all the stored acid and spite in the Solar System. She was tiny, a mite riding a bit of dander in a stadium. The vertigo that had trailed her all this time suddenly pounced, and she snaked her arms around the frond, as if she stood on a cliff. The rosette sank through the great cave in the clouds, and the puffy floor of the middle deck approached with the gentleness of a summer balloon ride. She was going to die. Venus would kill her, but had given her one last vision of wonder.

Marie-Claude rode her magic carpet to the bottom of the clear air and sank into the thick cloud of the middle deck. Like a drowning swimmer, Marie-Claude looked upward as the darkness swallowed. The repair drone broke out of the upper clouds a kilometer above, and then everything was out of sight.

A new rain of sulfuric acid fell as her oxygen display began winking yellow.

There was no oxygen recharging station around, and perhaps she would never see one again. She had to take what she needed. She was an engineer, but like everyone she'd read the ecological papers produced by the colony's part-time researchers.

The clouds, filled with dust, were a perfect crucible for Venusian life, cycling between low pressure and high, sunlit and dark, concentrated and dilute acidity, evaporation and condensation. Whole classes of acidophiles, psychrophiles, and thermophiles had life cycles the *colonistes* hadn't had the time to study. The microbes captured the wavelengths of light penetrating the middle and upper cloud decks within cell walls hardened to maintain buoyant gas pressures. Presumably, some of these autotrophs had evolved into floating mats that inflated and deflated as needed, and then, over millions of years, into hardened wooden balls, and finally, in an accident of tissue innovation rivaled by the Cambrian explosion on Earth, the balls had clustered into rosettes, and the cloud trawlers that lived in the deeper atmosphere.

The six chambers of the rosette beneath her feet were filled with oxygen, a byproduct of photosynthesis. Oxygen was buoyant in Venus' carbon dioxide atmosphere, but Marie-Claude couldn't take any of it without jeopardizing her foothold. She needed some of the spherical plants, or blastulae, that she'd seen.

She looked for a long time before she spotted a cluster floating perhaps a kilometer below, moving almost in parallel to the rosette she rode as she sank. Rosettes drifted with the wind, partly driven by their high fronds. Marie-Claude set her feet into the sludge at the base of the frond and tugged and pulled and leaned until the frond, like a small sail, angled to the wind so that slowly, her rosette began drifting leftward.

The rosettes were not easy to steer, but slowly, over some thirty minutes, she moved it across the wind, approaching the cluster of blastulae that contained an adult form—several buds and a pair of adults still connected by sticky ooze. Marie-Claude threw her parachute over the cluster and hauled it in.

The blastulae had nothing to do with embryos, but reminded many of the hollow-ball-of-cells phase of embryonic development, and no one had time to find a better name. They were hollow, woody balls that reproduced by budding. Adult blastulae floated with crowns of smaller buds, which grew to adult size and then detached when the difference in buoyancy between parent and offspring overcame the stickiness of the mucus gluing them together.

Her oxygen tanks had emergency hand pumps that could be fitted to the hoses in case the power failed in the habitats. The hoses contained anhydrous crystalline filters to neutralize sulfuric acid. She set up her pump and pulled one of the blastulae from the parachute.

Her helmet light revealed a brown skin pigmented to absorb the yellowed light reaching these depths. Transparent mucus slicked the blastula, beading off the raining acid.

Suddenly, the blastula hissed around six stomata. The carbon dioxide of the Venusian atmosphere flowed inward, and the blastula lost its buoyancy. Marie-Claude turned it over, and it hissed again, letting in more carbon dioxide.

Photoreactivity. Why? If an updraft carried a blastula into the upper atmosphere, sunlight would burn it. Its stomata must have dilated to allow heavy carbon dioxide in, to lower its buoyancy. Her lamp had tricked the stomata.

She let the blastula go. It tumbled slowly over the edge of the rosette. At some point, it would reach a depth where it would float. Then, further photosynthesis would create oxygen which would buoy it more. *In extremis*, blastulae had been observed to pump out some air from their cavities to correct their buoyancy more abruptly.

Marie-Claude switched off her helmet light and let her eyes adjust to the gloom of a rainy sundown. Then she pulled out one of the immature blastulae. She traced with her gloved fingertips until she found the stomata, tiny closed mouths, six of them, ringing the underside.

She cleared away the mucus and placed the hose against a stoma. With the other hand, she took a small hand light and lit just that part of the blastula. The stoma relaxed and Marie-Claude inserted the hose into the plant before too much carbon dioxide could rush in. She pumped the oxygen from the blastula into her tank. When she finally pulled free the hose and released it, it bobbed up and away, carried up like a cork in water.

She repeated her vampiric feast on all the blastulae in her parachute, watching each one shudder up into the clouds upon release, like bubbles rising in deep water. Seven of the woody balloons disappeared into the sky before her oxygen display edged into yellow-green. She had some oxygen, but she needed more.

But, as she stowed her equipment, she realized that acid had rasped the fabric of her parachute raw.

Les colonistes did not design their equipment to operate in the heavily acidic environment below the super-rotating winds, but something could be refitted in that time. The food paste in her suit had the calories, and the water recycler might keep her hydrated. Sweat dripped in her eyes. The temperature had topped fifty degrees and now hugged her with a full atmosphere of pressure.

A light shone in the distance above her. A machine whined. The drone was not designed to operate so deep. The steels used to build drones were more vulnerable to hot acids than her suit of fiber-reinforced plastics. If she could survive four days, they might be able to rescue her.

Marie-Claude's mother had also come to a new world, in one of the waves of Haitian refugees to Québec. Her mother had married *un Québécois pur laine*, pure wool, a man whose family counted French, or at least European blood, for generations. Her parents bequeathed to her two identities, one of belonging by blood, another of alienness by color of skin.

So, from birth, her country was both hers and not hers. The new nation of Québec consumed its children with politics of identity and place, self-referential and pastward-looking. Québec offered no place free of the acidity of the cultural insecurity. So Marie-Claude had come to Venus for the freedom and even-handedness of ground without footprints.

She might have immigrated to Mars or the asteroids for a frontier life, but as much as the Québécois infuriated her, she was Québécoise herself, by blood and language. *Le grand geste* seemed perfect for a time, but it turned out not to have been the frontier. *Les colonistes* had carried with them the panels and studies, the committees and language laws. Instead of thinking new thoughts, they argued over resource budgets, work schedules, and culture by proposing motions and agendas in committees. Marie-Claude liked engineering problems. Calculations of force and pressure and resistance and pH were simple things, an escape from politics that seemed to materialize wherever two people met. Marie-Claude's competent, forceful plain-speak led inevitably to her election as the chair of the engineering union.

Marie-Claude was not the only one restless for something they could not articulate. No one knew yet where they were going, but never a people to stop at one poorly conceived *grand geste, les colonistes* surviving in the clouds of Venus quickly began to speak of their own state. A country of our own. *Un pays pour nous.* And so, *les séparatistes* were born, even though *les colonistes* needed Québec to foot the bills for metals and volatiles.

A greater gift could not have been offered to the new nation of Québec. Québec did not have the budget to sustain the colony. They derived no benefit from it, not even respect. One might admire Quixote, but one did not respect him. Despite being faced with so convenient an escape from its responsibilities as the mother country, it surprised no one that *l'Assemblée* denounced any talk of secession. And so were born *les nationalistes.* The factions on the habitats spun webs of arguments for *une Vénus indépendente* or *une Vénus coloniale.*

Marie-Claude considered both ideas criminally impractical. Whether the colony declared its independence from Québec or not, Venus intended to kill them. Tempers burned, sometimes into open violence. Renaud Lanoix, the *séparatiste* leader, dreamed of a new nation, and saw Marie-Claude, chair of the powerful Engineering Union, as the key to unlocking it. He'd been waiting for her to choose her side. Someone else had not.

—From *Persephone's Descent: The Biography of Marie-Claude Duvieusart*

Marie-Claude sailed her rosette with the wind, slowly sinking. The atmosphere thickened, but the rosette was still not able to support her weight. After several hours, the Stygian clouds broke again, into the kilometer of clear air beneath the middle cloud deck.

This great cavern in the clouds was somber. Other rosettes floated in the distance, like dark specks, failing to give perspective to the vastness and too far away to help her with buoyancy or oxygen.

She must be only fifty kilometers above the surface now, almost twenty kilometers below the *Laurentide* and the other habitats. No one would be able to come this far down to rescue her.

Marie-Claude sank through the hot air and into the lower clouds of Venus, a thick yellow haze of sulfuric acid, veined with lines of brown and green mineral dust and chlorine. Few photosynthesizers would survive at these depths, leaving the clouds open to webs of chemotrophs, living off what volcanoes and storms churned upward.

A rain of hot acid fell, until, through the cloud, she spotted a cluster of blastulae beneath her, directly in her downward path. But her two-edged luck persisted; the blastulae were full of oxygen, but they were gummed to the side of a trawler.

Trawlers were shaped like rosettes, darker in color, radially symmetric, with six buoyancy chambers, but were much larger, serving as the platform for many kinds of life. Blastulae sometimes stuck parasitically to the great trawlers, absorbing nutrients from the rain they were not large enough to collect on their own.

Trawlers were not photosynthesizers. They occupied a more dramatic ecological niche. A conducting carbon filament hundreds of meters long hung beneath the trawler, ending in a bob. As the trawler drifted with the wind, the conductor joined clouds of different static charges and altitudes, drawing an electrical current along its length. More dangerously, trawlers were lightning rods in the storms of the middle and lower cloud decks. It was not healthy to be near a trawler.

But she needed the oxygen. The trawler and its crown of blastulae floated half a kilometer beneath her.

Marie-Claude's battery display suddenly flashed, edging from yellow to orange. The suit's heat exchanger shifted to a power-saver setting, and the suit's radio antenna turned off.

Merde.

She slipped her battery out of its pack behind her. The hand light trembled.

Merde, merde, merde.

Grainy acid leaked out of the fiber-reinforced plastic on one side of the battery. Its lifetime was measured in minutes, hours if she was lucky.

This shouldn't have happened. These plastics were hardened to survive in the Venusian atmosphere. Not exactly true. The fiber-reinforced plastics were resistant to the low concentrations of sulfuric acid at the cooler temperatures sixty and seventy kilometers above the surface. They reacted very differently to higher concentrations of sulfuric acid.

Over the beating rain, a regular machine sound thrummed. With the increasing pressure, sound warbled and direction deceived. She spun. The drone closed from only a few hundred meters away, scarred by patches of acid corrosion. Marie-Claude had nothing with which to damage it. And now she would cook far sooner than the drone would dissolve.

It neared.

She was trapped.

She couldn't see more than a few hundred meters through the rain. No sign of a storm. No thunder.

The drone was fifty meters away now.

She slipped the battery back into its pocket, switched her helmet light to its brightest, and shone it on the rosette, along with both hand lamps. The rosette opened all six of its stomata, flooding its buoyancy chambers with heavy carbon dioxide.

Marie-Claude's footing shuddered as the rosette tipped and sank. She held the frond tightly as the sludge on the rosette poured into clouds. Marie-Claude's feet slipped off and then there was nothing beneath them. One of her flashlights spun into the gloom below. She and the rosette fell sideways toward the trawler.

When the top of the trawler was fifteen meters below her, the rosette began drifting with the wind. She was going to miss her landing. And after the trawler, nothing separated her from the surface of Venus except forty-eight kilometers of crushing, hyper-acidic, broiling atmosphere.

She let go of the frond.

She spread her arms and legs. She hit the top of the trawler hard, the blow accompanied by a powerful static shock. She splashed in the pooled acid and organics, and bounced, nearly to the edge. Venusian epiphytes had colonized the trawler thickly, clutching with stringy roots or sticky mucus. They slowed her slide. She let her flashlight and parachute go and pulled free a pair of screwdrivers. She scraped the points along the top of the trawler until she stopped.

Slowly, she pulled herself away from the edge.

She ached all over.

The rosette she had ridden all the way down to the lower clouds ascended lazily past the circling drone. The gloom pressed in. Even though it had only been a further half kilometer down, she could have sworn that the temperature had risen, and that the atmosphere pressed tighter against her suit.

The trawler was not evolved to carry an extra ninety kilos of rider and survival gear. It began sinking, but more slowly than the rosette had. The lower cloud deck thinned around her, and she descended into a dark, yellow haze. The temperature outside her suit had risen almost to the boiling point of water. She was now beneath the upper, middle and lower cloud decks. The browned, cooked bellies of the lowest clouds on Venus lay above her head. This sub-cloud haze was a zone of thermal dissociation.

She took the blastulae stuck to the trawler, one by one, and pumped the oxygen into her tank until it was fully in the green. Her battery icon still blinked orange-red.

Something stung her leg, like a wasp sting. She jerked and patted at her leg. The sulfuric acid, at this heat and pressure, had bored a hole through the fiber-reinforced plastic of her suit.

The spite of Venus.

She huddled under the remains of her parachute and pulled the suit repair kit out of a pocket. She neutralized the acid, cleaned the hole, applied the adhesive and slapped the patch on. It was a drilled movement, automatic, thoughtless. It was now natural. What had her stupid plan been? Would she have one day taught children how to thwart the lashing of a chemically predatory planet? That was no birthright. The *séparatistes* and the *nationalistes* could have the whole damned place.

The last part of the drill was to get to shelter to replace the suit. Leaks bloomed in clusters, just like blastulae. She inspected the parts of her suit she could see. Patches of discoloration showed that her suit would not last even one day more in the hot rain. The acid delighted in dissolving all the cleverness of people. It might not matter. The heat would kill her soon if she didn't fix her battery.

The Hadean rain poured again as she sank. It jumped and spattered the surface of the pool in the depression in center of the trawler's platform, and overflowed the depression, running over the edge and out of sight, to fall until it evaporated, long before it ever came close to the surface of Venus.

She ran a finger through the slime on the surface of the trawler. Murky organic strands shot through its translucence. It repelled water, and probably contained bases to neutralize any acids that penetrated it. That was how an engineer would have designed a plant on Venus.

Marie-Claude scooped a handful of the slime and rubbed it on her suit and the parachute. If she guessed wrong and it was just a viscous acid, it would be a terrible way to die. It didn't seem to be hurting her suit, so she applied more, and soon, she looked like she'd been dipped in egg white. But the rain no longer touched her suit.

The battery reading flashed red. She needed to run the heat exchanger on full refrigeration. She had to do something.

She pulled a pair of needle-nosed pliers from her tool pouch and cut her parachute cables, tying them together to make a cable about forty meters long. With nothing to act as a piton, she rammed the pliers into the woody shell of the trawler and hammered them deep into the thick wood near the trawler's axis with her boot. She tied the cable around it, tested her weight, and then slipped over the edge.

The surface of Venus baked forty-three kilometers below her boots. But it would never get a chance to kill her. Too much of the rest of the planet wanted to try first. As did the repair drone. A light shone into the rain high above, and the sounds of a propeller working carried. The drone relentlessly descended, as if it were necessary for it to finish the job.

The long cable grown of carbon and wood and slime hung below the bulk of the trawler like a plumb line. Thick as her whole body, it flexed, resonating with the constant wind to form standing waves that hummed in her bones. Other winds would find different resonances, and many others would find only discordance. She imagined ageless flocks of trawlers moving through the lower cloud deck, playing eerie, subsonic hymns to Venus as she bathed them in poison.

She lowered herself and swung, trying to reach the lower side of one of the buoyancy chambers. She didn't know how long her pliers would survive as a makeshift piton. She found one of the trawler's six stomata on the lower curve of the buoyancy chamber. It was larger than the stomata on the rosette. She shone her helmet light on full. Its faltering light ought to have opened the stoma, but the vegetable lip remained shut. On the rosette, her helmet lamp had been enough to open a single stoma, but the trawler was bigger and far more complex. It probably opened all its stomata in unison, triggered by photoreceptors. She couldn't trigger them all from here.

Acid rained over her as she dangled. The stalk of the cable was still wide at this level, and slippery, but on the end of a swing, she wrapped her legs around it.

She produced a screwdriver from its pocket sheath and pushed it into the stoma. The stoma opened slightly, and inflowing gas hissed. She wiggled the screwdriver back and forth, loudening the hiss. She had a small pry, useful for corroded access hatches on the habitats. One end was flat, the other tapered to a blunt point. She jammed the blunt end into the stoma, beside the screwdriver. Air wooshed in, until the pressure inside equilibrated. She strained the lip wider. The first inch resisted, but then she must have reached some point that triggered the rest of the opening cycle. The stoma dilated to about fifty centimeters.

Marie-Claude tossed her tools in and wedged her elbows and head through. She got a better grip and pulled herself awkwardly in. The stoma slowly contracted behind her.

She collapsed against the curving walls. The chamber was round and nearly tall enough to stand in. She struggled to catch her breath in the heat, when her parachute cord suddenly slacked and then tugged lightly at her waist. She reeled it in. Only a corroded fragment of the pliers still dangled from the end. If she'd been a few seconds later, she would be plummeting through the brown haze right now.

The stoma shut completely and the drumming rain sounded hollow on the top of the trawler. Her faltering head lamp showed small sacs in the sides of the chamber beginning to inflate and deflate. She crawled closer. They were fleshy, transparently thin, their muscular flexing slowly pumping air out of the chamber. Regaining buoyancy.

Remarkable.

She shut off her helmet lamp to save the last of her power for her suit's cooling system and switched on her last flashlight, a small one for looking at the guts of machinery. A woody frame webbed the chamber, covered with a tough skin. Her light fell on dark patches above her that contracted in apparent response, simultaneous with a slight irising of the stomata, letting in more of the Venusian atmosphere, reducing the chamber's buoyancy further. She turned her light away from the patch.

Unlike the rosette, the trawler had ribs and webs of vasculature. Marie-Claude followed them. Most cells in a rosette were photosynthetic and each made their own food, like a cooperative. That was not true in a trawler, so it needed a complex vasculature to separate its functions. The cable moving through the atmosphere generated electricity, and something must carry either chemical or electrical energy to the rest of the body. Her flashlight showed dark lines within the skin of the chamber, all leading down the axis of the trawler to the cable. Other thick lines led from the axis to long cylindrical nodules beneath the floor of the chambers.

That was what she was looking for.

There must be times when the trawler had no chance to collect electricity. The trawler must store food somewhere for those times. Those nodules might be it.

Her red battery display flashed faster.

She slipped her leaking battery from its pocket.

She sawed through the tough vegetable flesh of the buoyancy chamber with the flattened end of the pry. She peeled back rubbery flaps, exposing a red, woody cylinder, like a stack of disks. The living carbon wiring of the trawler led into and out of the cylinder. She pulled a small voltmeter from a sealed pocket and pressed the needles against one of the wires leading into the cylinder. The voltmeter shot up and wobbled. She checked other wires. They were all live, with large variations in potential. The cylindrical stack showed a large, steady potential across its ends, like a capacitor, or the electroplaque of an eel. Something for times of famine.

She hesitated. The electricity was dirty, changing potential rapidly, even past the capacitor. But the alternative to recharging her battery was seeing how she liked one hundred and ten degrees at three atmospheres of pressure. She had continued dropping and might be as low as thirty-nine or thirty-eight kilometers above the surface.

She looked for the best place to attach alligator clip wires to the capacitor and finally chose a spot. The battery display in the visor of her helmet did not change. It blinked red as if mocking her. If this were a world that did not want to kill her, she would have lightly touched the battery to see how much the charging had heated it. Or to swat the *bebbits*. But the deep dark of hell had her. Her voltmeter showed a variable current for long, changeless minutes. Still no new charge. She examined the battery more closely with the flashlight.

The walls of the battery bowed like a melting toy. The acid exposed by the hole in the battery bubbled like magma.

"Merde!"

She yanked the wires, but the walls of the battery liquified and its sludge poured onto the floor of the woody chamber.

No more main battery.

Her backup battery was nearly used up. The hot suit against her skin was beginning to sting. She was going to pass out from heat exhaustion soon. Marie-Claude pulled the wires that had connected her suit to the battery, and hesitated over the capacitor and its dirty electricity. Then, she hooked her suit directly to the trawler, downstream of the electroplaque.

The displays in her helmet lit. The electrical icons expanded brightly, showing graphs of incoming voltage and current, their frequent surges. Little alarm symbols in different suit systems flashed yellow and red as fuses clicked, blowing and resetting every few seconds. Her backup battery was recharging. The suit's heat exchanger whirred, circulating hot fluid through tubes in her suit. She wondered how much it could refrigerate at this depth.

She wilted, but imagined that it was becoming cooler. She felt as frayed as her suit, as melted as the battery. The clock display showed that twenty-six hours had passed since her plane had been attacked. In that time, she'd descended almost thirty kilometers, from the cold, thin photochemical zone past the three cloud decks and into the haze beneath. Venus had not succeeded in killing her yet. Venus was cunning, but Marie-Claude was learning her tricks.

She watched the displays for a long time, making sure that the trawler didn't blow the suit's electrical system. And then finally, too tired to manage anymore, Marie-Claude lay as flat as she could and slept.

Venus hated them with blinding sulfuric acid, biting cold, ferocious winds, and if they were foolish, with crushing pressure and melting heat. Venus killed them with the slowness of a lion picking off gazelles, one by one: the slow, the unlucky, those who made small, human errors.

These were bits of heroic news in *La Presse* or *Le Devoir* in Montréal and Québec, testaments to the bravery of Québécois astronauts. *La République* had heroes, until the sinking of *Le Matapédia*.

The upper atmosphere had corroded one of the buoyancy tanks of the floating habitat. As *Le Matapédia* sunk into the killing depths, kilometer by kilometer, many of the inhabitants had been rescued, but the public mood back home changed. The Québécois were proud, and they could stomach the sacrifice of the unlucky and the slow, but Venus had tried to execute a whole herd.

Governments changed, throwing new equipment and fresh colonistes into the clouds. Venus did not care. She could not be outnumbered, and she did not relent.

—From *Commentaries
on the Foundation of the Venusian State*

Marie-Claude dreamed of heat and suffocation. A terrible dry thirst and a bath of sweat choked her, and she could neither wipe her face nor drink. Someone called her, incessantly, penetrating the thickness of dream without breaking her free. Against an oppressive exhaustion, she opened her eyes.

"Marie-Claude! Marie-Claude! Can you hear me?"

"Renaud," she said. She couldn't place where she was. Static swamped his voice. The lights on her suit were uneven, but, for the most part in the yellows.

"Marie-Claude! You're alive! Where are you?"

She checked her readings. Two atmospheres. Had the trawler climbed as she slept? She had been at three atmospheres, but the temperature had risen to one hundred and twenty degrees.

"I'm not sure. Have you got a fix on my signal?"

"Faint one. It looks like you're at thirty-three kilometers."

She rechecked her barometer and then shone her flashlight on the little pumping sacs on the wall of the chamber. They had dropped the pressure in the chamber, increased its buoyancy, but the trawler still could not hold her up. Thirty-three kilometers. She'd travelled halfway to the surface.

She explained where she was.

"Inside a trawler?" Renaud crackled. "That's incredibly dangerous!"

Marie-Claude checked the time. She had slept almost twenty-four hours. It had been fifty hours since the sabotage. "How long have I been down here? Four days haven't passed."

"No. We got back to the Laurentide and refitted the planes to fly ahead. I'm almost all fuel. There are eight of us up here looking for you. The habitats will be over tomorrow, but I'll be arriving on your position in about four hours."

"No plane can reach this depth," Marie-Claude said.

"A special plane will be dropping a deep probe tomorrow. Can you survive twenty-four hours?"

She looked at the makeshift wiring, the only thing keeping her alive. Her backup battery gave her a reserve of perhaps an hour.

"I don't know."

Renaud's silence dragged so long that she thought maybe they'd lost contact.

"What do you think would happen to a trawler if it goes into a storm?" he finally asked.

"What? Where is there a storm?" Venus had big polar storms, as stable as the ones on Saturn or Uranus, perhaps even as long-lived as the Great Red Spot. But below the super-rotating winds, the equatorial air frequently tore itself into short-lived storms of lightning and ripping winds.

"About an hour from you."

"How big?"

"It's a storm."

She understood. Researchers had dropped probes into the equatorial storms. None had survived the violent shifts of pressure, temperature, and acidity.

"This might be the way out," he said. "You might catch an updraft."

"Renaud, I've been standing on the edge for two days. I don't want to talk about luck."

"I'm sorry. I'm just glad you're alive. Everyone is going to be happy you're alive. The habitats are in turmoil. All the talk is about change. The constabulary has made arrests in the attempt on your life. The tracks led back to the office of the *parti nationaliste*. People are calling for a referendum on separation from Québec, but the parties are waiting on your safe recovery."

"Or death," she said.

"We'll get you! You're the hero of the day. You've seen Venus deeper than anyone ever has."

Thunder, distant and faint, sounded.

"Why are you saying this?" she asked.

"The agents of the *Gouverneur* tried to silence your voice, but they've only given you a larger audience."

"I'm not even *séparatiste*," she said.

"Everyone will be listening to your voice when you're rescued. Despite the passions, the referendum is no sure thing. The engineering union will almost certainly tip the balance. And you sway the union. You could give us our own nation. *Un pays pour nous.* We deserve it."

"Maybe we do deserve Venus," she said. "Who but idiots would deserve a burning land wrapped in poison?"

"You mastered Venus," Renaud said. "We will tame Venus."

"I did not master Venus."

"You are learning the ways of the land, like the first *coureurs des bois*."

Coureurs des bois. She tasted the phrase. It was an old one, from the times of the foundation of Québec by France, a word to speak of boys and men raised among the Algonquin and Montagnais natives to become the bridges between the *colonistes* and the new land. Renaud had used a term laden with history, as politicians and demagogues often do, careless of truth. But his words found a resonance in her heart, unexpected and potent.

A second radio signal chimed in her helmet, devoid of static and interference. Close. She chilled. The drone had heard her radio.

"*Merde.*"

"What is it?" Renaud demanded, so, so far away, safe in his plane.

"I thought I'd lost it. But it's homing in on my radio signal."

"The drone can get to you?"

"It's probably in worse shape than me, but its tools can break through the walls of the trawler. I've got no way to stop it."

"Shut down your antenna and radio," Renaud said.

"I'm not shutting down the radio. It will already have colocated my signal with the electrical noise of the trawler, but I'm not going to die by myself."

"What are you going to do?"

"Venus, the drone, and I are going to have this out."

"You just said you couldn't stop the drone."

"I know."

"What about the storm?"

"Be quiet," she said. "I've got to think."

She had little left in her tool kit. She pulled out copper wiring, a small knife, clamps of corroding reinforced plastic, a pockmarked screwdriver, and a small steel hammer. She slitted the wire and stripped away the insulation. The copper wouldn't last long in the rain, or even in this chamber, but she only needed it to survive until the storm.

For the first time, a rumble, a subsonic vibration, touched her bones. The storm, Venus' final offer in her negotiations, closed on Marie-Claude.

She wound the copper wire around the hammer, and then tied one of her two parachute cords to it. She swung the makeshift weapon experimentally on its cord. A flimsy thing against a machine.

She tied the end of her second, longer, parachute cord to the screwdriver, and then pounded it deep into woody flesh between the six buoyancy chambers, all the way to the rigid, charged spine of the trawler, and wrapped it tightly around. Static tingled through her gloves. She tied the cord to her harness.

The drone's signal was very close now.

She unplugged herself from the trawler's electroplaque, leaving her suit and its heat exchanger to run on the emergency battery. Perhaps an hour.

"You got a fix on me, Renaud?"

His voice crackled. "You're at thirty-three kilometers and sinking. What's your plan?"

"Just keep the fix and keep quiet."

The darkened patch on the top of the buoyancy chamber, the photoreceptor, had a dark filament running away from it, toward the axis of the trawler. She followed this line until the tough vegetable skin obscured it. With her screwdriver and her little hammer, she dug into the flesh, being careful not to dig far enough to break the outer skin of the trawler. She tore, following the filament to where it met five similar filaments and dove with them down the trawler's spine. She whispered a quick, unaddressed prayer, and severed the trunk of filaments with tip of her screwdriver. No more photoreceptors for her trawler.

She crawled back to the stoma and put her tools back into their little pouches before she took a hot breath. Then, she wriggled her finger into the sealed hole of the stoma. The atmosphere outside hissed in, hot. Her ears and sinuses ached.

Her suit crushed against her, and her tank released more oxygen to compensate, while the heat exchanger whirred to full. Almost seven atmospheres of pressure and one hundred and seventy degrees Celsius. Her suit was rated to five atmospheres, and one hundred and fifty degrees. Engineers understood tolerances; the designers would not wear this suit under these conditions.

But here she was.

She pushed two hands into the opening, pulling the edge wide to stare down into the sub-cloud haze. The trawler's cable flexed chaotically in surging winds, as crackles of blue-white arced along its length, shedding charge against particulate debris in the air. The trawler was a beautiful machine, a masterpiece of biological engineering, evolved to live and love this terrible world.

Marie-Claude wriggled free of the buoyancy chamber and slipped down her cord. The inconstant wind spun her. Her legs and arms swung and jerked as she tried to straighten. She paid out all her cord, until she hung twenty-five meters down the trawler's cable. She fluttered in the wind, meters from the trawler's cable, with nothing beneath her for thirty-three kilometers.

She tried to grab the cable, coming close to its slick, arcing surface. She wished that this was the most dangerous part of her plan, but it was only one part where she might be killed. And the longer she dangled in the wind, the more potential difference she accumulated relative to the cable. Her wet cord, as a conductor, mimicked the trawler's cable. If she didn't ground herself on the trawler's cable again, when she finally reached it, she would shock herself, possibly into unconsciousness.

The storm rumbled again, shaking her bones. She reached for the trawler's cable, and almost touched, before an arc of electricity leapt between them, shocking her. She snapped her hand back. The drone approached, its lamps lighting the mist from nearby. And the wind still kept her from the cable.

She climbed the cord, getting closer to the trawler's cable. She steeled herself as she grabbed it and electricity convulsed her. Displays in her helmet winked out momentarily. With spasming muscles, she slid her way down the shaft, wrapping her legs around it.

The repair drone broke through the mist. Two of its three lamps, despite being encased in glass, were dark. Its corroding claw gaped at her.

Marie-Claude reached her arms around the cable to tie the end of her second parachute cord around it, the one with the hammer and copper wire tied to one end. Rain whirled around her in gusts, discoloring the steel hammer and speckling the copper with powdery, blue-edged holes.

And then the rain stopped, the wind stilled, and the air brightened.

She twisted her body to see what was happening. Awe seized her. The haze opened into kilometers and kilometers of clear air. Dark, bruised clouds rimmed the open air, veined with flashes of blue-white lightning. A great vortex, a hundred kilometers across. The center of the storm pierced the bottom of the sub-cloud haze, revealing Venus, unclothed, terrifying and beautiful. A great plane of dark basalt lay beneath the storm, pocked by high, shiny lava domes. And thirty kilometers beneath the center of the storm's clear air, a flat volcanic mesa shot bright red lava and black sulfuric smoke into the sky.

Naked Venus. Terrifying. Beautiful.

She and the drone were sucked into the quick-moving winds scouring the edges of the clouds. Blue-tinged lightning decorated the walls of the great column with branching forks. The drone neared from the side, avoiding the trawler's shaft. It could measure electrical charge better than Marie-Claude.

She swung her hammer on the end of its cord and threw. The hammer dragged the wet parachute cord across the few meters and laid it across the top of the grabbing arm.

Electricity cracked across the wet cord. The drone's last light popped and smoke puffed out.

Whatever static charge the drone had acquired in the two days in the deep had not been the same as the trawler's. Now it was.

Marie-Claude hauled in the drone and lashed it to the trawler's shaft.

Thunder rumbled. Deep, bone-touching vibrations quickened primal fears.

Her fingers trembled as she opened the access panels of the drone and peeled away burnt acid barriers. Half-melted wiring lay over fuses charred in their brackets. She yanked the surviving wires free by the handful and began wiring the trawler shaft above her to the drone's hydrogen cells. Then, she connected the hydrogen cells to the shaft below the drone. Her fingers tingled as a light current passed through the wires.

She had to get out of here. The wind whipped the trawler past wrinkled walls of cloud, faster and faster. Marie-Claude struggled up the cord, on aching muscles, to the stoma.

The clear space opened wider, and the diffuse brightness of the light lent the gloom the tincture of dawn. Venus had spent almost three days testing her. She had survived. Venus respected Marie-Claude now, but had not finished with her. That was Venus' message in the gesture of opening the clouds. But Marie-Claude would use Venus' spite against her.

Her fingers scrabbled at the opening of the stoma, prying, pulling, until she could force her arms in and pull herself up. She kicked. Hard. Fast. Not much time.

Marie-Claude slipped into the chamber, but did not reconnect her suit to the electroplaque. She untied the parachute cord from her harness. She didn't want to be close to any of the trawler's electrical vascular systems. She huddled against the wall, her knees tucked close to her.

"Renaud?" she asked. "Renaud?"

Static. Then "Marie-Claude! Are you okay?"

"Have you got a fix on me?"

"Yes. It's really faint."

"Keep the fix. I might need a pick-up soon."

"The deep-dive vehicle won't be here until tomorrow, Marie-Claude," he said sadly, "and even then, I don't know if we can get close to the storm."

"Keep the fix," she said.

Thunder boomed closer. Lightning lit the walls of the chamber like a flashlight behind a hand, silhouetting reticulated vasculature. She'd never been close to lightning on Earth, but she felt, even without seeing it, that Venusian lightning was larger, angrier. Soon, the lightning would choose to travel through the stalk of the trawler for part of its journey. She didn't know what would happen to all the things that parasitized the trawler as a platform upon which to live. They might be burnt to a crisp, cleansing the trawler, or perhaps in the way a forest fire opens ground for new growth, new life might be quickened by the lightning, and given space in which to grow. She did not know if she would survive. She was now a seed in a pod, wondering if the casing was strong enough to survive the trial that preceded birth.

Distantly, through a wall of static, Renaud yelled. "You're descending. Are you in a down-draft? Marie-Claude! You're at thirty-one kilometers and dropping!"

The world exploded around her. Painful brightness. Bone-shaking noise. Heat. Sizzling shock seizing her muscles. The world became transparent. Fragments of overloaded sensation were simultaneous with a shuddering explosion below. Where the repair drone had been, a bright flash of orange and purple lit the thin floor of the chamber. The trawler shook, as if it were about to come apart.

Then the world dimmed.

Lightning cracked farther away, lighting the walls of her world like new moments of creation.

Her muscles trembled from electrical shock, even though she'd been grounded to the trawler and not in the path of any of the current. She felt heavy. The chamber continued to shake in turbulence. She was heavy. It was not the electrical shock. The chamber shook in the turbulence of its own rapid ascent through the atmosphere. It had worked. Igniting the hydrogen cells on the drone had severed the trawler's heavy cable.

"Renaud!" she cried.

Her antenna icon was red. Her operating system was rebooting. Renaud couldn't hear her. She wasn't transmitting her location. Her emergency battery was failing. And the trawler's severed shaft could not produce electricity anymore. But the electroplaque might still be charged.

Marie-Claude crawled to the hole she'd dug in the woody flesh of the trawler. Her hands shook, her muscles still spasming from the shock. She clipped her suit to the electroplaque.

Some displays lit, but it became hard to think, to focus on what they were telling her. Her chest felt heavy. Her arms and legs ached. The decompression icon winked bright red in the middle of her faceplate. The yellow nitrogen icon flashed beneath it. Danger of nitrogen narcosis, despite the low nitrogen mix in her air tank. Going from six atmospheres to one was lethal. The trawler shuddered as it continued upward, and blackness invaded the edges of her vision. Like a fickle genie, Venus might have granted her wish but killed her anyway.

Duvieusart Inquiry Transcript, page 782

6:35, RENAUD LANOIX, ENGINEERING SUPERVISOR: We found Mademoiselle Duvieusart in the charred husk of a trawler at forty-nine kilometers. Her suit had rebooted on a failing emergency battery. We had initially thought the trawler had only been mauled in a deep storm but later on, we found explosive damage underneath the buoyancy chambers and in the remains of its cable. The chambers were still sealed at an atmosphere and a half.

6:35, CHLOE RIVERIN, CHAIR: In what condition did you find Mademoiselle Duvieusart?

6:35, RENAUD LANOIX, ENGINEERING SUPERVISOR: The media reports were accurate. Unconscious. Extreme heat exhaustion. Shock. And nitrogen narcosis. The safeties in her suit had tried to adjust the pressure more gradually, but it hadn't had enough power to do more than a half-job.

6:35, CHLOE RIVERIN, CHAIR: And then what?

6:35, RENAUD LANOIX, ENGINEERING SUPERVISOR: We had no access to a hyperbaric chamber, so the only thing we could do was put her in our own plane and dive as deep as the tolerances would allow. We managed to raise the pressure in the plane to almost two atmospheres for several hours.

Everything ached when she woke. The drone of a plane engine sounded, and she was strapped in, reclining, in one of the back passenger seats. Her suit was off, and bandages covered her arms. Renaud knelt, applying an acid-burn cream to her legs.

"Renaud," she croaked.

The wind outside the plane sounded wrong, and the pilot ahead of them fought violent turbulence. It was dark outside the cockpit window. The plane shook and bumped again.

"We're going to be riding some rough weather until we can get you safely to higher pressures. Then we can take you home to the *Laurentide* to a hero's welcome. You're big news, even on Earth. The story of your three days in the clouds has had more hits than any other story on Earth, Mars, or the asteroids. Everyone is waiting to hear what you decide."

"*Les séparatistes?*" she asked.

"I sure hope your choice isn't *nationaliste.*"

"Neither," she said.

"Everyone has to choose," he said. "This will go to a vote, and there's only yes and no."

She shook her head. It hurt. "Whether we are a territory of Québec or the nation of Venus, we're still living in floating cans, losing the race. It doesn't matter who comes first in a losing race. The solutions that work elsewhere won't work here."

"What do you want? You're in no shape to lead anything right now."

"We have to learn to live off the land. Smaller habitats have to be more independent, riding deeper in the atmosphere, where we can learn from the life that already thrives here. We have to become the new *coureurs des bois.*"

THE END OF THE SILK ROAD

★

by David D. Levine

And now for a very different take on the second planet from the sun. Venus was once a lush, swampy jungle world, filled with deadly aquatic and amphibious life—at least that's what a bevy of science fiction writers told us. Then, of course, the probes said different, proving that nothing lurked under that inscrutable Venusian cloud cover but rocks and poisonous gas. Lucky for us, David D. Levine didn't let reality get in the way of a rousing good story. Here then, a tale of the Venus of old and a private eye on the trail of a conspiracy.

I GOT OFF THE RED CAR at the Port of Los Angeles stop, knocking some geezer in the knee with my suitcase as I did. "Sorry, Bud," I reassured his scowl. "Nothing personal, but I'm in a hurry."

Somehow I managed to cross the street, dodging between delivery vans laden with bananas and speeding Hudsons, without losing my suitcase, my fedora, or the ticket envelope clutched in my hand. The ticket said Pier A, Berth 152—May 24, 1936—3:40 PM.

My watch said 3:05.

Pier A stretched ahead of me, a huge yellow-painted shed looking as long as five football fields.

I jammed the suitcase under my arm, held my hat on with the other hand, put the ticket in my mouth, and ran for it.

The Three Planet Air Lines steward was just closing the gate as I rushed in, wringing with sweat, and presented my soggy, tooth-marked ticket. He gave me the fish-eye at first, but when he saw the words FIRST CLASS at the top his attitude changed completely. "Welcome aboard, Mr. Drayton," he said, and waved me up the gangplank with a broad smile.

Halfway up, I took a moment to mop my brow and admire the view.

The Port of Los Angeles sprawled out below me, an enormous model railroad set complete with life-sized trucks, trains, and cranes. Off to my left were the sea terminals, where oil tankers went out and banana boats came in. To my right, the interplanetary cargo docks, mostly workaday marswood freighters plus a few of the new cargo airliners, shining silver whales with dozens of propellers on each wing. One of the marswood ships was just taking off as I watched, rising into a clear blue sky under a white cloud of its own: sixty or more Venus-silk balloons full of hot air straining at their tethers. And behind me . . .

The *A. S. Santa Fe* loomed at the top of the gangplank like a streamlined skyscraper with wings, floating low in the water with a full load of fuel and supplies for the two-week flight to Venus. Gleaming with fresh paint in Three Planet Lines yellow, her engines already roaring, she was fast, clean, modern, beautiful—everything Victor Grossman was not. He ought to hate her; she and her speedy sisters were making a hash of his business. Yet that hidebound old silk merchant had sprung for a first-class ticket aboard her . . . for a beat-up old private eye whose guts he'd hated for twenty years.

Why?

It was that mystery, as much as the very substantial retainer accompanying the ticket, that had overcome this little fly's quite understandable reluctance to accept the spider's invitation to his silken parlor.

That, and Maria, of course.

The steward at the boarding door was gesturing impatiently. I waved my hat in the air, called out, "So long, L.A.! Be back soon!" and hurried to meet my fate.

The First Class Observation Lounge was pretty swank, with a magnificent bar at one end, enormous curved windows at the other, and a broad expanse of plush sky-blue carpet in between scattered with little tables. I ordered an orange juice and received two surprises: the drink came in a spherical aluminum container, all Deco and streamlined with a little sippy-straw, and it was on the house.

There was a time I would have made the management regret that decision, even for the price of a first-class ticket.

I sipped my orange juice and wandered to the window, where Brooks Brothers suits jostled elbows with each other at the rail, to watch the takeoff. From here we had a great view of the eight enormous propellers on each wing, each bigger than my house, but even as the engines spun up to speed, their no-doubt-deafening roar was reduced by the double glass to a throaty hum like a Rolls Royce.

There was almost no impression of motion as we thrummed forward, leaving a broad V-shaped wake behind us, then lifted from the water as smooth as a swan. The captain banked and turned in a big half-circle as we climbed, giving us a fabulous view of the glittering City of Angels, then rising still higher over the brown hills and the desert beyond. Details fell away as we climbed, California dwindling to a carpet of brown traced with highways upon which Hupmobiles and DeSotos crawled like ants, then even the highways faded to invisibility. Pretty soon we'd gone so high that we could see Baja and the Gulf of California to our right and the Rockies ahead, the horizon visibly curving away in all directions and a few puffy clouds drifting by below us.

A loudspeaker in the ceiling cleared its throat, then politely requested that passengers return to their staterooms for the passage through the turbulent zone. Quite a contrast with my last such passage, I thought, when it had been a Marine sergeant bellowing, "All right, you leathernecks, strap in!"

Back in my stateroom, I found that the steward had unpacked my bag and left a brochure about the passage, titled *Rounding the Horn*, on the bed. After putting my things back in the suitcase—I travel light and I like to know exactly where my gear is—I read about how the Earth's atmosphere, rotating along with the planet, collided with the interplanetary atmosphere to create a perpetual zone of turbulence which had claimed many a ship in the days of "Marswood Ships and Iron Men." But aboard the *Santa Fe* I need have no fear; her mighty engines and modern appointments would guarantee a swift and comfortable passage through the zone.

And, indeed, though the leather armchair was fixed to the deck and equipped with a seat belt, I never needed it. Even at the worst, the liner's gentle jostling did nothing more than rock me to sleep.

After breakfast, a remarkably tasty concoction of bacon and eggs wrapped in something I'd call a tortilla but which the menu described as a crêpe, I drifted back to the observation lounge, where I slipped my feet under the straps by the rail and sipped coffee from one of those spherical Deco things while I contemplated the globe of the Earth, floating like a big glass marble in the endless cloud-flecked blue of the sky.

From here, all mankind's schemes, ambitions, and fighting had dwindled to nothing. Dust bowls, floods, wars and rumors of wars . . . all were as invisible as the petty thefts, embezzlements, and infidelities that usually bought me my daily bread. I couldn't even see where one continent left off and another began, never mind countries.

My reverie was interrupted by a splash, a thud, and a petite little shriek as a soft, silk-clad form caromed off my shoulder, leaving a sphere that smelled of gin and vermouth spinning in the air between us.

Slipping my feet out of the straps, I held onto the rail with one hand and reached up with the other, grasping the dame by one slender wrist and pulling her down out of the air to where she could reach the rail.

Nice gams, I thought as she struggled to compose her dress, her hat, and her purse, all of which were trying to float off in different directions. Most of the other female passengers were wearing trousers; apparently this one hadn't read the brochure.

Her drink, I noted, was getting away, a spiral of shimmering droplets spilling from the end of the straw as it tumbled. I snagged the sphere out of the air and snapped it to one of the magnets lining the rail for that purpose, next to my coffee. I was just wondering what to do with the spilled martini droplets when an automaton waiter appeared, smoothly sweeping them up in a pristine white napkin. Just as well; it would have been uncouth, as well as stupidly self-destructive, for me to slurp them up out of the air with my tongue.

"First time in free fall?" I asked the dame after the waiter had refreshed our drinks.

"And here I thought I was hiding it so well," she replied, arching one plucked eyebrow in self-mockery as she daubed at a spot on her Venusian-silk sleeve. She was about my age but still a looker, honey-blonde with some meat on her bones. Just the way I like 'em. "And you?"

"Not my first spin on this merry-go-round, no." Droplets of blood wobbling in smoky air and the smell of gunpowder. I took a big swig of coffee to wash the memory out of my mouth.

We chatted for a while, and I couldn't help but notice that as she sipped her drink she was inspecting me from beneath the questionable cover of her hat's veil. I'm not sure just what she saw in a craggy forty-seven-year-old P.I. with a broken nose and graying temples, but she made her move after the second martini.

"Is it true what they say," she said, tilting her head downward and looking at me through her eyelashes, "about what two people can get up to in free fall?"

"I've known people who were quite enthusiastic about it," I replied, not admitting any specifics.

She turned from me and looked out the window, where the Earth was just vanishing behind the wing. "Pity about the view," she said. "I wonder if we can see it from my stateroom?"

The *Santa Fe* really did have the very latest word in passenger comforts, including some strategically-placed straps and grab bars on the bed frame. After we'd tried them all out, the blonde turned on the lights, lit a cigarette, and just looked at me for a time, the smoke mingling with her drifting hair before it curled away toward the ventilation grille on the wall. I looked at her, too, admiring the way her creamy breasts bobbed gently in the air.

"Who was it?" she asked.

"Who was what?"

"The girl you were thinking of instead of me." She took another drag on the cigarette. "I mean, don't get me wrong, I had a good time. But I know when a man isn't paying attention."

I looked out the window as I considered my reply. We'd left the curtains open; no one but the whole shining Earth was out there to look in on us. "Someone I haven't seen in over twenty years," I said.

"Must have been quite a girl, to hold your attention that long."

The Earth stared back at me. Wars and rumors of wars . . . all invisible at this distance, but still there nonetheless.

"I didn't deserve her."

Cooksport had changed a lot in twenty years, and not for the better. The small and shabby passenger dock from which I'd departed had been replaced with a grand palatial terminal, which had itself fallen into disrepair, with chipped terrazzo and falling plaster and only five of the sixty slots on the arrivals board occupied. I was sure the cargo terminals had seen even bigger changes, following the silk industry's rising and falling fortunes.

Emerging from the terminal, whose ceiling fans were tarnished but still slowly turning, was like stepping into a sauna. "Ah, Venus," I said, fanning myself with my hat. "How I haven't missed you."

Though it was just past noon, the sky above the port was a curdled mess of gray cloud and weak, fitful light, the best old Sol could manage even at a distance much closer than Earth's. Wormlights, each sucking a sugar-teat at the top of a light pole, illuminated the square fronting the terminal, where a row of cabs awaited the arriving passengers.

"Superior Silk," I said to the cabbie as I tossed my suitcase into the cab's howdah, clambering up after it.

"Office or plant?" the cabbie gurgled from the driver's saddle. He was a froggie—a "Venusian aboriginal," to be polite—crammed into a human-style cab driver's outfit, complete with a uniform cap that perched unsteadily behind his bulging eyes. His collar and cuffs were frayed, and damp with the moisture that oozed continually from his pale, greenish skin.

"Office, I guess."

The cabbie's throat-sac worked in acknowledgement. He pushed the flag on the meter down with one webbed hand and goaded the cab with his heel-spurs. The cab whuffled and gurgled as it rose unsteadily to its six suckered feet, then took off down the street at a shambling run, leaving me hanging onto the grab bar with one hand and my hat with the other. The suitcase I wedged between my hip and the howdah's side.

The breeze helped a little, but not much.

★ ★ ★

The Superior Silk Corporation of Venus sprawled across a half-square-mile plot not far from the port—which wasn't surprising, given that almost all of their product was exported to Mars and Earth for use in airship balloons. Seven vast hangars, each one an arched wooden structure as long as a football field and over a hundred feet tall, stood in an arc around the manufacturing plant, a blocky collection of greenbrick buildings topped by dozens of smokestacks. Only about a quarter of those stacks were sending their black fumes up to join the gray and muddy sky. But the cabbie drove his mount toward a building that stood out from that great industrial agglomeration like a Chrysler hood ornament on a woodpile.

Superior Silk's office block held itself aloof from the ugly, utilitarian buildings where the actual work was done. It was built to impress, three stories of streamlined aluminum and glass, all Art Deco curves and parallel lines. A large neon sign, reading only SUPERIOR, cast its harsh blue-white light over the buildings, streets, and swamps nearby.

A huge, stylized aluminum sculpture of a Venusian silkworm loomed over the main entrance. As I passed beneath it, I couldn't help but notice that the electric light that illuminated its left eye was burned out.

After I presented my card to the receptionist—MIKE DRAYTON, PRIVATE INVESTIGATOR, it read, with the old address crossed out and the new one written beneath in pen—she used the intercom to call the executive offices.

A minute later, the chairman's secretary appeared to take my hat and suitcase and lead me up to his office. I was not at all surprised that she was honey-blonde, zaftig, and very pleasing to my eye; Grossman's tastes had always matched my own.

"Mr. Grossman is expecting you," she said as she gestured me through the double doors.

Grossman's office was even more deluxe than the exterior of the building, the aluminum and steel joined by marswood and oak trim that would never have withstood Cooksport's spring rains. An electric fan whirred silently overhead.

"Welcome to Venus, Mr. Drayton," said the great man, extending a hand with something that could have been mistaken for sincerity. "I trust you had a pleasant trip?"

"I lost a hundred bucks on zero-gravity billiards," I replied, taking the hand with something that could have been mistaken for respect.

Victor Grossman was still tall, lean, and impeccably dressed—white silk from collar to spats, of course, with the shine and luster of the *really* expensive stuff. But in the twenty years since I'd last seen him he'd lost the last of his hair, picked up some wrinkles, and added dark bags under his eyes. Bags crafted of the finest Venusian silk, I was sure.

"You're probably wondering why I've asked you to come all this way," he said, seating himself behind his broad, immaculate desk and gesturing me to the supplicant's chair.

"The thought had crossed my mind. Especially considering the first-class airline ticket. For which thanks, by the way."

"I have an immediate requirement for a man to perform a . . . confidential task," he said, steepling his fingers. "A man of great personal integrity. A man with bravery, wit, and keen investigative skills. In short, a man with your unique qualities."

"I'm flattered. Also surprised."

He waved a hand dismissively. "I know we have not always seen eye to eye on every issue, Mr. Drayton, but I am not a man to carry a grudge."

That, I knew, was a bald-pated lie, but the weight of Grossman's retainer in my bank account held my mouth shut. "So why'd you send all the way to L.A. for this paragon of virtue?"

"Because there is no one on Venus I can trust."

That made two of us. The corrupt swamp of Venusian politics and jurisprudence made the Wugunta Bog look like a rose garden, which was one of the things that had driven me off of the planet in the first place. Grossman, of course, had been another. "All right, I'm here. What's the gig?"

He unlocked a desk drawer and extracted a file folder. The first thing I found in it was a photograph of a fat froggie with a scarred snout. "That," said Grossman, as though indicating a slug that had crawled onto his rosebush, "is Uluugan Ugulma, a prominent local fungus dealer. His very successful legitimate business in construction fungi is a front for an even more successful *ulka* ring."

"Hunh." *Ulka* was one of the nastier products of the fecund Venusian biosystem, a drug with a powerful kick and even more powerfully addictive. "So what's it to you?"

"My brother George is an *ulka* addict. He has gone into substantial debt to Mr. Ugulma's syndicate."

"Sorry to hear that."

"He is a weak man, Mr. Drayton, but he is my brother. I need you to investigate and document Mr. Ugulma's little side business so thoroughly that even the Cooksport police can't overlook it."

"That's a tall order, Mr. Grossman. They can be extremely myopic."

"I'm confident in your abilities, Mr. Drayton. Once I have your documentation in hand, I can offer it to Mr. Ugulma in exchange for forgiveness of my brother's debt."

Drugs, blackmail, and a focus on the money over his own brother's welfare . . . that was Grossman to a T. "That won't keep your brother from going right back into hock."

"Leave that part to me, Mr. Drayton. It's Ugulma I want."

I flipped through the file folder. It had names, addresses, schedules, a few more photographs. "I can work with this. I get fifty a day, plus expenses."

"Agreed. And there's a five-hundred-dollar bonus for you at the end of the job."

I raised one eyebrow at that. "I assume this is on the down-low?"

"Extremely confidential, yes. All payments henceforth will be in cash."

"My favorite flavor."

I closed the folder and tapped it on the desktop to settle the papers I'd disturbed. The job smelled fishy—I'd expected nothing better from the moment I received Grossman's radiogram—but his story was self-centered, underhanded, and nasty enough that I almost believed it.

I could spend the retainer on a week of high living at the Lugwunta Bay casinos, tell him I'd found nothing, and use the return ticket to fly back to sunny L.A.

Or I could do the job, milk him for all I could get, and maybe catch a glimpse of Maria.

I extended my hand, this time with a measure of genuine warmth. "All right, Mr. Grossman, you've got yourself a P.I." We shook on the deal.

I resisted the impulse to count my fingers afterward.

★ ★ ★

After the conclusion of our deal, Grossman's secretary—her name was Lillie—gave me the nickel tour of the plant. We started at Hangar One, where millions of Venusian silkworms dropped a hundred feet from the ceiling, dangling on their shining threads. The smell was as appalling as I remembered.

"Hell of a life," I said. "Start at the top, work your way to the bottom on a string you pull from your butt, then when you get where you're going they take away everything you've accomplished and make you start all over again."

"At least they're well fed." She tilted her honey-blonde head. "You know a lot about silkworms for a detective, Mr. Drayton."

"My dad was a silk salesman. He dragged us to Venus when I was twelve, and I worked in the hangars for a while before I became a cop." A business that stank even worse than silkworms, as I'd learned. "Then I joined the Marines."

"Is that where you got the broken nose?"

I looked down in embarrassment. "That was in a bar fight, actually."

"It gives you character." Her smile was heartbreaking. "You must have some fascinating stories. Would you care to join me for dinner?"

If only I were twenty years younger, I thought. "Sorry, miss, I've had a long day. In fact, I think I'd better cut this tour short and find my hotel. Get a fresh start tomorrow."

"Some other time, perhaps?"

I should have told her to back off but I didn't want to bruise her little heart unnecessarily. She looked like such a sweet, innocent kid. "Perhaps," I said.

Leaving the plant, I found myself in the middle of the departing shift-change crowd, humans and froggies chatting amiably together as they made their way home by bus, boat, foot, or flipper. I listened in as I walked.

Beneath the casual talk of weather, kids, and squabbleball there was an undercurrent of concern. Everyone knew that with the rise of airliners—metal-bodied internal-combustion contraptions using wings instead of balloons to reach the interplanetary atmosphere— the silk trade was changing. Fat military contracts were going the way of the sandsnake and fashion wasn't picking up the slack. But Superior appeared to be doing better than its competitors, at least.

Then, as I reached the street and raised a hand to hail a cab, I heard a voice that stopped me in my tracks.

"Darling!" she called from the rear window of a black eight-cylinder Duesenberg that had just purred up to the curb. Importing it from Earth must have cost ten times my annual income for the shipping alone, but hearing that voice and seeing that face again were worth far more to me than the car.

Maria Grossman, née Keene, still had the bluest eyes, the sweetest smile, and the silkiest honey-blonde hair of any girl on Venus. Maybe that's just infatuation talking, but I don't think so. The years might have made her a little plumper, a little paler, and a little sadder around the eyes, but from where I stood she still looked just as good as she had when I'd left Venus twenty years ago.

But before I could return her endearment and run to her arms, I heard another voice, almost as familiar but not nearly so pleasant, from behind me.

"Sweetie!" It was Grossman, of course, striding from Superior's offices with the brisk, confident step of a rich man whose beautiful and much younger wife had just called him "darling." She swung open the door as he reached the car, they kissed, and he climbed in.

She hadn't seen me at all.

I stood at the curb like a statue of *The Sucker* while the car purred away to their luxurious home in Bentwood or Wunguunna or some other neighborhood with servants and swimming pools and real Earth trees.

Right then I was wishing real hard I was still a drinking man.

I spent most of the evening sitting in the hotel bar anyway, pounding down glass after glass of soda water as though I had something to prove. Which I did. If I could sit within arm's reach of a whole bar full of alcohol and not touch a drop, I'd prove that I was still my own man, not a slave to the bottle.

Of course, at the moment I was Grossman's man. But the principle was still sound.

"She was the one who left me," I told the bartender, who listened as attentively as you might expect for a barman whose only customer was paying a dollar thirty-five a glass for soda water and tipping heavily. I'd say he was all ears, but froggies don't have external ears. "I wish to hell I knew what I could have done to keep her."

"Kugna," he gurgled.

"What?"

"Kugna. It's a kind of fish. A courting gift. Dames love a guy who brings them lots of fish."

I sipped my soda and listened to the sweat trickling down my back. The barman had something there. Even though Grossman was fifteen years older than me and not particularly handsome, with the fat military contracts he'd landed in the early days of the war he could offer Maria a hell of a lot more fish than I could.

But there had been something between us—something real, something bigger and better than money. And she'd proved it that night in Lugwunta Bay, eighteen months after the wedding, when we'd met by chance at the casino. We wound up in bed together less than half an hour later.

When I woke up and saw her beautiful, sleeping face in the wormlight that oozed through the hotel window, I knew if I stayed on Venus we'd both regret it sooner or later. I didn't wake her up to say goodbye.

I'd run off to the Marines that very morning. And after beating the Krauts at Ceres and Io, and losing a lot of good friends while suffering nothing worse than a broken nose myself, I'd crawled into the bottle. When I managed to drag myself out again I found myself back in California, where I'd been born and raised, and that's where I'd stayed. Because I knew if I ever went back to Venus I'd regret it sooner or later.

Well, now it was later.

I'd come back.

And I regretted it.

I stared at the ceiling fan all night, thinking and sweltering instead of sleeping, but by the time Venus's lame excuse for dawn rolled around, at least I'd made up my mind. I'd come here to do a job . . . I would do the job, take as much of Grossman's money as I could, and get out.

After breakfast, I hailed a cab and gave the cabbie Mr. Ugulma's business address. I always like to verify any information my clients provide, especially when the client is someone as trustworthy as Grossman.

Ugulma's shop was on the swampier side of town, a typical Venusian structure that looked like a banyan tree topped with a slice of peat bog. The sign out front read UGULMA FUNGI in English with two lines of Venusian squiggles below it, presumably the same thing in the two major local languages. I had the cabbie drive past and drop me a few streets beyond it, then walked around to the back to scope out the place for myself.

Although the front of the building wasn't much different from its neighbors, the back of the property was secured on three sides by a high greenbrick wall topped with broken bottles—not at all the sort of thing you'd expect of a legitimate fungus dealer. Score one for Grossman's story.

As I inspected the wall, I got one of those feelings that a P.I. learns to respect—an itching at the back of my neck, like I was being watched. I whipped my head around as quick as I could, but saw nothing behind me.

But was that a splash I heard? Someone vanishing around a corner?

I crouched low and stayed still for a while, but nothing jumped me.

Returning to the street, I approached the shop's front door just like an upstanding citizen. The door croaked a greeting as I approached— a habit of the local architecture I've always found disquieting—and as it opened itself, I was immediately met by the proprietor, Mr. Ugulma himself. He was just as plump and ugly as his photograph had promised, and his wide, shining eyes oozed suspicion.

"Can I help you?" he gurgled curtly. He spoke English with a German accent, which did not endear him to me. It wasn't the froggies' fault that the whole continent of Thugugruk had been German territory before the war, I told myself, but that accent still made me twitch.

"I'm looking for . . . something in the fungus line," I temporized as I inspected the merchandise. The place looked not unlike a soggy version of an Earth lumberyard, though all of the planks and beams were actually slices of giant mushroom and it smelled of loam rather than cut wood. But I wasn't really paying any attention to the goods on display—I was looking behind and between the stacks for signs of Ugulma's other business.

"Fungi we've got," he replied, gesturing to indicate the whole shop. But his froggy eyes didn't budge from mine. It was as though he expected me to walk off with a whole bundle of toadstool two-by-fours the minute his back was turned.

"I'd like some . . . some, ah, fancy trim work," I said, naming something I didn't see that he might plausibly carry. "You know, detail molding. Like you might find in a nice house."

"Nothing in stock. But we've got a catalog. Special order."

"Can I see it?"

He gave me a long, hard look, then muttered, "Yeah, sure," and ducked behind the counter. I heard the office door croak, which was interesting. I took advantage of his absence to peek a little more nosily into and behind his stock, but when the door croaked again, warning me of his return, I had learned nothing new.

Nor did I learn anything from perusing the catalog, other than the difference between an architrave and a dentil crown. I excused myself as quickly as I plausibly could. Ugulma seemed happy to see the back of me.

The door croaked at me again as I left. "Same to you, pal," I sneered to it under my breath.

I looked around, all casual like, before I hailed a cab back to my hotel. But though I didn't see anything out of the ordinary, I still couldn't shake the feeling I was being watched.

Even though the sun barely peeps through Venus's perpetual clouds, for some reason the natives are strongly diurnal. So when I returned to Ugulma's shop after dark, creeping through the moonless, starless blackness between the widely-spaced wormlights, I could be pretty sure I wouldn't encounter anyone. But I still brought my gat, plus a few other things.

The alley behind the shop was completely black, so I risked a quick flash of my cigarette lighter to make sure I was where I wanted to be before proceeding.

Was that movement? In the murk beyond the lighter's reach?

I doused the flame immediately and crouched stock-still—holding my breath, gun in hand, ready for any attack. But the Venusian night stayed silent as ever, and after several long minutes I decided that what I thought I'd seen had been just a trick of the lighter's flickering flame.

My hotel was pretty cheap—cheaper than my expense report to Grossman would indicate, anyway—but in this case that worked in my favor because the rough woolen blanket they'd provided worked just fine to cover the broken glass at the top of the wall. Even if it got torn, I figured no one would ever notice. Who uses a blanket on Venus, anyway?

I scampered up and over the rough greenbrick just as quick as if it were a wall on the Marines' obstacle course, then dropped to the ground on the other side without a sound.

From my jacket pocket I pulled a little gizmo like a perfume atomizer and squirted it at the door as I approached. The door relaxed, making no sound as I pushed it open a crack and squeezed inside. One of the many useful tricks I'd picked up during my sojourn as the only mostly-honest cop in Cooksport. The office door got the same treatment.

The croak I'd heard from that door on my earlier visit had been a significant clue. Living doors provided security as well as a polite greeting, and they weren't cheap, so the froggies generally only had them as outside doors. For Ugulma to install one of them as his interior office door indicated that there was something more than usually valuable inside.

The office had no windows, so I used my lighter to take a good look around. It had the usual sort of things you'd expect to find in a fungus dealer's office—papers, ashtray, spore casings—plus a large and very sophisticated safe.

Bingo.

The safe's nameplate read "Schlosserei Döttling GmbH" in that almost illegible black-letter type the Krauts are so fond of. It was a name I knew—quality German engineering, nearly impossible to crack. And, given the cost of shipping from Earth, far more expensive than any mere fungus dealer could possibly justify.

But even a perfect safe is worthless if the owner doesn't lock it, and you'd be surprised how often that happens. I reached for the handle to check it . . .

Suddenly I heard the gurgle of a Venusian squelch pistol being cocked. "Hands up, Mr. Drayton," came a familiar German-accented voice, "and turn around slowly."

I did as I'd been ordered, the flickering lighter still in my hand.

Ugulma was standing inside the open door that I myself had silenced. Damn it. "Shouldn't good little froggies be in bed by now?" I said.

"I was told you'd try to steal my notes," he replied, leveling the squelcher right at my family jewels. His grin showed that he knew just how much this was going to hurt.

"What's that behind you?" I cried, and threw the lighter in his face.

It might be the oldest trick in the book, but in this case I really *had* seen something moving behind him.

The lighter smacked him right between his bulging eyes. It went out with a hiss, followed immediately by the liquid cough of the squelcher's discharge. But I had ducked to the side as soon as I tossed the lighter and the shot only caught my sleeve.

I rolled under the desk, drew my gun, then crept out into the pitch blackness as silently as I could. Making for the door, hoping to slip past Ugulma in the dark.

But although froggies don't have ears, they still have excellent hearing. Just before I got to the door, I felt a warm, wet pressure behind my ear—the squelcher's business end.

"Goodbye, Mr. Drayton." The squelcher gurgled . . .

Suddenly a brilliant, blinding flash of light stabbed me in the eyes. Ugulma shrieked in pain, throwing the hand that held the squelcher across his eyes.

My gun was still in my hand. I aimed at Ugulma's afterimage and fired.

The muzzle flash showed Ugulma's startled face . . . and a second figure in the office, a skinny froggie with a fedora and a big camera like a reporter's. What the hell?

Darkness returned with a thud, the sound of Ugulma's body hitting the floor. I leapt at where I thought the froggie with the fedora might be.

Somewhat to my surprise, I connected.

We rolled over and over on the office floor, both grunting as we struggled, banging into furniture, wastebaskets, icky fungus things, and Ugulma's heavy, slimy body. Then there came a crunch of breaking glass and a gasp of froggy pain.

That gave me the opening I needed. I shifted my grip, got my thumbs under his throat-sac, and squeezed. Hard.

He fought back, but Earth's gravity is higher than Venus's and I work out at the boxing gym every week. Pretty soon he stopped fighting, his movements growing weaker and then stopping altogether.

I kept up the pressure long enough to be sure he wasn't playing possum, but not long enough to kill him.

By the time he came to, I'd handcuffed him to the safe, tickled the wormlights awake, and retrieved my gun. His pockets held a nasty little two-shot squelcher, some spare flashbulbs, and no identification. And though he was bleeding from a cut on his face where he'd rolled over and broken his own camera's flash unit, most of the green blood on him, and on me, was Ugulma's. The fungus dealer was dead, shot through the throat.

Whoever the froggie with the fedora was, he was tough and ruthless and good at his job; despite my advantages in strength and weight, I'd only beaten him by luck. So I sat in the chair a good ten feet from him, with my fully-loaded pistol trained on him and Ugulma's squelcher ready in my other hand. Fedora's own squelcher was in my pocket—I didn't trust it.

In any Earth city the size of Cooksport, the sound of gunshots would have brought the police by now. But I'd been a Cooksport cop for almost five years and I knew we wouldn't be disturbed until morning.

He groaned and sat up . . . or tried to, until the handcuffs holding him to the safe's thick steel foot stopped him. Then he looked around, spotted me, and immediately rose to a crouch, ready to spring if he got an opportunity.

"Settle back down or I shoot," I said conversationally.

He settled: butt on the floor, facing me, with his hands behind him. Which showed that he understood English and that he wasn't dumb.

"Who are you?"

"My name is not important." His English was good for a froggie, with no regional accent I could detect.

"Who sent you?"

Silence.

"Why were you following me?"

Silence.

I stood up, took one step closer to him, and drew back the hammer on my revolver. I find that the click it makes is extremely persuasive. "Who sent you, and why were you following me?"

I'll give him credit. He held his silence right up until I put the barrel between his froggy eyes and started to squeeze the trigger.

"I don't know who hired me!" he spat. "The money came through a blind drop."

I stepped back, still keeping the gun on him. "What was the job?"

"To get pictures of your death."

That explained why the camera had flashed just as Ugulma was about to pull the trigger, and strongly hinted at the employer. "You were a bit premature."

"I didn't know it would be so *bright*." If froggies had teeth, he would have been gritting them.

But something didn't quite fit. "How did you know Ugulma would show up and try to kill me?"

He smiled, and it was an ugly thing. "I told him to."

Ugulma had said something along those lines . . . "You told him I'd try to steal something of his. What was it?"

He didn't say anything, but his eyes flickered fractionally in the direction of the safe.

"So the *ulka*'s in the safe," I probed.

At that he blinked. "*Ulka?* Not even Ugulma's stupid enough to sell *ulka* here. This is Gurundi territory."

Curiouser and curiouser. "So what's in the safe that's so important Ugulma would risk killing a human over it?" Humans and froggies in Cooksport had separate-but-equal judicial systems. For a froggie to kill a human was a maximum crime under froggie law—he'd have to be truly desperate to even consider such a thing.

"Notes."

"What kind of notes?"

"I wasn't told." His throat-sac pulsed, then slowly deflated—a froggy shrug. He really didn't know.

"Whatever those notes are," I mused, "your employer knew that if Ugulma thought I was trying to steal them, he'd kill me. So he told you to warn Ugulma I was coming to do exactly that, and then follow me to photograph the hit."

"Pretty smart for a human."

I felt like I had all the pieces, but the puzzle still wasn't fitting together. "You're pretty good yourself. So if whoever-it-was wanted pictures of me dead . . . why didn't he just have you kill me?"

Again the ugly grin. "Look behind you."

It might be the oldest trick in the book, and I'd just used it myself, but even so I nearly fell for it. I started to look . . . then immediately caught myself and turned back.

Somehow he'd managed to work one hand out of the cuffs while they were behind his back. He was leaping right at me, fearless, the handcuffs swinging toward my face and the other hand reaching for my gun.

But even though my head had started to turn, the gun hadn't. I pulled the trigger right before he slammed into me.

He was still trying to claw my eyes out when he died.

So there I was with two dead froggies, a ruined suit, and a safe full of secrets. I straightened the place up a bit while I thought about what to do next.

Even though the cops wouldn't come by until business hours, whoever had hired Fedora Guy—and I had a very good idea who that might have been—was extremely interested in the contents of Ugulma's safe and certainly had resources of his own. I suspected he'd find out what had happened and try for the safe himself right away. And if he did, and if I could catch him in the act, that would be a very interesting conversation.

I squeezed myself between two file cabinets and waited in the dark.

I didn't have long to wait. It was less than an hour later when the door croaked—apparently it had recovered from the mickey I'd slipped it—and a little guy in a trench coat and slouch hat entered, carrying a pocket wormlight.

The light illuminated what he was looking at, not him, so I couldn't see his face. But he was much shorter than the gross man I'd expected. I took a firmer grip on my pistol and waited to see what he'd do.

He looked around the place a bit, obviously unnerved by the blood and the two bodies, but as soon as he saw the safe he went right to it. He knelt down in front of it, pulled a folded paper from his pocket, and dialed in the combination.

The click of the latch was followed by another click, this one from my revolver. "Okay, Bud," I said, "hands up and turn around slowly. Leave the safe open."

He did as he was told.

And I got a surprise. It was Lillie, Grossman's secretary.

"Mr. Drayton?" she gasped. "You're alive!" Her relief was palpable.

"No thanks to your employer. He tried to have me killed. Twice." I gestured to the two bodies.

"My father would never do such a thing," she protested.

Father? I took another look at the girl's face.

No wonder I'd been attracted, despite my reluctance to rob the cradle. She looked a hell of a lot like her mother had at her age . . . same face, same figure, same honey-blonde hair, same blue eyes.

Blue eyes.

The same as mine.

Grossman's eyes were brown.

"What's your birth date?" I snapped, using the cop voice that compels an immediate answer.

"February 16, 1917."

Subtract nine months . . .

Lugwunta Bay. Give or take a week.

"Holy cow," I muttered.

This changed everything.

"Listen, kid," I said, holstering my pistol, "you seem like a nice girl, and this is a very nasty business. You need to get the hell out right away or you're going to get hurt. Pack one bag, take a ferry to Nuglunda or a zep to Waknuuke, change your name, start a new life. I can front you some cash if you need it. Just go, and go now."

"I won't do that." She was strong-willed and defiant, just like her mom. And her real dad, come to think of it. "I'm sure this is all some kind of mix-up." She planted her feet and bunched her hands into fists. "I'd never betray my father like that."

This little twist made a difficult situation even stickier. If Lillie wouldn't go, then I couldn't sic the cops on Grossman without hurting her—she was an accomplice, and besides, she clearly idolized the man. Which meant that if I just shot Grossman, it would hurt her even more. Telling her he wasn't her real dad was also unlikely to fly. I had to come up with some other way to deal with him.

"What did he send you here to get?" I asked her. More information couldn't hurt and might help.

She handed me the paper. It had Ugulma's address, the safe combination, and the word ACHILLES. "I was to collect everything from the safe with this word on it."

There was one file folder with that label, a fat one. Flipping through it revealed a lot of handwritten notes. It would take a while to sort out.

I thought for a moment. "Okay, tell you what. Go back to Grossman and tell him the combination didn't work. You saw the two bodies, but you didn't see me and you didn't get anything. I'll take this information and I'll . . . I'll try to find some way to fix the situation without hurting your father." I did not clarify who I meant by that last. "Will you do that for me?"

She frowned, but after a moment she nodded. "All right."

I knew I was using her affection for me to manipulate her. I felt like a heel, but it might just keep her alive and out of trouble.

"You're a good kid," I said, and I gave her a quick kiss on the forehead. Her smile broke my heart, for the second time in two days. "Now run home. I'll find some way to let you know what's going on. And . . ." I closed my eyes and swallowed. ". . . and *don't* tell your mother you saw me. Okay?"

"Okay." She took one long, lingering look over her shoulder at me before leaving.

I sat in Ugulma's blood-spattered desk chair for a moment after she left. "Oh boy," I said, with my aching head in my hands. "Oh boy, oh boy, oh boy." Then I hauled myself to my feet and got back to work.

With the safe open, all it took was a screwdriver to change the combination. I used my pocket knife to change it to some random number, closed the door, and spun the wheel—now no one would be able to get it open without high explosives, safecracking expertise, or both. That would buy me some time.

I touched my hat brim to the two dead froggies. "Nice doing business with you, gents." Then I tucked the file folder under my arm and headed out the way I'd come in.

The damn door croaked at me on the way out, so I shot it.

First thing the next morning I had the hotel call a tailor to measure me for a new suit. Nothing too fancy, but I sprung for Venusian silk—when would I ever have a better opportunity? Besides, it was on Grossman's nickel.

After the tailor left, I ordered room service, sat in my skivvies on the bed, and read through Ugulma's notes. They weren't in code, but they were dense and elliptical and Ugulma's writing wasn't tidy. A lot of it was in Venusian squiggles, and some of the rest was in German, but between the English and what little I remembered of the German I managed to piece the story together.

No wonder Grossman had sent his own daughter to get these notes. And no wonder Ugulma had risked the maximum penalty to keep them.

Murder. Fraud. Smuggling. War crimes, even. Grossman was worse than I'd thought. And I had to find a way to take him down while keeping Lillie and Maria out of it.

I put on a shirt and slacks and went out to do what I do.

"Nasty piece of work," I said as I played my pocket wormlight over the destructor's glass casing. I'm not sure whether I was referring to the destructor or Grossman.

I'd walked in the tradesman's entrance at Superior bold as you please, slipped onto the work floor while the guard's back was turned, and made my way to the basement with the thundering silk mill's dark corners, pounding noise, and chemical stink to hide my passage.

The biotic destructor was right where Ugulma's notes had said it would be—twenty glass carboys full of an evil-looking dark green sludge, all connected to their sonic detonators and each other by wires and tubes. It was a Venusian invention, but it was Fritz who had used it on our doughboys back in the war; we'd called them "mold bombs" and now they were prohibited by the Geneva Conventions. They were extremely touchy; when I served a stint in the ordnance division our CO had ordered us not to attempt to disarm or move one if we should come across it in the field.

I didn't know for sure why Grossman had hired Ugulma to use his German contacts and biotics expertise to set up a mold bomb under his own factory, but I had my suspicions. In any case, simple possession of just one of these carboys would be enough to put him in jail for the rest of his life, and Ugulma's notes would tie them to Grossman so tightly even a Cooksport lawyer couldn't get him loose.

But I couldn't send him to jail without involving Lillie.

I sat on the filthy basement floor, staring at the evil thing and considering my options.

None of them was very good.

Three days later I was looking at myself in the wardrobe mirror, admiring my new Venusian silk suit. It was comfortable, stylish, cool, and made me look great. I'll give the froggies this—Cooksport tailors are the best on three planets. They work fast and turn out an excellent product. He'd even thrown in a matching hat, which also suited me perfectly.

Only the dark circles under my eyes spoiled the effect. I hadn't managed more than two or three hours' sleep at a snatch since landing on Venus. But I'd done everything I could to set my plan in motion, and now it was time for the final act. Any delay would only increase the risk of something going wrong.

I left the key in the room. One way or another, I wouldn't be coming back.

But before I departed the hotel, I made three calls from the pay phone in the lobby.

Grossman was inspecting his own reflection in his office window as I entered—with the lights on inside and the night so black outside, the glass made a perfect mirror. Not even the plant, which was of course visible from Grossman's office, showed any lights; with business so slow, no one was working the third shift.

"Nice suit," he said without turning around. His reflected eyes met mine without apparent fear. "You can put the gun away."

"It's just insurance," I said. I didn't lower it.

"I'm not going to try to jump you. I'm an old man, Mr. Drayton. I get what I want with money and power. And I understand from your telephone call that you have something I want."

"I do." I set down my suitcase, opened it left-handed, and pulled out Ugulma's file folder. "Does the name Achilles ring a bell?"

At that he did turn around, though his face showed neither surprise nor concern, just a cold disdain. "I suspected that item was what you were referring to. How did you get it? Did you seduce Lillie the way you did Maria?" My face must have shown my reaction, because he continued, "Oh yes, Mr. Drayton, I know all about Lugwunta Bay."

"And despite that you hired me for this job."

"I hired you *because* of that. Remember how I told you I needed someone of your unique qualities? I wasn't lying. I needed someone with bravery, wit—but not too much wit—and keen investigative skills, because no one else would put himself in front of Ugulma's squelcher for me. And I also needed someone I wouldn't mind seeing dead. You fit the bill for all of those criteria."

Something about the way he said it reminded me of his priorities. Money over family, over relationships, over everything. "So my death wasn't the main point of the plan."

"Only a delightful side effect." He chuckled. "The point of the plan was to photograph Mr. Ugulma in the process of committing the crime. You do recall what the penalty is for an aboriginal who kills a human, don't you?"

"Death by desiccation."

He held up one finger. "*And* destruction of the murderer's property."

Of course! I'd been so stupid to overlook that part—it was the linchpin of the entire scheme. "Which gets rid of the safe, and any other evidence connecting the destructor to you. Very clever. But your plan didn't quite work out."

He shrugged one silk-covered shoulder. "It seems to have worked out well enough in the end. With Mr. Ugulma dead, I only need to obtain and destroy his notes, and now you have brought them to me. I assume you will require some form of payment in exchange for them?"

"Yes. Three things."

"Name them."

"Item one: money. Payment of my fee, in cash, including the completion bonus and my expenses. Which were rather larger than I'd anticipated." I pulled a paper from my suitcase and skimmed it across the desk at him.

He picked up the paper, noted the bottom line, unlocked a file drawer, and tossed me a bundle of bills. I caught it left-handed and put it in my pocket without looking.

"Don't you want to count it?" he asked.

"I trust you when it comes to money. Item two: information. Why blow up your own factory?"

"For the insurance, of course! I'm surprised you even have to ask. I can read the writing on the wall as well as anyone . . . the age of balloons is over. If I destroy the plant now, while it's still a going concern, the payout will be more than enough to keep me and mine in style for the rest of our lives."

"Won't the insurance company find the explosion suspicious?"

Grossman chuckled again. "You underestimate me, Mr. Drayton. With a little help from my friends in the police department—you may know some of them—I've planted evidence tying the biotic destructor to the Silk Workers' Union. Which not only directs suspicion away from me, but under local law it allows me to claim the union's pension fund as damages." He raised an eyebrow. "Is that information sufficient payment for your item number two?"

"It is. I'm impressed—not only do you put your own workers out of a job, you steal their pensions."

"Thank you, Mr. Drayton. I've always suspected we have more in common than our taste in women."

"Which brings us to item three." I tightened my grip on the pistol. "Maria."

"Really, Mr. Drayton." He seemed disappointed. "After all these years?"

"That item is nonnegotiable. Divorce her, or I take Ugulma's notes to the police. No—the union."

"What makes you think she still wants you?"

"I only hope that she does. But even if she doesn't, at least this way she's out from under your thumb."

His brown eyes held mine for a long, considering moment. Then he nodded. "Done. You can have her. I'll file the papers with my lawyer in the morning."

I blinked. "I didn't expect it to be that easy." Frankly, I still didn't believe it.

"Even the shiniest toy palls with age. I'll even buy you a ticket to California for her." I didn't mention that I'd already included her ticket, and a few other things, in my heavily padded expense report. "So, may I have the file now?"

I handed it over. But there was a fourth item, which I hadn't mentioned until now because if I called too much attention to it, he might not say what I needed him to say. "Just one more thing. How could you send your own daughter to do your dirty work for you?"

He didn't look up from flipping through the papers. "Don't be disingenuous, Mr. Drayton. I know whose daughter she really is. Surely you don't think I'd send my own flesh and blood into such a dangerous situation?"

"You're even colder than I'd thought."

"Thank you for the compliment, Mr. Drayton." He closed the file folder, and now he did look up. "I trust you can find your own way out? I have important business to attend to."

"Of course." I tipped my new silk hat. "It's been a pleasure doing business with you."

I closed the door without any appearance of undue haste, then rushed as fast as I could down the stairs to the reception area.

Where I found Lillie crying at the front desk, the intercom's green light reflecting off her beautiful, tear-streaked face. She'd heard the truth, just as I'd promised her in my second phone call. "Sorry you had to get the news this way," I said, "but I knew you wouldn't believe it if you didn't hear it from his own mouth."

"He won't really give her up," she sobbed. "He'll just have you killed."

"I'm sure that's his plan." I took her hand, pulled her toward the front doors. "But I know his priorities: money over family. Now that the evidence is in his hands, he'll want to blow up the plant right away. Come on, *move!*"

She stumbled along behind me, not resisting me but not really cooperating either. I think she was still in shock from the news. "Why do we have to leave?"

"The bomb has a sonic detonator," I said as I hustled her out the front door and down the walkway to the street where the cab I'd come in waited. "A certain frequency of whistle sets it off. It has a range of up to a mile."

"I don't understand . . ."

We had just reached the cab when a strange high-pitched sound caught our ears and made us both look back.

A moment later came a horrible squelching bang, and the illuminated window of Grossman's office was suddenly splattered with green. Green with streaks of red.

The green immediately began to spread, oozing through the cracks the explosion had made in the office windows, creeping over the outside surface of the building. Inside, I knew, it would be even worse, all that shining aluminum and steel vanishing under a rapidly spreading carpet of highly corrosive mold.

And what it did to human flesh and bone . . . well, it was a crime.

"Come *on!*" I said, and hustled Lillie up into the cab's howdah.

I'd moved just one of the carboys from the factory basement into Grossman's office, disconnecting the detonators from the others. I hoped it would destroy only the office block, leaving the plant intact. At least then the workers would still have their jobs, for a few more years at least, and their pensions after that. But I couldn't be sure, so I wanted to get as far away as possible as quickly as possible.

Moving the carboy hadn't been easy, or safe, but it wasn't the first time I'd disobeyed my CO's orders and it probably wouldn't be the last.

"Take us to the port," I told the cabbie. "We have an airliner to catch."

When I saw Maria in the terminal bar, the tension that had been gripping my temples eased . . . and then immediately returned, even stronger.

I'd been too chicken to phone her directly. Instead, I'd called an old mutual friend and asked her to pass a message. I'd been worried she wouldn't follow through, or that the message wouldn't reach Maria in time, or that she'd get the message and pass on it. But she was here, sitting on a bar stool, clad all in black silk, with those magnificent legs crossed at the ankle. Smoking a cigarette, staring off into space, just waiting. Waiting for me at the bar, the way we used to do for each other back in happier times.

But when she heard what I had to say, she'd probably want to kill me.

As we approached, Lillie took away any opportunity I might have had to break the news gently. As soon as she saw Maria she ran toward her, sobbing over and over, "Daddy's dead!"

Maria took the girl into her arms and held her tight. It made my heart ache, remembering those arms around my own shoulders, but I held back to give the two of them a moment together.

After a time, Maria raised her head from her daughter's shoulder and looked me right in the eye.

She was dry-eyed.

"Mike," she said. Just that, just my name, even as she patted her baby girl on the back.

"Maria," I replied in kind. "It's been a long time."

"Yes, it has." She squeezed Lillie again, gave her a silk handkerchief from her purse, and led her to a booth. They sat on one side, the daughter sobbing with her head on her arms, the mother stroking her back; I sat opposite them, noticing how similar and yet how different they were. Maria ordered gin-and-tonics for both of us—our favorite tipple, back when—and ginger ale for the girl.

"How did it happen?" Maria asked me after the waiter left. She didn't look happy, but she wasn't devastated either, just subdued.

The G&T sat in front of me like an accusation. I folded my hands on the worn Formica and composed my thoughts before proceeding. "Grossman was planning to destroy the factory for the insurance money," I explained. "I caught him at it, but he went ahead with his plan anyway, there was an accident with the bomb, and he was killed. The office block is a total loss, I'm sure. The plant might be okay." Was there anything important I'd left out? Oh, yeah. "I'm sorry about your husband."

She didn't even acknowledge my pathetic attempt at solace. "It isn't just a coincidence that you're here," she said.

"No, it isn't. He brought me here as part of his plan—he was hoping to kill me as well as blow up the plant. But I got away." I was trying to tell the truth, but in a way that wouldn't hurt anyone more than necessary. I was failing miserably on both counts. "Oh, and one other thing. Before he died, he admitted in Lillie's hearing that he isn't her real father."

Lillie raised her head from her arms. There was mascara all over the sleeve of her white silk jacket. She looked at her mother accusingly. "Why didn't you *tell* me?"

Maria's face changed completely as she turned to her daughter, showing the deep, unbending love she'd once given to me. "I *couldn't*, darling. I couldn't hurt you like that. If you'd known, you would have had to choose . . . all day, every day. Do you pretend a love you don't feel, and maintain the luxurious lifestyle to which you've become accustomed? Or do you admit your true feelings, and get thrown back into the swamp with the other little fish . . . with the enmity of one of Cooksport's richest and most powerful men as an additional weight around your neck?" She returned her attention to me, her expression going back to neutral. "I would never wish that choice on anyone."

"You don't have to choose any more," I told her, and reached into my jacket pocket. "I got us tickets to L.A. on the *San Pablo*, leaving tonight." I laid the envelope on the table, pushed it toward her. "It's not first-class accommodations, but I got us a family suite, with two bedrooms. For the three of us. A real family, finally, after all these years."

Maria's face softened into the one I remembered . . . a little older, a little wearier, but still as full of hope and love as the one I'd known before the war.

And then it hardened again, and she slid the envelope back to my side of the table.

"I made my choice twenty years ago, Mike," she said, and took a sip of her G&T. "Now I'm a society matron. I have responsibilities. I can't just run away for love." She looked down into her drink. "Someone has to keep Superior Silk running, for another few years at least, or this whole town will fall right into the swamp. "

"Who cares?"

"*I* care, Mike. The workers . . . the aboriginals need us. We've taken so much from them . . . I couldn't just abandon them."

"You don't have to do this . . ."

"I don't know how to be a detective's wife!" she snapped. "I can't make a happy home on just sunshine and oranges." Then she seemed to gather herself up, and reached out and took my hand. "I'm sorry, Mike," she said, with a sweet, sad smile that showed she really meant it. "I'm too set in my ways to change now. Just leave me here with my mansion and my swimming pool and my million-dollar life insurance payout. I'll struggle through."

I picked up my G&T, tilted it back and forth. Watched the way the alcohol beaded on the inside of the glass.

Then I set it down.

"What about Lillie?" I asked.

They both looked at me. Both of their eyes so blue.

"It's not too late for her," I went on. "Let me take her out of this overcast, overheated swamp and back to L.A. where it's sunny and clement all year round. I can't offer her a mansion, but I make a decent living." I turned to my daughter. "And I could use a good secretary."

Lillie looked at her mother. Her mother looked back.

The connection that I saw pass between them was something I've never felt in my whole life—not with a woman, not with my own mother or father, not even with my wartime buddies.

And Maria nodded.

"Now boarding," came the amplified voice of the terminal announcer, echoing across the terminal's chipped terrazzo, "the *A. S. San Pablo* for Los Angeles. All aboard!"

The two women hugged and kissed and promised to write while I paid the tab, gathered up my suitcase, and marveled at what I'd seen pass between them.

It was a moment of shared sacrifice, mutual respect, and deep trust that would tear my cynical heart apart like a two-stroke lawnmower trying to run on high-test aviation fuel.

And I hoped to God that living with Lillie would teach me how to trust like that.

Maria let go of her daughter and, finally, gave me a hug. "If you let anything happen to her," she whispered in my ear, "I'll kill you."

"I'll do my best," I murmured back.

"That's what I'm afraid of." And she let go of me, except for one hand, and continued in a normal voice. "Take good care of my daughter, Mike."

"She's my daughter, too."

"All aboard!" repeated the announcer, and we skedaddled. I looked back one last time as we walked away, but she was already gone.

It was still night when the airliner broke through the clouds, and for the first time in weeks I saw the stars—clean and bright and pure. A gleaming white pinprick for every regret in my life.

And then the liner passed out of Venus's shadow and they faded away, replaced by the pure eternal blue of the sky between planets.

PICKET SHIP

★

by Brad R. Torgersen

When the mantis aliens attack an outpost colony, it's up to Chief Warrant Officer Amelia Schumann to get word of the renewed threat to Earth. But a crash landing on a hostile planet complicates things. What's more, Amelia and her crew aren't the only ones planet-side. The world on which they've landed is being primed for mantis colonization, and the mantis Queen Mother has given her hive-mind children a clear directive: exterminate all humans.

THE SEVEN-MAN picket ship bucked and slewed wildly as it flew through thick, turbulent air. Tall spires—the trunks of temperate marshland trees—whipped past the forward canopy while Chief Warrant Officer Amelia Schumann fought for control. Computerized alarm bells screamed in her ears. There had been too much battle damage. Coming down from orbit had made things worse. Schumann slammed her throttles wide open, pulling the control stick into her stomach and willing the vessel to gain altitude.

No good. The little spacecraft shuddered horribly. Piece by ragged piece, chunks of the starboard retractable aero wing peeled off. The control surfaces of the tail planes also remained frozen—their power leads cut by hostile fire.

A large hill loomed in the distance. It was all Amelia could do to nudge the nose of her vessel a few centimeters to port, hoping desperately to avoid the bluff.

Too little, too late.

The belly of the picket ship caromed off the top of the hill, sending it ass-over-teakettles, to come crashing into the middle of the huge trees on the other side. Chief Schumann screamed, every muscle in her body clenching up—waiting for the end to come. Branches and leaves smashed through the ruined canopy, whipping the cockpit and tearing viciously at her flight armor.

Cloudy water suddenly flooded the cockpit and immersed Amelia's helmet as she hung upside down in her seat. The flight armor should have sealed tight to the helmet when the cockpit was compromised, but something was wrong. Water began to flow around Amelia's scalp, reaching upwards to cover her eyes, then her nose. Amelia screamed and fought with the restraints of her seat as the water flooded her sinuses, cut off her air supply: stinking, choking, *killing*. Schumann writhed and banged back and forth in her seat, the straps holding her in a death grip as her wrecked spacecraft sank, sank, sank—

Amelia suddenly blinked. There was complete silence, save for the sound of warbling insects. Not precisely Earth crickets, but similar. The bright stars of night filled Amelia's vision. Sweat dripped off her face, and her throat felt ragged. There was a firm grip on her right hand and she realized that she was shaking.

"Are you all right, ma'am?" said a concerned, deep voice.

Ladd, Amelia thought with a sigh. *Thank God!*

"I . . . I think I'm okay," she whispered hoarsely.

Sergeant Warner Ladd held a canteen to Amelia's lips, and she found herself greedily gulping at a stream of lukewarm, clean water.

"You were dreaming," Ladd said, deadpan.

Amelia sat slowly upright, becoming aware of the other Fleet soldiers who surrounded her. They were barely visible in the night light, but they were there, watching.

The tension was palpable. Amelia could feel their uneasy contempt. For her. For putting them all in this predicament. Instead of being well on their way back to Sol System—to warn Earth—they were now grounded. Unable to complete their primary mission. And in serious jeapordy of getting killed. This wasn't what they'd trained for. This wasn't how the war was supposed to go.

Amelia almost laughed at the absurdity of her thoughts. *War.* What did any of them really know about fighting? She was an astronaut, after all. And the others were technicians of one kind or another. Their rank had been largely thrust upon them when the mantis aliens had crushed the human colony known as Marvelous. A lone starship—fleeing in the wake of Marvelous's destruction—had managed to warn Earth. And Earth had slapped together a hasty defense.

The Fleet: a drafted amalgam of existing civilian and military personnel. Not to mention existing ships and space stations.

Dozens of little vessels like the one Amelia had flown—and lost— were hastily constructed, and posted in orbit around every human world. So that if the aliens struck again . . .

That the mantes had attacked New America meant that they might be striking elsewhere too. It was the job of the picket ships to send word of attack, while the bigger ships took the fight to the enemy. And gave Earth—and the other worlds under Fleet's protection—enough time to prepare a response.

But the space surrounding New America had been quickly flooded with enemy ships. The few missiles Amelia had managed to fire, had died impotently against what she could only describe as translucent energy shielding.

There'd been almost no chance for escape.

Which didn't make Chief Schumann feel any better. She was the pilot. It had been her job to make a quick exit. She'd acted too slowly. The jump apparatus could not be operated in close proximity to a gravity well as deep as that of New America. When a mantis missile had proximity detonated near her spacecraft . . .

Amelia wiped at her eyes.

"Ma'am, I think we should pick up and move on," Ladd said. "The mantes have no doubt been searching for us since we left the crash site, and that muffled scream you just let out will act like a beacon for any mantis within a thousand meters."

Ladd's voice held no hint of emotion. To Chief Schumann, his manner was relieving and infuriating at the same time. The rest of the crew blamed Amelia for what she had done to them, so why not Ladd? She almost wished he would simply chew her out for her mistake. She deserved it. Yet, he remained nonplused and professional—the picture of a model NCO.

"You're right again, Ladd. I . . . I'm sorry," Amelia said. "We should get away from this place. And try another call to the *Aegean*."

Ladd voiced agreement, and Amelia levered herself off the root bed she had been sleeping on. Then she dropped into the hip-deep water that surrounded her. The wetlands were humid, and cool, and it was only the vacuum-capable combat armor—worn by all—that kept them from falling prey to hypothermia. Amelia shouldered her compact pilot's rifle by its sling, and followed Ladd as he waded his way back to where the other five survivors of the crash were huddled amongst the trees.

It moved over the water with its siblings—the many acting in unison, to almost form a single entity. Like wolves following the trail of their prey, they hunted, tracing the taste of machine oils, metal, and human flesh. The creature—using the sensory capacity infused by its saucer-shaped, biomechanical carriage—surmised that its tactical group had indeed discovered the location of the crashed hostile spaceship.

The mantis group leader's orders had been clear: exterminate all humans. This order had come from the very top. The Queen Mother was very angry that such a prime, vital planet as this one, had been violated by the presence of the soft, bipedal aliens. It was an affront to mantis supremacy in the galaxy.

Human intelligence was dangerous. Much too random. In mantis society, every individual knew his or her place from the moment awareness was attained. The humans, meanwhile, were messy. Disorganized. They built haphazardly, they lived haphazardly, they were stupid, and they were *in the way*. So, the Queen Mother's forces came to this world—which would make an excellent future mantis colony, by the looks of it—to cleanse, and prepare the way.

The tactical group found the human crash site.

Like the insects that they were, the mantes swarmed over the ship, probing for any signs of life. The scent of humans was still strong in the area, but there was no sign that the human crew had loitered. They'd fled further into the wetlands. Either towards what they thought would be safety, or away from pursuit. The group leader surmised that it mattered not. His force was good. If the crashed human ship was any indication, the fugitive crew numbered few. And the mantes could glide through the trees with ease, while the clumsy humans slogged.

When eventually the tactical group caught up with its prey, the humans would be no contest.

Signalling for his troops to follow, the group leader hurried off.

Amelia could almost sense the enemy lurking out beyond the farthest trees, waiting for the chance to spring, and pull her human crew to pieces with their serrated forelimbs. Grainy digital camera footage from the ship that had fled Marvelous told the story: the mantis aliens were carnivorous beasts. With bulbous insect-like eyes, and fearsome beaks filled with terrible teeth that vibrated when the aliens were aggressive. Or feeding. The footage seemed to indicate that there was little difference, once battle was joined. And those flying saucers the aliens rode on . . . nightmarish!

Still, while the company was true, hope flickered like a candle.

Chief Schumann watched Sergant Ladd's back, and wondered about the man. He had served ten years in the United States Army, and fought in no human wars of which she was aware. Being pressed into Fleet service seemed to make no difference to him. He knew his job, and he knew his people, and he didn't seem to worry about that which didn't need worrying about.

Which just made Amelia's guilt worse. The crew were clearly Ladd's to command. Not hers. Oh, there had always been a degree of deference. But Chief Schumann was only a Chief by accident: utility pilots of all description being accorded the middle-step rank of Warrant Officer in Fleet's laddered heirarchy. If Amelia flew the ship, Ladd clearly drove the men. Each of whom regarded the sergeant with trusting eyes.

For Chief Schumann, there were only wary glances.

She kept her eyes forward and pushed through the knee-high water. New America's alien trees began to thin out, and the remnants of the picket ship's crew soon found themselves in a wide, shallow patch of marsh which was only ankle deep.

Overhead, the bright stars sparkled and danced. But the eastern horizon was just becoming visible as dawn approached. Little lights maneuvered crazily in the sky overhead. Occasionally one of them would flare brightly, and die. Loud booms sounded in the distance—explosions from the mantis planetary invasion? The nearest city was over a hundred kilometers off. Perhaps other human craft had crashed? The bigger Fleet ships had numerous escape pods . . .

Amelia stopped, and called everyone to a halt. Ladd didn't need to be told what to do. He hastily erected their portable emergency satellite dish. He tapped a few codes into the wrist key pad on his left arm and waited for his armor's internal communications computer to uplink to any of the human-made ships that should have been in orbit. The *Aegean* being the newest, largest, and theoretically toughest. If any Fleet ship would be giving it back to the enemy, it would be the *Aegean*. Alien shields, or no alien shields.

There was a long pause, followed by static in the crew's ears.

"Awwww, man!" Specialist Shaw drawled with much displeasure.

"We be effed," came the voice of Corporal Powell, a heavy-weapons engineer who knew a picket ship's missile bays like the back of his hand—and was the only troop large and muscular enough to tote their single squad weapon through the uneven, flooded terrain of the wetlands.

A cacophony of groupwide bitching suddenly errupted. Ladd tried to interject, but the crew had had enough, and were jawing at full steam, drowning out the Sergeant's barritone barking. A day and a night of forced marching had rubbed nerves raw. Men went chest to chest. Somebody shoved somebody else.

That did it. They were dogpiling like children, splashing and shouting and filling the air with profanity.

Amelia tried to drown out the noise with her own sullen thoughts, but it was impossible. Even if there was no contact with Fleet in orbit, they still had to find a way to evade detection. Get back to civilization. Find a way to make a *difference*.

A hot spark of anger suddenly flared up within Amelia. Maybe it was the deep exhaustion, or the sudden hopelessness, or the bitter resentment at her own guilty self-pity that caused her to snap.

"Have you lost your minds?" she bawled. "Do you really want to draw them down on top of us, like hawks on a pack of rats?"

The crew, not used to taking sharp orders from their young Warrant Officer pilot, froze in place.

"Keep your effing mouths shut!" Amelia barked. "The next person that says a single word is getting my boot in his balls!"

Chief Schumann's chest heaved with anger as she spat her last words. And, for the first time, something barely approaching respect appeared in the eyes of the crew. Also appearing for the first time was a slight smile on the lips of Sergeant Ladd.

"Sergeant?" Amelia finally said, motioning a palm to Ladd as she plodded back over and retrived the satellite unit from its watery perch.

"Right," Ladd growled low and strong. "You people heard the Chief."

Amelia continued. "We're still Fleet. We can't accomplish our primary mission. But maybe we can do something else constructive. Those lights moving in orbit tell me that *somebody* is still fighting. We should see if we can too. We're all from Earth, I know, and this isn't our world, really. But for hell's sake, as long as we're stuck here, we should defend it like it *is* Earth! Because if we don't, then what we're seeing above us might soon be replayed in Earth's night skies. Do we want mantis ships dropping down over New York or Hong Kong or Paris?"

The crew muttered negatives.

"Then let's get moving," Ladd said. "And keep an effing lid on it."

Amelia was already heading away from the group, her back ramrod straight in disgust, her legs making strong, swirling strides through the muck and water. Adrenaline warred with hesitation. Anger brought with it a certain bravado, that would drain away very quickly. She'd surprised them. She wouldn't be able to surprise them again. Her only choice was to try to prove to them—and to herself—that they still had value *as soldiers*. That they could make the mantis aliens *pay* for daring to attack another human world.

One by one, the others fell in line, Ladd hauling up the rear.

They slog-marched for almost an hour, nobody saying much, eyes and ears wide open, looking for any hint of trouble. The sky grew brighter and brighter, until the first rays began to peak over the far horizon. The mantes could be anywhere in this morass, waiting to spring. That much was certain. But the crew was small, and if they put their minds to it, they could move quickly when they wanted to.

Eventually, Ladd called for a break. None of them had rested much during the night. All eyes were growing dim and weary.

Chief Schumann clutched her pilot's rifle tightly and continued to brood, standing in the water, until the strong, gauntlet-clad hand of

Sergeant Ladd gripped her shoulder. She turned her head and found herself face to face with the older man.

"That was a good thing you did back there," Ladd said warmly, a smile on his face. "I was wondering when you were going to pull yourself out of your sulking."

"I only wish I felt as strong as I talked," Amelia replied glumly, eyes avoiding Ladd's smiling face. "Christ, Sergeant, I don't know what the hell I'm doing here."

"Listen," Ladd interrupted, "I know you feel like scum for what happened. You were muttering every detail in your dreams. But these guys are starting to get a different angle on you. And frankly, so am I."

"Thanks, Sergeant," Amelia replied honestly.

"Right," Ladd said, squeazed her shoulder again, then dropped back into the group. Amelia watched him go, a silent *thank you* in her mind.

The scent was *hot*.

The mantes and their group leader slipped easily through the trees to the clear patch of shallows where the human smell was strongest. Here, the bipedal aliens—with their clumsy weapons and cheap, artificial carapaces—had stopped for some purpose. The group leader swept outward from the middle of the shallows, seeking the new direction of the trail, and quickly found what he wanted. An unvoiced computer message flowed from the group leader's disc, and that message was heard by the others. The command simply said, *follow me!* And the horde of praying-mantis-like cyborg creatures shot forward into the trees once again, sensing that their quarry was not far away.

The group leader eventually dispatched a scout to snoop ahead—the scout's natural pedator's senses combining with his artificial carriage-enabled awareness to ferret out the humans. It wouldn't be long now. The group leader wondered what it would be like to kill one of the aliens. Mantes had done it before, on other worlds. Long ago. Would humans die easily? Or die hard?

The group leader grew anxious to find out.

Private Wang Li had relieved his comrade at the rear of the little column, and slogged through the water, grunting at the weight of his automatic rifle and cursing the partly-cloudy sky. Though Li dreaded the thought of face-to-beak combat—for which he'd received what he thought was minimal training—he also hated the never-ending anticipation. Waiting was always the worst part of anything unpleasant.

Then, unexpectedly, Wang got his wish. Looking over his shoulder, he realized he was staring at one of the enemy. The creature had maneuvered stealthily through the trees, using its flying saucer to stay above the water, such that nothing was heard. Until now, suddenly, it was too late.

An instant of alarmed recognition passed—human to mantis.

Aiming his weapon from the hip, Private Li flicked off the safety and squeezed the trigger. For the first time since Initial Entry Training, Li felt his weapon feed round after round through the firing chamber. No brass casings were ejected. None were needed on Li's space-age rifle. Both the propellant and the soft casing were vaporized the instant the firing pin punctured the thin wall separating the two halves of the propellant proper.

Spouts of water flew up around the lone mantis. Several rounds impacted solidly on the creature's disc, causing metal and sparks to fly.

Amelia froze, as all around, her rifles began to belch propellant and bullets in every concievable direction. The hammering noise of the guns was only bested by the incoherently terrified cries of the crew.

A chortling *WHAM-WHAM-WHAM* could be heard as Corporal Powell churned up the water with his powerful squad gun, which fired a larger, more potent shell. The lone mantis was burst into fragments of alien gore and splintered machinery that fanned outward and splashed into the water.

"Cease fire! Cease fire!" Ladd yelled.

All of them crept toward the remains of the mantis that drifted in the foamy water. It was the first time any of them had seen the enemy up close and in person. Private Li himself was in a near-daze, his chest heaving mightily and his eyes bugged out so far, Amelia thought they were going to pop from their sockets.

Then, the noise of the mantis soldier's commrades could be heard. The humming sound of multiple discs far off in the trees, but growing louder as they grew closer.

"Must have signalled the rest of his squad," Ladd said, watching in the direction from which the noise came.

"How many?" Chief Schumann asked, her pilot's rifle leveled from her shoulder, but the barrel wavering just slightly as adrenaline made her arms shake.

"Damned if I know," Ladd said. "Everybody get behind a tree and shoot at the first mantis you see!"

When no one moved—their eyes still transfixed on the alien gore that drifted in the water—Amelia hissed, "Do what the Sergeant says! Go!"

Seven humans slipped behind fat tree trunks as several disc-riding mantes came into view. They moved over the water—the liquid beneath each disc making strange patterns that swirled and distorted according to whatever force it was which kept the discs in the air. None of the aliens spoke, nor made any sound. Their instect-like eyes and heads scanned furiously. Until they saw what was left of their commrade.

At which point both Chief Schumann and Sergeant Ladd shouted for the group to open fire, and again the air was filled with the ear-splitting reports of rifles. Only, this time, it wasn't just human bullets chewing up the scene. Mantis rounds smacked and popped against tree trunks, bursting off great splinters of bark and wood. Amelia flatted behind her own tree as at least a dozen mantis rounds chewed into it. She almost fell to her knees, she was so instantly petrified.

But when she peered to the side and saw Sergeant Ladd still up, and still firing, she forced herself to mimic him, peeking around her tree and popping off shots at the mantes as they scattered between the trunks. At least three of the mantes appeared down, their discs half subermged into the water and their exposed upper thoraxes split open, with fresh mantis ooze pouring from the lethal wounds.

Amelia felt a sudden, almost insane surge of pride. If she'd been unable to fight back in orbit, at least down here, humans could successfully defend themselves. That the aliens had fallen at all suddenly gave the mantes a mortal quality which they'd lacked before, in Chief Schumann's mind. Amelia remembered a line from a very, very old two-dee motion picture entertainment she'd once seen. *If it bleeds, we can kill it.*

Though fictional, the two-dee movie seemed oddly appropriate, given Amelia's present circumstances.

But then the firefight turned nasty. The remaining mantes ringed the humans, and suddenly everyone was shooting at everyone else. Human had to be wary of shooting at human, while attempting to shoot at the mantes, and suddenly the picket ship's crew were diving from behind their trees, risking exposure to enemy fire while they tried to regroup. Lacking the kind of concentrated squad-level maneuvering skills a proper infantry element might possess, the crew was quickly routed, and sent fleeing east—for their very lives.

Amelia ran fastest of all.

The tactical group leader held his force back, letting the humans go. The patrol had lost five of their number, having achieved no significant human casualties that the group leader could detect.

Except for one.

The human who lay in the water was not dead. Not yet. He dragged himself along, clearly wounded in the leg, and trailing a thick plume of human blood behind him as he want. The tactical group leader called his fellows to him and together they hovered over the human, who'd thrown away his weapon when it became empty of ammunition.

The group leader pointed with a serrated forelimb at the bleeding human and said—in the silent carriage-to-carriage language of his kind—*Observe here, the enemy of our people. An animal. Vermin. We are here on this planet to pave the way. Soon, the Quorum of the Select will launch the Fourth Expansion, and evey human on every world will fall to us. Wherever they may be. Look at this one, and remember. Remember how easily they die.*

With that, the group leader dipped the leading edge of its carriage, scooped the screaming, bleeding human up—serrated forelimbs holding the squirming human fast—and began to feed.

After many minutes of frantic flight, Amelia heard Corporal Powell ordering them all to stand down. Amelia was so exhausted, she literally sank to her knees and panted, eyes staring into the murky water. Her ears thundered with the beats of her own heart, and she would have gotten back up and run some more, if not for the fact that she simply couldn't get enough oxygen into her blood to make her muscles work.

A minute later, Powell's voice prodded her.

"Ma'am?" He said in a half-worried tone. "Are you hurt? Ma'am?"

Amelia didn't respond. She just turned her eyes this way and that, counting bodies as they crouched behind tries, faces flushed and mouths open, taking in great gulps of air.

"Sergeant Ladd?" she said. "Where is the sergeant??"

One by one, she met their eyes, and very quickly she realized the truth. He'd not made it. When they'd broken cover and run, she'd heard someone yell in pain. She hadn't realized it was him. Of all the people to fall, it had to be the one troop upon whom Amelia felt she could rely with any degree of security.

She let her chin hit her chest, and closed her eyes against the gentle sob that was trying to tear itself out of her.

The tactical group was thin now. The leader became worried. He had lost almost half his attacking force in the melee with the humans. At the cost of many, his group had destroyed only one of the enemy. And while the feast had been glorious—what a thrill to devour human meat!—the present casualty ratio was not going to yield a successful end to the chase. New tactics would have to be employed. The humans had not gone far. But the water and abundant life forms of the wetlands made it difficult to distinguish the humans from their surroundings. If the group leader sent out a scout, would the scout be any more successful than his fallen sibling? The humans might have been few, but they were heavily armed—something else the tactical group leader had not expected. For a moment, he considered the idea of calling in reinforcements.

It was the logical thing to do. If the humans had proven much more difficult to deal with than expected, overwhelming force would be best. It had worked in orbit. Already, the tactical group leader knew that almost every human craft had been destroyed, or forced to land, whereupon the occupants were slaughtered.

Still, even mantes had their pride.

No. The group leader knew he just needed to be more patient. Calling for help at this stage would be a sign to his superiors that he was not fit for his station. A warrior did not cry for assistance at the first sign of difficulty! A warrior adapted, and overcame.

Using his silent contact with his troops, the group leader dispensed a series of new instructions.

Chief Schumann and her crew dragged themselves from the water and flopped onto their backs at the bank of a small stream filtering into the wetland. At last, they had found truly solid ground. Having spent almost all of their duty time where it was dry and clean—Fleet spaceships and space stations being fastidiously neat and orderly—being put through the hell of the swamp march had almost taken the the life out of them. They lay or curled on the solid ground, dragging in breath, eyes unfocused; and practically pushed to the point of uncaring.

Amelia's body felt leaden from the forced march. They had only traveled a handful of kilometers, but it felt as if she had walked the circumference of the entire planet. Most pilots had to be in better-than-average shape to pass the standard flight and Fleet physicals. But nothing had prepared her for this. Her body was chafed raw where the flight armor had rubbed against skin, and her legs and feet and thighs were a quivering chorus of agony.

She rolled over and muttered something about the satellite dish.

"I've got it," Private Li said. "I almost dropped it a few times. But it's our only way to talk to Fleet now."

Off in the distance, a new noise: the whine-and-thunderclap of hostile ship's guns could be heard. Only, this time they were firing in-atmosphere. Amelia was just curious enough to crawl her way across the ground to where a pile of half-rotten logs gave her a little elevation. Across the hard ground to the south she could see a stupendously large craft sitting on three thick, extended legs. It was ringed with what seemed to be smaller craft. Or cargo containers? Troop pods? Amelia couldn't be sure. They hugged the side of the mother ship. Occasionally one of the nozzle-like weapons on the ship's crown swiveled skyward, and blasted a shot into the sky. What the enemy could be shooting at—when Amelia could not even see it herself—was a mystery.

Suicide. Amelia thought glumly. *Leading the crew past this is totally out of the question. But we can't stay here! And we can't go back into the swamp. It will kill us, as surely as the mantis patrol will kill us. Sooner or later we'll run out of ammunition and then . . .*

Chief Schumann did not want to contemplate what would happen then. Poor Sergeant Ladd had been the first to fall. She felt a desperate need to make his death count for something.

Dear God, I am so tired, Amelia thought, as her eyes closed.

An indeterminate amount of time passed, and she drifted. At once present, yet not present. Her consciousness swirling away into nothingness.

The ground suddenly rumbled and rocked beneath her. Amelia sat up groggily, her mind racing to catch up with the action taking place around her. How long had she drifted off? What was happening now? The rest of the crew were also getting to their feet, the hot rays of New America's yellow-dwarf home star blinding them slightly as they looked towards the horizon, and the source of the trembling.

A great mushroom of fire and debris spouted high into the air in the distance. Directly in front of the huge mantis ship.

Amelia stared dumbly at the sight, and crawled forward trying to understand what was happening. Then, a finger of fire seemed to fly from the sun itself and arc downward, towards the alien craft. Its shields flickered and sparkled. A third strike from the sky left a massive divot in the turf near where the first shot had fallen. Soil and smoke drifted. Another mushroom rose to join the first, and together they began floating away in the breeze.

Amelia scrambled back and grabbed at the satellite uplink Private Li still husbanded. She unfurled its umbrella-like dish, tying quickly in to her suit's communications computer. Then she aimed the dish a few degrees off the limb of the sun, in the direction from which the tongue of fire had come, and pressed the HAIL key.

Moments ticked by, and then a sharp, clean transmission broke through.

The crew huddled close, and all listened as Amelia identified herself. It was not the communications officer of the *Aegean* who answered, but a tactical officer from the *Tycho Brahe,* one of the new, swift Fleet destroyers, specifically designed for stealth.

The voice from the *Brahe* was quick and to the point: those few Fleet ships that were still left were playing a hit-and-run game with the mantes out beyond the third asteroid belt. Most of the mantis ships had been drawn away as a result. But mantis reinforcements were expected from out-system, and the *Tycho Brahe* had been detailed to return and aid the very few recovery teams that had already been dispatched. New America was officially being abandoned. Any civilians or Fleet personnel still left alive were being picked up prior to the *Brahe* leaving for Earth.

"We've got a big mother of a mantis craft sitting right in front of us," Amelia said. "You're shooting at it, but not causing any damage."

"The governor's private entourage was downed a few kilometers from where you are," said the *Brahe's* tactical officer. "We're trying to keep that beast diverted while we execute a pickup, copy?"

"Copy," Chief Schumann said, and considered. The same shields that had stopped her missiles in orbit were stopping the *Brahe's* kinetic kill strikes as well. They might very well be able to keep the mantis ship occupied while the governor got picked up, but that wouldn't mean a damned thing for Amelia's crew if they couldn't hope for a recovery as well. The only way they were getting off-planet now was if something—or someone—found a way to get through those shields and neutralize the big bastard where it sat.

Might as well wish for the moon, Amelia thought bitterly.

But then, there didn't seem to be any ground troops active around the mantis ship. All of its attention seemed to be on the *Brahe*. Amelia watched for a few minutes while the mantis ship cracked off another round, and then another, and then still another. Each time it did, the air around the craft shimmered just briefly. At which point a small period of clarity could be discerned. As if the milky shielded air around the alien ship resolved into . . . emptiness.

"It has to drop its shields in order to fire," Chief Schumann deduced, letting a small smile curl up the corners of her mouth for the first time since the invasion of New America began.

"We didn't receive that, over?" said *Brahe*.

"Never mind," Amelia said into the satellite gadget. "Just keep up your firing pattern. I think I might have discovered a way to help you."

And to possibly help my crew, too, she thought.

Chief Schumann looked from face to weary face. They were all tired and worn down to the nub. There was no exhilaration of battle in their eyes. Just exhaustion. However, they pulled their weapons to the ready and waited.

"What you got in mind, Chief?" said Powell.

It was the first time he'd ever said that word to Amelia. In the past it had always been *ma'am.*

Amelia did not want to throw all their lives away. She did not feel brave or heroic in the slightest. But she had come this far, and she owed it to Ladd to make a final push. Then, and only then, would the crew get their long-awaited dust-off.

And if they didn't make it . . . well, it wouldn't matter anyway.

★ ★ ★

The group leader and his forces were searching the small streams that flowed from a low rise of packed soil that overlooked the wetlands. Beyond, far in the distance, a mantis drop-pod super-carrier had landed, and was presently engaged with a human ship that drifted somewhere in a very low orbit, just out of reach of the mantis guns. At that altitude, the human ship must have been expending tremendous energy to loiter over the drop-pod carrier's present ground coordinates.

The group leader signaled to the super-carrier, announcing his renewed intent to find and destroy the survivors of the crashed picket ship. The commander of the drop-pod super-carrier replied that he had no way to assist. Having emptied all of his troops on a human settlement far to the west, he'd set down in his present position to await further instructions, when the bombardment from the elusive human ship began.

How the human ship was evading the super-carrier's targeting sensors was not known. Suffice to say it was difficult to get a lock on the human vessel; at least a lock which would last long enough to launch missiles. The super-carrier commander was therefore engaging the human ship until such a time that mantis capital ships could return from the asteroids, and clear the sky once more.

The super-carrier commander was fairly certain that a refugee crew of humans—armed with only rifles—could not do him any harm. The group leader was instructed to conduct his search and take care of the humans. The super-carrier commander would relay news of the group leader's success to their superiors, when it was all over. There would be potential for advancement in such a victory. Perhaps even the possibility of mating.

The group leader shuddered with anticipated ecstasy.

Mating was reserved for males of significant rank and ability only. Never in his wildest imagination had he dared to think of such a thing. But now?

The group leader encouraged his depleted force to redouble its efforts. The humans could not hide forever. They would be found eventually. Oh yes, they would be found.

Loam and fire flew into the air as the mantis shields swept away another blow from the *Tycho Brahe*. Amelia and her group were now just a few hundred meters from the low rise upon which the alien craft sat. Like a great elongated egg—mated to a dozen smaller elongated eggs—it perched there: a shimmering dome of energy rippling above it in the blue-green sky, and great, thick landing pylons balancing it on the turf.

A concussion wave from the *Brahe's* latest shot knocked Amelia's crew flat, yet the great egg remained motionless amongst the maelstrom.

"We can't go much further," Corporal Powell said at Chief Schumann's ear. "We're pinned down here. By our own artillery, for hell's sake."

"I know that," Amelia said back, "but there has got to be a way of getting in closer. We just have to time it right. When the *Brahe* hits, and when the mantis ship drops its sheilds for a shot. The real trick is going to be getting in without them seeing us."

Both of them began to scan around for any conceivable natural form of cover, when Powell's eyes fell upon the group of aliens floating towards them. It was a much smaller group than the one they'd faced before. Could it be the same mantes? Or a different patrol altogether?

Though still a very long way off, it was clear the mantes had spotted the crew.

So, it had come down to this. Caught, not even in the act . . .

Suddenly, an idea leapt into Chief Schumann's head. She turned her gaze from the onrushing mantes to the great egg on the hill, then back to the mantes. A realization hit her like a bolt of lighting. Then she was ripping the last bandolier of squad gun shells from Powell's back, and before he could protest, she was up and running.

Powell yelped, trying to pull her down, but she was too quick. The crew screamed after her as she tore past them, and then they were up on their own feet chasing after her, howling like Zulus.

"No, no, NO!" Amelia puffed into her headset. "Stay behind and give me cover! The mantis patrol will follow *me!* It's the ship they'll be protecting!!"

Powell and the others slowed and stopped.

It was true.

The mantis aliens—riding their discs—had turned away from the crew and were now zooming straight as an arrow at the shrinking figure of their commanding officer. Powell and the rest of the platoon watched in amazement as every last mantis ignored them and pursued Chief Schumann.

"Awright, you heard the lady!" The big corporal snarled. "Up and ready!"

Each of the crew dropped to one knee and raised his or her weapon up to the shoulder, telescopic sights whining as they focused on the retreating images of the mantes.

Rifles cracked to life, sending bullets into the cluster of aliens that were right on Schumann's heels. The creatures broke, trying to avoid the incoming fire, but still maintained their pursuit. Powell, using the last free round for his squad gun, adjusted the weapon's trajectory and drew a bead on the lead mantis.

The group leader died, as did three of its kindred. The dream of mating—so wonderful, so fleeting—was terminated in a hail of anti-personnel shrapnel.

Amelia Schumann's ears pounded loudly as her heart forced blood to her brain. Her legs pumped like pistons, muscles burning, but running on pure adrenaline, while her lungs hurt with each ragged breath. The grass and weeds flowed under her feet in a blur, yet the distance to the mantis mother craft shrank ever so slowly. She could hear the hideous squeals of the cyborg bugs as they died behind her, and the reports of the crew's weapons as they fired. She almost fell as one of Powell's shells decimated the head of the pack. But desperation drove her onward.

Thus far no one had even put so much as a scratch in the alien ship. The *Brahe's* rail guns were hurling everything short of nukes, and they ran off the egg's shields like rainwater. Dissolving into nothingness. The only way anyone was going to get to that thing was to go right up to it and shove a shell up its ass. And Amelia had a whole bandolier of shells.

The drop-pod super-carrier commander watched as one of the bipedal creatures—still some distance away—destroyed the tactical group leader who was leading his patrol to defend the ship. The group leader had been on the heels of the smaller biped that now rushed toward the commander's home. The commander had not given these humans enough credit. They'd proven to have remarkable tenacity, even when faced with overwhelming numbers and technology.

The commander tried to make contact with one of the other mantis troops in the patrol group, and impose his will upon it. But the patrol was too single-minded in their focus now. The little human who ran was clearly all that mattered to them.

The little alien biped sped towards the commander's armored battle fortress.

Deciding that caution was best, the commander temporarily took his attention away from the pesty human ship in low orbit, and re-concentrated his weapons systems on the planet's surface around the ship. There were guns for anti-ground attack too. All he needed to do was drop the shield system long enough to squeaze off a few bursts, and the running human would be finished.

Not like a single little alien could do much to hurt the drop-pod super-carrier anyway. The little runner seemed almost cute, in a pathetic manner. The commander regretted that it would be too easy.

Amelia saw the guns emerge, and she leapt violently to her left as a burst fried the air above her head and smashed into the ground several meters behind. Blinded with fear, she ran onward, tears streaming from her eyes, and her breath coming in gasps. The alien craft was less than twenty meters away now. Just a few more meters was all she would need.

More shots lashed out, hitting the ground just behind the Chief. The alien guns were quick, but they could not compensate for her sudden jerking and weaving movements; so close to the point of origin. Burst after burst missed Amelia, but the shield system stayed down.

If the *Brahe* were on its game, it would give the mantis ship a triple strike right now, and finish the job. But the human ship hadn't fired in over a minute, and Amelia began to wonder if perhaps the giant mantis craft's sisters in space had returned and gotten rid of the *Brahe?*

No matter, Chief Schumann had but one last chore to complete. Her eyes fell on the huge, thick landing leg nearest her. The bandolier of shells came off her back. Giving off a hoarse cry, Amelia slipped a hand grenade into one of the empty ammo pouches on the bandoleer, flipped off the grenade's spoon handle, and then hurled the bandolier at the leg. That done, Amelia then threw her whole body to the right, tucked into a ball, and rolled.

She kept rolling until she dropped—rather painfully—into a muddy runnel which had been worn in the low rise. It was perhaps a meter deep. No more.

The bandolier had landed in the metal gearworks that made up the "ankle" at the base of the leg. The grenade's timer fizzed towards zero.

A blinding flash was followed by a boom that muted out every other sound in Amelia's universe. Poking her head over the lip of the runnel, she saw the mangled mechanisms at the base of the leg begin to buckle and split. The massive mantis ship tilted crazily as the leg finally gave out.

Surprise.

That was the drop-pod super-carrier commander's only emotion as he felt his ship shudder underneath him. The pilot and technicians who surrounded the commander's creche all eyed him; the semi-soft portions of their carapaces flushing with confused tension. How could one little human have done so much damage?

The commander told himself he'd be more careful in the future.

Take off now, the commander ordered the pilot, who signaled his obedience, and started up the super-carrier's lift engines. Just before the ship could lean dangerously out of whack, the repulsor effect kicked in, and the ship began to fly. Slowly, at first—being so massive. But then gradually with more power. The remaining, good legs left the ground, and the commander began to consider his next options, when true disaster struck.

Two consecutive rounds from the *Tycho Brahe* broke the skin of the super-carrier—now far above the ground, and drifting north at speed. The commander had forgotten to re-erect the shield system. It was a simple error. A momentary lapse. Losing the landing leg had broken the commander's concentration. And it was an error the commander would never get to make twice.

The wounded super-carrier augered in some six kilometers from where it had taken off, at a velocity of approximately one hundred and sixty kilometers an hour. There was nothing the mantis commander or crew could do but scream oaths into eternity as their ship fractured, then exploded like a tiny fusion bomb.

Amelia swam in a murky pool of calm. Her body was nowhere to be found, and all she could hear was a slow, steady rumble that seemed to emanate from everywhere. Where had she been? It didn't matter anymore.

"Hey, are you okay in there?"

Corporal Powell's voice. It was soft, and filled with respect.

At first, the sound was completely out of place. Why was *he* here? Amelia's heart saddened at the thought that she could have caused Powell's death too. Then she noticed that the rumble was getting louder and that there was a warm, firm hand on one of her arms.

Arms?

Amelia's eyes opened slowly. Everything was terribly blurred.

There, a certain blur looked familiar.

Working hard to focus, Amelia recognized the face of Powell. There were other faces, too: Corporal Bybee, Privates Li and Shaw, and the others. They each had various bandages and healing sleeves wrapped around their extremities, but they all seemed healthy and, yes, very much alive.

"I . . . we . . . I . . ." Amelia rasped. Her throat felt funny and her body seemed to be immobilized. Powell placed a hand on her lips and gestured to the rest of the crew.

"We're all okay, Chief. It's been five Earth days since the *Tycho Brahe*'s slicks picked us up. The governor's party too. We're the lucky ones. The *Brahe* was the only capital ship that made it. New America is history. But we're now high-tailing it for Fleet headquarters. For *Earth*."

Amelia allowed herself a small moment of satisfaction. Perhaps she and her picket ship crew would get to accomplish their primary mission after all? The mantis aliens were impressive, perhaps even overwhelmingly so. But they weren't immortal.

Someone on Earth needs to know that, she thought. And let her eyes close once more. For Chief Schumann, her first battle was over.

For humanity, the war to survive had only just begun.

DECAYING ORBIT

★

by Robert R. Chase

Humanity is on the brink war with itself. Divided into three factions—the Dominion, the Eternals, and the Trans-Humans—each group vies for supremacy in a crowded galaxy. Dispatched to the Disputed Territories, the crew of a Specter Class IV ship comes across the wreckage of a TransHuman vessel of enormous size—and enormous potential. But unlocking its secrets may prove costlier than imagined.

THE SPECTER CLASS IV is a long-range reconnaissance vessel with a complement of a junior lieutenant who is also commander and the primary pilot, an ensign who is the alternate pilot, and a warrant officer who is chief technician, in charge of the esoterica related to impellers, quantum drives and environmental controls. You should not be able to see its exterior under most conditions, but if you could, you would see a long, tapering tube, pinched at its nose and bulbous at its base. It has the largest quantum *sur* space engine for its size in the Dominion fleet. Aside from its stealthing, it has little defensive capability and no offensive armament.

It also has the most claustrophobically uncomfortable quarters of any vessel to which I was ever assigned. I was still fuzzy-headed from cold sleep resuscitation when the battle stations alarm sounded. I launched myself down the narrow corridor Lieutenant Jansons had christened the birth canal. It was barely large enough for two crew members in horizontal position to float by each other and I banged my head on the exposed pipes. Those would have been covered over in a commercial vessel but Space Force rules mandate that they be left exposed for quick repairs.

Just ahead of me, Jeanine darted into her station. I reached mine, grabbed both handholds and inserted myself. The couch snugged me down in safety restraints as various screens flicked on. I tried to ignore a growing headache and make sense of the data they were throwing at me. The deck throbbed with barely repressed power; O'Connor, our chief tech, was holding the quantum drive just below critical excitation in case we had to leave quickly.

Interstellar politics were in a state of high confusion. If you asked a man or woman of a previous era "Is the human race at war with itself," there would have been a confident if regretful answer of "yes." In my lifetime, the answer had changed to "it depends." On what? On the definition of human. The TransHuman Confederacy boasted that the term had become obsolete with their embrace of the man-machine union. The Eternals, on the other hand, having granted themselves immortality, proclaimed themselves the endpoint of evolution. Both TransHumans and Eternals looked down on the minimally modified citizens of the Dominion, like me, as at best Neanderthal-like evolutionary dead ends.

Mere disdain would have been no more than an irritation. The problem was that both groups were expansionist. The Eternals recruited from both the Dominion and the far distant Terrestrial CoProsperity Sphere. Since the mortality rate of Eternals was less than one percent, they needed planets for their new members. TransHuman motivations were more opaque. Some said they had a missionary zeal to spread the blessings of the Singularity; to others, it looked like they were determined to eradicate any intelligence unlike their own.

When the Specter had been launched from its base on Victoria, Dominion Intelligence estimated that that there was a seventy percent chance that war between the two would break out in the next three months. As far as we were concerned, the optimal outcome would have been for each to blast the other back to the Stone Age. Since we could not rely on that happening, we had been dispatched to the Disputed Territories between the polities where war was most likely to start.

★ ★ ★

Jeanine and I each did a quick scan of half the celestial sphere. Emerging from *sur* space sends a pulse of Cerenkov radiation in all directions. Any potential enemies, Eternal, TransHuman or otherwise, could see it and would certainly come to investigate if they were anywhere in the vicinity.

"All clear," I said after a minute. Jeanine agreed a few seconds later.

"Keep a lookout," Jansons ordered.

She had put us into orbit around a super Earth, a world with three times Earth's mass illuminated by a Cepheid variable star. Hurricanes churned through the all-encompassing cloud cover, fueled in part, according to my heat sensors, by volcano chains stretching halfway around the planet. As far as I could tell, its only satellite was ahead of us, rushing into night side's shadow.

"That's artificial," Jeanine said.

"And . . . huge," I added.

It was larger than the space docks surrounding Gloriana. Large enough to service an armada, if that was its purpose. If it spotted us . . .

"Stand by, Mr. O'Connor." Jansons was having the same thoughts I was.

I scanned each data stream for any hint that the station was powering up an attack. Nothing. No neutrino flux to indicate a nuclear power source. Skin temperature identical to a black body at this distance from its star. It rotated slowly. A surface irregularity came into view. It became wider and much, much deeper.

The universe is a violent place. It is not that unusual to find a moon or planetoid that has been almost, but not quite, completely shattered by a collision. Something of that magnitude had blown a crater in this station, destroying an estimated twenty percent of its volume. A station that size was frightening enough by itself. Something that could pulverize it like this . . . was something I did not want to think about.

The station was in a lower, faster orbit. Jansons brought the Specter down and slowly closed the gap until we were only a hundred kilometers apart.

"I would like a full, remote inspection of that vessel," Jansons said. "I want to know if it is really completely dead. Who built it. How it was destroyed. Perhaps most importantly, I want to know if there is anything worth salvaging."

Putting the bogey scan on automatic, I called up one hundred twenty mini-rovers and, with three muttered commands, had them packed into two firing canisters and loaded them into the rail gun tubes while Jeanine took care of their last-minute programming.

"Ready, ma'am."

"Fire, Mr. Wu," Jansons commanded.

I pressed the appropriate button, which kicked them silently out the tubes. It would take them ten minutes to cross the gap. The next phase of this operation was likely to be intense and prolonged. Time to grab snacks and take a restroom break.

I was born in an arcology that was not a slum because slums were illegal on the planet Spencer. I had access to basic nourishment at the communal kitchens, basic education through the city's library net, and basic entertainment through joining or running from any of the dozens of youth gangs.

Near the top of the pyramid, while trying to hide from one of those gangs, I discovered an abandoned maintenance section. One of the rooms opened onto an exterior platform and it was there that I took myself, whether to watch one of the innumerable *Casablanca* remakes or read something as old and obscure as "The Ballad of Reading Gaol." Old entertainments, useless education. I knew I lacked the self-discipline to learn the skills that would free me from the arcology.

From that platform, when the air was exceptionally clear and the setting sun was behind me, I could see a silver ribbon stretching from the ground beyond the horizon to the sky. As dusk spread across the desert, the ribbon would dance and shimmer high above the ground. Sometimes I even glimpsed some of the Dominion's military spacecraft which, disdaining the use of the beanstalk, hurled themselves into space on their dark-energy impellers.

One day I realized I could watch them no more. I took a jump tube down to the base of the arcology, stepped out to the desert, and began walking to the spaceport. It took all day. As if guided by fate, the first thing I found that I could recognize was a Space Force recruiting station. I signed up after the most rudimentary physical and mental tests. To my surprise, they indicated that I had "intellectual promise."

I was put into a cram course for combat engineers. I learned a lot, sometimes painfully.

Now that I was near the end of my second hitch, I had decided not to re-up. The Dominion economy has good jobs for people with combat engineer training. I wanted to make something of my life. And I wanted someone to share it with.

Jeanine was cradling a coffee bulb by the time I made it to our galley.

"At least your final mission is proving interesting," she said. "In enemy territory, examining a mysterious derelict . . ."

I turned away from her to heat my own coffee. I was not trying to feign indifference. The truth was, I didn't dare look at her.

"What interests me right now is what I will be doing after this mission," I said. "And with whom."

"You are referring to that, ah, proposition you made to me back on Victoria?"

I wanted to make the sort of fervent declaration protagonists in ancient literature are always making. Instead, I cleared my throat and said, "Yes."

She seemed to be mulling it over. I stole a glance. Only then did I see the huge grin on her face.

"Yes!"

Micro-gravity has a way of making all the old clichés come true. Jeanine launched herself at me and I was knocked off my feet and, even within the confined quarters of the galley, found myself dancing on air. We spent the next few minutes cementing the agreement.

"Kipnis! Wu!" The voice of alternate pilot Shakeel rang in my earphone. "To your stations. The situation is becoming complicated."

"The problem is with the star," Shakeel said. I was snugged back into my station, viewing the graphics which accompanied Shakeel's explanation.

"We recognized it immediately as a Cepheid variable," he continued. "What I did not immediately realize was the effect that has on the planet below. The extra energy pumped into its atmosphere at the height of the star's pulsation makes it puff out. That in turn is causing the derelict's orbit to decay.

"According to my calculations, it should begin its terminal descent sometime in the next twelve hours."

"Stupid placement by whomever constructed it," Jeanine said.

"Probably not their fault," Jansons said. "I have been running attack scenarios, trying to account for the situation we see. Here is the best fit so far." A new set of graphics spread out before me. "I am assuming the derelict was part of a TransHuman power projection strategy. A base that large could be used to maintain and provision as many as a hundred X-5 fighter equivalents.

"The original orbit must have been much higher. For this scenario, I made it geosynchronous with the planet below. Pretty certainly, it was not finished when the Eternal strike force appeared. The battle seems to have climaxed with a small nuclear device burying itself thirty meters below the sphere's surface before detonation."

The battle station on my screen obediently exploded.

"Supposing that that hemisphere of the station was facing away from the planet at the time, the recoil from the explosion would have kicked the station toward the planet, lowering the perigee enough that it would brush the upper reaches of the atmosphere. With each succeeding orbit it would drop lower and lower. Which brings us to the current situation."

"If the Eternals won the battle, where are they?" I asked.

There was just the slightest hesitation before she answered. "This star system is as far from Eternal support as it is from TransHuman lines. A battle group could just manage to come this far and fight an action. There is no way it could maintain itself so far from home. I just hope they had to leave before they were able to loot everything of interest from the station.

"On the other hand, we are extraordinarily lucky to have arrived when we have. Another day, and everything would be lost."

Something about that statement bothered me, but I had no time to figure out why. The canisters, having reached their destination, disgorged the rovers. Half a dozen began circling the exterior of the derelict, sending detailed images of every hatch, gun port, and exterior sensor. The rest plunged into the crater and started mapping the interior of the structure.

"It does look like TransHuman work," Jeanine muttered a few minutes later.

"That has been the assumption," I agreed. "You have proof?"

She moved the part of the map she had been studying onto my screen. "Even though I don't understand the pattern as a whole, I can identify familiar parts: tubing to move gasses and liquids from one place to another; superconductor strip for power distribution. What I do not see are rooms for people to inhabit and corridors to connect them."

"What about these?" I asked, indicating apparent passageways that squirmed through the interior like lost intestines.

"Check the scale," Jeanine said. "They're even narrower than the corridor on this ship. Too small for humans. And the ones I have been able to trace start and stop without really going anywhere."

Too small for humans. One of the nastier rumors about TransHumans is that they have been devoured by their own creations. According to their propaganda, a combination of genetic tinkering and electronic enhancement has pushed them beyond the evolutionary horizon. But some say that the artificial intelligences they created decided years ago that everything would go more smoothly without their biological partners. You may see images of humans transmitted from TransHuman planets, but that is all they are. Or at best, the AIs have maintained a small human population, which they completely control to interface with the human polities like the Dominion. I had always discounted these stories as Dominion propaganda. Now I was not so sure.

The map became stranger yet. Our rovers came across interior voids perhaps explicable as areas where construction was never complete. But then there were elongated gaps between sections, like crevasses or certain cave formations. At first, I thought they had been sheared apart by the explosion that made the crater. The more I studied them, though, the more they seemed intentional. For what purpose I had no idea.

An hour into the exploration, we started losing contact with some of the rovers. The radio frequencies we were using to control the rovers could not penetrate that far through the metal of the station. I pulled some of them back to act as line-of-sight relays, but that only allowed us to proceed another ten levels. We were going to have to do something different.

"Choose one or two most likely approach routes and concentrate on them instead of investigating all avenues at once," Jeanine suggested. "We should have enough rovers to establish line-of-sight communication across the radius of the station."

"Two problems," I said. "How do you determine the 'most likely' routes? Even if you can, you are increasing the time to do a full examination of the station by an order of magnitude or more. If Shakeel is right, we don't have that long."

"I'm open to better ideas," she said.

I did not have any, but command did.

"Wu and Kipnis to the bridge."

Bridge was a grandiose name for a space that was little more than a cockpit. There was barely room for all three of us. Jansons was holding a pocket datascreen in one hand.

"I am about to read you on to ROGUE POSTULATE. ROGUE POSTULATE is a special access, higher than secret program. Unauthorized disclosure of any of the information you are about to learn is *per se* treason and may be considered a capital offense. Do you understand what I have just said?'

We did.

"Do you affirm that you will bear true faith with the Dominion and guard this information with your lives."

"Yes." The datascreen recorded our voices as legally unique identifiers.

Jansons cleared her throat. For the first time, I saw through some of the commanding-officer body language to the young woman underneath, a woman who was beginning to realize that she might be out of her depth.

"This is information that our people have gathered from Eternal sources. Their intelligence service has reason to believe that the TransHumans are attempting to engineer the creation of a white hole. This white hole would be a counterpart of the many black holes occurring naturally throughout the galaxy. Theoretically, it could be an infinite energy source. It could also lead to controlling gravity the way we now control electricity."

"If it has that much potential," Jeanine said, "why would they build it out here? They must have realized it would be vulnerable to attack. Why not locate it in the heart of their polity, where both construction and protection would be far easier?"

Janson's smile was grim. "You would put it as far away as practical because infinite energy is difficult to control. Make a mistake, and you may get an explosion which makes a supernova look like a firecracker."

Which certainly explained why the Eternals thought it worthwhile to send a strike force so far from home.

"The Eternal intelligence service obtained this picture of one of the crucial units necessary to generate the white hole," Jansons continued. A hologram glowed into existence between us. The image was oddly unimpressive: a light gray, rectangular solid with rounded top edges. There were small projections from the middle of each side of the base but the image was too fuzzy to identify them further. A measuring stick, added to the image during processing, indicated that each side was about a meter long.

"And here are some of the images the two of you provided that triggered a security alert when I fed them into my computer."

The picture changed and now we were seeing the feed from one of the rovers. It was in one of the rift zones. Scattered over the large, curved surface, looking almost like barnacles, were units identical to the one in the hologram from the Eternals.

"Our techs say that is a field distributor," Jansons said. "Or a power generator. My guess is they don't have a clue and won't get one until they actually get one of those things to examine. Which is just what the two of you are going to do for them."

In a display case in the Space Force's school for combat engineers there is a cartoon which goes back to the days before space travel. Two guys are standing in a hole in the ground. Both wear helmets identifying them as combat engineers. It's raining. Bombs are going off all around them. One guy says to the other, "Quitcher bitchin' or I'll send you back to the infantry."

That is hundreds of years out of date and still the most honest assessment of what it means to be in the combat engineers. Recruiting commercials may show you repairing starships, building orbital stations or constructing space ports. In reality, you are often called upon to do technically complex tasks under the most dangerous and uncomfortable conditions imaginable.

★ ★ ★

Fifteen minutes after being briefed by Jansons, Jeanine and I were suited up for vacuum in the Specter's forward compartment, just below the bridge. We checked our communications link and then our Omni-Tools, informally known as Otees. Depending on its setting, an Otee could be used as a signaling device, a knife, or a welding torch, or to put a hole through three inches of steel or twelve inches of human being. That done, I held the launching skeleton, looking like a gleaming coil of wire, above my head. I touched the activation button. The skeleton extended itself down the length of my body and then contracted until it fit snugly. Since I was now unable to move arms or legs, O'Connor had to attach the reaction tanks to the skeleton and slide me into the rail gun tube. He dogged the hatch at my feet.

It was completely dark. Have I mentioned claustrophobia before?

I felt the rail gun's kick all over my body. Then I was in space with the Specter receding rapidly behind me. The heads-up display on the inside of my helmet showed my position on a line extending from the Specter to the derelict. Numbers showing my distance to the target unreeled in a race to zero.

Jeanine was on my right, just barely within my range of vision. Far below, lightning flashes illuminated the swirling clouds. I seemed to be hanging motionless in space.

There was time to think. One of the things I thought about was why Jeanine and I had to do this instead of a robot. It would have been easy to blame the Dominion's prejudice against robots and artificial intelligence generally, but in this instance, involving TransHumans, it made some sense. A radio-controlled robot would be vulnerable to hacking. TransHuman technology was acknowledged to be better at that than we were at countermeasures. You might deal with that problem by removing the radio and giving the robot enough intelligence to complete the task. But then you would have no direct control. A robot with sufficient flexibility to surmount unforeseen problems might also have sufficient flexibility to reprogram itself.

"When we get there, I go in first," Jeanine said.

"Why?" I asked.

"I'm smaller than you," she said. "If I can't fit through a passageway, you certainly won't be able to."

"Makes sense," I said, not happy with the decision but with no logical counter.

The one weakness in the Space Force's analysis was the assumption that humans, like me, might not change their own programming. Not that I was a natural rebel or an agent of either the Eternals or the TransHumans. On the contrary, I was proof that reactionary views are sometimes correct, that if you put men and women in the same unit their concern for each other may outweigh their dedication to the mission. Under most circumstances, this would not matter. If anything went seriously wrong—if, for example, the derelict turned out to be an elaborate trap—we would both likely be dead before we knew what was happening. Yet I knew, without reasoning it out or weighing the alternatives, that if it came to a choice between Jeanine and the mission, I would abandon the mission without a second thought. Call this short timer's attitude if you like, or call it treason. It was who I was and what I would do.

The derelict was growing perceptibly larger with each second. Suddenly, one side of it seemed to ignite as it swung out of the planet's shadow. My helmet polarized to make the brilliance bearable. It activated its auditory warning.

"Deceleration commences in three . . . two . . . one."

No flames erupted from the launching skeleton, but I felt a pressure on my shoulders which quickly grew stronger as reaction mass jetted out in front of me.

The derelict transitioned from "over there" to "down below." As it turned, the crater came into view, looking like a huge mouth approaching to scoop me up. I fell within it.

Deceleration ended. The launching skeleton spread away from me in pieces. Half a dozen rovers, under O'Connor's control, swarmed around us as guides. Now the side of the crater was a wall bearing down on me implacably as I fell deeper. I fired a tether from my wrist, hoping the glue on the tip of the dart would work on whatever material it hit. The line went taut and swung me gently to the side. I bounced once and came to rest. A moment later, Jeanine was beside me.

"Our entry is about thirty meters further in," she said.

I followed her and experienced one of those shifts in perspective which literally make some people sick. As we had been approaching, visual cues made the derelict and the crater in particular seem to be "down." Now that we were on the side of the crater, however, the rotation of the derelict was providing a constant mild centrifugal force. As a result, we now had to climb "up" to move deeper into the crater. There was no shortage of handholds: sliced cables, shattered pipes, gaps which might have been designed for storage of some kind. Moving carefully, it took ten minutes to find our entry spot.

"Are you certain?" I asked when we reached it. "We passed at least three larger entries."

"All dead ends," she assured me.

"I confirm that," O'Connor said from his work station back on the Specter.

"A rover goes in first," Jeanine said, "then me, then you. The remaining rovers will trail behind you, establishing line-of-sight communications back to the Specter. Now let's hook up in case one of us gets stuck."

We did so, and then I followed her in. The first part wasn't too bad. My helmet provided enough light for me to see that I was in a featureless tube. The line connecting me to Jeanine stretched out ahead until it was lost in the dimness. I advanced with a microgravity swim, pushing myself forward with my toes, guiding my trajectory with my hands.

"It gets a little narrower here," Jeanine warned.

Narrower was not the word for it. The tunnel constricted itself into an S curve. I tried to imitate a snake and slither through. At the top of the curve, my shoulders wedged against both sides of the tube. My feet slid off the surface behind me. Trying to move forward on my elbows just wedged me in tighter.

"Jeanine, I'm stuck at the top of the S. I'm going to pull back and try a different angle of attack."

My feet still could not find any purchase. I imagined being stuck there indefinitely. My suit could recycle air but I would die of thirst.

"Stop trying to move either way," Jeanine said. "Just stretch your arms out in front of you as far as they will go. Relax. Go limp!"

"And if that doesn't work?" I asked.

"No problem. We'll just deflate your suit."

I did as instructed. There were two sharp tugs. Neither seemed a serious effort to extract me. Rather, she seemed to be testing her own leverage and how tightly I was caught. Then a prolonged pull of steadily increasing pressure. I was just starting to wonder if this could make a bad situation worse when I popped forward like a champagne cork.

"A diet is definitely in order," Jeanine said. I grunted agreement.

The passage widened considerably as we continued to zigzag our way into the interior under O'Connor's guidance. We were in a stomach-shaped room when we were drawn to one side with enough force that it became "down."

A white hole, Jansons had said, *could lead to controlling gravity.*

"O'Connor, is the station activating itself?" I asked. "Jeanine and I seem to be in the presence of a weak but very noticeable gravitational field."

"Negative," O'Connor said. "You are experiencing deceleration as the derelict passes through the outer edges of the atmosphere. It will cease soon."

In fact, it was already diminishing. I floated away from the side.

"However, our updated program shows your orbit to be decaying more rapidly than originally forecast. You have no time to waste."

"Roger that," I agreed.

"Jeanine," O'Connor said, "the next leg of your journey is through the meter-wide opening just above your head. It will lead you immediately into a chamber larger than the one you are currently in."

"Uh, there is no opening above my head," Jeanine said. "Are you sure you have my correct orientation?"

"Say again?"

"There is no opening above my head. In fact, there is no opening at this end of the room at all. Take a look." Three rovers floated around her, earnestly searching for the missing opening.

"Let me check—" O'Connor's voice stopped. There wasn't even static. The rovers drifted in random directions.

Jeanine and I turned to each other. "Now what?" she asked.

I accessed the rovers. There should have been signals from fifteen. Only ten showed up on the display. The image from the one farthest back showed a collapsed tunnel. None were under control.

"We will suppose that we have not sprung a trap," I said hesitantly, "because, if we have, our situation is likely to be hopeless."

Jeanine took control of the rovers. They darted through tunnels and chambers seeking a way out.

"Let's think this through," I said. "A nuke or something similar blasts out that crater above us. The remainder of the station looks solid enough, but in fact it has been shattered. You can't tell immediately because everything is at rest. But if sufficient force is applied, like plowing into the outer fringes of the atmosphere, the parts will shift into a new configuration. Old tunnels will close. New ones will open."

"Yes!" Jeanine shouted.

"Have you found a way out?" I asked.

"No," she said. "I have found a way in."

We went back about fifty meters. There, a narrow slit opened onto a passageway that seemed to have formed from interconnected bubbles. At their end, we came out on a cleft which must have extended all the way to the center of the derelict. And there, scattered across a surface which curved away to a rocky floor, were the field distributors—or whatever they were. A jagged rectangle of sunlight crept down the wall. Looking up, I saw far above a long opening one to two meters wide. Except for the brightness of the sunshine, I would have been able to see the stars marching by.

Jeanine bounded ahead of me and pried up one of the units from its substrate.

"Ow!" She dropped the unit. It settled to one side and began drifting slowly up the wall. "Minibots. One stung me!" She grabbed the unit and stuffed it in her backpack.

The shaft of sunlight swept over her and I could see dots swarming around her. Not swirling like insects, but zooming in straight lines broken by sharp turns. I unholstered my Otee and fired a test pulse at Jeanine. A green light flicked on, assuring me that it recognized Jeanine as a friendly and would not fire when pointed directly at her. I told it to define anything moving as a legitimate target and, pointing in Jeanine's general direction, squeezed the trigger. A dozen minibots exploded all around her.

"Are you all right?" I asked.

"One of them got me," she said. Pain was in her voice.

I examined her arm. A metal ovoid about the size of the nail on my little finger was embedded just below her elbow. Her suit was trying to seal itself over the wound. As I watched, the ovoid pushed itself further into her flesh.

I set my Otee to its lowest cutting power and narrowest beam. "This is going to hurt," I warned. I immobilized her arm between my left arm and my side. Then I put the short barrel directly on the ovoid and depressed the trigger. The minibot twisted violently as if trying to hide in Jeanine's arm. I depressed the trigger further, increasing the strength of the beam. The minibot blackened and ceased moving. I flicked a short blade out of the Otee and used it to dig out the pieces. Jeanine moaned and tried not to fight me. Her suit sealed itself when I was done. My hand was shaking. I blinked away a combination of tears and sweat. By the time I could see clearly, Jeanine had lost consciousness.

I wrapped her around my shoulders in a fireman's carry. I would have removed the unit from her backpack except that it had surprisingly little mass. Tentatively at first, I began to climb out of the cleft. The farther out, the greater the effect of centrifugal force. I had to be careful. If I lost contact with the wall, we would be ejected into the void.

I used the rovers to scout ahead for handholds. Near the rim, I sent two rovers over the top to look for the Specter. It was nowhere in sight. Instead there were three Eternal vessels about five kilometers out, making a cautious approach.

While Jeanine and I and the rovers were sending out a steady stream of signals. I shut down our communications network and pressed myself against the side of the wall. I had no idea what to do. The Specter had vanished and, under the circumstances, I could not blame Jansons. There was no way she could fight Eternal warcraft.

A decrypted message displayed itself inside my helmet. *Jump. Now.* I blinked, then resumed my climb, going faster and faster until the derelict threw me into space. I had just enough time to wonder if I had misunderstood the message when stars above me vanished and I collided with the interior of an airlock. The outer hatch sealed behind us. The inner hatch slid aside and Shakeel helped us into the Specter's interior.

"I've got them," he yelled up the companionway. Heat washed over my skin, the feeling you get when you make a quantum jump and the suppressor fields aren't precisely aligned. Five seconds later we were back in normal space.

"Eternals," I said as I opened my helmet. "What were they doing?"

"No idea," Shakeel said. "They just appeared fifteen minutes ago and seemed as surprised by the derelict as we were at first. They were moving in slowly, as if they thought the station might come alive and fire at them. When the Lieutenant realized that, she figured she could wait a few minutes to see if the two of you would make contact. She really wanted a white-hole unit and did not want either of you ending up in an Eternal interrogation facility."

Jeanine was still unconscious. I explained what had happened to her as Shakeel retrieved the unit from her backpack. ""We'll keep her in a cold-sleep capsule until we can reach a medical installation. You were lucky," he said. "A well-designed system would have overwhelmed both of you. Or maybe you just ran into the only one that had not been knocked out of commission."

I have a lot of beliefs that are considered odd by some people, but I do not believe in that kind of luck. And why should the Eternals have been so cautious about approaching a station they had already defeated?

Jeanine stirred. Her hands went to her helmet.

"Don't open that!" I said. She turned in my direction, but gave no indication that she recognized me or understood a word I said. Her fingers found the release switch.

"I said, don't open your helmet!" My Otee was in my hand, pointed at her.

"Wait a minute," Shakeel said. "What—"

I pulled the trigger and put a hole right through her heart.

Jansons was almost obscenely pleased with herself. "The entire crew will get medals, but that's arguably the least of it. If you re-up, you will be eligible for a five-year rejuve treatment."

"The white-hole unit was a fake," I said. "There is no such technology."

"Well, yes, and knowing that is valuable information by itself. But in discovering that, we also discovered a real TransHuman weapon, one that might have done incalculable damage if we had no warning of its existence. We have that warning because you were able to put loyalty to the Dominion above your personal feelings."

I had just sufficient self-control to turn away from her. Punching a superior officer is still frowned upon in the Space Force.

"Look, I understand that you are emotionally distraught right now. All I'm saying is that now is not the time for rash decisions. Give it time and I'm sure you will make the decision that's best for both of you."

I finally said something ambiguously positive just to get her to go away.

Jeanine had been put in stasis immediately in a cold-sleep unit and kept that way for the ten weeks it took us to get back to Dominion space. There she was delivered to a quarantined Space Force medical unit. All her blood was removed and strained, harvesting a crop of nanobots that made all the Intelligence techs *ooh* and *ah*. Her heart was too badly damaged for repair. The surgeon snipped it out, dropped in a standard heart for a woman her size from the refrigerator section, and zipped her up. They had also primed the heart with her DNA. Those cells would spread, replacing the standard cells over the course of a year, at the end of which she would truly have her heart back.

I was allowed to visit the third day after the surgery. Her room looked like a regular bedroom. Sterilized air, scented like the ocean during the day and like mountain jungles at night, blew through a fake window. This was done, not because she had ever lived in either habitat, but because her psych profile indicated that she wanted to and so would be most comfortable imagining herself in those surroundings. Circuits imprinted on her nightwear monitored her condition at all times. All surgical and resuscitation mechanisms were hidden in the walls.

I sat in a chair by her bedside, impatient for her to awake and afraid that she would do so.

"So, they say you shot me." Jeanine had opened her eyes while I was sunk in my own thoughts. Her voice was weak but clear.

"Technically speaking, I killed you," I said.

She stared at me dispassionately from her pillow. "You are sure you had a good reason, but you are not sure I will agree."

"Being shot by your fiancé might put a damper on romance for some," I allowed.

"This better be good," she said.

I took a deep breath, and it was like running up the side of the cleft and jumping into space.

"From the beginning, I was afraid the derelict might be a trap. I was just thinking of the kind that snaps shut and kills you. Not until it was almost too late did I think about traps baited with poison to be brought back to the nest and kill all the creatures exposed."

I shook my head, trying to order my thoughts. "Jansons said how lucky we were to have discovered the derelict when we did because it would burn up in the atmosphere in a day. That bothered me when I heard it, though I couldn't say why at the time. Subconsciously, though, I was remembering the astronomers' postulate that we do not occupy a specialized place in the universe. All apparent coincidences are suspect. And what could be a greater coincidence than discovering an abandoned station stuffed with secret technology a day before it would be destroyed?

"Then Shakeel pointed out another coincidence. You had been attacked by the one remaining active defense system. A system active enough to make us run with our loot but not active enough to stop us.

"There were other things equally strange. The way we were run like rats in a maze that kept opening some paths and closing others. The way the Eternal strike force approach the station so cautiously. Yet the Eternals were the ones who supposedly had defeated it. Why should they be cautious?

"The pieces didn't come together until we were back in the Specter. It had been no coincidence to find the station in a decaying orbit and no coincidence that you were attacked the way you were. The station was not a derelict at all. It was functioning as designed. It would always shift its orbit to appear a day from destruction. It would always attack raiders but let them go after injecting them with nanobots to take home and spread. We triggered a trap set for Eternals. If I had allowed you to open your helmet, they would have spread through the entire ship."

"So you shot me to keep all of us from becoming cyber-zombies," Jeanine said.

"Jansons prefers the story that I chose the Dominion over you," I said. "I would never have done that."

"Yet reasonable as all that is, you are worried that I may not forgive you," she said.

I gave a slight nod.

"Good," she said. "I needed something to hold over you. Guilt! You must be partly Jewish. Or Otho-Catholic. Whenever I want something in the future, and however compelling your reasons for saying no, all I will have to do is wail about the cruel brute who broke my heart and you will wilt immediately."

The talking had tired her out. She turned on her pillow and smiled, for all the world looking like a sleepy cat. "I think . . . this is the beginning . . . of a beautiful . . ."

MORRIGAN IN THE SUNGLARE

★

by Seth Dickinson

The tenets of Ubuntu taught compassion, understanding, humanity for all. But was that any way to win a war?

THINGS LAPORTE SAYS, during the war—

The big thing, at the end:

The navigators tell Laporte that *Indus* is falling into the sun.

Think about the *difficulty* of it. On Earth, Mars, the moons of Jupiter, the sun wants you but it cannot have you: you slip sideways fast enough to miss. This is the truth of orbit, a hand-me-down birthright of velocity between your world and the fire. You never think about it.

Unless you want to fall. Then you need to strip all that speed away. Navigators call it *killing your velocity* (killing again: Laporte's not sure whether this is any kind of funny). It takes more thrust to fall into the sun than to escape out to the stars.

Indus made a blind jump, fleeing the carnage, exit velocity uncertain.

And here they are. Falling.

They are the last of *Indus'* pilots and there is nothing left to fly, so Laporte and Simms sit in the empty briefing room and play caps. The ship groans around them, ruined hull protesting the efforts of the damage control crews—racing to revive engines and jump drive before CME radiation sleets through tattered armor and kills everyone on board.

"What do you think our dosage is?" Laporte asks.

"I don't know. Left my badge in my bunk." Simms rakes her sweat-soaked hair, selects a cap, and antes. Red emergency light on her collarbone, on the delta of muscle there. "Saw a whole damage control party asleep in the number two causeway. Radiation fatigue."

"So fast? That's bad, boss." Laporte watches her Captain, pale lanky daughter of Marineris, sprawled across three seats in the half-shed tangle of her flight suit, and makes a fearful search for damage. Radiation poisoning, or worse. A deeper sort of wound.

In the beginning Simms was broken and Laporte saved her, a truth Simms has never acknowledged but must know. And she saved Laporte in turn, by ferocity, by hate, by being the avatar of everything Laporte didn't know.

And here in the sunglare Laporte is afraid that the saving's been undone. Not that it should matter, this concern of hearts, when they'll all be dead so soon—but—

"Hey," Laporte says, catching on. "You *sneak,* boss. I call bullshit."

"Got me." Simms pushes the bottlecap (ARD/AE-002 ANTI RADIATION, it says) across. A little tremble in her fingers. Not so severe. "They're all too busy to sleep."

The caps game is an Ubuntu game, a children's game, a kill-time game, an I'm-afraid game. Say something, truth or lie. See if your friends call it right.

It teaches you to see other people. Martin Mandho, during a childhood visit, told her that. *This is why it's so popular in the military. Discipline and killing require dehumanization. The caps game lets soldiers reclaim shared subjectivity.*

"Your go, Morrigan," Simms says, shuffling her pile of ARD/AE-002 caps. The callsign might be a habit, might be a reminder: *we're still soldiers.*

"I was in CIC. Think I saw Captain Sorensen tearing up over a picture of Captain Kyrematen." *Yangtze*'s skipper, Sorensen's comrade. Lost.

Simms' face armors up. "I don't want to talk about anything that just happened."

"Is that a call?"

"No. Of course it's true."

Laporte wants to stand up and say: fuck this. *Fuck this stupid game, fuck the rank insignia, fuck the rules. We're falling into the sun, there's no rescue coming. Boss, I—*

But what would she say? It's not as simple as the obvious thing (and boy, it's obvious), not about lust or discipline or loyalty. Bigger than that, truer than that, full of guilt and fire and salvation, because what she really wants to say is something about—

About how Simms is—important, right, but that's not it. That's not big enough.

Laporte can't get her tongue around it. She doesn't know how to say it.

Simms closes her eyes for a moment. In the near distance, another radiation alarm joins the threnody.

Things Laporte already knows how to say—

I'm going to kill that one, yes, I killed him. Say it like this:

Morrigan, tally bandit. Knife advantage, have pure, pressing now. Guns guns guns.

And the ship in her sights, silver-dart *Atalanta,* built under some other star by hands not unlike her own, the fighter and its avionics and torch and weapons and its desperate skew as it tries to break clear, the pilot too—they all come apart under the coilgun hammer. The pilot too.

Blossoming shrapnel. Spill of fusion fire. Behold Laporte, starmaker. (Some of the color in the flame is human tissue, atomizing.)

She made her first kill during the fall of Jupiter, covering Third Fleet's retreat. Sometimes rookies fall apart after their first, eaten up by guilt. Laporte's seen this. But the cry-scream-puke cycle never hits her, even though she's been afraid of her own compassion, even though her callsign was almost *Flower Girl.*

Instead she feels high.

There's an Ubuntu counselor waiting on the *Solaris,* prepared to debrief and support pilots with post-kill trauma. She waves him away. Twenty years of Ubuntu education, *cherish all life* hammered into the metal of her. All meaningless, all wasted.

That high says: born killer.

She was still flying off the *Solaris* here, Kassim on her wing. Still hadn't met Simms yet.

Who is Lorna Simms? Noemi Laporte thinks about this, puzzles and probes, and sometimes it's a joy, and sometimes it hurts. Sometimes she doesn't think about it at all—mostly when she's with Simms, flying, killing.

Maybe that's who Simms is. The moment. A place where Laporte never has to think, never has a chance to reflect, never has to be anything other than laughter and kill-joy. But that's a selfish way to go at it, isn't it? Simms is her own woman, impatient, profane, ferocious, and Laporte shouldn't make an icon of her. She's not a lion, not a war-god, not some kind of oblivion Laporte can curl up inside.

A conversation they have, after a sortie, long after they saved each other:

"You flew like shit today, Morrigan."

"That so, boss?"

Squared off in the shower queue, breathing the fear stink of pilots and *Indus* crew all waiting for cold water. Simms a pylon in the crowd and dark little Laporte feels like the raven roosting on her.

"You got sloppy on your e-poles," Simms says. "Slipped into the threat envelope twice."

"I went in to finish the kill, sir. Calculated risk."

"Not much good if you don't live to brag about it."

"Yet here I am, sir."

"You'll spend two hours in the helmet running poles and drags before I let you fly again." Simms puts a little crack of authority on the end of the reprimand, and then grimaces like she's just noticed the smell. "Flight Lieutenant Levi assures me that they *were* good kills, though."

Laporte is pretty sure Simms hasn't spoken to Levi since preflight. She grins toothsomely at her Captain, and Simms, exasperated, grinning back though (!), shakes her head and sighs.

"You love it, don't you," she says. "You're *happy* out there."

Laporte puts her hands on the back of her head, an improper attitude towards a superior officer, and holds the grin. "I'm coming for you, sir."

She's racing Simms for the top of the Second Fleet kill board. They both know who's going to win.

★ ★ ★

I'm in trouble. Say it like this:

Boss, Morrigan, engaged defensive, bandit my six on plane, has pure.

And Simms' voice, flat and clear on the tactical channel, so unburdened by tone or technology that it just comes off like clean truth, an easy promise on a calm day, impossible not to trust:

Break high, Morrigan. I've got you.

There's a little spark deep down there under the calm, an ember of rage or glee. It's the first thing Laporte ever knew about Simms, even before her name.

Laporte had a friend and wingman, Kassim. He killed a few people, clean ship-to-ship kills, and afterwards he'd come back to the *Solaris* with Laporte and they'd drink and shout and chase women until the next mission.

But he broke. Sectioned out. A psychological casualty: cry-scream-puke.

Why? Why Kassim, why not Laporte? She's got a theory. Kassim used to talk about why the war started, how it would end, who was right, who was wrong. And, fuck, who can blame him? Ubuntu was supposed to breed a better class of human, meticulously empathic, selflessly rational.

Care for those you kill. Mourn them. They are human too, and no less afraid.

How could you think like that and then pull the trigger, ride the burst, *guns guns guns* and boom, *scratch bandit, good kill*? So Laporte gave up on empathy and let herself ride the murder-kick. She hated herself for it. But at least she didn't break.

Too many people are breaking. The whole Federation is getting its ass kicked.

After Kassim sectioned out, Laporte put in for a transfer to the frigate *Indus,* right out on the bleeding edge. She'd barely met Captain Simms, barely knew her. But she'd heard Simms on FLEETTAC, heard the exultation and the fury in her voice as she led her squadron during the *Meridian* ambush and the defense of Rheza Station.

"It's a suicide posting," Captain Telfer warned her. "The *Indus* eats new pilots and shits ash."

But Simms' voice said: *I know how to live with this. I know how to love it.*

I'm with you, Captain Simms. I'll watch over you while you go ahead and make the kill. Say it like this:
Boss, Morrigan, tally, visual. Press!
That's all it takes. A fighter pilot's brevity code is a strict, demanding form: say as much as you can with as few words as possible, while you're terrified and angry and you weigh nine times as much as you should.

Like weaponized poetry, except that deep down your poem always says *we have to live. They have to die.*

For all their time together on the *Indus,* Laporte has probably spoken more brevity code to Simms than anything else.

People from Earth aren't supposed to be very good at killing.

Noemi Laporte, callsign Morrigan, grew up in a sealed peace. The firewall defense that saved the solar system from alien annihilation fifty years ago also collapsed the Sol-Serpentis wormhole, leaving the interstellar colonies out in the cold—a fistful of sparks scattered to catch fire or gutter out. Weary, walled in, the people of Sol abandoned starflight and built a cozy nest out of the wreckage: the eudaimonic Federation, democracy underpinned by gentle, simulation-guided Ubuntu philosophy. *We have weathered enough strife,* Laporte remembers—Martin Mandho, at the podium in Hellas Planitia for the 40th anniversary speech. *In the decades to come, we hope to build a community of compassion and pluralism here in Sol, a new model for the state and for the human mind.*

And then they came back.

Not the aliens, oh no no, that's the heart of it—they're still out there, enigmatic, vast, xenocidal. And the colonist Alliance, galvanized by imminent annihilation, has to be ready for them.

Ready at any price.

These are our terms. An older Laporte, listening to another broadcast: the colonists' *Orestes* at the reopened wormhole, when negotiations finally broke down. *We must have Sol's wealth and infrastructure to meet the coming storm. We appealed to your leaders in the spirit of common humanity, but no agreement could be reached.*

This is a matter of survival. We cannot accept the Federation's policy of isolation. Necessity demands that we resort to force.

That was eighteen months ago.

A lot of people believe that the whole war's a problem of communication, fundamentally solvable. Officers in the *Solaris'* off-duty salon argue that if only the Federation and the Alliance could just figure out what to say, how to save face and stand down, they could find a joint solution. A way to give the Alliance resources and manpower while preserving the Federation from socioeconomic collapse and the threat of alien extermination. It's the Ubuntu dream, the human solution.

Captain Simms doesn't hold to that, though.

A conversation they had, on the *Indus'* observation deck:

"But," Laporte says (she doesn't remember her words exactly, or what she's responding to; and anyway, she's ashamed to remember). "The Alliance pilots are people too."

"Stow that shit." Simms' voice a thundercrack, unexpected: she'd been across the compartment, speaking to Levi. "I won't have poison on my ship."

The habit of a lifetime and the hurt of a moment conspire against military discipline and Laporte almost makes a protest—*Ubuntu says, Martin Mandho said*—

But Simms is already on her, circling, waiting for the outspoken new transfer to make *one* more mistake. "What's the least reliable weapons system on your ship, Morrigan?"

A whole catalogue of options, a bestiary of the Federation's reluctant innovations—least reliable? Must be the Mulberry GES-2.

"Wrong. It's you. Pilots introduce milliseconds of unaffordable latency. In a lethal combat environment, hesitation kills." Simms is talking to everyone now, making an example of Laporte. She sits there, stiff and burning, waiting for it to be over. "If the Admiralty had its way, they'd put machines in these cockpits. But until that day, your job is to come as close as you can. Your job is to keep your humanity out of the gears. How do you do that?"

"Hate, sir," Levi says.

"Hate." Simms lifts her hands to an invisible throat. Bears down, for emphasis, as her voice drops to a purr. She's got milspec features, aerodyne chin, surgical cheekbones, and Laporte feels like she's going to get cut if she stares, but she does. "There are no people in those ships you kill. They have no lovers, no parents, no home. They were never children and they will never grow old. They invaded your home, and you are going to stop them by killing them all. Is that clear, Laporte?"

Willful, proud, stupid, maybe thinking that Simms would give her slack on account of that first time they flew together, Laporte says: "That's monstrous."

Simms puts the ice on her: full-bore all-aspect derision. "It's a war. Monsters win."

The Alliance flagship, feared by Federation pilot and admiral alike, is *Atreus*. Her missile batteries fire GTM-36 Block 2 Eos munitions (*memorize that name, pilot. Memorize these capabilities*). The *Atreus'* dawn-bringers have a fearsome gift: given targeting data, they can perform their own jumps. Strike targets far across the solar system. The euphemism is "over the horizon."

Laporte used to wonder about the gun crews who run the Eos batteries. Do they know what they're shooting at, when they launch a salvo? Do they invent stories to assure each other that the missiles are intended for Vital Military Targets? When they hear about collateral damage, a civilian platform shattered and smashed into Europa's ice in the name of "shipping denial," do they speculate in a guilty hush: *was that us?*

Maybe that's the difference between the Alliance and the Federation, the reason the Alliance is winning. The colonists can live with it.

She doesn't wonder about these things any more, though.

One night in the gym the squadron gets to sparring in a round robin and then Laporte's in the ring with Simms, nervous and half-fixed on quitting until they get into it and slam to the mat, grappling for the arm-bar or the joint lock, and Laporte feels it click: it's just like the dogfight, like the merge, pacing your strength exactly like riding a turn, waiting for the moment to cut in and *shoot*.

She gets Simms in guard, flips her, puts an elbow in her throat. Feels herself grinning down with the pressure while everyone else circles and hoots: *Morrrrrrigan—look at her, she's on it—*

Simms looks back up at her and there's this question in her wary, wonderful eyes, a little annoyed, a little curious, a little scared: *what* are *you?*

She rolls her shoulders, lashes her hips, throws Laporte sideways. Laporte's got no breath and no strength left to spend but she thinks Simms's just as tapped and the rush feeds her, sends her clawing back for the finish.

Simms puts her finger up, thumb cocked, before Laporte can reach her. "Bang," she says.

Laporte falls on her belly. "Oof. Aargh."

It's important that Simms not laugh too hard. She's got to maintain command presence. She's been careful about that, since their first sortie.

You need help, Captain Simms. Say it like this:

This is the first time they flew together, when Laporte saved Simms. It happened because of a letter Laporte received, after her transfer to *Indus* was approved but before she actually shuttled out to her new post.

FLEETNET PERSONAL—TAIGA/TARN/NODIS
FLIGHT LIEUTENANT KAREN NG [YANGTZE]
//ENSIGN NOEMI LAPORTE [INDUS]
Laporte:

Just got word of your transfer. You may remember me from the *Nauticus* incident. I'm de facto squadron leader aboard *Yangtze*. Lorna Simms and I go way back.

Admiral Netreba is about to select ships for a big joint operation against the Alliance. Two months ago the *Indus* would have been top of the list, and Simms with it. But they've been on the front too long, and the scars are starting to show.

I hear reports of a two hundred percent casualty rate. Simms and Ehud Levi are the only survivors of the original squadron. I hear that Simms doesn't give new pilots callsigns, that she won't let the deck crew paint names on their ships. If she's going to lose her people, she'd rather not allow them to be people.

It's killing morale. Simms won't open up to her

replacements until they stop dying, and they won't stop
dying until she opens up.

I want the *Indus* with us when we make our move, but
Netreba won't pick a sick ship. See if you can get through
to Simms.

Regards,
Karen Ng

Laporte takes this shit seriously. When Simms takes her out for a
training sortie, a jaunt around the Martian sensor perimeter, she's got
notes slipped into the plastic map pockets on her flightsuit thighs,
gleaned from gossip and snippy FLEETNET posts: *responds well to
confidence and plain talk, rejects overt empathy, accepts professional
criticism but will enforce a semblance of military discipline.* No pictures,
though.

She knows she's overthinking it, but fuck, man, it's hard not to be
nervous. Simms is her new boss, her wartime idol, the woman who
might get her killed. Simms is supposed to teach her how to live with—
with all this crazy shit. And now it turns out she's broken too? Is there
anyone out here who *hasn't* cracked?

Maybe a little of that disappointment gets into Laporte's voice.
Afterwards, because of the thing that happens next, she can't
remember exactly how she broached it—professional inquiry, officer
to superior? Flirtatious breach of discipline? Oafishly direct? But she
remembers it going bad, remembers Simms curling around from
bemusement to disappointment, probably thinking: *great,* Solaris *is
shipping me its discipline cases so I can get them killed.*

Then the Alliance jumps them. Four Nyx, a wolfpack out hunting
stragglers. Bone-white metal cast in shark shapes. Shadows on the light
of their own fusion stars.

Simms, her voice a cutting edge, a wing unpinioned, shedding all the
weight of death she carries: "Morrigan, Lead, knock it off, knock it off,
I see jump flash, bandits two by two." And then, realizing as Laporte
does that they're not getting clear, that help's going to be too long
coming: "On my lead, Morrigan, we're going in. Get your fangs out."

And Laporte puts it all away. Seals it up, like she's never been able
to before. Just her and the thirty-ton Kentauroi beneath her and the
woman on her wing.

They hit the merge in a snarl of missile and countermeasure and everything after that blurs in memory, just spills together in a whirl of acceleration daze and coilgun fire until it's pointless to recall, and what would it mean, anyway? You don't remember love as a series of acts. You just know: *I love her.* So it is here. They fought, and it was good. (And damn, yes, she loves Simms, that much has been apparent for a while, but it's maybe not the kind of love that anyone does anything about, maybe not the kind it's wise to voice or touch.) She remembers a few calls back and forth, grunted out through the pressure of acceleration. All brevity code, though, and what does that mean outside the moment?

Two gunships off *Yangtze* arrive to save them and the Alliance fighters bug out, down a ship. Laporte comes back to the surface, shaking off the narcosis of the combat trance, and finds herself talking to Simms, Simms talking back.

Simms is laughing. "That was good," she says. "That was good, Morrigan. Damn!"

Indus comes off the line less than twelve hours later, yielding her patrol slot to another frigate. Captain Simms takes the chance to drill her new pilots to exhaustion and they begin to loathe her so profoundly they'd all eat a knife just to hear one word of her approval. Admiral Netreba, impressed by *Indus'* quick recovery, taps the frigate for his special task force.

Laporte knows her intervention made a difference. Knows Simms felt the same exhilaration, flying side by side, and maybe she thought: *I've got to keep this woman alive.*

Simms just needed to believe she could save someone.

Alliance forces in the Sol theater fall under the command of Admiral Steele, a man with Kinshasa haute-couture looks and winter-still eyes. Sometimes he gives interviews, and sometimes they leak across the divide.

"Overwhelming violence," he answers, asked about his methods. "The strategic application of shock. They're gentle people, humane, compassionate. Force them into violent retaliation, and they'll break. The Ubuntu philosophy that shapes their society cannot endure open war."

"Some of your critics accuse you of atrocity," the interviewer says.

"Indiscriminate strategic bombing. Targeted killings against members of the civilian government in Sol."

Steele puts his hands together, palm to palm, fingers laced, and Laporte would absolutely bet a bottle cap that the sorrow on his face is genuine. "The faster I end the war," he says, "the faster we can stop the killing. My conscience asks me to use every tool available."

"So you believe this is a war worth winning? That the Security Council is right to pursue a military solution to this crisis?"

Steele's face gives nothing any human being could read, but Laporte, she senses determination. "That's not my call to make," he says.

This happens after the intervention, after Simms teaches Laporte to be a monster (or lets her realize she already was), after they manage the biggest coup of the war—the capture of the *Agincourt*. Before they fall into the sun, though.

They take some leave time, Simms and Laporte and the rest of the *Indus* pilots, and the *Yangtze*'s air wing too. Karen Ng has a cabin in Tharsis National Park, on the edge of Mars' terraformed valleys. Olympus Mons fills the horizon like the lip of a battered pugilist, six-kilometer peak scraping the edge of atmosphere. Like a bridge between where they are and where they fight.

Barbeque on the shore of Marineris Reservoir. The lake is meltwater from impacted comets, crystalline and still, and Levi won't swim in it because he swears up and down it's full of cyanide. They're out of uniform and Laporte should really *not* take that as an excuse but, well, discipline issues: she finds Simms, walking the shore.

"Boss," she says.

"Laporte." No callsign. Simms winds up and hurls a stone. It doesn't even skip once: hits, pierces, vanishes. The glass of their reflections shatters and reforms. Simms chuckles, a guarded sound, like she's expecting Laporte to do something worth reprimand, like she's not sure what she'll do about it. "Been on Mars before?"

"Uh, pretty much," Laporte mumbles, hoping to avoid this conversation: she was at Hellas for Martin Mandho's speech ten years ago, but she was a snotty teenager, Earthsick, and single-handedly ruined Mom's plan to see more of the world. "Never with a native guide, though."

"Tourist girl." Simms tries skipping again. "Fuck!"

"Boss, you're killing me." Laporte finds a flat stone chip, barely weathered, and throws it—but Mars gravity, hey, Mars gravity is a good excuse for *that*. "Mars gravity!" she pleads, while Simms laughs, while Laporte thinks about what a bad idea this is, to let herself listen to that laugh and get drunk. Fleet says: no fraternization.

They walk a while.

"You really hate them?" Laporte asks, forgetting whatever wit she had planned the instant it hits her tongue.

"The colonists? The Alliance?" Simms squints up Olympus-ways, one boot up on a rock. The archetypical laconic pioneer, minus only that awful Mongolian chew everyone here adores. "What's the alternative?"

"Didn't you go to school?" Ubuntu never found so many ears on hardscrabble Mars. "They gave it to us every day on *Solaris*: love them, understand them, regret the killing."

"Ah, right. 'He has a husband,' I remember, shooting him. 'May you find peace,' I pray, uncaging the seekers." Simms rolls the rock with her boot, flipping it, spinning it on its axis. "And you had this in your head, the first time you made a kill? You cut into the merge and lined up the shot thinking about your shared humanity?"

"I guess so," Laporte says. A good person would have thought about that, so she'd thought about it. "But it didn't stop me."

Simms lets the rock fall. It makes a flinty clap. She eyes Laporte. "No? You weren't angry? You didn't hate?"

"No." She thinks of Kassim. "It was so easy for me. I thought I was sick."

"Huh," Simms says, chewing on that. "Well, can't speak for you, then. But it helps me to hate them."

"Hate's inhumane, though." Words from a conscience she's kept buried all these months. "It perpetuates the cycle."

"I wish the universe gave power to the decent. Protection to the humane." Simms shrugs, in her shoulders, in her lips. "But I've only seen one power stop the violent, and it's a closer friend to hate."

She's less coltish down here, like she's got more time for every motion, like she's set aside her haste. "Hey," Laporte says, pressing her luck. "When I transferred in. You were—in a tough place."

Simms holds up a hand to ward her off. "You can see the ships," she says.

Mars is a little world with a close horizon and when she looks up

Laporte feels like she's going to lose her balance and fall right off, out past Phobos, into a waiting wolfpack, into the Eos dawnbringers from *over the horizon*. She takes a step closer to Simms, towards the stanchion that keeps her down.

High up there some warship's drive flickers.

"I was pretty sure," Simms says, "that everyone I knew was going to die, and that I couldn't stop it. That's where I was, when you transferred in."

"And now?" Laporte asks, still watching the star. It's a lot farther away, a lot safer.

"Jury's out," Simms says. Laporte's too skittish to check whether she's joking. "Look. Moonsrise. You've got to tell me a secret."

"Are you fucking with me?"

"Native guide," Simms says, rather smugly.

"When I was a kid," Laporte says, "I had an invisible friend named Ken. He told me I had to watch the ants in the yard go to war, the red ants and the black ones, and that I had to choose one side to win. He said it was the way of things. I got a garden hose and I—I took him really seriously—"

Simms starts cracking up. "You're a loon," she chokes. "I'm glad you're on my side."

"I wonder what we'll do after this," Laporte says.

Simms sobers up. "Don't think about that. It'll kill you."

Laporte listens to the flight data record of that training sortie, the tangle with the Nyx wolfpack, just to warm her hands on that fire, to tremble at the inarticulate beauty of the fight:

"*—am spiked, am spiked, music up. Bandit my seven high, fifteen hundred, aspect attack.*"

"*Lead supporting.*" The record is full of warbling alarms, the voices of a ship trying to articulate every kind of danger. "*Anchor your turn at, uh—fuck it, just break low, break low. Padlocking—*"

"*Kill him, boss—*"

"*Guns.*" A low, smooth exhalation, Simms breathing out on the trigger. "*Guns.*"

"*Nice. Good kill. Bandit your nine low—break left—*"

Everything's so clear. So true. Flying with Simms, there's no confusion.

They respond to a distress call from a civilian vessel suffering catastrophic reactor failure. *Indus* jumps on-scene to find an Alliance corvette, *Arethusa,* already providing aid to the civilian. Both sides launch fighters, slam down curtains of jamming over long-range communications, and prepare to attack.

But neither of them has enough gear to save the civilian ship—the colonists don't have the medical suite for all her casualties; *Indus* can't provide enough gear to stabilize her reactor. Captain Sorensen negotiates a truce with the *Arethusa's* commander.

Laporte circles *Indus,* flying wary patrol, her fingers on the master arm switch. Some of the other pilots talk to the colonists on GUARD. They talk back, their accents skewed by fifty years of linguistic drift, their humanity still plain. One of the enemy pilots, callsign Anansi, asks for her by name: there's a bounty on her head, an Enemy Ace Incentive, and smartass Anansi wants to talk to her and live to tell. She mutes the channel.

When she stops and thinks about it, she doesn't really believe this war is necessary. So it's quit, or—don't think about it. That's what Simms taught her: you go in light. You throw away everything about yourself that doesn't help you kill. Strip down, sharpen up. Weaponize your soul.

Another Federation frigate, *Hesperia,* picks up the distress signal, picks up the jamming, assumes the worst. She has no way to know about the truce. When she jumps in she opens *Arethusa's* belly with her first salvo and everything goes back to being simple.

Laporte gets Anansi, she's pretty sure.

Fresh off the *Agincourt* coup, they make a play for the *Carthage*— *Indus, Yangtze, Altan Orde, Katana,* and Simms riding herd on three full squadrons. It's a trap. Steele's been keeping his favorite piece, the hunter-killer *Imperieuse,* in the back row. She makes a shock jump, spinal guns hungry.

Everyone dies.

The last thing Laporte hears before she makes a crash-landing on *Indus'* deck is Captain Simms, calling out to Karen Ng, begging her to abandon *Yangtze,* begging her to live. But Karen won't leave her ship.

Indus jumps blind, destination unplotted, exit vector unknown.

The crash transition wrecks her hangar deck, shatters her escape pods in their mounts.

She falls into light.

So Laporte was wrong, in the end. The death of everyone Simms knew *was* inevitable.

Monsters win.

Laporte stacks her bottlecaps and waits for Simms to offer her a word.

The game is just a way to pass the time. Not real speech, not like the chatter, like the brevity code. Out there they could *talk*. And is that why they're alive, just the two of them? Even Levi, old hand Levi, came apart at the end, first in his head when he saw the bodies spilling out of *Altan Orde* and then in his cockpit when the guns found him. But Simms and Laporte, they flew each other home. Home to die in this empty searing room with the bolted-down frame chairs and the bottle caps and their cells rotting inside them.

Or maybe it's just that Simms hated harder than anyone else, hesitated the least. And Laporte, well—she's never hesitated at all.

"It's my fault we're here," Laporte says, even though it's not her turn.

"Yeah?" Simms, she's got red in her eyes, a tremor in her frame.

"If I hadn't listened to Karen's note, if I hadn't done whatever I did to wake you up." If they'd never met. "Netreba never would've picked *Indus* for the task force. We wouldn't have been at the ambush. Wouldn't have watched *Imperieuse* kill our friends."

"All you did was fly my wing," Simms says. "It's not your fault." But she knows exactly what Laporte's talking about.

Simms picks up a bottle cap and puts it between them. "I'm transferring you to *Eris*," she says. "Netreba's flagship. On track for a squadron command."

"Bullshit." Because they're not going to live long enough to transfer anywhere.

Simms wraps the cap up in her shaking hand and draws it back. "I already put the order in," she says. "Just in case."

A dosage alarm shrieks and stops: someone from damage control, silencing the obvious. Beams of ionizing radiation piercing the torn armor, arcing through the crew spaces as *Indus* tumbles and falls.

Is this the time to just give up on protocol? To get her boss by the wrists and beg: wait, stop, please, let me explain, let me stay? We'll make it, rescue will come, we'll fly again? But she *gets it*. She's got that Ubuntu empathy bug. She can feel it in Simms, the old break splintering again: *I can't watch these people die.*

Laporte's the only people she's got left. So Simms has to send her away.

"Boss," she says. "You taught me—without you I wouldn't—"

Killing, it's like falling into the sun: you've got all this compassion, all this goodwill, keeping you in the human orbit. All that civilization that everyone before you worked to build. And somehow you've got to lose it all.

Only Laporte never—

"Without me," Simms says, and she's got no mercy left in her tongue, "you'd be fine. You'll *be* fine. You're a killer. That's all you need—no reasons, no hate. It's just you."

She lets her head loll back and exhales hard. The lines of her arched throat kink and smooth.

"Fuck," she says. "It's hot."

Laporte opens her hand. Asking for the cap. She doesn't have the spit to say: *true.*

Captain Simms makes herself comfortable, flat on her back across three chairs. "Your turn," she says.

"Boss," Laporte rasps. "Fuck. Excuse me." She clears her throat. Might as well go for it: it begs to be said. "Boss, I . . . "

But Simms has gone. She's asleep, breathing hard. It's lethargy, the radiation pulling her down. Giving her some peace.

Laporte calls a medical team. While she waits she tries to find a blanket, but Simms seems to prefer an uneasy rest. She breathes a little easier when Laporte touches her shoulder, though, and Laporte thinks about clasping her hand.

But, no, that's too much.

Federation ships find them. A black-ops frigate, running signals intelligence in deep orbit, picks *Indus'* distress cries from the solar background. Salvage teams scramble to make her ready for one last jump to salvation.

Laporte's waiting by her captain's side when they come for her. The medical team, and the woman with the steel eyes.

"Laporte," the new woman says. "The *Indus* ace. Came looking for you."

By instinct and inclination Laporte stands to shield her captain from the gray-clad woman, from her absent insignia and hidden rank. She can't figure out a graceful way to drop the bottle cap, so she just holds it like a switch for some hidden explosive, for the grief that wants to get out any way it can. "I need to stay with my squadron leader," she says.

"If I'm reading this order right," Steel Eyes says, though she's got no paper or tablet and the light on her iris makes little crawling signs, "she's shipping you out." She opens a glove in invitation. "I'm with Federation wetwork. Elite of the elite. I'm recruiting pilots for ugly jobs."

Laporte hesitates. She wants to stay, wants it like nothing she knows how to tell. But Steel Eyes stares her down and her gaze cuts deep. "I know you like you wouldn't begin to believe," she says. "I watched you learn what you are. We don't have many of your kind left here in Sol. We made ourselves too good. And it's killing us."

"Please," Laporte croaks. "I can't leave her."

The woman from the eclipse depths of Federation intelligence extends her open hand. A gesture of compassion, though she's wearing tactical gloves. "What do you think happens if you stay? You're not going to stop changing, Noemi. You're never going back to humanity."

She sighs a little, not a hesitation, maybe an apology. "This woman, here, this loyalty you have. You're going to be an alien to her."

Laporte doesn't know how to argue with that. Doesn't know how to speak her defiance. Maybe because Steel Eyes is right.

"Ubuntu," the woman says, "is a philosophy of human development. We have a use for everyone. Even, in times like these, for us monsters."

What's she got left? What the fuck else is there? She gave it all up to become a better killer. Humanity's just dead weight on her trigger.

Nothing but Simms and wreckage in the poison sunlight.

"You know we're losing," Steel Eyes says. "You know we need you."

Ah. That's it. The thing she's been trying to say:

Monsters kill because they like it, and that's all Laporte had. Until this new thing, this fragile human thing, until Simms.

Something worth fighting for. A small, stupid, precious reason.

Laporte gets down on her knees. Puts herself as close to the salt sand cap of Simms' hair as she's ever been. Says it, the best way she knows, promising her, promising herself:

"Boss," she whispers. "Hey. I'll see you when we win."

For Darius and the Blue Planet crew.

LIGHT AND SHADOW
★
by Linda Nagata

The skullcaps kept emotion at bay—anger, fear, hate. They kept the mind cold and calculating. A boon on the battlefield, a way to stay sane.

LIEUTENANT DANI REID was serving her turn on watch inside Fort Zana's Tactical Operations Center. She scanned the TOC's monitors and their rotating displays of real-time surveillance data. All was quiet. Even the goats that usually grazed outside the walls had retreated, taking refuge from the noon sun in a grove of spindly thorn trees.

The temperature outside was a steamy 39°C, but within the fort's prefabricated, insulated walls, the air was cool enough that Reid kept the jacket of her brown-camo combat uniform buttoned up per regulation. The skullcap she wore was part of the uniform. Made like an athletic skullcap, it covered her forehead and clung skin-tight against her hairless scalp. Fine wires woven through its silky brown fabric were in constant dialog with the workings of her mind.

On watch, the skullcap kept her alert, just slightly on edge, immune to the mesmerizing hum of electronics and the soothing whisper of air circulating through the vents—white noise that retreated into subliminal volumes when confronted by a louder sound: a rustle of movement in the hallway.

Private First Class Landon Phan leaned in the doorway of the TOC.

Phan was just twenty-one, slender and wiry. Beneath the brim of his skullcap, his eyebrows angled in an annoyed scowl. "LT? You should go check on Sakai."

"Why? What's up?"

"Ma'am, you need to see it yourself."

Phan had been part of Reid's linked combat squad for nine months. He'd done well in the LCS; he'd earned Reid's trust. She didn't feel the same about Sakai.

"Okay. You take the watch."

Light spilling from the TOC was the only illumination in the hallway. The bunkroom was even darker. Reid couldn't see anything inside, but she could hear the fast, shallow, ragged breathing of a soldier in trouble, skirting the edge of panic. She slapped on the hall light.

Specialist Caroline Sakai was revealed, coiled in a bottom bunk, her trembling fists clenched against her chin, her eyes squeezed shut. She wore a T-shirt, shorts, and socks, but she wasn't wearing a skullcap. The pale skin of her hairless scalp gleamed in the refracted light.

"What the hell?" Reid whispered, crossing the room to crouch beside the bunk. "Sakai? What happened?"

Sakai's eyes popped open. She jerked back against the wall, glaring as if she'd never seen Reid before.

"What the hell?" Reid repeated.

Sakai's gaze cut sideways. She bit her lip. Then, in an uncharacteristically husky voice, she confessed, "I think . . . I was having a nightmare."

"No shit! What did you expect?"

She seemed honestly confused. "Ma'am?"

"Where the hell is your skullcap?"

Sakai caught on; her expression hardened. "In my locker, ma'am."

The microwire net in Reid's skullcap detected her consternation and responded to it by signaling the tiny beads strewn throughout her brain tissue to stimulate a counteracting cerebral cocktail that helped her think calmly, logically, as this conversation veered into dangerous territory.

The skullcap was standard equipment in a linked combat squad. It guarded and guided a soldier's emotional state, keeping moods balanced and minds honed. It was so essential to the job that, on deployment, LCS soldiers were allowed to wear it at all times, waking or sleeping. And they did wear it. All of them did. Always.

But they were not required to wear it, not during off-duty hours.

The hallway light picked out a few pale freckles on Sakai's cheeks and the multiple, empty piercings in her earlobes. It tangled in her black, unkempt eyebrows and glinted in her glassy brown eyes. "You want the nightmares?" Reid asked, revolted by Sakai's choice.

"Of course not, ma'am."

Use of the skullcap was tangled up in issues of mental health and self-determination, so regulations existed to protect a soldier's right of choice. Reid could not order Sakai to wear it when she was off-duty; she could not even ask Sakai why she chose to go without it. So she approached the issue sideways. "Something you need to talk about, soldier?"

"No, ma'am," Sakai said in a flat voice. "I'm fine."

Reid nodded, because there was nothing else she could do. "Get some sleep, then. Nightmares aren't going to excuse you from patrol."

She returned to the TOC, where Phan was waiting. "When did this start?"

"Yesterday," he answered cautiously.

Even Phan knew this wasn't a subject they could discuss.

"Get some sleep," she told him. "Use earplugs if you have to."

When he'd gone, Reid considered reporting the issue to Guidance . . . but she knew what Guidance would say. So long as Sakai performed her duties in an acceptable manner, she was within her rights to forego the skullcap during off-duty hours, no matter how much it disturbed the rest of the squad.

What the hell was Sakai trying to prove?

Reid ran her palms across the silky fabric of her skullcap. Then, as if on a dare, she slipped her fingertips under its brim and took it off.

A cold draft kissed her bare scalp and made her shiver.

Her pulse picked up as fear unfolded around her heart.

You're psyching yourself out.

Probably.

She studied the skullcap, turning it over, feeling the hair-thin microwires embedded in the smooth brown cloth.

No big deal, really, to go without it. It was only out of habit that she wore it all the time.

The hum of electronics within the TOC grew a little louder, a little closer, and then, with no further warning, Reid found herself caught up in a quiet fury. Sakai had always been the squad's problem child. Not in the performance of her duty—if that had been an issue, Reid would have been all over her. It was Sakai's personality. She didn't mesh. Distant, uncommunicative, her emotions locked away. A loner. Seven months at Fort Zana had not changed her status as an outsider.

Reid's emotions were closer to the surface: she didn't like Sakai; didn't like her effect on the squad. There needed to be trust between her soldiers, but none of them really trusted Sakai and no one wanted to partner with her. No one believed she would truly have their back if things went hard south. Reid saw it in the field when her soldiers hesitated, thought twice, allowed a few seconds to pass in doubt. Someday those few seconds would be the last measure of a life.

Reid clenched the skullcap.

Fuck Sakai anyway.

Ducking her head, she slipped the cap back on, pressing it close to her scalp. Within seconds, her racing heart slowed. Her anger grew cold and thoughtful.

Sakai thought she could get by without her skullcap. Maybe she wanted to prove she had more mettle than the rest of them, but it wouldn't last. It couldn't. "You'll give it up," Reid whispered. "By this time tomorrow, you'll be back in the fold."

Reid finished her watch and went back to sleep, waking at 1900. She laced on her boots, then tromped next door to the TOC, where Private First Class David Wicks was on duty.

"Anything?" she asked.

"No, ma'am. No alerts at all from Command." He flashed a shy smile. "But my niece had her first-birthday party today." He pulled up a window with his email, and Reid got to watch a short video of a smiling one-year-old in a pretty blue dress.

"Your sister doing okay now?"

"Yeah, she's good."

Wicks sent money to his sister. It was a big part of why he'd signed up.

In the kitchen, Reid microwaved a meal, then joined Sergeant Juarez at the table. "Command thinks we've got a quiet night."

Juarez was no taller than Reid, but he carried fifty extra pounds of muscle. He'd been army for seven years, and Reid was sure he'd be in for twenty if he could pull it off. "You ever notice," he drawled, "how the patrol gets interesting every time Command says there's nothing going on?"

"Just means we're good at finding trouble."

Phan reeled in, with Private First Class Mila Faraci a step behind him. "How's it look tonight, LT?" Faraci asked.

"Quiet so far."

"That's what I like to hear."

Juarez finished eating. He got up just as Sakai came in the door wearing a fresh uniform, her cheeks still flushed from a hot shower and her head freshly denuded of hair, leaving her scalp smooth and pale under the ceiling lights with no skullcap to hide it. Phan and Faraci were waiting together by the two humming microwaves. Phan glared. Faraci looked shocked. "I thought you were shitting me," she murmured.

Sakai ignored everyone. She opened the freezer and pulled out a meal packet while Reid traded a look with Juarez.

"What the hell is with you, Sakai?" Faraci demanded.

"Faraci," Juarez growled, "you got a problem?"

Faraci was strong, tall, tough, and full of swagger, but she took care never to cross Juarez. "No, Sergeant."

Reid got up, dumped her meal packet, and left. Juarez followed her to her quarters, where there was barely enough room for the two of them to stand without breathing each other's air.

"What the hell?" he demanded.

"You know I can't ask. She hasn't said anything to you?"

"She doesn't talk to me or anybody. It's been worse since she got back from leave."

Skullcaps got turned in before a soldier went on leave. It was a harsh transition, learning to live without it. But taking it up again after your twenty-one days—that was easy. No one ever had a problem with that.

"She's just annoyed at being back," Reid decided. "If there was a real issue, Guidance would know. They would address it. Meantime, make sure our other noble warriors don't get in her face. I don't want to bust the kids when Sakai is the loose cannon."

"You got it, LT."

"This won't last," Reid assured him. "You'll see. She'll give this up tomorrow."

Reid was wrong.

Sakai wore the skullcap during the nightly patrols as she was required to do, but for three days running she took the cap off as soon as she hit the showers, and it didn't go on again until they rigged up for the next patrol. This generated its own problem: Sakai couldn't sleep well without her skullcap. It wouldn't be long before she was unfit for patrol.

Reid rigged up early for the night's adventures. Her armored vest went on first. Then she strapped into her "dead sister." The titanium exoskeleton was made of bone-like struts that paralleled her arms and legs and were linked together by a back frame that supported the weight of her pack. Testing the rig, she crouched and then bobbed up, letting the dead sister's powered leg struts do the work of lifting her body weight. The exoskeleton made it easy to walk for hours, to run, to jump, to kick and hit, and to support the weight of her tactical rifle, an MCL1a with muzzle-mounted cams and AI integration.

The rest of the squad was still prepping when she slung her weapon, tucked her helmet under her arm, and strode out into the small yard enclosed by the fort's fifteen-foot-high walls.

The night air was heavy with heat and humidity and the scent of mud and blossoms, but the clouds that had brought a late-afternoon shower had dispersed, leaving the sky clear and awash in the light of a rising moon. Reid allowed herself a handful of seconds to take in the night as it was meant to be seen. Then she pulled her helmet on. Seen through her visor, the yard brightened with the green, alien glow of night vision while icons mustered across the bottom of the display, one for every soldier wearing a skullcap: Juarez, Faraci, Phan, and Wicks.

A familiar voice spoke through Reid's helmet audio: "You're early tonight."

She smiled, though he couldn't see it. "So are you. Slow night?"

"Not too bad."

He was her primary handler from Guidance, codenamed Tyrant, the only name she knew him by. His job was to assist in field operations, overseeing data analysis and relaying communications with Command from his office, five thousand miles away in Charleston. Tyrant had access to the feeds from her helmet cams as well as the display on her visor, and he kept a close eye on all of it. "Where's Sakai's icon?" he asked. "You didn't give her the night off?"

The door opened and, to Reid's surprise, Sakai stepped through, already rigged in armor and bones, her pack on, her weapon on her shoulder, and her helmet in her gloved hand. But no skullcap.

And without her skullcap, she didn't appear as an icon on Reid's display.

"She's challenging you," Tyrant murmured, amusement in his voice.

Sakai shot Reid a sideways glance, but if she was looking for a reaction, she was disappointed. Reid's face was hidden behind the anonymous black shield of her visor.

Sakai turned away, setting her helmet down on a dusty table. Then, like a good girl, she fished her skullcap out of a pocket and put it on.

Her icon popped up on Reid's display. Reid gazed at it and a menu slid open. She shifted her gaze, selecting "physiology" from the list of options. Her system AI whispered a brief report: *status marginal; brain chemistry indicates insufficient sleep.* But as Sakai's skullcap went to work, stimulating the chemical factory of her brain, her status ramped up. By the time the squad assembled, Sakai's condition became nominal, and the AI approved her for the night's mission.

That night, they were to patrol far to the north. They spread out in their customary formation: two hundred meters between each soldier, with Reid on the east, Sakai on the west, and the others in between. The physical separation let them cover more territory while they remained electronically linked to each other, to Tyrant, and to the angel that accompanied them. The surveillance drone was the squad's remote eyes, hunting ahead for signs of enemy insurgents.

Reid moved easily through the flat terrain, the power of her stride augmented by her exoskeleton's struts and joints, while the shocked footplates that supported her booted feet generated a faint, rhythmic hiss with every step. Her gaze was never still, roving between the squad map, the video feed from the angel, the terrain around her, and the quality of the ground where her next steps would fall.

Threat assessment had gotten harder since the start of the rainy season. Stands of head-high grass covered what only a month ago had been bare red earth. Thickets had leafed out and the scattered trees had sprouted green canopies. Cattle liked to spend the hottest hours of the day beneath the trees, their sharp hooves treading the ground into sticky bogs. For most of the year this worn-out land was barely habitable, with the Sahara encroaching from the north. But for at least this one more year the rains had come, bringing life back—and providing extensive cover for an enemy made up of violent but half-trained insurgent soldiers.

Reid held her tactical rifle across her body, ready for use at all times as she searched for signs of disturbance that could not be accounted for by cattle or goats or the herdsmen who accompanied them. At the same time, video from her helmet cams was relayed to Guidance for first-pass analysis by Intelligence AIs—a process duplicated for everyone in the squad.

Tyrant remained silent as three hours passed with no anomalies found. Despite the uneventful night, no one's attention strayed. The skullcaps wouldn't allow it. If a soldier's focus began to drift, brain activity would reflect it, and be corrected. Every soldier remained alert at all times.

Near midnight Tyrant finally spoke. "Reid."

"Go ahead."

"Weather on the way. Nasty squall from the west. ETA twenty minutes."

"Roger that."

She switched to gen-com, addressing the squad. "Heavy weather on the way. That means any signs of hostile activity are about to get erased. Stick to designated paths plotted by Guidance and do not get ahead of the squad."

After a few minutes the wind picked up, bringing a black front with it. The squad map showed them approaching a road to the north, a one-lane stretch of highway paved in cracked asphalt, its position in the landscape marked by a cell tower rising above the trees. Reid spoke again over gen-com: "Wicks, you've got the tower on your transect. Use extra caution."

"No worries, LT."

Right. It was her job to worry.

The rain reached Sakai first. Then it rolled over Phan, Juarez,

Faraci, and Wicks. Reid was a few steps from the asphalt road when she heard the sizzling edge of the storm sweeping toward her. The rain hit, hammering with Biblical force, generating a chiming chorus of pings against the bones of her dead sister and enclosing her in a scintillating curtain that even night vision couldn't pierce. At her feet, a veil of standing water hid the ground.

"Hold up," Reid said over gen-com. "No one move until—"

An explosion erupted maybe two hundred meters away, a ball of fire that illuminated the base of the cell tower where it stood just south of the road. Reid dropped to her belly. A splash of muddy water briefly obscured her faceplate before a frictionless coating sent it sliding away. Her heart hammered: the squad map showed Wicks at the foot of the tower. "Wicks, report!"

"Grenades incoming," Tyrant warned as another icon popped up on the map: a red skull marking a newly discovered enemy position on the other side of the road.

Reid echoed the warning over gen-com. "Grenades incoming!" Clutching her weapon, she curled into a fetal position to minimize her exposure. A status notification popped up on her display, a bold-red statement of Wicks's condition: nonresponsive; traumatic injury with blood loss.

Goddamn.

The grenades hit. Two behind her, one to the east. She felt the concussions in her body and in the ground beneath her shoulder, but her helmet shielded her eyes and ears, and if debris fell on her she couldn't tell it apart from the storm.

She rolled to her belly, bringing the stock of her MCL1a to her shoulder as she strained to see past the rain to the other side of the road. "Tyrant, I need a target."

"Target acquired."

All extraneous data vanished from her visor, leaving only a gold targeting circle and a small red point that showed where her weapon was aimed. It took half-a-second to align point and circle. Then her AI fired the weapon.

The MCL1a's standard projectile was a 7.62mm round, but it was the second trigger Reid felt dropping away from her finger. The stock kicked as a grenade rocketed from the underslung launcher, looking like a blazing comet in night vision as it shot across the road, disappearing into the brush on the other side. Reid couldn't see the target, but when the grenade hit, the explosion lit up the rain and threw the intervening trees into silhouette.

A second grenade chased the first, fired from Faraci's position farther west. Reid used the explosion as cover. She flexed her legs, using the power of the dead sister's joints to launch to her feet. Then she dropped back, away from the road and into the brush as the squad icons returned to her visor. "Juarez! I'm going after Wicks. Take Phan and Sakai. Set up a defensive perimeter."

"Roger that." On the squad map, lines shot from the sergeant's icon, linking him to Phan and Sakai as they switched to a different channel to coordinate.

"Faraci, you're with me. Full caution as you approach Wicks. Take the path Guidance gives you and do not stray."

"Roger, LT."

Reid flinched as a burst of automatic weapons fire rattled the nearby brush. Another gun opened up. A glance at the squad map confirmed it was Juarez, returning fire.

"Got your route," Tyrant said.

A transparent, glowing green rectangle popped into existence at Reid's feet as if suspended just above the sheen of standing water. It stretched into a luminous path, winding out of sight behind a thicket. Reid bounded after it, running all-out—Hell-bent, maybe, because she could see only three strides ahead. If a hazard popped up in front of her she'd have to go through it or over it, because she was going too fast to stop. When she spied a suspiciously neat circle of rainwater, she vaulted it. Then she ducked to avoid a branch weighed down by the pounding rain.

Hell failed to claim her, and in just a few seconds the path brought her to the concrete pad that supported the cell tower, and to Wicks, who lay just a few meters behind it.

He was belly down in almost two inches of water and he wasn't nonresponsive anymore. He struggled to lift his helmeted head, but the weight of his pack and his injuries pinned him in place. His shoulders shook with a wracking cough as Reid dropped to her knees beside him.

"Damn it, Wicks, don't drown."

Another grenade went off, this one maybe a hundred meters away.

Reid flinched, but her duty was to Wicks. She pulled the pins on his pack straps and heaved the pack aside. Then she grabbed the frame of his dead sister and flipped him onto his back. He made a faint mewling noise, more fear than pain. The skullcap should be controlling his pain. As she shrugged off her pack and got out her med kit, she tried to reassure him. "Wicks, listen to me. We'll get you out of here. You'll be okay."

He groaned . . . in denial maybe, or despair.

"Tyrant, where's my battle medic?"

"I'm here," a woman said, speaking through her helmet audio. "Let's do an assessment."

Reid's helmet cams let the medic see what she saw. Wicks still had all four limbs, but most of his right calf was gone, and shrapnel had shredded the flesh of his right arm. Reid used her body to shield his wounds from the rain for the few seconds it took to apply a spray-on coagulant. Then she slipped off his helmet to check for head injuries. When she found none, she put his helmet back on.

Tyrant said, "Faraci's at twenty meters and closing fast. Don't shoot her."

"Roger that."

Juarez was still trading fire with someone to the north when Faraci burst out of the brush. She dropped her pack and then dropped to her knees beside Reid. "How's he doing, LT?"

"How you doing, Wicks?" Reid asked as she slathered wound putty across his chewed-up calf.

"*Fucked*," he whispered between clenched teeth.

Reid couldn't argue. She guessed he'd lose the leg, and then he'd be out of a job that he desperately needed for his sister's sake as well as his own. "Faraci's going to take care of you," she said. "You got that, Faraci? Do what the battle medic tells you, and get him stabilized."

"Yes, ma'am."

"And keep your head down."

Reid closed up her med kit and jammed it back into her pack. Then she shouldered the pack, along with her weapon. "Tyrant, I need a target."

"Look toward the road."

She did, bringing a new path into view on her display. Icons showed Juarez and Phan engaged two hundred fifty meters to the west, with

Sakai half a klick farther out. Maybe Juarez had gotten word of more targets on that side and instructed her to go after them. No time to ask.

Reid took off, water geysering under her footplates until the path expanded, indicating she should slow. The path ended at a tree with a fat trunk. Livestock had churned the ground into thick mud that sucked at her boots as she braced herself against the trunk and brought up her weapon. A targeting circle appeared in her visor, but just as she aligned her aim, her attention was hijacked by a bold-red status notification that popped up at the bottom of her display: *Contact lost with C. Sakai; position and status unknown.*

Her finger hesitated above the trigger. Contact lost? What the hell did that mean? Even if Sakai was dead, the angel should still know her position—

Focus!

Reid squeezed the trigger, firing a burst of 7.62mm rounds.

An answering fusillade hammered the tree trunk. She spun and dropped to a crouch, putting the tree at her back as bullets whined through the space she'd just occupied.

"Target down," Tyrant said.

"Then who the fuck is shooting at me?"

"Another target."

"How did Command miss all this, Tyrant?"

"Debrief later. You've got another target. Stay low."

The notification was gone from Reid's display. The squad map was back up. It showed Faraci still with Wicks; Juarez and Phan circling to the west. There was no icon for Sakai.

"Reid!" Tyrant barked as he blanked her display. "Target's moving in. You need to hit it now."

She twisted around, still on her knees, sliding in the mud. When the targeting circle came into sight, she covered it and fired. There was a scream, much closer than she'd expected. She fired again, and the scream cut off. "Where the hell is Sakai?" she demanded, as another exchange of gunfire rattled to the west.

"I don't know! Waiting to hear from Intelligence."

Gunfire ceased. There was only the sound of rain.

"Three targets remaining," Tyrant said. "But they're pulling back."

Reid stared into the green-tinted night. The rain was easing. Night vision could again make out the shapes of distant trees, but it could not reveal IEDs buried beneath the mud, or popper mines that the surviving insurgents might have dropped on their retreat. Command might be persuaded to send in bomb sniffers tomorrow, but tonight the other side of the road was a no-man's-land.

"We have to let them go," Reid said. "Tyrant, shift the angel west. I want it looking for Sakai."

The rain had stopped by the time she returned to Wicks. Faraci had sealed his wounds and gotten him out of his rig, but she'd left his helmet on, per regulation. His visor was tuned to transparent, so that Reid could see his face, his half-closed eyes. "He'll be okay," Faraci said.

Meaning that he would live.

Juarez and Phan emerged from the brush as a distant growl announced the approach of the medevac helicopter. While Juarez went through Wicks's pack, redistributing its contents, Reid stepped aside. "Tyrant, I want to see the video from Sakai's helmet cams."

It didn't show much. Rain had been coming down so hard that at first all Reid saw was falling water. Then a blur that resolved into the dripping branches of a thicket, luminous in night vision; then a splash of mud. Reid checked her display, confirming she was on a solo link before she asked Tyrant, "Did someone cut her fucking head off?"

"Negative. The skullcap would have picked up remnant brain function. Reid, her helmet was removed."

"That doesn't make sense. If she got jumped, we'd see—" She broke off in midsentence as the truth hit. "Sakai took off her own helmet. That's what you're saying."

Reid had been slow to consider it because all her training argued against it. LCS soldiers must never remove their helmets in the field. Even Wicks, grievously wounded, still wore his, because in a linked combat squad the helmet *was* the soldier. It was protective gear, yes, but it also marked position, monitored condition, allowed communication, enhanced the control of weapons and targeting, and provided a visual interface for the shared data stream that allowed an LCS to function.

If Sakai had removed her helmet it meant only one thing: she'd walked away.

She'd deserted.

The helicopter set down, kicking up a windstorm that flattened a circle of waist-high grass. Wicks shivered as the medics loaded him onboard. He was in their care now, so they took his helmet off. His expression was disconsolate. Reid squeezed his hand and lied to him. "It'll all work out."

Moonlight shone through rents and tears in the clouds as the helicopter took him away.

Reid tried to put herself into Sakai's head; tried to understand what Sakai had been thinking when she'd walked out on the squad, abandoned them, in the middle of a firefight. No love existed between Sakai and the others; no reason to think she gave a shit about any of them. The commotion had been a chance to slip away, that's all . . .

Except there was nowhere for her to go, no escape, no refuge, no way home.

No way to survive for long.

Reid found it easy to imagine Sakai as suicidal, but why hadn't Guidance known or even suspected?

Because Sakai had only worn the skullcap on patrol.

Until tonight, Sakai had been okay on patrol.

Some people were like that. They were fine so long as they were working, fulfilling whatever regimented role life had handed them, but leave them on their own and they could disappear down rabbit holes.

What twisted passage had Sakai wandered down?

Reid caught her breath, hit by a new worry: what if Sakai hadn't run away?

The night was warm and Reid's uniform had shed the rain so she was barely damp, but she shuddered anyway as the fine hairs on the back of her neck stood up. She looked over her shoulder, scanning the surrounding terrain, searching for motion in the brush or beneath the trees.

Tyrant noticed. "You see something?"

The drone had been sent to search from Sakai's last known position. "Tyrant, bring the angel back. Make sure Sakai isn't here, hunting us."

"Roger that." A few seconds later: "You really think she's turned on you?"

"I don't know. I just want to make sure." She switched to gen-com. "Everyone, stay low. Keep alert."

They all dropped into a crouch.

"Somebody out there?" Juarez wanted to know.

"We'll let the angel answer that."

The drone searched, but it picked up no sign of Sakai anywhere nearby. So Reid sent it south, toward the fort, but Sakai wasn't there either.

"Let her go," Faraci muttered. "Who gives a shit? She didn't do anything for Wicks when he went down."

"We don't abandon our own, Faraci," Reid snapped. "Remember that, next time you get in a tight spot."

"Yes, ma'am."

"This is now a search and rescue, and speed is critical." Alone, without her helmet, it was just a question of time and distance, not chance, until Sakai was found by some insurgent group. Maybe that was her goal, to get far enough away that there could be no rescue, no first aid, no helicopter evacuation while her heart was still beating.

Only four remained in the squad—Reid, Juarez, Faraci, Phan—but they still assumed their standard two-hundred meter interval, sweeping the terrain until they converged again on Sakai's last known position. Reid got there first and found Sakai's skullcap hanging from a branch. It felt like a message meant just for her. She shoved the skullcap into a pocket. Phan recovered Sakai's helmet from a thicket, finding it upside down and half-full of rain. Juarez located her pack. But her MCL1a didn't turn up. Neither did her stock of grenades, or her dead sister.

"We have two possibilities," Reid told the squad. "She's been taken prisoner, in which case we are obligated to effect a rescue and to recover her equipment. Or she's gone rogue. If so, we must assume she is mentally unstable. Without her helmet she doesn't have night vision, but she'll be able to see well enough by moonlight to be dangerous. Use extreme caution."

The rain had washed away any tracks that might have indicated the direction Sakai had taken, but it seemed logical to Reid that she would have headed west to northwest. "Either direction would allow her to avoid the angel's eyes while it was monitoring the firefight, but west means following tonight's patrol route and I don't think that's what she had in mind."

"Northwest then," Juarez said in disgust.

Reid nodded. "She's heading for the border."

They set off, moving fast on a no-choice mission. They had to find Sakai. Personnel did not go missing anymore. And they had to get the dead sister and the MCL1a back. That equipment could not be allowed to enter the black market. It had to be recovered, even if they took heavy casualties in the process.

"Tyrant."

"Here."

"Something happened when Sakai was on leave."

"No incident in her record."

"Go beyond the record! Something else happened just a few days ago. That's when she stopped wearing her skullcap. Something was going on inside her head. Something she didn't want the skullcap to fix."

"Stand by."

A figure of speech. Reid loped north, while her AI analyzed the feeds from her helmet cams. Every few minutes it highlighted a potential hazard: a shining thread that could have been a tripwire but turned out to be a spiderweb; a metallic sheen that might have been a cheap sensor but was only a foil wrapper, blown in from God knows where; an area of disturbed ground washed by the rain where there might be a buried IED. Reid skirted it, though she suspected it was just a resting place for cattle.

Tyrant spoke again, "Intelligence took a look at her email. She split with her boyfriend a few days ago, told him she wasn't coming back and not to worry about money, that she'd take care of him."

"Oh *fuck*," Reid said as enlightenment hit. "This is about her life insurance."

"It's about more than that. The boyfriend has a six-year-old kid. Sakai got crazy on leave, had a meltdown, slammed the kid against a wall—"

Reid didn't want to hear anymore. "That's bullshit. Sakai passed her psych quals. She's not like that. *None* of us are like that."

"Intelligence believes the boyfriend's story. He's been out of work a long time. Sakai's been sending him money. He didn't report the incident because he can't afford to break up with her. So he kept telling her everything was okay."

Sakai was not the kind of person who could do something like that and ever imagine it was okay; Reid didn't have to like her to know that. The life insurance was Sakai's apology, a way to make amends and to ensure she never harmed the child again.

A few minutes later Tyrant announced, "The angel has found her." He marked the position on Reid's map. Three kilometers east-northeast. Reid switched to gen-com. "Hold up."

A new window opened in her display, a feed from the angel that showed Sakai rigged in her dead sister, with her MCL1a in hand. Sakai surely presented a danger, yet without her helmet and her skullcap she looked fragile, her bare scalp like a gray eggshell in the sideways light of the westering moon.

"You got her, LT?" Juarez asked.

Reid sent him the feed and the location.

The map updated.

"*Shit*," Juarez breathed. "She's not alone."

Scanning the ground with its infrared camera, the angel had found three figures less than a hundred-thirty meters from Sakai—a distance rapidly closing as she advanced.

Half-hidden beneath the spreading branches of a thorn tree, they appeared at first as flashes and chips of bright heat. Then they emerged draped in infrared-blocking fabric that did not hide them completely but gave them the vagueness of ghosts as they passed through tall grass, moving in a line toward Sakai. The angel identified them from profiles compiled during the firefight: they were the three insurgents who had escaped alive.

They probably couldn't see Sakai past the vegetation, but they would be able to hear her. She was using her dead sister to trot at a careless pace, rustling grass and snapping twigs, with no way to know what lay in wait for her. They would gun her down before she knew anyone was there.

And wasn't that what she'd gone looking for?

Reid wondered if she'd fight back; wanted her to; resolved to force her to, if she could. Reid would not let death take Sakai by surprise. She would make her face it, and facing it, maybe Sakai would choose life instead.

Fuck the insurance.

Speaking over gen-com, Reid said, "Faraci, you've only used one grenade. Fire another, maximum range. In Sakai's direction."

"LT?" Faraci sounded perplexed. "Sakai's way out of range."

"Shit, Faraci, I don't want you to kill her. I just want you to put her on alert. *Now*, if that's all right with you."

"Yes, ma'am."

The grenade shot above the tree tops, hurtling northeast, to burst above the brush. The *boom* rolled past while through the angel's eyes, Reid watched Sakai drop flat, her training taking over despite the guilt and despair that had sent her north.

The insurgents took cover inside a thicket, no doubt trying to guess what the distant explosion meant for them. Caution should have made them retreat, but they wanted Sakai's weapon and dead sister.

"Let's go!" Reid barked. "Now, while they're confused. Fast as we fucking can. *Go, go, go!*"

Tyrant posted a path. Reid jumped on it, running flat out. The joints of her dead sister multiplied the power of every stride. She crunched through grass, slid sideways in mud, bounded over deadfalls and, carrying her tactical rifle one-handed, she used the struts on her other arm as a hammer to batter aside branches.

"Sakai's taken cover in the brush," Tyrant said.

It was hard to look death in the face.

Tyrant spoke again. "The insurgents are moving. They're closing on Sakai's position."

"Good."

Sakai would see them, she would know what death looked like, and she would fight back. She had to.

With two kilometers behind her, Reid heard the slow *tap, tap, tap* of small arms fire. "Tyrant?"

"They're trying to flush her from cover."

Reid ducked under a tree and then battered her way along a cattle trail between two thickets. The terrain was so monotonous she felt like she was getting nowhere.

A larger-caliber weapon spoke. Reid well knew the sound of an MCL1a.

"She got one," Tyrant reported. "Damn good shot by moonlight alone."

Half a kilometer to go.

"The survivors are retreating."

Too soon.

Reid heard the worried bleat of a goat just ahead of her, the sound so unexpected she almost threw herself down and started shooting.

The goats were just as frightened. They must have been sleeping in a thicket. Startled at her approach, they fled straight toward Sakai.

"Reid, get down!" Tyrant shouted. "Get down! She's got her weapon turned on you!"

Never before had Reid heard that level of emotion in Tyrant's voice. It scared her but she kept running, because the goats were a distraction that she could use. They were cover. Sakai wouldn't hear her coming past the noise of their stampede.

The goat herd funneled together as they raced between two tall thickets. Then they spilled into a grove of seven or eight trees with only bare ground beneath them. Branches filtered the moonlight into shards and polygons that painted the mud and flashed over the hides of the fleeing animals.

Hidden in shadow, unseen by the frantic goats but clear to Reid in night vision, was Sakai. Reid saw her in profile, crouched and trembling with her back to a tree trunk, weapon held close to her chest, shoulders heaving, her hairless head tipped back, and amazement on her exhausted face as she watched the goats dart past.

With no night vision to aid her, she didn't see Reid.

Briefly, Reid considered a negotiation, verbal persuasion, but she didn't want to have a conversation while Sakai held onto her MCL1a and her stock of grenades.

So Reid tackled her. Shoulder to shoulder: their arm struts clanged as they both went down. Reid got a hand on Sakai's rifle, got it loose, heaved it away—but that was only step one in disarming her. She still had a full complement of grenades in her vest, and her dead sister was a lethal weapon in hand-to-hand combat—though Reid had no intention of letting it come to that.

Scrambling free, she came up on her knees in a patch of fractured moonlight, her MCL1a braced at her shoulder. *"Don't move!"*

Sakai wasn't there anymore. She wasn't wearing her pack, and without it she was more agile than Reid expected. She had rolled away, rolled onto her feet. She stood looking down at Reid with a shocked expression.

What did she see with her unaided eyes? Gray bones and the negative space of Reid's black visor? Maybe nothing more than that, blind in the night.

No.

This close, there would be a glimmer of light from the MCL1a's targeting mechanism.

Reid corrected her aim. "Very slowly," she said, "crouch, and release the cinches on your dead sister, starting at the ankles."

Sakai frowned. She turned her head, perusing the shadows, wondering maybe if they were alone. "Come on, LT," she said in a low voice as she looked back at Reid. "Do it now. No one's watching."

"Someone's always watching. You know that. I'm not your ticket out."

The goats had fled. The night had gone quiet. Reid had no idea where the insurgents were, but she trusted Tyrant to warn her if it looked like they would interfere.

"Do you have it with you?" Sakai asked. "My skullcap?"

"Do you want it?"

"No! *No.* I don't want it." As if trying to convince herself. "I don't want to die with that thing on my head."

"You mean that when you wear it, you don't want to die at all . . . right?"

Sakai shook her head. "You know what I think? I think we all start off as light and shadow, but the light seeps away when we wear the skullcap. It moves out of us and into the wires, so when we take it off, there's only darkness left in our heads." Titanium struts gleamed in night vision as she brought her gloved hand up to tap the center of her forehead. "Punch it, LT. Or I'm going to take you out."

Reid waited, and when Sakai sprang she squeezed the trigger. The round caught Sakai in the shoulder, pancaking in her armor. It didn't penetrate, but the impact spun her around so that she landed face down, a rag doll mounted on a metal rack.

Juarez stepped out of the shadows with Phan behind him.

"Get her unstrapped," Reid growled.

Sakai had tried to turn her into an executioner. Now, in the aftermath, fury kicked in.

Maybe I should have complied.

But Reid's skullcap responded, modulating her outrage, defusing her brittle frustration, bringing her back to a logical center. Because that's what it did, she decided. It didn't control what she thought or who she was. It didn't make her a different person. It kept her tied to who she really was. It was a shield against anger and guilt; against the emotional scar tissue that could consume a mind.

Juarez and Phan turned Sakai over; they popped her cinches while Reid checked the squad map, confirming Faraci on their flank, ready, if the two surviving insurgents made the poor choice to return.

Sakai's chest spasmed. She sucked in a whistling breath and tried to sit up, but Juarez pushed her back down again while Phan finished removing the ordnance from her vest.

"Cuff her," Reid said, handing Juarez a set of plastic restraints.

He got Sakai into a sitting position. She offered no resistance as he bound her wrists behind her back.

Sakai had always been a problem child, but she'd been a good soldier. The army should have protected her. Command should have required her to wear her skullcap. No soldier had the option of going naked into battle—and battles didn't always end when the weapons were racked.

Reid crouched in front of Sakai. In night vision her face was stark; her features dragged down as if by the gravity of despair. At first she didn't acknowledge Reid, but after a few seconds she looked up, fixing an unflinching gaze on the featureless void of Reid's black visor.

"Is that you, LT?"

Shadow, unblended with light.

"It's me." She reached into her pocket and got out Sakai's skullcap, holding it so that a triangle of moonlight glinted against its silky surface. "I want you to wear this."

"No."

"You'll feel better."

"You think I want to feel better?"

"So you lost your temper with a kid! You want to kill yourself over that?"

"I didn't just lose my temper. Sixteen days without the skullcap and

I was fucking out of control. If Kevin hadn't been there, I might have killed that sweet baby. And that's not who I am . . . or it's not who I was."

"It wasn't the skullcap that made you do it."

"Shit yes, it was! When I was wearing it, it hid all the crap I couldn't live with. Made me feel okay. Didn't even know I was falling apart inside until it was too late."

Is that what the skullcap did? Hide the rot?

Did it matter? They had a job to do.

Reid jammed Sakai's skullcap back into a pocket, and then she stood up. "Tyrant, we need to evacuate Sakai."

"Chopper on the way," he said. "ETA thirteen minutes."

"Rest while you can," Reid advised the squad.

They still had two insurgents to hunt and the second half of their patrol to finish—a long night ahead of them, followed by a few hours of sleep and then another patrol where their lives would be at risk every moment until they were back inside the fort. Thinking about it, Reid felt a looming abyss of emotional exhaustion, there and then gone, washed away by the ministrations of the skullcap.

ICARUS AT NOON

★

by Eric Leif Davin

Once abuzz with human activity, the solar system is now all but devoid of life. Robots do the work faster, better, and safer than their biological counterparts, and the people of Earth have returned to the planet that bore them, content to experience life through a screen. But for one man, the last untouched piece of real estate in the solar system beckons.

HELL FILLED THE SKY. The seething cauldron of the Sun, only 17 million miles away and thirty times larger than it appeared from Earth, began to pour fire across the horizon. Soon its thousand-degree heat would begin cooking Santiago de la Cruz. Facing Sol as it grew larger, de la Cruz sat cross-legged in the Lotus position, bobbing gently, as if underwater, above the burned and blackened surface of Icarus. Almost eighty million miles from home, de la Cruz prepared to die.

It wasn't supposed to have been this way. It was an accident. It was because he shut down the damn computers on the final approach. No machine was going to have anything to do with touching down on this last "untouched" world. It was going to be one small step—for a man!

Santiago de la Cruz came in slow in the small cone of darkness trailing out from Icarus like a windsock. He wanted to park the ship in a close parallel orbit, then glide down in a suit. He miscalculated. Alarms blared, retros fired, and he plowed into the side of the asteroid in slow motion.

The ship's oxygen gushed out into the void of space as the scarred side of the asteroid ripped into the ship. It was a long horizontal slash—not enough to demolish the spacecraft. But enough to disable it. It would never make it back to Earth. It now drifted as a companion body to the tiny world and would join it in its long 409-day journey around the Sun. Somewhere amid the wreckage floated a spacesuit. In the suit was Santiago de la Cruz.

Santiago de la Cruz was an old hand. He had thrilled at the stark beauty of the Martian hinterlands and walked the bubbling surface of Io. He'd commanded every type of craft. He'd supervised bases on Mars and Io, built the Deep Space Observer on Pluto when almost everyone else said it couldn't be done. And because he was an old hand, he understood the logic of withdrawal. It made dollars and sense.

Besides, anyplace he'd been he could return to via VR tours. Anything seen by a robot or a human with a camera was easily accessible to anyone else thereafter. All you had to do was buy the appropriate virtual disk, slip it in, and you were there once more—or for the first time! You could hunker down to outlast a Martian sand storm, plummet through the stygian depths of the Jovian atmosphere, stand on the edge of an erupting volcano on Io. When virtual reality was as real as reality—who needed dangerous reality? But it still ate at him. "It's just not the same," he insisted to himself.

All around him Serenity Moon Base was a hive of activity, but as de la Cruz surveyed the installation he saw no humans. Worker 'bots scurried everywhere, intent on their work. Some of that work was ongoing astronomical observations. Other work entailed the industrial production of oxygen, hydrogen, and other raw materials for lunar and space-based industries. Mass-production industry no longer took place on Earth. It was cheaper and safer off-planet, where raw materials were plentiful and transportation was easy. Finished products were then dropped down the gravity well to Earth. The home planet consumed what the Solar System provided.

What the robots of the Solar System provided, de la Cruz thought bitterly to himself. Just as worker 'bots swarmed over Serenity Moon Base, so they swarmed over the entire System, from Mercury to Pluto and Charon. Indeed, they pushed out even farther than the System, as robot probes explored the edges of the Sun's gravitational field and headed toward the nearest stars.

It's been like this from the beginning, de la Cruz thought bitterly. Machines got here first, now they're everywhere. The Russians weren't the first in space. Back in 1957 it was Sputnik, a piece of Russian metal, which got into space first, announcing to everyone down below as it beeped away in the night sky that a machine got up here first. The first spacecraft from Earth to reach another world was another hunk of machinery, the Russian Lunik, which crashed on the Moon back in 1959. It was another Russian robot craft which reached Mars back in 1971. And so it went, planet after planet, probe after probe: Venus, Mars, Jupiter and Saturn and their moons, Halley's Comet, the asteroid belt. After Sputnik and Lunik it was Mariner, Pioneer, Viking, Pathfinder, Galileo, Magellan, Voyager. The machines always got there first.

And now they'll be here last, de la Cruz thought to himself. The human presence in space was but a brief intrusion. It just didn't make sense to have all those fragile and expensive pieces of protoplasm in harm's way. They weren't needed. Robot stations on Mercury and Venus, on Vesta and Mars, on Io and Pluto, could carry out all the observations and experiments any human could, and for a fraction of the cost. All the expensive life support systems needed to maintain human life could be jettisoned, making for a smaller, streamlined, high-performance facility operating on a shoestring. And it was safer, at least from the human viewpoint. When a catastrophic failure occurred at some far-distant outpost, all that was lost was some machinery.

And so the United Nations Space Agency had declared space gradually "off-limits" to humans. The human presence slowly pulled back from the fringes of the Solar System as human-staffed facilities were closed down one by one and put on automatic pilot. Serenity Moon Base, half-buried under the Moon's Sea of Serenity, was the last to be staffed by humans. And, as the personnel went home at the end of their turns, it finally came down to Santiago de la Cruz. He was "The Last Man on the Moon." It was his job to turn out the lights.

Santiago de la Cruz continued on his tour of inspection. It was for the most part redundant. The automatic systems ran everything, checked everything. But, it was his job, at least for the time being, and so he did it. He entered the hermetically sealed hangar where the Prometheus Project was nearing completion. Robot technicians scurried here and there running diagnostics on the craft. Soon it would be launched to the last unexplored piece of real estate in the Solar System, a small world previously overlooked. The all-conquering robots weren't quite everywhere just yet and, almost as an afterthought, the final blank spot on the map of the Solar System was going to be filled in. How ironic, de la Cruz thought, that the craft was named Prometheus, after a man who stole fire from the gods.

De la Cruz paused to admire the ship. It was a beautiful piece of machinery—manufactured right here at Serenity Moon Base. Like everything else on the Moon—or on Earth—it was untouched by human hands, entirely produced by robot techies in an automated facility. "That's just the problem," thought de la Cruz. "Who needs people? We're all redundant."

Indeed, humans weren't needed for any productive work. They were almost literally useless. Computers and robots produced everything—and they produced megatons of it, whatever it was. Thorstein Veblen had predicted it long ago. The "inordinate productivity of the machine," he said, would soon produce wealth far beyond the fevered dreams of Midas. And it did. About the only job left for humans was to consume the wealth.

For those who could. Most could not. Earth had become a hellhole for the common person. There were no jobs. And there were no handouts. The "freeloading parasites" who comprised most of humanity had become an idle underclass locked out beyond the gates of Eden, where the equally idle rich frolicked. And when the underclass became too restive, there were lots of prisons just waiting for them. Santiago de la Cruz was not a member of the "owning" class, so no comfortable and well-guarded high-rise condo waited for him. And when a robot could do his job just as well and cheaper, no job awaited him. Instead, the underclass beckoned him. As soon as he finished supervising the closing of Serenity Moon Base to humans, he would join it. "Just what the hell am I going to do down on Earth?" he thought. "May as well be dead."

The purpose of the Prometheus mission was to secure the Helios Station on the surface of Icarus, the hottest hunk of rock in the Solar System. Orbiting Sol inside the orbit of Mercury, Icarus was a two-mile-diameter nickel-iron asteroid. Even smaller than Deimos, the smallest Martian moon at seven-by-nine miles, there was nevertheless enough of it for a ship to approach in the shadow and touch down on it. The ship, however, would be as light as a feather. With gravity 1/10,000th that of Earth, a man, even in a bulky spacesuit, would not be able to walk across the surface of Icarus. He'd have to traverse the 15 square miles of jagged and sun-blackened surface by his hands, like a buoyant scuba diver pulling himself along the bottom of a Caribbean lagoon.

Once planted, the Helios Station would be a permanent, cheap, and fully automated solar observatory. It would monitor the various layers of the Sun's roiling solar gases, the photosphere, chromosphere, and corona, with their varying temperatures, directions, and visual characteristics. Based on Icarus, its orbit would never decay, as had so many other robotic solar observer spacecraft, plunging them into the Sun.

In addition, the four-hour rotation of Icarus meant there would also be a period of night during which useful observations could be made of the chromosphere and corona, the layers of hot gases just above the Sun's photosphere, or visual surface. While those layers actually shine by themselves, they are overwhelmed by the intensity of the direct surface glare. Blotting out that glare would bring the upper two layers into prominent view. Nighttime conditions would also make it possible for the Helios Station to observe the oval, gray, hazy glow of the inner Zodiacal light caused by sunlight reflection off dust particles along the plane of the Solar System, also erased in the full glare of the Sun.

And, with a wildly elliptical orbit, Icarus at perihelion—its closest approach to the Sun—dwarfed any hell Mercury could offer. On Mercury, the Sun was only twice the size as seen from Earth. On Icarus it filled the sky. With a brightside surface temperature of 797 degrees Fahrenheit, Mercury was hot enough—but at high noon on Icarus a week from perihelion, the temperature hit 1,000 degrees F. And Prometheus was going to rendezvous with Icarus at perihelion.

As Prometheus became more fully operational, de la Cruz spent more time in the facility, becoming more and more familiar with the last spacecraft he'd ever get to see up close and personal. Finally, he made a decision. Santiago de la Cruz had almost singlehandedly built the Deep Space Observer on Pluto at the very edge of the Solar System. He'd be damned if a robot spacecraft was going to set up Earth's outpost at the other end of the System. He began programing instructions to alter the design and construction of Prometheus. He didn't want too much changed. Just enough to support a single human occupant.

And who was to stop him? He was the only man on the Moon. And since he supervised all reports to Ground Control, it was easy enough to conceal what he was doing. By the time his superiors down on Earth found out what he was up to, it was too late. He was already in space.

"De la Cruz!" they radioed. "Abort immediately and return to Serenity!"

"No chance," he replied. "I'm on my way to the Sun. I've got a rendezvous with Icarus at high noon."

"De la Cruz, are you insane? This is suicidal!"

"Yeah, pretty irrational, alright. What'ya gonna do? Terminate my career?"

"Why are you doing this?"

"Like Sir Edmund said, 'Because it's there!'"

"De la Cruz, you are jeopardizing the success of a multi-trillion-dollar scientific expedition!"

"So arrest me," de la Cruz radioed back, and then broke communication with Earth. He knew they'd be after him, but not before he got to Icarus first.

When Santiago de la Cruz regained consciousness, he seemed to be floating just above the steeply curving surface of a small hill. In all directions the dark and broken land fell away from him. A momentary wave of vertigo engulfed him and his head swam. Then he realized where he was and his vision steadied. The small hill below him was the entire near side of Icarus. Above him in the darkness of the asteroid's night side floated the wreckage of Prometheus. Then, off to his side, the disorientingly near horizon flickered with fire as the Sun began to rise.

The Sun galvanized de la Cruz into action. The sudden impact of its hellish temperature would quickly overheat his suit's cooling capacity. Soon, he'd be boiling like a lobster in its shell. He doubled over, reached down, and touched the surface of Icarus. "That's one small handhold for a man," he said, "one giant reach for all Mankind."

Then he reached out and grabbed another handhold on the surface. He pulled himself forward and reached with his other hand for yet another outcropping. Then another. And another. Weighing less than an ounce in his suit, he made rapid progress as he pulled himself across the face of Icarus. As the asteroid's rotation speed was only one mile per hour, de la Cruz soon saw the giant thermonuclear furnace of superheated gases which was the Sun sink back below the horizon behind him. He plunged deeper into the blessed -60 degree F. temperature of the Icaran night. In a short time he was in the middle of the asteroid's nocturnal zone. All he had to do, he thought, was just keep moving. That way, he could always outrun the dawn. And, with the slight exertion such movement required, he could keep it up forever. Or until his suit ran out of oxygen.

De la Cruz continued pulling himself slowly across the darkened surface of Icarus, pacing himself so he didn't use more oxygen than absolutely necessary. It was only a temporary solution, he realized. Eventually, he'd run out. "The Sun's going to get me," he thought, "just as it got the original Icarus."

He paused and bobbed gently above the Icaran surface, tethered by a light handhold on a piece of rock. He turned and looked back in the direction he'd come. There was a hell hound coming for him from just beyond the horizon. He couldn't outrun it much longer. Why not greet the inevitable face-on?

Santiago de la Cruz drifted into a sitting position inches above the surface and crossed his legs, assuming the Lotus position. He began to breathe in a slow, regular rhythm as he calmed his heartbeat and composed his thoughts. The problem, he thought, is rotation. And oxygen. If this damn piece of rock didn't rotate, I'd be able to hide in its shadow indefinitely. And if I had more oxygen . . . But there was nothing he could do about either.

Up ahead in the expanding aurora of the Sun, de la Cruz noticed a brilliant point of light, as if a morning star shined in the heavens to presage the Sun. It grew larger, however, as the slow rotation of Icarus brought him nearer. Suddenly, de la Cruz realized what it was. It was the Prometheus! It was still there, where the collision with Icarus had left it, drifting now about two miles above the surface as the asteroid rotated beneath it. While Icarus turned constantly toward the Sun, the wrecked Prometheus hovered in stationary position, orbiting the Sun parallel with Icarus. De la Cruz's heart leapt within him as he thrust aside thoughts of stoic acceptance. "There's my shade!" he thought. "And oxygen, too, if the tanks weren't ruptured!" Two miles up. So close—and yet so far!

De la Cruz coiled his legs beneath him, calculated his trajectory, and kicked off from the Icaran surface as hard as he could. Arms stretched out in front of him, like a diver in a slow-motion arc, de la Cruz aimed for the derelict hulk. His leap carried him into the full blaze of the Sun. The temperature soared on the shell of his suit and harsh UV radiation flooded over him. But he spread his wings and flew. The leap to the ship seemed to take forever. "If I miss it," he thought, "I'll end up diving into the Sun."

But he didn't miss it.

Nor did the rescue ship miss his emergency beacon. De la Cruz floated in the welcome shade of the Prometheus as he waited for the ship from Earth. They'd arrest him, he thought. Maybe imprison him. It'd be the last time a human was allowed in space. It wasn't important. What was important was that a human had gotten to the last world in the Solar System before the robots. A human had flown to Icarus at high noon—and his wings had not melted.

Santiago de la Cruz looked out into the blackness of space. Hard pinpricks of starlight punctured the dark. They'd always called to him. They'd pulled him into space and across a dozen worlds. Their harsh reality would test him no more. But it doesn't matter, he thought. Even if unattainable—the stars still beckon.

SOFT CASUALTY

★

by Michael Z. Williamson

The former colonists of the Freehold of Grainne are fed up with the occupation of their planet by the UN forces of Earth. No longer content with lobbing missiles at the opposition, the locals intend to go that extra step. And now Jandro Hauer is about to find out that even a trip to the local bazaar can be an invitation to horror.

JANDRO HAUER waited in the hot, bright light of Iota Persei for his shuttle to clear for boarding. On his forearm was a medication patch feeding a steady dose of strong tranquilizer. Above that was an IV line from a bottle hanging off his collar. He'd be in orbit in a few hours, and then transferred to a starship home. Perhaps then he could calm down.

"Hey, Soldier," someone called. There were eighty or so people at this boarding. He looked toward the voice to see another uniform. A US Marine with a powered prosthesis on his right leg gave a slight wave.

"Hey, Marine," he replied. "Soldier" wasn't strictly accurate for the combined South American Service Contingent, but it was close enough.

"I noticed the meds," the man said, pantomiming at his own arm. "Are you a casualty? If it's okay to ask."

Jefferson was a beautiful city, or at least it had been before the war.

Jandro Hauer looked out from his quarters. This building had once been apartments for the middling wealthy. The enlisted people had a good view, the officers were lower down. That's because the locals occasionally fired a missile. Usually Air Defense intercepted it. Usually. Three floors up there was a hole, and a sealed-off area, where one had gotten through and killed two troops. That's why he was inside the window with the lights off, not out on the balcony. He could see the towers of brilliant white clouds rising over the coastal hills just fine from here.

Support troops spent a lot of time indoors, not interacting with the planet or its residents. It was safer that way. That, and it meant not having to deal with the bright local light, thin air, and vicious fauna.

He still didn't get it. The former colonists were so willing to fight the UN and Earth they'd destroy their own city in the process, which would just guarantee whatever was rebuilt would look like all the other major colonial cities. Being independent had let them develop a unique architecture and style. That wasn't going to last with them reverting to Colony status.

It was 1900, but still full light here. The local day was twenty-eight and some odd hours. The UN Forces stuck to Earth's 24-hour clock. That led to some really surreal days where it would be midnight at noon.

A chime at the door indicated his roommate returning. He stepped aside because . . .

Jason Jardine swiped the lights on as he stepped in.

"Off!" Jandro shouted.

Jason scrabbled with the touch plate. "Sorry," he said as the room darkened.

"Always check the window first, Jase," he said. Jase was a Senior Corporal in Finance, but had only been here a week. He was still adapting. It was his first offworld mobilization.

The man nodded. "Yeah."

Some troops even kept the windows opaque 24/7, or 28/10 here. That was safer, but it didn't let them have a view.

"Goddamn, it's a hell of a city," Jardine said, walking over to the window.

"It is. That concentration of wealth thing is pretty dang good, if you're the one with the wealth." He looked around inside.

Troops had scribbled notes, art, tags and names on the walls. There had been decorations. Even though war trophies weren't allowed, there were ways to get stuff out.

Jardine looked where he was looking.

He said, "Just pay some local a few Marks to sign it over as something sold to you, and as long as it passes Customs, you're fine. The guy you replaced picked up quite a few neat things in town."

"It's that easy?"

"Depends. If they have kids to feed, they'll sell just about anything. You know prostitution was legal here, right?"

"I heard. Not just legal, but unregulated."

"Pretty much. So some of them are still in business, and others are freelance."

Jardine said, "Just wear an all-over polybarrier."

"Not really. Most are actually clean. That was one of things they were very strict on."

"I heard they're cheap, too." Jardine stowed his day pack on a rack by the door.

"I've heard that. Never tried, not planning to. I also hear some of them made a fortune."

"Doing what?"

"Doing rich guys. Apparently when you have a lot of money, you want to spend it."

"Makes sense. Almost like a tax."

"Hah. Good." He hadn't thought of it that way. What would you do if you had all that money? "Heading for chow?"

Jase said, "Nah, I was wondering if we could go out and eat? Into the compound area, I mean. I know there's vendors out there. Do you know much about them?"

"Yeah, I'll go with you. I've eaten at several. That will be a change from the chow hall. They're doing lameo chili again anyway." He hated military chili. It wasn't chili with paprika and rice and whatever else they put in to make it international. It was nothing like the chili he'd had when visiting Texas, or that you got in a restaurant back home. He'd also had enough sandwiches lately. He didn't want another bland burger thing.

He took a step, looked down, and said, "Let me change into casuals." He was still wearing a battle uniform, even though he never went out on patrol. They had orders to "support the battlefighters." That meant dressing up like them during the work day.

He went to his room, undressed and tossed the battle uniform onto the bed for later. It was a nice room. Most of the furnishings were still there and in good shape. The dresser was real wood of some figured sort. He grabbed a clean casual uniform from the top drawer and pulled it on. He was back into the common room in two minutes.

"Let's go," he said to Jase.

Six squares of this area was controlled compound, barricaded off with triple concrete and polyarmor walls. Inside that were military and UN contractors only. Outside that was another four blocks of restricted area, where local contractors took care of nonessential functions. Outside that, chaos.

Though even there, most of the fighting was subtle. It wasn't until you got outside of the metroplex that violence started in earnest. Here, they didn't even need armor. As long as it was stored in their quarters, it was considered "within reach."

They walked the two blocks to the inner perimeter and berm, scanned out through the gate, and entered the Gray Zone. It was patrolled by bots with cameras, and there were a few MPs rolling around in carts. He still wasn't sure how many, but there was usually a cart in sight. He looked both ways and saw one patrol. There were probably a hundred troops in sight, more around the rest of the perimeter.

The local sun was gradually going down. It was late summer, and it was merely hot, not scorching. It reminded him a bit of Rio, except for the thin air and higher gravity. The sky was clearer, though, and this city had a split personality. Most of it continued to function, its business and politics monitored by the Interim Government in this compound and in those two buildings to the south, protected by lots of heavy floater platforms, manned air support and ground-based lasers. Very little got shot at it these days, but occasional gunfire happened to little effect.

This area was a low-intensity war zone.

To punctuate that, his phone chimed a message.

He looked fast, wondering if there was something inbound, some political change.

It was from Kaela Smith at the MP station.

The screen read, "Jandro, the sniper casualty earlier today. Moritz got shot. Sorry. —Kay."

He didn't even swear, he just wiped the screen.

Jase asked, "Something bad?"

He realized he was tearing up. "That sniper this morning at the West side? Got Sammy Moritz."

"I'm sorry. Were you close?"

"No, it's just . . ." he took a deep breath, because this was scary. "Right after we secured this area and set up for the diplomats and provisional government, they shot some guy at the gate. Just dropped him from a distance and that was all. He got replaced by someone else. They got shot. Moritz was the fifth or sixth person in that duty slot."

"That's sick." Jase apparently hadn't heard about this yet.

"Very. They're not targeting battlefighters or staff. Just people at random, or in this case, not random. It's been six people in about three months in that slot."

"Glad I'm not an MP. At least not that MP."

"It's creepy. I wonder which poor bastard gets it next." He didn't want to think like that, but he couldn't help it. One field unit kept losing cooks. Convoys got disrupted. They needed live drivers because automated ones got waylaid or hijacked. The enemy was outnumbered, but technologically smart and vicious.

He always wondered if they'd come after Logistics some day.

Jase asked, "Can't they rotate around?"

"They do. But they seem to follow the slot, not the location."

"Sheesu."

"These fuckers have no sense of decency. We laughed, it was hilarious, when they abducted Huff, stripped him naked and made him walk back. But if you're a prole, you're likely to just wind up dead."

"Is that why the no fraternizing order?"

He nodded. "Absolutely. Outside the second line, nothing is safe."

"Almost makes me glad to be stuck in here."

"Almost. Would like to actually fight, though. Or support it. Something." He actually wasn't sure about that, but he kept telling himself that.

"Yes, but logistics is what wins wars," Jase said. "And my family's glad I'm safe," he added.

"Hey, at least you're here, doing something." They crossed into the plaza that had been a park of sorts. Much of the greenery was chewed up from troops walking and playing. One of the trees had been used for climbing until the CO stopped it.

Jase nodded. "You're right about that, and so was the Captain. These people really don't want us."

He said, "It's resistance to change. In twenty years, their kids will love life and wonder why anyone lived this way." They were told that, and he wanted to believe it.

"I hope so. The poor people must appreciate it."

"So I'm told. I see interviews."

Jase gave him a disgusted look. "Oh, come on, you don't think those are faked."

Jandro sighed. That hadn't come out right in English. "No, not at all. But everyone I've met locally has a couple of different things going. I've also read that civilians will tell occupying forces anything to keep them happy. And I can't imagine a lot of frustrated rich people are shooting at us."

"No, but maybe the people doing the shooting need money badly enough to do it for them. Or are held hostage some other way."

"Or maybe they're just afraid of us from propaganda. Hate isn't rational."

"Yeah. Okay."

Good. Jase didn't like the conspiracy nuts any more than he did. Sure, there were problems back home, but no one started a war just for a political edge. Paid bribes, manipulated language, made economic payoffs, but not start wars.

"So what looks good?" he said. There were ten or so little carts and knockdown kiosks offering food.

"Pizza's always good. Or I always like it. But it just doesn't taste right here."

"They grow different grain breeds."

Jase looked over. "That must be it. Don't they use real animals, too?"

"Yes, raised out in the open air and then killed."

"That's awful. It's so awful I want to try that, just to stare at people and tell them."

"Hah. It was really trippy the first time. I got used to it. It's just meat. You realize that's in the dining hall too, right?"

"I didn't." Jase looked at him with distrust.

"All food has to be locally sourced. There's just no effective way to bring in that much meat from outsystem, process it in orbit and land it. So we get it here."

"Why don't they tell everyone?"

"It's inspected and approved. There's some sort of BuAg exemption until we can build enough facilities here. So they don't mention the source in case it disturbs people."

"I guess I can see colonies needing that, but once you get to cities," he waved around at the surroundings, "shouldn't you be building vatories?"

"Exactly. So you've already eaten dead stuff, and these people either don't have a choice, or actually like it."

"The chow hall meat is a bit stronger tasting than home, I guess. Wow. Suffering animals. One more way we're tougher than civilians."

"You can't really brag about it. Someone will call a counselor."

"I know. But part of it is knowing, and part of it is tossing it out there when someone wants to try to measure up."

He nodded. "There is that. I feel sorry for the grunts. You can't boast about being in combat. It's seen as some sort of moral and mental handicap. No wonder they all burn out."

"Six months is a long time. I've been here a week and it's getting old fast."

"So what are you eating?"

"How's the bratwurst?" Jase asked, and pointed at a cart under a broad tree that was warping the plascrete walkway.

"Spicy and greasy. Occasionally there are small bone chips from processing."

"How spicy?"

"Middling. Hot for Europe, medium for Tex."

"Let's do it."

"Looks like he's closing, too. Better run."

They jogged over to the cart, and looked over the menu. It was posted on a scrolling screen in English, Mandarin, Arabic and Russian. Next to the screen was a tag certifying inspection and authorization to be in the Gray Zone.

The cook looked up and nodded.

"You're just in time. What can I get you?"

Jandro said, "I'll take a cheddar brat."

The man nodded. "Got it."

Jase said, "The 'Meatlog.' That sounds suggestive."

"I had one before. It's good. Savory and salty as well as spicy."

"Sure. That's two hundred grams? I'll take two."

The cook, Gustin, per his nametag, flipped three sausages off the grill, said, "That's all I had left. You're in luck," and rolled them around to drain on the rack. Then he rolled each into a bun, and pointed to the condiments. "What would you like?"

Jase considered and pointed. "Lemme get the dark chili mustard, onions, relish and banana peppers."

The man didn't stint on the toppings. Each boat-shaped bun was overflowing.

They paid him in scrip he could exchange later. It was supposed to cut down on black marketing, but Jandro had heard of so many ways around it. He wasn't really interested in scamming stuff, but it wasn't hard.

He pointed to a bench under another tree. It was made of wooden timbers locally, not extruded.

"I was on Mtali for a while, too, when I was just out of training," he said.

Behind them, the man closed his cart, unfolded the seat and drove off. It was a fueled vehicle, not electric.

"Oh?" Jase asked.

"That was much worse than this place. Here they're opportunistic. There, they were crooked."

"How crooked?"

"We had to open every package, test every delivery, and no local help at all. They'd steal it in front of you, toss it over the fence to a buddy, and insist they never saw it."

"Hah. Lameo."

"Very. It was pathetic. These people are creative at least." And scary. He'd swap that for incompetently dishonest any time.

"The food looks good."

Jase squeezed and stuffed the bread around the contents, angled his face and got a bite. He chewed for a moment, and flared his eyebrows.

"Damn. If all dead animal tastes like this, I could be a convert."

"Hah. Just don't say that around the cultural officers."

"Oh, hell no. But it's different from vat raised. Stronger tasting? Something. Good stuff."

The cheddar brat was good as always, and he tried not to think about dead pig. On the other hand, he'd seen pigs up close. They were pretty nasty creatures.

Jase took another bite and made it disappear.

"Is stuff like this why people stay in? Seeing all parts of the universe?"

"All parts we know about. It does cost a veinful to travel. We get to see the bombed out ruins. Chicks in New York and Beijing and Nairobi pay good money for that."

He munched the brat. Yes, once you got used to the ugly fact of a dead living being, rather than one raised in a vatory with no head, they were tasty. Did the animal's emotions and life flavor the meat? That was a bit creepy, and a bit taboo.

He bit something hard. There was something in it, probably a bit of bone. He worked it around and pulled it out with his fingers. It was gray. He wiped it on the boards and kept chewing.

There was another.

"Damn, they need a better butcher. I'm getting bone bits."

Jase took another bite and twitched, then pulled back with a confused look.

"What the . . ." He reached into the bun, grabbed something and pulled it out. It was a long, gray piece of polymer. It took a moment to recognize it, and then it was instantaneous.

It was a shredded dogtag, and it had been inside a sausage. That meant . . .

Jase screamed through the entire audio spectrum, then he vomited a meter, gushing and squealing and choking and trying for more.

A moment later it hit Jandro, and he puked and puked and kept puking. He realized he'd blacked out, and was leaning over the table. Then he heaved again. It felt as if he'd emptied his entire tract, and he hoped he had.

Someone nearby asked, "What's wrong, are you alright?"

"Water!" he demanded. "Ohdioswater!"

A bottle was placed in his hand. He cracked the seal, rinsed, spat, rinsed, spat, gargled, and kept going.

★ ★ ★

Everything blurred out as two people helped him walk to the clinic. There were MPs around, and camera drones. Someone handed him two pills and another bottle of water, and he tried to swallow them, but spat the water out. The pills went with it.

He didn't want to swallow anything.

Someone waved an inhaler under his nose and he passed out.

He woke up in a bed, wrapped in a sheet, and a South Asian woman in casuals sat next to him. The lights were at half. He could tell he that was medicated.

"How are you doing, Alejandro?"

"I feel ill," he said. Very ill. He'd eaten . . . oh, God.

"I'm Doctor Ramjit from Emotional Health and Wellness. You're safe here."

"I know. I'm just . . . it was awful. Jase pulled out that tag . . ."

"What do you think it was?"

"A shredded dogtag."

"The investigators say they're not sure of that."

He sat up and shouted, "*It was a maldito dogtag*!" As she recoiled, he added, "Ma'am." If he wasn't careful, he'd wind up in some long term facility.

She reached out and offered a hand. He took it and clutched at it.

She said, "It may have been. If so, it may have been a prank."

"I hope so." Yes, that was entirely likely. Like stripping the General, or the doped sodajuice one time. The locals wanted to find ways to screw with the troops. He hoped that was it.

"Did they get the vendor?"

She hesitated a moment.

"No, and he's not responding to contact."

"I feel okay otherwise. How long am I here?"

"When you feel fit you can leave. We will do trace analysis on the regurgitate. We'll let you know what we find."

He wasn't sure they would. If they said it was clean, would he believe them?

"Can I get something for the stress?"

"Yes. I've prescribed some tranquilizer patches. You're welcome to come talk to us any time, or the chaplains. You're on quarters for tomorrow so you can de-stress."

"Thank you," he said.

He gave it a few minutes, decided he could walk, and signed out. He made his way back to the dorm, and slipped inside.

Jase's room was dark, but the door was open.

"Jase?"

"Yeah."

"How are you?"

"Sick."

The man didn't want to talk more than that.

He went to bed, and the tranquilizer did help him sleep. He woke up twice, hungry, but shook in terror at the thought of food.

He was still awake on and off, and a glance at the wall said it was 0500. The chow hall was open, and he was hungry. He'd slept in casuals, so he wore those down.

He walked into the dining hall, and walked right back out. They had sausage in there, and pans of other meat. He couldn't do it.

He went to the dispenser in the rec room and swiped his hand. He went to select a bag of vegetable chips, and his hand froze. They were local, too.

Perhaps he wasn't hungry yet.

Two hours later he was back in the clinic.

Doctor Ramjit saw him at once.

"Please tell me," he said. "I have to know what you found."

"The sausage contained human flesh," she said evenly.

He'd known it would be bad news, because he couldn't have trusted the good. He closed his eyes and felt dizzy, as if spinning.

"It was only a trace amount," she said. "Probably a piece of muscle tissue. The identag was deliberately placed to draw attention to it. It was intended to be morally horrifying, and it was."

It was intended to be morally horrifying. What she was didn't seem to grasp is what that implied. The troops knew what had happened, and everyone had been eating local food for months. There was no way to be sure how much of it was contaminated with their buddies, and there was no way to be sure how much wasn't.

It was worse than that.

That was the moment Jandro knew there was no line the rebels wouldn't cross. They'd spent a year and a half escalating the moral outrage, humiliation and fear. The executions of the MPs, and this, had been a message.

We will hunt you down relentlessly, remorselessly, tirelessly. Regardless of your power and the damage you inflict, we will violate the sanctity of your mind. We will make you question reality and yourselves. And we will never stop.

He wanted to go home. There was nothing here but hatred, no one to be liberated, no one to be brought into line with modern thought. They were atavists and savages who could not be reasoned with.

The UN Forces alliance had come here to save them from rampant repression. He'd seen some of the poor in images from patrols. Out of the city only a few kilometers, some people lived in shacks without power or plumbing, because it was cheap. No one should be forced to make that "choice." There wasn't even a right to due process. That had to be paid for in cash, in an annual tax that they insisted on calling a "resident's fee," even though it was a tax. Fail to pay, and you had no status.

Yet, when the Forces arrived to help them, dirt poor and super rich alike homogenized into one people, intent only on fighting them.

"Whose tag was it?" he asked.

She blushed and stammered.

"I don't have that information."

"You do," he said. "It was a real person's tag, wasn't it?"

"It was." She nodded, looking queasy herself.

"Who?"

"Binyamin Al-Jabr. The first MP shot at the gate."

His head spun again.

"That's not for release," she said. "At all. But I'd rather you had the truth than a rumor."

It was orchestrated terror. They'd shot the man and taken his body. They'd shot everyone who replaced him in the last three months. The MPs were near rioting in terror. Then they'd chopped him, or parts of him, up and fed him to Jase and Jandro.

He really didn't want to know what muscle they'd used. Nor how many batches they'd made.

"I can't eat," he said, and erupted in tears. His lips trembled as he mouthed, "I have to go home."

"I will arrange it," she said. "I've documented both emotional trauma and post event trauma. We'll get you home. We've got other people distressed as a result, though of course, none had the direct experience you and Senior Corporal Jardine did."

"I can't eat," he said again. "Please hurry."

Doctor Ramjit seemed compassionate, but someone in the chain didn't believe him. A sergeant from Commisary took him over to the kitchen, to watch the food being prepared. It arrived in ground and cut form, and he watched a steak go from freezer to grill. He could smell it, too, dead meat. But the cooks were all contracted locally, brought in every morning and searched. A couple of them stared at him, then there were a couple of giggles.

"Didn't you see that?"

"See what?" his escort asked.

"They're laughing at me."

"It's fresh steak. Or you can choose a vegetarian option." Though the man looked unsure himself. He kept glancing furtively at Jandro, and at the cooks.

"I . . ." He had no ability to trust them.

The smell caught him. Somewhere there was pork, and he remembered bratwurst, and there it was again. He ran from the kitchen.

They took him back to the clinic and dosed him again. He felt needles, and they said something he didn't follow.

He almost limped, almost staggered back to the dorm, escorted by a medic. He carried a case of Earth-sourced field rations. He had that, and sealed bottles of expensive, imported spring water. That would have to suffice until he left.

Jase wasn't there. He was probably at the clinic, too. He might even be worse off, since he'd gotten the whole dogtag.

That set him reeling again, and he quickly brought up some landscape images from Iguaçu National Park.

Two hours later he stared at the open packets before him. He'd even placed them on a plate and microheated them, so they'd look more like real food.

He couldn't.

He knew it was perfectly safe, packaged on Earth, and was real food, but he couldn't.

Maybe in a day or two.

The door chimed and opened, and Sergeant Second Class Andreo Romero walked in quietly.

"Hey, Jandro."

"Hola."

"Jase is in the Emotional Health Ward. They reassigned me here."

On the one hand, he needed company. On the other, he knew a suicide watch when he saw one.

"How is he doing?"

"Not good. Homb, they officially haven't said anything, but there were witnesses. Everyone knows what happened."

"Did they find the vendor yet?"

"No one knows where he is."

"Not even the other sellers?"

"They say they've never heard of him. They're also gone. No more local carts. All food is going to process through the dining hall now, for safety."

It might well be. But Jandro couldn't eat it. He pushed back from the table and left the food there.

"Is Jase coming back?" he asked.

Andreo shook his head. "No, he's pretty much sedated and prioritied to return home. He took it pretty hard."

"I took it pretty hard."

There was awkward silence for several moments.

"Well, if you need anything, I'm here. They say you're on extended quarters until tomorrow, then you're on days."

"Days" didn't really mean much here, since each shift would be four plus hours out of synch with the local clock. It was a gesture, though.

Andreo said, "The cooks are all going to be offworld contractors, too. Pricey. We put in a RFQ already, and have some interim workers from BuState and elsewhere. The chow hall is going to be substandard for a while, but that's better than . . ." He faded off, and shivered.

Jandro nodded. Lots of people had eaten from the local vendors.

Andreo asked, "Can I finish that ration if you're not going to?"

"Sure."

At least someone could eat it.

That local night, another MP was shot. Officially they were told counterfire had demolished the sniper's hide, along with a chunk of that building, but he didn't think it would matter.

He twitched all night, between wakefulness and dozing. The next morning, he was ravenous. He opened another field ration, and managed two bites before nausea caused him to curl up.

It's from Earth. It's vatory raised chicken. There's eggs and vegetables. It's guaranteed safe.

Maybe lunch.

He walked into the Logistics compound, into the bay, and got greeted.

"Hey, Jandro. Good to see you back."

"Danke," he said. Johann Meffert was German.

He had materiel to process. Three huge cargontainers sat in the bay, pending sort. This shipment was ammunition, spare parts, tools, generators and nuclear powerpacks for them. He had units and their transport chains on cue, with quantities needed. Those always exceeded quantity available. He broke them down by percentage, then applied the urgency codes to adjust the amounts. Once the Captain signed off, the loader operators would dispense it to be tied down and depart for the forward bases.

He ignored Meffert's periodic stares. Everyone was doing it.

"Ready for review, Captain," he said into his mic.

He sat back and stretched for a moment. It did feel good to do something productive.

"Looks good so far, Jandro. But those KPAKs need sorted, too."

He looked at his screen. He'd missed four pallets of field rations.

"It's not my fault!" he shouted at the bay. "I didn't plan to eat him, I didn't want to eat him, and I didn't put him in the food!"

He stood up and walked out, back to the clinic.

"You really must try to eat something," Doctor Ramjit said. "Vegetables should be fine. I've switched to that myself. It's perfectly understandable that you don't trust the meat."

He sat in a reclined chair, surrounded by trickling fountains, soft images, and with a therapy dog for company. It responded to his scratches with a thumping tail.

"They're from on planet," he said. Had they urinated on the plants? Grown them in poison? Fertilized the ground with dead troops?

"How are you managing with field rations?" she asked.

"Better," he said. "I've eaten part of one."

Her frown was earnest. "That's not enough for three days. You've already lost weight."

"I know," he said. "But I can't. I just . . . can't." He hoped she understood.

"It's not just the food," he continued. "It's this place. All of it. I can't be around people like this. The cooks were giggling. Our people stare at me. They get the gossip. They all know. Jase has already gone. Please send me, too."

"I'll try," she said. Her frown came across as pitying. He didn't want that, either.

He untangled from the chair and dog and left in silence, though she said, "Good luck, Alejandro. You have our wishes."

As he entered his room, his phone pinged a message. He swiped it.

"Alejandro, you are scheduled to depart in fifteen days. The clinic will fit you with a nutrient IV to help you in the interim."

"Yes," he said to the Marine. "I'm a casualty."

"Good luck with it, then. I'm sorry, at first I'd figured you were a base monkey. They don't know what the point is like."

"No, most of them don't," he agreed. He looked around at the other people on the rotation. Some were military, some UN bureau staff, some contractors. They might know what had happened, but they had no idea what it felt like. Thankfully, none of them recognized him.

The Marine said, "But I saw that," pointing at the IV. "I hope you're recovering?"

"Yes. It shouldn't take long. Good luck with the leg."

"Thanks. They say three months."

He boarded the ship and found his launch couch. The shuttle was well-used, smelling of people, disinfectant and musty military bags. He settled in and closed his eyes, not wanting to talk to anyone around him. They bantered and joked and sounded cheerful to be leaving. He wasn't cheerful, only relieved.

When they sealed up, pressure increased to Earth normal. He breathed deeply.

The acceleration and engine roar took a faint edge off his nerves. Soon. Off this nightmarish hellhole and home.

The tranks worked. He had a scrip for more, and a note that said he should not be questioned about them. Doctor Ramjit had said that wasn't unusual for some of the Special Unit troops, and even some of the infantry. "The ship infirmary should be able to refill you without problems," she'd said. "Especially as we've put out a bulletin about personnel generally suffering stress disorders. We haven't said why."

They even helped with launch sickness. He felt blissfully fine, not nauseous.

He zoned through until the intercom interrupted him.

"Passengers, we are in orbit, and will dock directly with the *Wabash*. Departure for Earth will be only a couple of hours. Final loading is taking place now."

Good. He eyed the tube on his arm. He could have them unplug this, and he could eat real, solid food from safe, quality-inspected producers on Earth.

Well, he'd have to start with baby food. Fifteen days of the tube had wiped out his GI tract. He'd have to rebuild it. That would be fine. And he'd never touch a sausage again.

He unlatched when the screen said to, and waited impatiently. He wasn't bad in emgee, knowing how to drag himself along the couches and guide cable. Several passengers didn't seem to know how, and some of them were even military.

Shortly, he was in the gangtube, creeping along behind the Marine and a couple of contractors rotating out.

There was a small port to his right, looking aft along the length of the ship. He looked out and saw the open framework of an orbital supply shuttle detach a cargotainer from the ship's cargo lock, rotate and attach another in its place.

He flinched, and nausea and dizziness poured into him again.

The cargotainer was marked "Hughes Commissary Services, Jefferson, Freehold of Grainne."

He fumbled with his kit, slapped three patches on his arm, and almost bit his tongue off holding back a scream.

PALM STRIKE'S LAST CASE

★

by Charlie Jane Anders

Fleeing crime-ridden Argus City for the colonial world of Newfoundland, Luc Devereaux, also know as the vigilante Palm Strike, thought he'd left his crime-fighting days behind him. But Newfoundland is not the paradise he was promised. Crime and drug abuse run rampant. The colony needs a savior—and Palm Strike has found his last case.

1.

PALM STRIKE'S costume has never been comfortable, but lately it's pinching his shoulders and chafing in the groin area. Sweat pools in the boots. The Tensilon-reinforced helmet gives him a blinding headache after two hours, and the chestplate is slightly too loose, which causes it to move around and rub the skin off his stomach and collarbone.

The thing that keeps Palm Strike running past water tower after water tower along the cracked rooftops of Argus City, the thing that keeps him breaking heads after taking three bullets that night, is the knowledge that there are still innocents out there whose lives haven't yet been ruined.

Kids who still have hope and joy, the way Palm Strike's own son did before Dark Shard got him. When the bruised ribs and punctured lung start to slow him down and the forty-pound costume has him dancing in chains, he pictures his son. Rene. It never fails—he feels a weight in his stomach, like a chunk of concrete studded with rocks, and it fills him with rage, which he turns into purpose.

Argus City is full of disintegrating Frank Lloyd Wright knock-offs and people who have nothing to lose but someone else's innocence. This was a great city, once, just like America was a great country and Earth was a great planet.

Palm Strike catches a trio of Shardlings selling dreamflies in Grand Park, under the bronze statue of a war hero piloting a drone. The drone casts deep shadows, and that's where they hunker in a three-point parabolic formation. They're well trained, maybe even ex-Special Forces, and decently armed, including one customized 1911 with a tight-bore barrel. Dark Shard must be getting desperate.

Once they're down, Palm Strike feeds them their own drugs, baggie by baggie.

"You know my rule," he growls. The process is not unlike making foie gras. One of these men is so terrified, he blurts out the location of Dark Shard's secret lair, the Pleasuresplinter.

Ambulance called. These men will be fine. Eventually. Palm Strike's already far away before the sirens come. Losing himself in the filthy obstacle course of broken walls and shattered vestibules in the old financial district. Leaping over prone bodies. He doglegs into the old French Quarter. All of the bistros are shuttered, but a few subterranean bars give off a tallowy glare, along with the sound of blues musicians who refuse to quit for the night. Cleansing acrid smoke pours around his feet.

Turns out Dark Shard's Pleasuresplinter is hidden right under City Hall. But service tunnels from the river go all the way, almost. Catacombs, filthy and crawling with vermin. Palm Strike's boots get soaked, both inside and out. Men and women stand guard at intervals, but none of them sees Palm Strike coming. Palm Strike's main superpower is the stupidity of his enemies. He sets charges as he goes, something to be a beacon for first responders, firefighters and EMTs. And police. But don't trust the police, *never* trust the police.

Palm Strike crashes through the dense mahogany door just as all the charges he set in the tunnels go off. Smoke billows up out of the fractured street behind him. The door explodes inwards, into a beautiful marble space—a mausoleum—with a recessed floor like a sauna, and a dozen little dark alcoves and nooks. Red drapes. Gray-suited men sporting expensive guns and obvious body armor with the trademark broken-glass masks.

In one of those nooks, just on the far side of the room, he spots the children: all in their teens, some of them barely pubescent. Their faces wide open, like they are in the middle of something that will never leave them, no matter what else they see or do.

Everyone over eighteen is shooting at Palm Strike. Lung definitely collapsed. Healing mojo has crapped out.

First priority: get the children out. Second priority: bring this den of foulness down on these men's heads. Third priority: find Dark Shard.

Children first, though.

One of the bullets goes right through Palm Strike's thigh, in spite of the ablative fibers. Femoral artery? No time to check. This place probably smells like candy floss and cheap perfume most of the time, but now it's laced with vomit, blood and sewage. Clear a path to the exit for the children. Drive the armed men into cover, in the far alcoves. Be a constantly moving whirl of anger, all weapon and no target. Unleash the throwing-claws and smart-javelins. Find one brave child, who can be a leader, who will guide the rest to safety. That one, with the upturned nose and dark eyes, who looks like Rene only with lighter, straighter hair. "Get them out," Palm Strike says, and the kid understands. Throwing claws have taken out most of the ordnance. Children run past Palm Strike, stumbling but not stopping, into the tunnel.

Palm Strike blacks out. Just for an instant. He snaps awake to see the boy he'd appointed leader in the hands of one of the top Shardlings—you can tell from the mask's shatter pattern. Stupid. Busting in here, with no plan. Dumb crazy old fool. The kid squirms in the man's grasp, but his little face is calm. Palm Strike has one throwing-claw left. He hears the first responders in the tunnels behind him, and they've found the children who got away.

Palm Strike's throwing-claw hits the pinstripe-suited thug in the neck, and slashes at him on its way to find a weapon to disable. An angry insect, made of Tensilon, stainless steel, and certain proprietary polymers, scuttles down the man's neck. The man pulls the trigger—just as the throwing claw's razor talons slice the gun in two. The recoil takes half the man's hand, and then the boy is running for the exit. Palm Strike wants to stay and force-feed this man every drug he can find here. But he's lost a lot of blood and can't breathe, and the shouts are getting close.

Palm Strike barely makes it out of there before the place swarms with uniforms.

The Strike-copter is where he left it, concealed between the decaying awnings of the Grand Opera House. He manages to set the autopilot before passing out again. Healing mojo works for crap nowadays. After only three years of this, he's played out. He regains and loses consciousness as his limp body weaves over the barbed silhouette of downtown, and then the squat brick tops of abandoned factories. At last, the Strike-copter carries him up the river, to a secluded mansion near Mercy Bay.

Josiah, his personal assistant, releases him from the copter's harness, with practiced care. Josiah's young, too young, with curly red hair and a wide face that looks constantly startled. As usual, he wears an apron over a suit and skinny tie. "You really did it this time," Josiah says, prepping the gurney to roll Palm Strike through the hidden doorway in one of the granite blocks of the mansion's outer walls. Josiah removes the headpiece, but before he can attach the oxygen mask, Palm Strike says: "The children."

"They got out okay," Josiah responds. "Ten of them. You did good. Now rest."

Some time later, a day maybe, Palm Strike wakes with tubes in his arms and screens beeping ostentatiously around him. The healing mojo has finally kicked in. He still feels like hell but he's not dying any more. He sits up, slowly. Josiah tries to keep him bedridden, but they both know it's a lost cause.

"You've received a letter," Josiah says as Palm Strike scans newsfeeds on his tablet. "An actual piece of paper. On stationery."

Palm Strike—now he's Luc Deveaux, because he's out of costume—shrugs, which makes his ribs flare with agony. But then Josiah hands him the letter, already opened, and the Space Administration logo sends a shiver through Luc before he even sees the words.

"Congratulations. You have been selected to join the next colonization wave . . ."

2.

THE SPACE AGENCY interview process is the last vivid memory Luc has of Rene. And he remembers it two different ways.

First version: They were happy, a family, in this together. His son leaned his head against Luc's shoulder in the waiting room, with its framed Naïve-art posters of happy colonists unsnapping helmets under a wild new sun. Rene joked about his main qualification being his ability to invent a brand new style of dance for a higher-gravity world, and even demonstrated high-gravity dancing for the other families in the waiting room, to general applause. Rene aced the interviews, they both did, and Luc was so proud of his son, as he gave clever answers, dressed up in a little suit like a baby banker.

In that version of the memory, Rene turned to Luc in the waiting room and said, "I know our main selling point is you, your geo-engineering experience. But they'll need young people who are up for literally whatever, any challenge, to make this planet livable. And that'll be me. You'll see, Dad."

So. Damn. Proud.

The other version of the memory only comes to Luc when he's half asleep, or when he's had a few single malts and is sick of lying to himself. In that other version, Rene was being a smartmouth the whole time—in the waiting room, in the interviews, the whole time—and Luc had to chew his tongue bloody to keep from telling his son to put a sock in it. They both knew that Luc was the one with the land-reclamation skills the colony would need, and all Rene had to do was shut his trap and let them think he'd make himself useful and not be too much of a smart-ass. That's all.

Luc can just about remember the stiffening in his neck and chest every time Rene acted out or failed to follow the script in those interviews. Rene had to get cute, doing his high-gravity dance and annoying all the other families. It's a close cousin to the anger that keeps him laying into Dark Shard's thugs every night, if he wants to be honest with himself, which he mostly doesn't. Except after a few single malts, or when he's half asleep.

Both versions of the memory are true, Luc guesses. If he really wanted a second opinion, he could ask Josiah if he was too hard on Rene when his son was alive, but he never does.

He has too many other regrets crowding that one out, anyway. Like, why didn't he pick Rene up from school himself that day? And keep better tabs, in general? Or, why didn't he get Rene off this doomed planet before it was too late to save him?

3.

NOW LUC GRIPS the letter in both hands, wondering whose idea of a joke this is.

"You have to go," Josiah says. Luc is already crumpling the letter into a ball, aiming for the recycling. "You have to go. Sir. If you stay, you'll die."

"My work here is not done." Luc realizes he's slept through most of the day. Almost time to suit up. "Dark Shard still needs to pay. For Rene. And all the rest."

Luc can't find his headpiece. A jet-black scowling half-mask, with a shock-absorbing duroplex helmet built in, it usually isn't hard to spot in the midst of civilized bedroom furnishings and nice linens. But it's gone. Now he remembers—Josiah took it from him when he was strapped to the gurney.

"How do you think you'll best honor Rene's memory?" Josiah is touching Luc's arm. "By throwing your life away here? Or by following Rene's dream and going to another planet, where you could really make a difference? You've destroyed Dark Shard's lair. Which will weaken him a little, but also drive him further underground."

"Where is my headpiece?" Luc asks. Josiah won't answer. "Where did you put my helmet? Tell me."

Josiah backs away, even though Luc still walks teeteringly.

"You could help build something new," Josiah says. "Instead of breaking things, over and over, until you're broken in turn. You could build something."

"That part of me is dead." Luc is already thinking about alternatives to the headpiece. There are prototypes, which he hid someplace even

Josiah doesn't know about. Flawed designs, but good enough for a night or two, until Josiah comes around. "This is all I have left."

The nanofiber-reinforced lower half of his costume still has that bullet-hole, and his leg is so heavily bandaged that the pants barely fit. This could be a problem, especially if the rip widens around the bandages. He could end up with a big white patch on his leg, like a target for every thug to aim at in the darkness. Stain the bandages black? Wrap black tape around them?

"Luc. Please." Josiah grabs his arm and shoves the letter, which he's retrieved and uncrumpled, in Luc's face. "I helped bury your son. I don't want to bury you." He has tears in his eyes, which are also puffy from sleepless nights caring for Luc's slow-healing wounds. "There's more than one way to be a hero. You taught me that, before all this."

Luc stares at the letter again. Departure date is in just a few weeks, and there are a lot of training sessions and tests before then. Someone must have backed out, or maybe washed out. "If I go," he growls at Josiah, "I won't leave you any money. I've spent every last penny on my fight."

"I know that, sir," Josiah says, smiling wearily. "Who do you think has been keeping them from taking the house? We've restructured your debt five times in the last two years."

In the end, Luc says yes, even though every instinct rebels against it. Not because Josiah hid his mask, but because something inside him, his core, is suddenly too exhausted to do anything else. Sleeping for a hundred years sounds perfect. Maybe he'll wake up having understood something. Maybe he won't wake up at all—even better.

After that, Luc's trapped in the clutches of officialdom. Imprisoned. Every spare minute goes to medical tests—even with the healing mojo, he still has to explain the scars and old broken bones—and briefings on absolutely everything they know about Kepler, which people are calling Newfoundland. The same facts are repeated over and over, like the fact that Newfoundland has 1.27 times Earth gravity and a year that lasts fifteen Earth months. Only one of the seven continents is habitable, the south pole. Blah blah blah. There is a whole three-hour talk on what to do if you wake up early, and five days devoted to how to convert the ship into a survival module on landing—the crew should know, but if the crew are dead, then the colonists may need to know, too. The other colonists in the briefings are cute, fresh-faced. Mostly around Luc's age, but he feels much, much older.

And meanwhile, all of Luc's sources in the underworld suggest that Dark Shard has blown town, and his organization is in disarray.

At last, the day comes. Two days of fasting, then Luc strips naked and climbs inside the decontamination vat—which sears off a few layers of skin—and then the cryo-module. The technicians close the lid over his face, and he feels the ice threading through his veins and into his muscles and joints.

Just as the paralysis starts to take hold, he's dead certain he hears someone say, "Palm Strike." With a chuckle.

Palm Strike hears his name and comes to life. But it's too late. Palm Strike tries to fight the cold tendrils immobilizing his body, to stay awake. He almost sits up in his tiny chamber. He only needs to pull out these tubes. He battles with everything he has, kicking against the top of his coffin. But the clammy grip pulls him under, into an ocean with no surface.

4.

FALLING FOR YEARS, drowning in slow motion, Luc sees Rene's corpse over and over. The bullet hole in his side, the tell-tale dilated pupils, the broken capillaries in his face. Mouth frozen open in a last abortive yell. They made him identify the body.

He only met Dark Shard once—and it was as Luc, not as Palm Strike. Palm Strike didn't even exist yet. A few nights after he buried Rene, there was a shape in his window. A shadowy form, wearing a cloak over a chestplate, with a mask that appeared to be constantly exploding outward with black crystal pieces.

Luc heard something and sat up in bed. The light wouldn't turn on.

"I came to convey my regrets," Dark Shard said in a voice like the grinding of broken glass. His hands were obsidian fragments, flexing. "Your son was not meant to die. It was an unfortunate mistake. The responsible individual has been disciplined."

"What . . ." Luc stammered. Naked except for filthy boxer shorts. Half drunk since the funeral. He couldn't remember, later, what he said to Dark Shard, but none of it had any dignity. He may have begged for death. He was sure he cried and tore his own sheets. He tried, over and over, to imagine that meeting if he'd been Palm Strike.

"Your son was not meant to die," Dark Shard said again. "We do not waste lives in such a fashion. We would have taken him for ransom, held him in our Pleasuresplinter a day or two, but he would not have been molested in any way. He might have been allowed to sample our dreamflies, which are highly addictive, depending on whether we desired a single ransom payment or an ongoing relationship."

"Why are you telling me this?" Luc still didn't know the answer to that question, all this time later. If Dark Shard hadn't shown up to apologize for Rene's death, he might not have felt such intense hatred. Luc might have remained a regular broken wreck instead of spending the fortune he'd made from his land-reclamation projects becoming Palm Strike.

The way Dark Shard explained it, they had seized Rene, as a hostage, but then they'd gotten caught in a shootout with a rival group, the Street Commanders. Rene had taken a bullet to the gut, and he was bleeding out. So one of the Shardlings, a man named Jobbo, had cradled Rene in his arms and given him something for the pain.

Rene might have survived if Jobbo hadn't given him the drugs. The dreamflies thinned his blood and prevented coagulation, so he bled out faster. Plus Rene's final moments were spent under the effects of a dissociative drug that made him feel lost to the world and slowed everything to a hideous crawl. He died not knowing who he was, or who loved him.

Luc has imagined Rene's death a million times since Dark Shard described it to him. But in this frozen sensory deprivation tank, he's living it. Rene's eyes, like empty wells—the image keeps tormenting Luc. The harder he tries to swim, the deeper he sinks.

5.

WHEN THE FROZEN WAVES recede and light invades, Luc cries out from deep in his strangulated throat. He's sure he can't face reality again, after the endless nightmare. But the light is remorseless, and the cold abandons him. He can move his arms again. At last, the lid of the cryo-module opens, and he's looking up at a young round face. A girl. Twelve or thirteen. Red hair, in braids.

"I did it," she says. "Hot wow, I can't believe I did it."

"Did what?" Luc tries to sit up, but he's still too weak. She raises a sippy-cup of something hot and bitter, and pours it down his throat.

"I finally got this thing working. It's been my project, for years."

"Years?" Luc blinks. Something is wrong. He can see the chamber behind the girl's head, and it looks old, broken. The gray serrated walls are bare except for some torn fibers and rough edges, as though every last bit of technology was stripped away long ago.

"Oh, sorry. Yeah." She leans over further, so she can make eye contact. Her eyes are hazel. "Better start at the beginning. The Endeavour landed, like twenty years ago. Your module was busted, the wake-up sequence failed. There was no way to revive you without killing you. But I've been tinkering, every spare moment."

"Everybody needs a hobby," Luc grunts.

"Take it slow, okay?" The girl puts a threadbare blanket over him. "There was a lot of stuff here, originally. Procedures and things. You were supposed to watch some video that explained that a hundred and three years have passed on Earth and everyone you knew is dead. Plus any last messages from your loved ones back home. And there was an acclimation chamber to help you adjust to the air and gravity. But that stuff is all gone. Sorry, guy."

"What's your name?" This time Luc does manage to sit up.

"I'm Sasha Jacobs. Anyway, you should be glad. We almost ate you. More than once. The whole colony's starving. Nothing grows here any more—the soil just kills all our crops. You were supposed to be some kind of big-time agriculture expert, right? I figured maybe you could help."

"Geo-engineer." Luc shrugs. He's naked under the blanket. He glares at Sasha until she hands him some pants. "But that was another life, a long time ago. These days, my main skill-set involves finding bad people and making them pay. Someone sabotaged my casket. And whoever it was, they're going to learn my rule."

He tugs the itchy red pants on under the blanket and lifts himself up out of the cryo-module, only to collapse in a heap at Sasha's rawhide-covered feet when his legs won't support his weight. He twitches and grips his own knees, dry-heaving.

"You might not want to rush into anything," Sasha says.

6.

LUC AND SASHA emerge, not from a spaceship or a survival module, but from a crude hut covered with some kind of rubbery wood, attached in overlapping wedge-shaped slats. There's no sign of any source of that wood, though—the surrounding area is barren and the ground has a crumbly furrowed consistency, like the surface of a brain made of pale clay. Luc sees no other buildings or signs of civilization, which makes him wonder if they really did hide his cryo-module to save him from being eaten, after all.

The sun is too bright and pale—reminding Luc of the time he experimented with night-vision lenses and someone shone a floodlight in his eyes. In the blanched daylight, Sasha looks a little older. She's a rangy girl, with arms too long for her torso and a shiny blue dress that might be made out of the upholstery fabric from one of the ship's escape pods. Her face has freckles and a thin nose that appears to twitch constantly, perhaps in amusement or maybe because he smells bad.

"The air is higher in nitrogen than you're used to, and the gravity—"

Luc cuts her off. "I remember the briefings. Where's the colony?"

"Down the hill, a kilometer and a half away." Sasha gestures. "Everyone is going to want to meet you, if you're up for it."

"I'm up for it." The sooner Luc meets the pool of suspects, which is everyone who was an adult when the ship left Earth, the sooner he can start narrowing it down.

Sasha leads Luc along an unsteady slope covered with loose rocks that jab at his bare feet, and he stumbles repeatedly as the gravity catches him off guard. She keeps talking about the planet, how the other six continents have temperatures too extreme for humans to survive most of the time, but contain massive jungles full of megafauna, including nine-limbed mammoths that swing through a canopy of carnivorous fronds. She wants to visit someday.

They walk maybe three quarters of a kilometer before they reach the first buildings, which are laid out in a pinwheel pattern around the center of the colony, set in a kind of valley. Most of the buildings are made of that same spongy wood, which looks like pumice, only softer. Pipes come out of the houses and disappear into the ground. Wires snake along their rooftops, connecting to junctions on poles.

And then the ground levels out, the buildings grow denser, and the stench clouds Luc's eyes just as the sights become unbearable. The crumbling shacks, made of a mixture of prefab construction materials from the ship, plus spongy wood, weak drywall and local rocks. The river clogged with effluent, running through the middle of Hopetown. The lashed-together pieces of failing technology. And above it all, the rank odor of wounds and sores that won't heal properly due to the malnutrition. Luc saw a lot of nightmares, when he was helping to turn Benin into the world's last breadbasket and visiting the Arkansas refugee camps. But here, no relief workers are coming. He passes a group of teenagers playing listlessly in the street, with arms like twigs and swollen torsos. Older people slump against the unstable walls.

But there's something else, too—some of the people standing around that ugly modern-art sculpture made of cannibalized spaceship parts at the center of it all have a vacant look in their bloodshot eyes that he knows at a glance. And festering trackmarks on their arms. Luc files that away, for now.

The Survival Module—all that's left of the Endeavour—is at the other end of Hopetown from where Luc and Sandy came in, along the filthy river and to the right. The dinged-up white structure, the size of the Opera House back home, has been dressed up as a town hall, with a podium and sound system out front, plus someone has painted a decorative gold leaf motif around the entrance using some local plant sludge. Sasha waves hi at the people sitting at desks inside the building, then runs off to tell her mother her amazing news.

"Oh, my lord," says a middle-aged lady, maybe around fifty, sitting in a repurposed cockpit chair at the rear of the Survival Module, behind a big desk covered with data tablets. "Sasha actually did it. Mr. Deveaux, you don't know any of us, but you're famous around these parts: the agriculture expert who didn't wake up."

"Tell me what went wrong," Luc says.

7.

HERE'S THE SECRET that almost nobody ever guessed about Palm Strike: he was a brawler. The name "Palm Strike" was an intentional misdirect, to make people believe he was some kind of martial-arts wizard and then catch them off guard with his total lack of skill. People tended to overestimate him, and then underestimate him. He'd had months, not years, of training, but he mostly relied on the healing mojo and the enhanced strength. His detective skills, too, mostly involved punching people and asking questions.

So Luc sits there, for hours, and listens to the colony's leaders talk about their incredibly meticulous terraforming process and all the things they did before and after planetfall to prepare the soil for farming. The tests that revealed nothing wrong, and the excellent early harvests. Inside, he's still raging and traumatized by his endless cryo-nightmares, but he maintains a totally blank expression. Luc has to believe that whoever sabotaged his cryo-unit also made the voyage here—maybe even Dark Shard himself—and at some point Luc will have someone to hit. And that person will already know that Luc is Palm Strike, and will therefore fear him. He studies each of these people, looking for the signs of that fear. He's a lousy detective, but he knows all about fear.

"We brought bioengineered microbes from Earth that were supposed to neutralize any toxins in the soil and correct the pH balance," one burly man named Ron McGregor is saying, "but most of them died in flight, due to cosmic radiation exposure in that section of the ship." McGregor's the right age and almost the right build, but he's a fussy bureaucrat whose biggest worry is that Luc will make him look incompetent. He's neither afraid of Luc nor happy to see him.

They're in a conference room behind the town hall, which turns out to be the ship's flight deck with all of the equipment and panels removed and a big table made out of some kind of polished slate, surrounded by a dozen chairs. Luc begins to feel weary after just a couple hours of this briefing. The gravity takes its toll, as do the aftereffects of years of deathly cold and cryo-nightmares. But he wants to look all these people over while they're still surprised by his return from the dead.

Luc keeps drinking the hot brew, made from some kind of noxious weed that they also use for clothing, and it keeps him awake.

"We tested the soil and it was perfect." The governor, or president, of Newfoundland, is that woman from the town hall, Rebecca Hoffman. Attractive for her age, which is roughly the age Luc would be if he'd woken on time. Hair in a messy gray bob, blouse made of some local algae. "Five or six years of decent harvests. And then the crops just . . . stopped growing."

Ron McGregor keeps interrupting himself and nodding at his own points. He talks about the heavy terraforming engine that cleared the local vegetation, removed the biggest obstructions, and wiped out the local pests—these horrible bugs got everywhere and into everything, at first.

Happiest to see Luc is probably Bertram Cargill, an old man who has hair coming out of his ears that matches his fuzzy vest. And open sores on his knuckles and wrists. Cargill took over as the water and soil expert when Luc didn't wake up, and he found the river that provided irrigation and drinking water, one tributary of which is now a sewer running through Hopetown. Plus the geyser and hot springs that supply heat and geothermal power to their dwellings.

"Geyser," Luc says at last. "That explains the brain-like furrow pattern I noticed on the ground when I arrived. Soil near a geyser is often highly acidic. Plus those hot springs probably have bacteria living in them, kilometers under the surface, and they could be producing toxins we've never even encountered before."

Everybody pauses—even McGregor—waiting for Luc to finish his thought. "The mystery here isn't why the soil stopped being fertile," he says. "It's why it ever was."

Luc catches up with Sasha, who's hanging around the edge of town, basking in her heroism. Everybody in the world has been patting her on the back, and she's got a crowd of other kids standing around listening to her triumphant narrative of how she cobbled together a new wake-up circuit out of spit and dead branches. The kids are all Sasha's age, give or take—chances are, nobody's wanted to have children in this colony, since the food started running out.

"Hey," she says. "How did it go? Want to meet my mom? She's dying to meet you."

They walk toward the edge of Hopetown, the opposite direction from the hut where Luc woke up. He's going to need some shoes, or better yet boots. Along the way, he sees plenty more emaciated people shuffling like the living dead, with tiny punctures in their arms. Even amongst the starving people with hair like dead grass and skin like bedsores, the addicts stand out.

"Tell me about the drugs," Luc says when they're far enough away from the center of town, where the ramshackle huts are spaced further apart.

"I don't use them," Sasha says, shrugging even as she swings her arms mid-stride. "I'm not that dumb."

"Good for you," Luc says. The exhaustion and strain are catching up with him, and he's about to keel over. He's famished, too, which means he's becoming a real citizen of Newfoundland.

"Every now and then, Hoffman's peacekeepers turn the town upside down, looking for the source. She gives speeches. And they've actually executed a few drug-dealers, just beheaded them. But you gotta understand, we've been starving a long time. People need something to distract them from the inevitable."

"Even here." Luc is clenching his fists, staring at the worry-lined earth. Not dirt. Dead microorganisms. "Even here. Goddamnit."

"From what I hear, they have a recipe," says Sasha. "The ship's engine still had a lot of coolant left over after landing, and they siphoned everything out of the cryo-units, except yours, of course. Plus some fungi that grow on the coast have hallucinogenic properties, in very tiny doses. They trade it for food rations, or bits of Earth clothing and personal items."

A few weeks of the year, the nearest continent cools down enough for humans to travel there and do some big game hunting. But the last expedition never made it back, and the colony won't survive long enough to make another hunting trip, Sasha says.

Sasha's mother is a cheerful, leather-faced woman named Clarissa, with curly hair that was probably dirty blonde but has gone platinum thanks to the unrelenting sun. She insists that Luc sit down at her dining-room table, which is made of that same rock as the table back in the conference room. She gives him some of her dead husband's clothes, including a decent pair of boots that made the trip from Earth. (Luc's own personal effects from Earth were stolen years ago.) Like every other adult here, her tongue is swollen, making her diction hard to understand at first. She fusses over Luc, feeding him a watery stew with some tough roots in it. Then she insists that Luc should rest—there's a kind of hammock in the front room of the four-room house, that he can sleep in.

Luc lays on the hammock, but he can't close his eyes without seeing Rene bleeding out, now filtered through his cryogenic visions. The broken-off piece of rock inside his stomach that kept him going out every night and pummeling criminals is back, sharper than ever, since he spent a hundred and twenty years having the same nightmare.

8.

In the morning, Sasha's mother is gone, but Sasha gives Luc a single strip of pungent jerky left over from some great beast they killed on their last successful sortie to the jungle continent to the north. "Save your food," Luc says, but she insists and he chews a bit of it. The best he can say is that digesting it will keep his stomach busy for hours. The house is dusty—that loose soil gets everywhere—and it makes him itch. Soil erosion. Wooden structures everywhere, but no trees.

"They gave me a few days off my chores and studies," Sasha says, "to help you acclimate, since I was the one who brought you back. This ought to be planting season, but that's been delayed indefinitely."

Luc walks around the colony, trying to get used to the gravity, letting everyone get an eyeful of him. Something about that cryofreeze has recharged his healing mojo. Old aches hurt less, even in 1.27-G. Looking everybody in the eyes, he sees signs of long-term starvation, worse even than what he saw in Arkansas—but also lots of dilated pupils (painful in this more intense sunlight, he guesses), no teeth, and puncture scars. Junkies: They assault anyone who comes too close, with a terrifying fury but no strength. Too far gone. Even if he could feed those people, he can't save most of them.

Becky Hoffman shows Luc the last of the seed vault, with Sasha on tiptoes behind them. Corn, wheat, some sorghum. But not much of any. Even with a bumper crop, you couldn't plant enough to feed 3,000 people for another 15 months.

"Don't tell anybody what you've seen here," Hoffman whispers. "I'm frankly terrified of what will happen if people discover how hopeless it is. We already have a huge drug problem, and a lot of unrest." A lot of people took to eating the clay near the river last year, just to feel full, until dysentery and some excruciating thistle-shaped parasite killed a few dozen within a month, she says.

Luc glances over at Sasha, and can't read anything from her face.

Many colonies, back on Earth, died within one generation. Of the ten extrasolar planets that humans have colonized thus far, only three still have people living on them. Including Newfoundland.

The seed vault, behind the town hall, is one of two places in Newfoundland that has a guard, wearing body armor and toting a Brazelton fast-repeater, the kind they used for crowd control back on Earth. The other place is the food dispensary right off the town square, where Sasha goes once per day to collect her family's food rations in a red box while two people with clubs and guns watch carefully.

Luc heads into the fields, stretching out to the horizon, where Cargill irrigated using river water, and can't find egregious fault with Cargill's work. The soil, though, is toxic, arid, acrid, a dead waste. He kneels in the dirt, his skin getting burnt and then unburning as the healing mojo works. He leans against a wooden post.

The sun goes down and the first of three moons is already up. Sasha comes to find Luc, who is kicking the dirt and cursing, punching the wooden post until his hand is bleeding and crammed with splinters.

"Hey, calm down," Sasha says. "You're going to hurt yourself."

Luc's only answer is a roar and another swing of his fist, hard enough to smash the wood to splinters. He looks at his own bloody hand and backs off, shaking off Sasha's attempt to see to him.

"It's hopeless," he says. "I could have done something. I could have stopped this. You didn't all have to die. But somebody sabotaged my capsule. Whoever did that has murdered this colony, and I'm here just in time to watch it rot. And they're probably the same person who's profiting off all this misery. Selling drugs to people who are living in hell."

The wounds on Luc's hand are already closing. He sits in the dirt, convulsed with pure anger, lurching into his own knees again and again. He can't think, he can't see a way forward. Nothing but dead soil all around him.

"For the first time ever," he says when his rage has spun down, "I believe my son was lucky."

Sasha sits near him, but keeps her distance, probably because he looks as if he'll take her head off if she gets too close.

"I'm sorry," Luc says. "I didn't mean to go nuts on you."

"It's okay," Sasha says. "I guess this is a big adjustment. You get used to seeing people lose their minds, around here." She hesitates, then: "Hey, I wanted to ask you something."

"Sure."

She's studying him. "When I first got you out of your coffin, you said something about your main skill being justice. I can't remember the exact words. What were you talking about?"

"I lost someone, back on Earth. The people who did it needed to pay. So I turned myself into something else. A crime-fighter. I spent millions of dollars to become this whole other creature. When I got out of my casket and it was twenty years too late, I had a moment of bravado. It was like a defense mechanism. Forget it happened."

"So you're not going to get justice? For your cryo-unit, and everything else?"

"I don't know," Luc says, realizing that's the truth. "I've been biding my time these last couple days, but now I'm not sure what the point would be. The guilty and the innocent will both die the same way, soon enough."

"When I was working on your cryo-pod, I had this idea that I would wake you up, and you would burst out of there and save us all. Maybe with a fanfare, like in that videox they let me watch before the ship's entertainment system finally gave out. And when I did wake you up and you said all that stuff, part of me was thrilled because you really sounded like . . . I don't know, like someone who saves people."

The light of the first moon draws shadows under her eyes, while a second moon sneaks up on her, illuminating her hair and her rough jacket. She looks as if she's in the middle of one of those rite-of-passage moments where you surrender some of your illusions on the way to adulthood. Something is breaking forever inside her. He has no idea what he's supposed to do about this.

What would Palm Strike do? He wouldn't be sitting here in the dirt kissing his knees. Palm Strike would find a way to save the colony and take down the pushers.

"Can you help me get some gear?" he asks Sasha. "I need a helmet, body armor, gloves. It needs to be black, or I need some dye. Do you know where I can score some?"

She stares at him, her eyes ginormous. Then, slowly, she nods.

9.

PALM STRIKE never had a sidekick. For a while, he let Josiah create a fake identity as his partner No-Shadow, not to do any actual fighting but to talk to the cops once they stopped trying to kill Palm Strike. No-Shadow's outfit was all cape and full-face mask, plus some gloves with spikes coming out of them. Ridiculous.

One night, Palm Strike got back from busting heads but No-Shadow was nowhere to be found. Turned out No-Shadow had gone on a ride-along with a pair of detectives, Lancaster and Marsh, so they could talk his ear off.

"They think you're doing more harm than good," Josiah explained when he got home. "You shut down the Street Commanders and took out some of the Shardlings, but in the process you've only strengthened Dark Shard. Both by eliminating his competition and culling his weakest people."

"You shouldn't judge an exterminator halfway through a job," Luc grunted.

"But that's the thing. It's like, during the Great Leap Forward, Mao sent every peasant in China out to kill sparrows, on the theory that sparrows were eating seeds and reducing the harvests. But once the sparrows were all gone, turned out they had been eating locusts, which had been eating the grain. It was an ecosystem. When all the sparrows were gone, everybody starved."

Josiah said these things while he was making a sandwich for Luc, still wearing his big black cape and unfeasibly spiky gloves as he stood at the marble kitchen counter.

"Maybe Palm Strike isn't the best solution," Luc said after he stopped laughing at No-Shadow. "But he's all I'm capable of, right now."

The next few days, Luc spends every waking hour traveling around and taking soil samples, and every night watching the rotating cast of hoodlums selling drugs in the town square. He hasn't seen much in the way of "peacekeepers" in this town of three thousand souls, but the dealers are there from sundown to sunup. They mostly trade drugs for food, which means there's a stockpile somewhere.

You wouldn't want to be the only one eating when everyone else is starving to death. You'd find out the hard way that nobody is an island.

One day, when Luc's sitting in front of the house, Clarissa comes out and sits with him. He is trying to nibble his breakfast so he can give most of it to Sasha. She's growing, and he has his healing mojo. "Starvation isn't as cool as when I was a teenager trying to be a ballerina back on Earth," Clarissa says, with sympathy. "It's more like a chronic pain, and exhaustion. I can't think straight and I feel like I'm constantly getting sick. It just sucks."

"Starvation was pretty widespread back on Earth, too," Luc says. "It's just that here, there's no class of people who aren't starving. It's more egalitarian."

"God, this colony is such a clusterfuck." Clarissa kicks the white dirt. "We all had jobs, most of which turned out to be irrelevant. I was supposed to be the marine biologist. We've barely studied the ocean here. We cannibalized the diving equipment early on and we haven't been able to catch any marine life at all. It's a joke. So now I'm Becky Hoffman's assistant instead."

"I bet Hoffman's an okay boss," Luc says. Clarissa just snorts.

There's a long pause, both of them watching the sky turn pale. "Be careful with Sasha," Clarissa says out of nowhere. "That whole time she was working on your pod, she was trying to develop her mechanic skills. But I also caught her looking at your face sometimes, as if she thought you were going to replace her dad or something."

"I'm very comfortable having people project onto me," said Luc.

"Just don't break her heart, okay?" she says. Luc nods, slowly.

At night, down near the dirtiest part of the river, people gather in a three-walled structure and sing, holding hands and swaying on their feet. Luc hears their muffled chanting as he stakes out the drug dealers, hiding behind the Town Hall's partially disassembled ancillary cockpit.

Two dawns in a row, Luc tries to follow the dealers when they leave the town square with their ill-gotten food supply. But both nights, the food disappears. He can't see where they're stashing it. They leave their cozy perch, walk around that ugly sculpture, go through the tight space between the two municipal buildings, then out toward the polluted estuary that runs through Hopetown. By that point, they've ditched their crate of food and they're swinging their unladen arms, eager to crash out. Their route takes them right near the guard watching the food dispensary, but she doesn't worry about people carrying food around, just about them taking food from the communal store. Luc searches every spot the dealers passed on their route. No sign.

Sasha has found him a banged-up helmet, a chest-plate, and a single ancient glove. "When do we make our move?" she asks every few minutes.

Luc keeps thinking about Mao and the sparrows. The pests that turned out to be essential. And then he thinks about the terraforming process.

On the fourth morning since he woke from his long sleep, he gets up and tells Sasha he needs to do something on his own. Then he takes off walking, toward the polar geyser. He walks for hours, until his feet are throbbing and the sunburn overtaxes his healing mojo. He hasn't taken a long walk in the wilderness since Rene was born, and he's forgotten how giant the sky can loom, or how it feels to be miles away from other people. His mind empties as the landscape unfolds, ridge after ridge, and he's weirdly calm. But he's also stewing. He's jaw-grinding mad at Sasha for waking him up in the first place, at Clarissa for telling him not to break Sasha's heart, and at this whole colony for being so perfectly self-destructive. He keeps yelling at people in his head. As he passes the geyser, it seems totally inert, a dry depression, but it could blow without warning. He keeps walking, the sun in his eyes, until he sees the first silhouettes on the horizon. The sun is behind him by the time he gets to the trees.

Up close, the white spikes rise up so far they seem to converge in the sky. Thousands of them, singing with the wind. Zigzag spikes extend from them, and they remind him of a power-staff Palm Strike experimented with wielding for a few months. Luc hasn't felt anything like joy since he lost Rene, but he feels an unaccustomed thrill of wonder in the middle of all this.

Then he crouches down and opens his bag of equipment. Time to get to work. He grabs a soil sample and adds nanosensors to it.

The sun's almost gone and two moons are taunting him, and he still can't make sense of how these things live, or what they're doing. They have no roots, no leaves. They fix the soil and make it fertile, that much is clear from his first samples—but they're too far from the colony's current site to farm here without relocating everyone. Which could actually be impossible, given that the colony only has a few small ATVs, and the exertion of moving would kill most of the colonists even quicker.

But if Luc could figure out what these things are, and how they live . . . He takes samples of their "bark," he digs around them, he makes scans. He has a grinding headache, but he keeps working.

It's almost a relief when Luc hears a loud crack and feels a gouging pain in his chest, and looks down to realize he's been shot. He keels over, painting the white dust crimson. His chest is spurting blood like that geyser. He feels everything going black for a moment.

A moment later, he hears three sets of footsteps, feels their heavy tread as they stand around him. "We'll bury him out here," one woman says. "They'll never know."

"They better not find out," a man says. "They still think this clown can feed the starving masses."

"We had no choice," a second man responds. "He was getting too close to the truth."

The man who spoke last kicks Luc's body. And Luc grabs his foot with both hands and twists, snapping the man's ankle. As Luc rises, he flings the first man at the second, and they both fall in a tangle. The woman is the one with the gun, and she's raising it to aim at his head. He knocks it out of her grasp.

Fighting in high gravity is everything Luc feared. He keeps misjudging his swings and overbalancing. And then just as he finally connects with the second guy's neck, he remembers to pull his punch. His whole fighting style is adapted to a world of paramedics and ambulances. But even a fairly minor injury could wind up being fatal this far from any doctors, and he has no idea how bad sepsis can be here with the local bacteria. So he can't afford to hurt these people too much, even as they're trying to kill him. They take turns kicking him and lashing him with their fists, with each blow landing harder than it would on Earth. Luc's head rings, and it dawns on him that he's on a pretty good trajectory to lose this fight.

The one bright spot is they've lost their only gun somewhere down in the billowing dirt. He finds it first, with his foot, and he steps down on it until he hears metal splinter. After that, he staggers out of the way of the larger man's roundhouse and grabs him, bringing his head and the woman's together with as much gentleness as he can manage. They fall on either side of him. The last man, the one whose ankle he broke, cowers as Luc grabs his stubbly throat.

Time to put on the best Palm Strike voice. Sounds throatier in the high-nitrogen air. "Where is Dark Shard?" he bellows. "Who sabotaged my cryo-unit?"

"I don't know." The scrawny man weeps. "What are you talking about? I don't even understand." Broken Ankle is staining his pants, and Luc believes he has no idea what Luc is asking. At least Broken Ankle gives up the location of the lab where the drugs are manufactured: the basement of a red house upriver from the town where the water isn't too polluted.

Luc lets Broken Ankle fall next to his friends, then notices that the "tree" he was examining now has a hole in it, thanks to the bullet that went through Luc's chest. And he catches a glimpse of something dark in motion. A lot of somethings, in fact.

Luc puts a swab inside the hole, and pulls out a number of tiny mites, the biggest of them no more than a centimeter wide. They're bright red with yellow stripes, and they have long proboscises and a dozen crooked legs each. If you happened to notice them, you'd think they were akin to termites. They're not, though. They do eat the "trees" from the inside, but they also consume the surrounding soil and detoxify it, releasing nutrients in a form that the tree can use. Symbiosis. He puts one of the mites into a soil sample he collected earlier, from the barren fields near the colony, and dumps them into a continuous monitor tube. Pretty soon, the soil shows up as fertile.

Luc analyzes a few of these mites using every test he can think of, then on a hunch he bends over Broken Ankle's face with his swab full of bugs. "Open up," he growls. Broken Ankle tries to clamp his mouth shut, but Luc threatens to smack him again, so he opens up and takes his medicine. And seems to suffer no ill effects, at least not during the time it takes Luc to haul him back to the thugs' vehicle, an all-terrain buggy parked on a nearby rise, and drive him back to the colony.

"That's the nicest thing I've ever force-fed to someone like you,"

Luc tells Broken Ankle, who has wiry gray hair, freckles and a habitual look of terror and alarm. Habitual the whole time Luc has known him, at least. Broken Ankle tells Luc again where they make the drugs, but not where they put the food they collect from the addicts.

Luc leaves Broken Ankle in a ditch within crawling distance of Hopetown, then he goes back to Sasha's house. When he gets there, there's no sign of her anywhere. Clarissa is sleeping in a chair near the door, but she wakes up when Luc comes in. "Where's Sasha?" Clarissa asks, before Luc can ask her the same thing. "I thought she must have gone off with you."

"No," Luc says. "I've been gone all day, and half the night."

Luc searches the house and its surroundings for any sign of Sasha, convinced that the same assholes who tried to kill him must have sent someone to take care of her. He feels the familiar jagged rock in his stomach. If they harm her, he will forget his earlier mercy; he will rain permanent injury down on them.

Just as Luc is about to run back to interrogate Broken Ankle one more time, Clarissa notices her oceanographer kit is gone, including the binoculars and the special shoes that keep you from getting yanked away by the dangerous waves. "She's gone to the beach," Clarissa says, as if this is something Sasha does a lot. Go to the beach, in the middle of the night. "It's where her father is," Clarissa adds. She shrugs and shakes her head when Luc asks if she wants to come along.

Sure enough, Sasha is sitting on a giant rock, dangling her giant shoes in the froth kicked up by the giant waves. Luc comes and sits beside her, but he doesn't say anything.

"My dad went on one of those expeditions to the northern jungle," Sasha says, staring at the rough surf. "He hated hot weather. We buried his body right over there." She points at a rockpile that's half underwater.

"I was worried about you," Luc says.

"I thought you had decided to ditch us," Sasha said. "Or something happened to you. You just took off, without any explanation. I figured we'd seen the last of you."

"I'm not used to having to explain myself to anyone." The moons lace the angry water with silver lines. The air is brine-scented. "I had to do something on my own. And I'm not sure you want to be around for what I'm going to do next, either."

She turns and looks at him. "Why's that?"

"I just . . . You know all of these people, right? You grew up with them. This is a small town, I keep forgetting how small. I just hurt some people and I'm about to hurt some more people. I figure that could be hard for you to watch."

"I want to watch." She looks fierce. "I want to help. My dad died for this place."

"Okay. Did you find me a second glove?"

"Yeah," she says. "I have a complete outfit, in a crate under my bed. It's even sort of black, sort of."

"Okay. One more question," Luc says. "Do you know anything about setting explosives?"

She shakes her head.

"Would you like to learn?"

Sasha nods, slowly.

10.

WHO WAS DARK SHARD? Was Dark Shard even a person? Did different people take turns wearing that costume? Luc spent all this time thinking of Dark Shard as his nemesis, but he knew nothing about him. Luc is slowly letting go of the idea that Dark Shard might have made the trip to Newfoundland, because the more he sees of the local drug dealers, the less they resemble Dark Shard's crew. He's never going to get perfect closure, no matter what happens. This isn't even about him.

Somehow, realizing this makes Luc feel lighter, even as his improvised Palm Strike uniform is weighing him down. He has a tough time conjuring the menace of Palm Strike with a tween girl on his heels chattering loudly about righting the colony's wrongs.

"Listen," Palm Strike tells Sasha. "When we get to the drug lab, I'm going to need you to hang back, okay? You to see what happens next, that's fine—but don't get in harm's way. I can't be hurt, not really, but you can."

"I'm going to get hurt, one way or the other, if we don't fix this. I chose to come along and help. We're in this together."

"Yeah. Just, I don't know, be careful. Your mom would kill me."

Upriver from town, where the water is still relatively clean, a red building houses an industrial laundry facility. A dozen people with guns and machetes are guarding it in the middle of the night.

Palm Strike signals for Sasha to take cover, and uses the river to mask his footsteps, sloshing only slightly as he wades upstream. Then he climbs a jagged rock, leaps, and catches the edge of the building's roof with one hand. Moments later, he drops off the other side and lands on top of the man with the biggest gun. After that, it's one big knife fight in close quarters, with Palm Strike using the high gravity to his advantage for a change, staying low and letting his opponents overbalance. He brings his forearm down onto one man's neck, while headbutting the woman who's trying to choke him. Gently. No life-threatening injuries. He executes one move straight out of Rene's high-gravity dance routine, but there's no time to dwell on the past.

In the midst of the fracas, Palm Strike keeps moving, heading for the door they were guarding, which leads to a basement.

In the basement, there's a giant vat of ochre sludge, surrounded by people wearing masks and smocks. They're all shooting at him. He's finally starting to like this planet.

11.

Becky Hoffman is still asleep when Palm Strike comes through her bedroom window. The tableau is so reminiscent of Dark Shard visiting Luc's bedroom that he has to shudder. He gets out of the way long enough to let Sasha slip in behind him. Hoffman sits up in bed and stifles a gasp when she sees his dark shape looming over her bed. "Deveaux?" she says. "What the hell are you—"

"I solved the food problem," he growls. "There are billions of tiny mites that live in the soil around those trees, the ones you destroyed with your terraforming procedures. They eliminate the toxins and acidity from the soil. They'll have to be reintroduced to your growing areas, which will be a slow painful process. In the mean time, though, the bugs themselves are high in protein, renewable, and easy to transport."

"That's great news." She blinks. "Why didn't you just come to my office in a few hours to tell me?"

"Because three people tried to kill me tonight. I couldn't figure out what secret was so important they'd be willing to kill to protect it. Everybody knew they were trading drugs for food, so that couldn't be it. And meanwhile, I still couldn't work out where they were putting the food they collected from the addicts. Until I finally realized: there was only one place on the drug dealers' route at the end of the night that they could be leaving the food. The colony's food dispensary. Where it came from in the first place. And that led me to you."

"It's a perfect system." Misery displaces Hoffman's last traces of sleepiness. "We hand out the same food rations, over and over."

"That's insane," Sasha says, from the foot of Hoffman's bed, where she's standing. Hoffman startles, noticing the girl for the first time.

"We would have run out of food by now," Becky Hoffman says to Luc. "We would all have starved."

"Don't explain to me," Palm Strike snarls. "Explain to *her*." He jerks a gloved hand in Sasha's direction. "She's one of your people. She was born here. This colony is all she's ever known. You have to explain to her."

"You're too young to understand," Hoffman pleads with Sasha. "We—I—had to make impossible choices. There wasn't enough food. And it was a mercy. The people who use our drug don't feel any hunger pains, and they don't even notice their bodies shutting down. It gives people like you and Clarissa, good people, a chance to survive."

Sasha stares at the colony's leader, her mom's boss, with tears streaming down her face. Luc has to remind himself she wanted to see this. "I don't . . ." she gropes for an unaccustomed formality. "I don't recognize your authority any longer."

"I didn't set up the drug operation," Becky Hoffman says. She's sweating, and inching her hand toward something under her pillow. A silent alarm? Her guards are already taken care of. "I found out about it. I told them they could work for me, or be executed. I turned it into a way to save the colony. This was the only way to ration the food that wouldn't lead to riots."

Becky Hoffman makes her move, pulling out a power-welder of the sort that you'd use to repair hull damage on a starship in flight. It's the size and shape of a big fork, like you'd use on a pot roast. At close range, it would tear a hole in Palm Strike that even his healing mojo couldn't begin to fix. He's already on her, trying to pin her wrist, but she slips under his guard. She brings the power welder up and activates it, bringing it within a few centimeters of Palm Strike's chest.

"Now," he tells Sasha.

Sasha squeezes the remote she rigged up, and an explosion in the distance rattles the survival module so violently the emergency impact alarms go off, like a dozen electronic goats bleating. Hoffman's grip loosens on the power-welder long enough for Palm Strike to knock it out of her grasp.

Palm Strike looks into Hoffman's tear-soaked face and unleashes The Voice. "That was your drug lab. Next time, it'll be your office. Your days of choosing who gets to live are over. You are going to help me fix this mess." And then Palm Strike gestures for Sasha to go back out the window they came in. He takes the power-welder with him.

12.

LUC DIGS until his arms are throbbing, and he's waist deep in the hard, unyielding earth. Probably deep enough—he doesn't want to hit one of those underground hot springs. Then he clambers back out, and tosses the helmet, safety vest, gloves and leggings into the hole. It's not like burying the actual Palm Strike costume, but close enough. And if he needs safety gear later, he'll know where some's buried.

"Do you want to say some words?" Sasha asks. She's hit a growth spurt, and her wrists and ankles are miles long. Even in the higher gravity, you get human beanpoles. Amazing.

"Don't be stupid," Luc grunts.

"We are gathered here today to remember Palm Strike," Sasha intones.

"Cut it out," Luc says. "Seriously."

"He was a good man, even though we never knew who he really was. Some said he was a sea slug that oozed inside some old safety gear and pretended to be a man. But he fought for justice."

Luc tunes out her terrible funeral oration, starts filling in the hole. He pauses just long enough to turn and look out at the farmland, where they've managed to transplant a handful of the "trees" from the other side of the geyser, and a few acres of sorghum are being planted. Too close together. You'll want at least a couple feet between plants, or the mites will shred the roots. He'll need to talk to McGregor about that. He's almost done filling the hole, and Sasha is still nattering.

"—and he dedicated himself to helping people, unless they had really gross teeth or bad breath, in which case they were on their own."

Luc slings the shovel over his shoulder, and wrestles with the temptation to tell her to shut the hell up for once. Instead, he just shrugs and says, "I knew this was a bad idea."

The sun is going down. The parade of moons begins. Luc turns and walks back the way they came. Sasha doesn't quit blabbing the whole way back to the colony, which is still filled with the susurration of a thousand people moaning in the grasp of drug withdrawal, like souls crawling out of hell. Part of Luc feels compassion at the sound, but another part of him finds the din weirdly comforting. It sounds like home.

BROOD

★

by Stephen Gaskell

Growing up on Mars, Lena had heard tales of the Slicers—augmented soldier, more machine than human, left over from the Fringe Wars. She'd thought them boogeymen made up by parents to frighten willful children into obedience. Now, she knew different.

LENA HAD TO HAND IT to her brother. He didn't shy away from the system's most inhospitable places. She'd used to think he was testing her, testing to see how far she would go to forge a bond with him, but now, twenty-seven years after she'd become his little sister, she wasn't so sure. Maybe he did want to be alone, and she should just stop trying. She could certainly do without his so-called *charm*.

They'd lost contact with his research team hours ago. They'd swept past the same pitted plains, the same mountainous ridge of volcanoes, the same abandoned derricks, four times in their low-slung orbit. He'd known something was up, but all she'd got out of him was a dismissive "You can't land yet" before the link had turned to white noise.

"I say we set down." Nik Magyar, the Miura-Sagan Prize-winning journalist, spun head-over-heels, bored out of his mind.

Lena sighed.

She wasn't cut out for chaperoning. She didn't know how much longer she could hold him off. Corporate-sponsored gigs like this weren't his usual bag. This was a man who was used to working alone, getting his own way—much like her brother, Artem.

"I said 'I say we set down.'"

"I heard you. And *you* heard my brother. We're not—"

"They might be in trouble."

Possible, but unlikely. More likely a fried RF relay or EM interference had crippled the comms. She had to be careful. Obtaining the license for the experimental trial had taken the better part of a year of legal wrangling with the Astronautical Control Agency, the United Interplanetary Space Authority, the Biotech Ethics Committee, and the rest. It might never be granted again. Artem—not to mention the Genotech board—would be mighty pissed if rockstar writer Nik Magyar saw something he shouldn't. They wanted a PR coup, not a PR disaster. "We wait."

"Do you do *everything* he tells you?"

His question needled her. "I trust him."

Nik shrugged. *If you say so.*

Lena liked that even less. "I'll tell you what. We're not landing, but maybe we can take a closer look."

Nik smiled. "Now we're getting somewhere."

Ancient lava flows coated the crust in a glittering mineral of deep red hue. Sea-green gashes laced the ochre fields where shallow impacts had exposed the olivine mantle. In places, meadows of purple grass clung to the stone. It was a form of needlegrass geneered from archea microorganisms, and one of Artem's greatest triumphs. It survived solely on solar energy and silicates, a marvel of resilience—and a steady source of food for the harvesters.

"There," Lena whispered, spying one of the giant insects.

Nik studied the lone forager, rapt. "Surreal."

"On Mars their size would cripple them."

Nik shook his head, disbelieving. "How do they survive?"

"Mucus."

"Mucus?"

"Their bodies are coated in the stuff. Traps enough air and warmth for them to survive outside for a time."

Lena explained how after Vesta's precious ores had been excavated, cleaned, and brought to the surface, a specialized flinger caste would toss it into space. Through reference to the star field—and this was another stroke of genius on her brother's part—the flingers could be trained to send the ore through solar windows like the Kirkwood Gap, ensuring their capture at the Lagrange points or in Earth's or Mars' gravitational wells. From there, orbital mining scoops would collect the ores. "This is going to be revolutionary."

Twenty years ago they'd lost their father in a drilling accident on Ceres. Extraction tech hadn't fundamentally changed since the pre-space era, and Artem dreamed of dragging the industry into the rwenty-second century, breaking the corps' monopoly of medieval practices.

"Now we definitely have to land," Nik said.

Lena rattled the small aerosol can of pheromone. "You know, this stuff hasn't been tested yet."

The chemical had been manufactured in the Genotech labs from data transmitted back by the Vesta team. A fine spray over their suits would identify Lena and Nik as members of the insect colony, and allow them to wander unchallenged—that was the theory, anyhow.

"Nik," Lena gasped. "Look."

On the holo an entourage of smaller insects swarmed around one of the colossal flingers. Lena's mouth went dry. The smaller insects weren't cleaning the flinger as they should've been. They were *attacking* it. She watched on, couldn't help herself as they slashed and tore at the behemoth, gouging its eyes, puncturing its carapace. It fought back, but its immense size hindered its attacks on its small, nimble foes. Straw-yellow ichor spilled from its wounds, marking the rocks.

"You okay?" Nik asked.

She shook her head. "I'm afraid for Artem, for the others."

"Shit, you don't think—"

"I don't know!" Lena imagined the insects clashing in the dark, musty tunnels of the nest. It'd be no place for a person, pheromoned or not. Stupidly, she felt guilty too. She'd been angry when they'd last spoken, lived up to the childish image he had of her.

"Lena—"

"What?"

"Easy there. I was—"

"*Easy there?* My brother's down there, not a fucking story!" She raked her hands into her hair, pulled hard. "I'm sorry."

They stared at one another, the silence festering. Landing would be suicidal. Backup was weeks away. They were both about to speak, when the navigation holo blinked to life. A compact object tore into the heavens not twenty klicks away. Lena neuralled the holo, began instructing it for an object composition analysis.

"Don't bother," Nik said. "I'd recognize that trail signature anywhere." He spun towards the vacsuit lockers. "That was a rescue flare."

The survivor trekked across a crystal plain, gunmetal vacsuit contrasting with the prismatic red stone. He—Lena assumed it was a he from the survivor's languid bearing—waved. His lack of urgency unnerved Lena. She tried hailing him on the close-range frequency, but only got static.

"Funny," she said, speaking into her helmet's mic, "radio's off."

Like Lena, Nik had put on his vacsuit. He stood by the entry hatch, impatient, eyes glued to a small holo that relayed a grainy feed of the survivor. "Maybe he can sign?"

Lena didn't appreciate the joke. "I just want to know who it is."

"So do I. And before they're made into very modern art."

They set down on a small plateau, not two hundred meters from the survivor. "Hold tight," Lena said.

The hatch groaned open. Lena felt a chill enveloping her, the buzz of her thermal sleeve responding. She didn't like the sensation, didn't like the situation, either. "Off and on, Nik. No dallying." She listened to herself inhale, exhale, the noises amplified by the helmet. "Nik? You get that?"

Nik hunkered down, staring out the hatch. "I got it," he said, distractedly.

"And watch your step, you'll be practically weightless."

She wondered who it would be—maybe Carlson, or Petronis, or perhaps it was Miera, the short, tough Brazilian. She didn't dare imagine that it was Artem—

"Get us out of here!" Nik's footsteps thrummed through the starsloop's metalloceramic skeleton. He jammed himself into the co-pilot's seat. "Now!"

Lena blinked, confused. Survivors need rescuing.

Nik didn't wait a second time, leaning across Lena and wrenching her command field into his lap. His fingers rippled through the light. The starsloop lurched upwards pressing Lena down hard.

"What is it?" she stuttered.

Nik ignored her, slammed his right hand forward. The starsloop responded likewise, plowing forward, engines screeching. Lena's head cracked against the headrest with a dull thump. Pain bloomed. The external cam was still slaved on the survivor, and in a dozy slo-mo she watched the man begin to raise his arm.

Poor soul, she thought.

Except what she'd thought was a last desperate plea *wasn't*. A pulse of earth-sky blue flashed across the vacuum, followed by a tremendous crash. They went into a terrifying spin, the whole craft churning and whining and shaking, while everything blurred. Nik shouted something, but his words were lost as his teeth chattered and the warning sirens blared. She tasted blood on her tongue.

The low gravity prolonged their descent into a long drawn-out affair, putting klicks between themselves and their attacker. Lena's life didn't so much flash as amble before her eyes.

Then, with a thunderous rumble, the ground reared up and swallowed them.

She woke dazed and bruised in darkness.

Down was sideways and up was somewhere else. Her arm felt sore, trapped. With a determined effort she cracked it free. She waved the other arm, carved out some space in front of her, and neuralled on her shoulder-mounted torch. Shockfoam, white and crispy like meringue, had saved her life. She kicked her legs, amazed they were still willing and able, broke the foam. Suit vitals on the inner arm indicated that its integrity had held, but comms, meds, and data were all shot. A red light on the sleeve blinked every few seconds; air supplies were low but not critical. She must've been out for the better part of an hour. No sign of fear. Perhaps she was still in shock. Whatever, at least she could think straight.

She breathed calmly, excavated Nik from his foam crypt. His body was doubled up, hanging. She pressed her helmet against his, her busted comms meaning he wouldn't hear a peep without direct contact. "Nik! Wake up!"

He groaned, slowly came round.

"Check your vitals."

He gazed at his arm then gave her a groggy thumbs up.

The starsloop had corkscrewed in the crash. Getting out was no
picnic. After swinging and grappling and climbing, they stood on the
starsloop hull surveying the carnage. Thank Sol we hadn't closed the
hatch before we were hit, Lena thought. The starsloop was deader than
Mercury now, even the emergency hydraulics were busted good. Nik
pointed to the rough track where it had skidded to rest.

S-'s that way, he mouthed.

"What?"

He loomed close, cracked their helmets together harder than he
intended. "I said, the slicer's that way." His voice sounded hollow,
distant.

The slicer? She'd get the story later. Right now they had to get
inside, avoid asphyxiation. "Let's head away from him."

"Where's the nest entrance?"

Good question. The vacsuits couldn't help them, their data cores
corrupt or broken. Lena scanned the dead horizon. Nothing. Nothing
except the odd flutter of motion. Insects. And insects meant access—

The pheromone! "Do you have the aerosol?"

Nik cursed, then peered down into the dim interior of the
starsloop. He clambered inside, moments later hoisting up a couple of
compact harpoon guns and a couple pairs of Hi-Gain IR goggles. As
Lena clutched the second gun her eyes wandered back in the direction
of their arrival.

Something glinted in the sunlight, far off.

The slicer? She went horizontal, pressed herself against the
starsloop shell, and motioned the danger to Nik. He hauled himself
out, touched helmets. "If you can see him, he can see you. We go. Now."

"Where's the aerosol?"

"Lost." He grabbed one of the guns, stuffed the goggles into a pouch
on his vacsuit. "Come on."

Lena picked up the other gun, clasped the barrel of the harpoon
gun tight, glad to feel its heft. Then, crouching, they scampered down
the curved belly of the starsloop and onto the asteroid. The stone was
cold and hard. Dread assailed her. This was supposed to be a
cakewalk—babysit a journo, collect some hard samples, go home.

She slapped her helmet as she ran. *Stop it.*

Nik was a few paces ahead, his steps controlled but fast, as if he was
running on the spot. The microgravity was a nightmare, and she tried

to emulate his action, all the while keeping her eyes peeled for outcroppings or loose rocks. And then they needed to find an insect—

The whole ground shook. She nearly tumbled.

Nik turned, pointed into the sky. She twisted, watched a piece of debris pirouette between the stars and crash mere meters away. Burnt and mangled as it was, she still recognized it as the remains of the landing ramp. Beyond it the starsloop was a blackened smoldering thing.

Nik gestured with his head. *Come on.*

She nodded, tried to ignore her hammering heart. She pointed at a dead insect ahead and to the right, not two hundred paces away. They moved fast, and not long after, wheezing hard, Lena pulled a hunting knife from her shin pocket. Hand shaking, she crouched down and began examining the underside of the insect's head with the tip of the blade. A thin film coated its exoskeleton.

There.

The gland was easily visible beneath the insect's leathery skin, a thick rope of a vessel. She beckoned Nik over, motioned for him to cup his hands. He did, and she sliced through the gland. Hot spurts of fluid pooled in his makeshift bowl, dripped between his fingers. He threw the liquid over himself and rubbed it into the folds of his vacsuit. Lena did likewise with the ebbing flow.

It felt like a pathetic shield against the insects.

She shook away the thought, found herself listening to the quickened beep of her sleeve. Oxygen supply was getting low.

Not waiting to speak, they hiked up a gentle rise. A vast expanse of the magenta needlegrass stretched across the shallow valley beyond. Foraging insects toiled in the field, coming and going from a fissure in the cliff on the far side. Hundreds of kilometers of nest tunnels, not to mention the team research station, lay within.

Lena nodded. *Onwards.*

An insect approached as they slid down loose rock. Lena tried not to hesitate, tried not to quicken her breathing, but she couldn't help it. She wanted to run, but she held firm as the insect loomed close. Feelers roved over her, analyzed her chemical signature. A bulbous head, less than a foot away, rocked from side to side, while its sharp jaws flexed in slow pulses. She hadn't felt so uncomfortable since she'd been subjected to Artem's withering gaze after she'd flunked her Highers all those years back.

Eventually, satisfied, the insect moved on.

They headed for the fissure. At the thick spongy membrane—five paces wide and twice as tall—that sealed the entrance to the nest, Nik turned and shrugged. *Open sesame?* he mouthed.

Lena placed her hand, palm flat, against the membrane. The organic material was semi-translucent, but the multitude of layers made the whole thing opaque, like staring into deep water. She pulled her hand away, gelatinous tendrils caught between her fingers. As she studied the strands, marveling at the ingenuity of the system, motion within the membrane drew her eye.

Dark forms shifted, grew.

Lena bundled into Nik, moving both of them out of the way.

Two legs came first, then the antennae, then the head. Remarkably little of the material adhered to the insect as it passed. The membrane wobbled, then stilled.

"Amazing," Lena whispered. As she said the word, splinters of rock exploded from the cliff, rained over them. She glanced back, watched the figure descending on the far slope. It fired off a few more pulses, killing any approaching insects in a cloud of gore and dust.

Nik untangled himself from Lena's grasp. He took a few steps back, rocked on his heels, and sprinted forward, harpoon at his hip like an infantry charge. Lena neuralled her torch on, swept it up and down where he'd entered.

No evidence of his passage remained.

She took a few paces backwards and charged. The membrane was deeper than she'd imagined and she found herself trapped as if a fly in amber. Her breaths came in shallow gasps as she struggled. The vacsuit beeped faster than her heart. The pain in her chest worsened. Ahead, in the attenuated light of her torch, his outline fractured and morphed by the membrane, she thought she could see Nik moving freely.

His form got bigger, before his harpoon gun speared into the area to her right. She flexed her fingers, slowly moving her arm until she could clasp the end of the barrel. She tugged as best she could to indicate she had purchase, then gripped tighter.

Three heaves later, chest burning, arm feeling like it'd been wrenched from its socket, she was inside.

Save for the lances of light emanating from their shoulder-mounted torches, the interior of the nest was pitch black. Lena swept her beam down the passage, fighting a growing sense of claustrophobia. The pockmarked walls looked ancient and alien. Occasional motion blurred the edge of her vision. Part of her wanted to take her chances with the slicer. *What would Artem do?*

She drew the light back to Nik, who blocked the beam with his hand. She dipped the light. He gestured with his hands. *Remove the helmets?*

She nodded. As Nik lifted off his helmet, Lena unclasped her own. A faint hiss accompanied the outrushing high-pressurized mix, before she caught her first breath of the nest. The air was warm and thick, rich with an unpleasant yeasty scent. Strange clicks and tapping noises could be heard from distant tunnels. Nik spluttered.

"It's the fungi." Back on Mars, Lena had helped geneer the carbon-dioxide fixer.

She'd been proud. "You'll get used to it."

She slipped on her goggles. The darkness transformed into a web of ochre filaments, the contours of the passage walls clear. Dead insects littered the tunnel. They ran. Despite the low gravity, lifeless carapaces and spindly limbs cracked under their feet. As they made their way deeper, their weight would only lessen from this point. Their passage would be a mixture of scrabbling on all-fours as much as hiking. "That thing outside," Lena shouted, "you've seen it before?"

"Maybe not one and the same." Ahead, beyond the splayed forms, the passage opened up into a bigger chamber. Bright flashes of cadmium orange and sodium yellow slashed across Lena's vision. More insects. "But I've seen others like it—other slicers. It's a remnant of the Fringe Wars."

Fringe Wars. Lunatic factions fighting bitter wars for Europa, Titan, and the rest.

What the hell was it doing here?

Nik seemed to read her mind. "That war made a lot of crazies, a lot of killers," he said, breathing hard. "Deadly, augmented crazies more machine than man. We called them *slicers*. Some of the more sane ones do a steady line as guns for hire."

She recalled the name now. On Mars, children were told that slicers roamed the red plains outside the domes looking for easy kills. It helped keep kids away from the 'locks. First she'd feared them. Later she'd thought them no more real than ghosts. Now she knew different. "You think the mining corps sent it?"

"Makes sense. They've got the funds—and the reasons."

They stumbled into the cavernous chamber, came to a halt. The smell of butchery was almost overwhelming. The place thronged with insects. Some were clearing the fallen—hoisting severed limbs, cutting gasters into more manageable pieces, scampering off with their bloody pillage—while others raced from one side to the other. They paid little heed to the two newest members of their colony.

Nik gagged, his vomit a sickly yellow color in the infra-red. A small worker ate it up. "What *happened* here?" he asked, wiping the back of his hand over his mouth.

"Looks like the colony went to war with itself."

"Why?"

"Starvation? Disease? I don't know." A heavy rumble from the passage they'd left broke Lena's train of thought. The slicer.

"Which way?" Nik asked, beads of perspiration hot on his brow. A dozen passages led off in a myriad directions.

Lena glanced around the chamber, watched a couple of workers carry off their booty through a tunnel high and to the left. They'd be taking the bodies to the garbage pits, close to the fungal gardens—and the source of food for the team. The research station would be nearby. "Up there," she said, pointing.

She didn't wait for a reply.

"Now I feel safe," Nik said, sneering.

They'd torn through the dark riddle of tunnels, descending and climbing when they'd had to, sweating hard, not speaking much. They'd pretended that was to conserve their energy, but the reality was something else: they didn't want to be heard.

The maze-like place was their best ally and worst enemy. The tunnels forked and multiplied so much that there was no chance the slicer could've followed them, but equally, the sense of being lost, of being at the whim of the deranged geometry of the nest, was a nasty, itchy feeling that only got worse with each step.

They'd made it to the research station, though. Lena blinked, dazzled, as she ran into its artificial white light. The yeasty smell was still strong, but here it battled with more familiar aromas: coffee, disinfectant, plastics. Somebody or something had trashed the room, the wall of computing cores smashed, glass crunching underfoot. Lena sifted through the electronic rubble left on the large table that dominated the middle of the room, but anything that wasn't in pieces had been wiped.

"Nothing," she said. No clue as to Artem's or the others' whereabouts. No clue as to how they might escape.

"What now?" Nik's suit, like hers, was in tatters, ripped and useless. He fumbled a packet of flashfeed, scattering the freeze-dried contents over the floor. "Dammit!"

She needed his smarts, not his anxieties. "Why'd you think it came now? Why not two years ago?"

"What?" Nik crouched, ferrying morsels of food into his mouth with his fingers.

"Genotech's been here two years. Why did the corps wait two years before they sent this thing?"

Nik looked up, stopped chewing. "Maybe they never thought this crazy idea would come to anything." He got up, ferreted about. If he got out of this, he'd have one hell of a story to tell. "Or maybe sending the slicer was a last resort after the usual channels failed." He proceeded into an adjoining room—the researchers' dorm by the look of things— and his voice grew quieter. "You know, the bribes, the—"

There was a loud crash from the other room.

"Nik?" She felt her stomach pit.

"Don't come in."

What had he seen? She had to know. If it was Artem—

Nik came out of the dorm, stood in the threshold. He raised his hands in a stopping motion, using his frame to block her view. "They're dead," he said. He grabbed her wrists. "And messed up."

His words only made her more frantic, and she tried to writhe past him. The room smelt rancid. "Let go of me, for dust's sake!"

He didn't.

Lena stopped struggling. "I need to know if it's him." She held his gaze, and finally he relented, flinging her arms down before letting her past. She should've taken a moment to compose herself, but her eyes were drawn to the spectacle like vultures to a carcass.

No surface or fixture had escaped the blood. Misty, ferrous-colored arcs daubed the walls. Congealed slicks caked the bunks. Thick plum-shaded puddles pooled around the bodies. The scene had a surreal, artistic quality—at least until Lena caught a glimpse of a man's face. Despite some decomposition, she recognized him.

It was Carlson, the myrmecology expert.

They were only acquaintances, but she remembered a snatch of conversation they'd shared in the Genotech cafeteria. She retched, tasted bile. She took a deep breath, then moved closer to one of the other bodies that slumped upside-down off a lower bunk. Please don't let it be Artem, she thought, hating herself for it. She twisted her head—

Petronis. Climatology.

Last one. The body was splayed on the floor, face down. She pivoted, careful not to step in the surrounding viscous fluid, and crouched. She steeled herself, then rolled the body. She gasped. The face was bruised and bloody. She tugged free the corpse's arm, spat on the sleeve and scrubbed away the gore.

It was Miera. The team petrologist. Lena and the man used to play shuttle ball together. She stumbled backwards, fighting another wave of nausea.

She turned round, fell into Nik's arms, numb. She squeezed her eyes shut as if she could undo all of this in that simple act. They stood holding one another for a long while, gently swaying. When she opened her eyes, she cried out in shock.

Somebody was standing in the doorway.

It was her brother, Artem.

He placed a finger over his lips, then led them in silence through the wrecked research station and out into the musty passage. They hadn't gone five paces when he pointed to an area high on the tunnel side. He clambered up and disappeared into the wall. Next moment an arm shot out with an open hand. Lena went first, Nik second, and shortly the trio sat in a tiny cubby hole, legs tangled.

Lena pressed the palm of her hand against her brother's face, grateful to feel his warmth, but he swatted it away, angry. She was going to say something, but his glare made her hold her tongue. He nodded at the small hole through which they'd scrambled. Over their breaths, Lena could hear the sounds of the nest—unsettling clicks and burrs— and something else . . . a whirring sound . . . regular . . . *artificial*. It grew louder, and she realized what it was: mechanized servos.

The slicer.

It grew louder still, and Artem indicated for them to hunker down as best they could. Lena's heart was beating so hard, she was sure the slicer must've been able to hear it.

The noise of the servos stopped.

She pictured it mere paces away, gaze combing the walls. After a long moment it moved off. She could still hear it, though. It must've gone into the research station. Her body ached, and she felt a pain where a sharp tuft of rock dug into her side. Her legs went numb. Eventually the slicer came out of the station, strode past them, rock quaking at its every step. When all they'd been able to hear was the sounds of the nest for several minutes, Artem spoke in a low whisper. "You shouldn't have come here."

"We had no choice!" Lena snapped back, immediately regretting her tone.

Nik nodded. "That thing shot us out of the sky."

Artem dropped his head between his knees.

Lena gripped his hand. "The corps sent it, didn't they?"

"Only after I told them where to shove their money." He pulled his head up, met her eyes. "I was stupid, Lena. I thought I could handle them alone."

They sat in silence for a while. "Why are the insects fighting?" Nik asked.

Artem narrowed his eyes, glanced between the pair of them, calculating. "My guess is that that thing brought some kind of phage that sent them into a frenzy."

He pulled a holostick from his coveralls. A complex web of light filled the space between them. "This is a map of the nest." He delved a hand into the holo, and a green path appeared. "And this is your route to safety. The phage hasn't spread to this area yet. There are emergency space-rafts here."

"You're not coming with us?" Lena could hardly believe Artem wanted them to split up already.

Artem clicked off the holostick. "The others might still be alive—"

"Then we'll look for them together."

"No, we won't."

Lena had heard that tone many times over the years. Conversation closed. "Fine."

★ ★ ★

They grabbed essentials from the research station—water, food, meds, power modules—then trekked off in silence, twenty yards apart. Nik took point. It was slow going checking the map all the time. Shallow veins of color—the residue of excavated minerals—marked the sides, drawing the eye away from the dangers underfoot. Every passing insect unnerved Lena. Her knees, elbows, and shoulders became grazed from where they had to get down on all fours and squeeze through choked channels.

Often, Nik disappeared from view as the passages turned hard or pinched tight. At these moments, Lena would up her pace, terrified that he'd be gone by the time she turned the corner, but he was always there, a ghost of hot light in the darkness. Sometimes her mind played tricks on her and she thought she could hear a mechanized whirr. The fact they'd left Artem to fend alone gnawed at her constantly.

Ahead, she noticed Nik had stopped. "I need some chow," he said when she caught up with him. He slung off his pack, and flopped down. Even in the thick yeasty air, she could smell his sweat. He needed a distraction.

A worker approached. Before she lost the nerve she leapt in front of the insect and tapped out a complicated pattern on the side of its head. The bristled carapace felt like coarse sandpaper against her knuckles. She'd learnt the simple stimulus-response action from some researcher's notes she'd read on the journey out, thinking it would've made a nice party trick. The insect twitched, disgorged a clotted clump of regurgitate, and scuttled off. A layer of mucus clung to the food, but underneath it felt doughy in her hands. She tore off a piece, offered it.

"You're shitting me," he said, but he took the food, curious. He sniffed it. "Eughh. After you."

Lena broke off another piece and wolfed it down. It tasted like rich, chewy bread; weird, but not unpleasant. "Beats the slop blocks."

Nik nibbled a corner, devoured the rest. "Not bad."

They ate the remainder in silence, listening to the weird clicks and taps of the nest. A faint and odorous breeze, rich with a yeasty scent, blew past.

Lena said, "I shouldn't have left him."

"He didn't give you any choice."

"It wasn't his choice to make. It was mine. And I left him."

Nik got to his feet. "Stop beating yourself up. He didn't want us with him." He slipped on his pack.

Lena hauled herself up, wondering if she'd ever see her brother again.

Ahead, the passage opened up into a low-ceilinged chamber. An explosive profusion of fungi sprouted wildly from its sides and roof. Delicate swollen saucers, tangled spaghetti-like tubules, and massed bifurcating thickets crowded every surface. A dim mist of exhaled spores charged the air, the moldy smell overwhelming. A couple of workers scurried past, jaws loaded with long shoots of needlegrass.

A fungal garden.

Nik cupped his hand over his mouth and nose, coughing. "Let's stock up and get out."

Lena nodded, slipping off her pack. At the sides of the chamber, where the workers had dumped the needlegrass, other smaller castes worked the organic matter. One type chewed down the grass, then added it to a growing mound of vegetative pap, while another distributed the mulch to the roots of the fungi. She watched one wind its way down a hanging tendril—

Hell.

Near the base of the tendril slumped a human. Her head was shaved, her hands and face filthy, and her body so emaciated her jumpsuit looked like a deflated balloon, but there was no doubting it was a woman.

"Ana?"

The technician lay on one side, barely alive, the rise and fall of her chest slight, her eyes closed in peace. Laser scorch marks streaked her midriff, her flesh blistered and seeping.

Nik joined Lena. "What—"

Ana's eyes opened. She screamed, began trying to scramble away, her body flexing in ugly spasms. The insects in the chamber responded to the shrieks, spiraling around in tight circles. Workers streamed in, alert and ready.

"Ana," Lena said, but it was to no avail, the woman's mind reeling.

Nik crouched down, the aim of his harpoon gun shifting between the chamber's three exits. "Calm her down!"

"Ana!" Lena grabbed the woman's shoulders. Up close, she stank of burnt flesh and decay. "It's me, Lena—from Pavonis Majoris, from Genotech!"

The woman still floundered, but less aggressively.

"You're safe now," Lena said. "No one's going to harm you."

"Lena?" Ana asked in an awestruck tone, as if the name were a foreign word. One side of her face was red raw where it had scraped the ground. Spittle flecked her chin.

"Yes. Lena." She stroked the woman's cheek with the back of her fingers, wiped off the saliva as best she could. She cradled the woman in her lap for a long while, waiting until her breathing calmed before giving her a few mouthfuls of water. "We're going to help you get out of here," Lena said, pulling a med kit from her pack.

She pressed a sterilizing pad against the first wound, making the woman gasp in pain. After the lacerations were cleaned and dressed, Nik tapped Lena on the arm. "Give her this," he said, pushing a slop block into Lena's hand. "She must be sick to death of this fungal crap."

It was a smart move. The block would help distance her from the place. Lena offered the food. "Here. Eat."

Ana snatched the slop block, tore open the wrapper, devoured the bar in three bites. Afterwards, she almost retched it straight back up.

Nik helped the woman to her feet, arm around her shoulder, while Lena swathed her in a creased flash blanket. "For a second there, I thought we'd run across some infected insects."

"Infected?" Ana looked confused.

"Yeah. Infected with the phage-virus from the slicer."

Ana tottered as she glanced around the chamber. "Who told you that?"

"Artem. We were with—"

"Where is he?"

Lena glanced at Nik, her stomach pitting. "He's looking for the others."

Ana wrapped the blanket around herself tighter. "The others are all dead."

Artem had lied. There was no phage virus.

The insects were fighting, Ana explained, because Vesta contained not one, but two, insect colonies. The second had never been planned, but when the researchers had discovered that the original queen was suffering a terminal, degenerative disease—a disease that would one day stop the flow of precious ores dead in its tracks—Artem had argued in favor of a second colony with a tweaked geneline.

The team had been divided.

The second colony would have to be kept secret, since Genotech had only been given license to establish one insect colony, not two. "Semantics," Artem had argued. "We owe it to the drilling crews who risk their lives every day."

Eventually, the dissenters had backed down.

"Everything was working out okay," Ana whispered, "until that thing arrived."

Nik shifted his weight, Ana still leaning on him. "Are you saying the slicer caused the fighting between the colonies?"

"Yes." Ana coughed, brushed away a handful of spores that floated by her head. "The slicer hacked the commsat, eavesdropped on us. It must've realized there were two colonies—and that making them meet would cause chaos."

"And how did it do that?"

Ana laughed bitterly. "It used one of the abandoned drilling rigs to connect the nests." Lena was sure Artem would've appreciated the irony.

Ana went on, eyes on the ground. "It was only me and Artem who weren't torn to pieces during the first wave of attacks. We holed up while the insects fought. Afterwards, as we fled, it found us." She stroked the laser wound on her side. "I couldn't go on. I told Artem to carry on without me." She glanced up, must've seen the unspoken question in Lena's eyes. "My life was saved by my brood."

Brood. The bond between Ana and the insects was strong, familial. The notion unsettled Lena. "My brother isn't looking for Nikerson or Singh—or anyone else, is he?"

Ana shook her head sadly.

Lena bit her lip. "What then?"

Ana met Lena's eyes. "He's hunting the hunter."

They went their separate ways from the fungal garden. Ana and Nik, arms draped over one another, headed for the space-rafts, while Lena headed deeper into the nest.

Before they parted Ana had explained that Artem would've made for the second colony's queen to ambush the slicer. "He knew that thing wouldn't be content until this place is a lifeless rock again," she'd said. "Killing the healthy queen is the only way to be sure that no more ore leaves Vesta."

"I didn't think there were any weapons here."

"There aren't."

She'd decided there and then that she would go back—try and find him before the slicer did, before he threw his life away. Nik had tried to argue her out of it, but a stubborn streak she was all too familiar with made her hold her ground. She'd glanced at the passages out of the gardens. "Which way—?"

"You can't waltz in like the slicer." Ana had leaned close, reeking of sweat and piss. "With the scent of this nest you'd be swarmed."

"I have to—"

"There's another way," Ana had said. "But you must hurry. Listen."

She moved as fast as she dared, harpoon gun in hand, keeping light on her feet. Sometimes she tripped, grazed a knee. Sometimes she stumbled, slammed a shoulder. Scrapes and bruises littered her body.

Nest activity increased as she made for the heart of the original colony, the insects dug in, guarding their dying queen. Workers carried the scars of fighting—broken antennae, missing legs, fluids seeping from cracked carapaces. The air was thick with the smell of acrid blood. Terrifying, alien shrieks echoed from afar. A party of soldiers hightailed past. Lena followed, fighting the urge to flee, the noises growing louder. Fallen insects, reeking fluids seeping from their wounds, clogged the route. Their splayed limbs crunched and cracked underfoot. Some were probably soldiers from the invading colony, but she had to be sure so she carried on.

Rounding a corner, she was nearly pitched into the front line of the fighting. Legs and jaws blurred as the two sides clashed. Gouts of blood sprayed the air, accompanied by awful, spine-chilling wails. The enemy ranks stretched away as far as the eye could see, only the narrow passage preventing the defenders from being overrun.

The original colony wouldn't hold out much longer.

Lena ducked backwards, tripping as she avoided the lunge of an enemy soldier. Instinctively, she raised her harpoon gun to shield herself. The insect's head surged forward. Its jaws clamped around the barrel with a terrible gnash. It drew back for a second attack. And a third.

Saliva dripped onto her cheek, hot and putrid. As she warded off more blows, she imagined Artem laughing at her. *You, little sister? Save me?*

She fired. The bolt ripped through the insect's head, and the monster went limp. She scrambled back and let out a deep breath, then gasped in pain. When she brought her fingers back from her cheek they were dappled in blood, her face sliced wide.

At least she had her enemy insect. With shaking hands, she collected its glandular fluid in a small canister. One spilt drop on herself would see her ripped apart. A few paces away the two colony's insects crashed together like the armies of old, a tremendous din reverberating around the choked tunnel. A scrambling leg knocked her arm, but she held firm. She screwed on the cap, allowed herself a small sigh of relief.

She didn't have much time, though. At the head of the tunnel that led to the queen, a phalanx of an elite caste bristled, barring her way. They didn't attack, but they made it clear she wasn't to pass, raising their forelegs while they nipped at her arms. She wasn't the enemy, but she had no place there.

Ana's words came back to her. *If the entrance to the queen's nest is blocked, look for a tunneller.*

It didn't take long to find one, the tunneller ambling across an intersection, uncertain. It was a strange paddle-limbed beast, its head a mass of sharp grinding jaws and blunt armored acid spouts. Before she could change her mind, Lena grabbed onto one of its chitinous plates and heaved herself up onto its segmented body. *If you could see me now, Artem.*

The tunneler barely acknowledged her presence, carrying on its way. Bobbing up and down, legs rubbing against its prickly exterior, Lena shifted her pack about, pulled out the holostick, and flicked on the map. There was only one path into or out of the queen's chambers—and the nurseries beyond—but some of the surrounding tunnels skirted close. Hanging tight, she waited to where she thought the walls came closest, then tapped out the quick-fire pattern that Ana had shown her on the tunneler's head, careful to avoid its vicious jaws. The monster responded, pitching right and going to work on the rock.

Splinters of mica and basalt ricocheted from the wall-accompanied by a heavy grinding sound. Now and then, the tunneler edged backwards to shoot geysers of acid or paw away the growing mound of debris underfoot. Steam fizzed from the rock face, shone white hot through Lena's goggles.

After it had broken through, Lena rapped out a retreat command, and the tunneler padded away. She stepped through the breach to an overpowering smell of mucus and decay. The chamber was enormous, cathedral-sized, matched by the colossal girth of the colony queen. Its spiracled abdomen bulged, while rounded billows of soft flesh undulated with machine-like churning and gurgling. A slow stream of eggs coated in a thick hormonal paste emerged from an orifice near the rear. Even from this distance Lena could tell the spawn was rotten. Workers inspected the latent, diseased offspring, before carting them off to a nearby graveyard pit. From the entry passage where her way had been barred, she heard shrieks and the clash of battle. The colony was in its death throes, a last stand being made against a new wave of invaders.

Lena hurried onto a nursery chamber off to one side. A few workers tended a depleted collection of larvae, bedding them down on discarded cocoons. Soon the larvae would be plundered by the invading army and taken to *their* nurseries. There they would be chemically instilled with new allegiances. There they would forget their true lineage. Nature's means could be profoundly frightening at times.

Lena stepped to the nearest larva—a rubbery oval, half a man tall—and roughly cut a slit along its top, releasing a putrid stench. She delved her hand inside, coating herself in the nutrient goop, and sought out the rudimentary form. Finding it, she pulled it out with a puckered slurp and cast it away. She tipped the larva over and let the goop sluice out.

A mighty squeal came from the adjoining chamber. Nursery workers rushed past to defend their imperiled queen. Enemy soldiers swarmed over the matriarch's bloated abdomen, stabbing and tearing and biting. Spouts of clotted fluid sprayed from her wounds. She made a half-hearted effort to shrug them off, tossing a few off with a flaccid crunch, but their numbers were too great.

The larva was a hollowed-out shell now. Lena stared at it, heart pounding. *Artem, you sure as hell better show me some gratitude.* She clambered inside, wiping the lubricant over herself as she hunched down into a fetal position. She nearly gagged from the stench, but forced herself to pull the slit closed, leaving only a small gap for air. The last thing she heard before the enemy surged into the nursery was a lurching crash and an awful, otherworldly screech.

In the darkness and decay, she waited.

Soon enough, Lena was hoisted up by an enemy worker. She dared not move, but by tilting her head she was able to catch glimpses of the world outside. Most of the view was obscured by the underside of the worker's head—a thick bristled hide, tapering to its claw-like mandibles—but she also saw the enormous gasters of others ahead. With the constant patter of the insect's legs against the rock, it felt like she was in the middle of a stampede.

Tensed up, it didn't take long before her muscles began to ache. Then burn. Her right arm went dead. She gritted her teeth against the pain, tried to transport her mind somewhere—anywhere—else. She wondered what she'd say to Artem to make him listen. He wasn't easily swayed once he'd made up his mind.

Her bearer slowed up.

Was she there already? The insects moved fast, but it didn't feel like she'd traveled far enough. *Maybe some kind of bottleneck?*

And then she glimpsed it.

Head shaved down to fine stubble. Two whirring, mechanized eyes—hot coals in a cold inhuman face. A muscular arm with a metallic exoskeleton. The slicer. Oh yes, slicer was the right word, no simple mercenary here. This *thing* was an efficient blend of sinew and purpose and engineering. It was heading in the same direction, gaze roving over the passing insects. She prayed it hadn't found Artem yet.

She ducked a little deeper into the cocoon, held her breath. The sound of the slicer's motorized rhythms receded. The stampede settled down into a more ordered march. She was in enemy territory.

She risked a small stretch, releasing the pressure on her arm. She lost track of her bearings, their path a hodgepodge of sharp turns and inclines. Without a decent map—the second colony's nest still largely uncharted—she was terrified that she might never find her way back. She sought landmarks wherever she could: a skein of minerals in a chamber ceiling; the shape of an arch; an unusual rock formation.

If the nest was anything like the first—a chaotic riddle of thousands of passages and hundreds of chambers—it was probably an exercise in futility. She might walk dozens of kilometers and never find her way out. She repeated a mantra to herself, mouthing the words in the darkness. *Artem will know the way. Artem will know the way.*

She tried not to think of the unspoken conditional: *If he's still alive.*

They left her with the rest of the stolen larvae and pupae in a cavernous storage chamber. When she could only hear the background hum of the nest, she heaved herself out of her cocoon. She stripped off her sodden undergarments, lodged the clothes in the pod, and swiftly applied the new colony's pheromone.

A worker at the chamber entrance rushed over. It seemed confused to find her there, but after probing her it turned its attention to a pupa that was nearing maturity. Lena rapped out a pattern on its head. Ana had taught her the action—a command to retrieve fungal pap for the queen. The worker set off. Lena grabbed her pack and jogged after it, grateful that it paused at the chamber entrance to pick up the right trail. She kept her harpoon gun in hand, ready to fire.

Unlike the original colony, the tunnels teemed with activity. She encountered several castes she hadn't seen before: a small, frenetic beast that ferried debris away from tunneling sites; a type with a proboscis-like extrusion sensitive to mineral deposits; and a lumbering insect with a long balloon-like sac on its underbelly. The last was one of the fabled kamikaze caste. An insect loaded up with more toxic acids than Genotech's entire biochemical division. The other nestmates gave it a wide berth. Lena did likewise.

After the worker collected some pap in a nearby garden, it led her off to an almighty chamber. The chatter of several hundred insects and a thousand myriad rumblings filled the cavern, while the smell of moist organics prickled Lena's nose. In contrast to the dying queen, this gargantuan matriarch positively glowed with vitality. The great curving bulk of its abdomen shone, while its flesh beat with powerful pulses. Lena wondered if it had any inkling its colony had won the battle for Vesta.

"Lena!"

Artem. Thank God.

Lena tracked the sound of his voice to one of the side vestibules, where she found him gesturing her over. She went to embrace him, but he grabbed her hard and pulled her down amongst the giant fungi. "What the hell are you doing here?" he spat, keeping his voice low.

Only trying to save your ungrateful ass.

"How did you find me?" His face lit up. "It's Ana, right? She's alive."

His mind worked fast. Too fast, sometimes. Lena nodded, glad to be the bearer of good news.

Artem's smile was short-lived, though. "If you've come to talk me out of this, forget it. And if you've come to give me help, I don't need it."

"Like you didn't need help when the corps came knocking?" It felt good to stand up to him for once. "Look where that got you."

He blinked, shocked.

"I'm not blaming you." She took a deep breath. "You don't have to fix everything on your own, Art."

He bobbed his head up, looked across the chamber towards the entrance. "Were you followed?"

"Shit, Artem, are you listening to me?" Lena punched a saucer-shaped fungus head. "No, I wasn't followed."

"Good, we've still got time then."

"Artem, stop! You got a death wish? For what? Revenge?"

"Revenge? You think this is about revenge?" He gritted his teeth, stared hard at Lena. "Okay, I admit it. I won't be sorry to put this animal down, but that's not it. I'm doing this for all those miners who live short, shitty lives, for those guys who if they don't cop it out in the belt, die of the raddies when they get back home. If she dies,"—he nodded at the monstrous queen—"belt mining stays in the dark ages."

"No, stupid. If she dies, we lose six months' work. If *you* die,"—and here, suddenly, a knot of emotion choked her—"we lose everything."

He examined her face, which she held up, proud. Then he picked up a loose rock, rolled it in his hands, while he stared across the chamber. "She's beautiful, isn't she?"

Lena didn't say anything, just listened to the rhythms of the nest, inhaled the pungent smells of life and death. There was a harsh beauty to this world.

After a while, Artem got to his feet.

They left together.

★ ★ ★

She thought he was leading her to safety.

She thought their fleetness of foot, their silence, their persistence in keeping to minor passages, were tactics to *avoid* the slicer. Any moment she thought they'd emerge from the riddled, evolutionary-honed chaos of the nest and come across the clean engineered lines of the space-rafts.

She thought wrong.

Artem wasn't *avoiding* the slicer, he was *tracking* it. The realization came too late to argue the toss—came when they almost ploughed straight into the back of the monster. It was trudging away from them, crossing a large pit-shaped chamber, the space churning with insects. She imagined they would've met a swift death if it hadn't been for the noise and motion of their nestmates.

Artem ducked down, pulling Lena with him so they were hidden by the monstrous bodies. A din of clicks and burrs and taps echoed off the hard igneous walls, but Lena could still hear the whirring, metronomic stride of the slicer. *Zzzt-klank. Zzzt-klank. Zzzt—*

It stopped.

She would've been furious if she wasn't so shit scared. She slowed her breathing, held herself still. Her legs trembled, muscles exhausted. Artem motioned for the harpoon gun. *Wait*, she wanted to say, but his face was hard and unyielding. She leaned over to pass him the gun, the reflex to obey as natural as blinking. Still the compliant sister, a small part of her whispered, taunting. *Only as a last resort*, she tried to tell him with her own face set stern. It was almost in his hands, when she had an idea. She drew it back from him, delicately twisted the pack off her back, and retrieved the aerosol from inside.

Artem's eyes lit up, understanding. The aerosol held the original colony's scent. If he were forced to fire, dousing the slicer in the scent would give them a fighting chance of escape. She passed him both the gun and the aerosol.

The slicer began moving again—began moving away from them. Lena let her head slump, felt her tension draining. Then she turned to Artem, and watched in horror as he stood up, jammed the aerosol can into the harpoon tip, and took aim—

Stupid, stupid, stupid.

The slicer turned full about, unleashing some type of explosive pulse.

Artem fired.

A tunneler took the full brunt of the pulse—its heavy abdomen flying apart with a terrific crack—but they were still thrown like rag dolls by the blast. The spiked harpoon must've hit the slicer because around it a storm of fighting broke out. The shot didn't have the consequences Artem had intended though. The slicer was like the calm eye of a hurricane, impervious to the carnage that whipped about it, blade fields cutting its opponents to pieces in a carnival of false color. This thing—this cold-hearted killer, this inhuman machine of flesh and blood and metal, this monster of rhymes and nightmares— would kill them.

She couldn't move, could barely breathe for the thought. "Artem," she screamed.

No reply.

Artem wasn't going to save the day. Artem was still down, keeping a low profile, licking his wounds—or worse.

Dazed, she watched the strange caste of insect with the pendulous, bulbous sac amble past. Before she lost her nerve, she clambered onto the bloated insect, gripped its antennae like reins. She wheeled it about to face the slicer, struck a simple pattern on the side of its head. As the insect charged, its enormous sac inflated. Ten yards from the target, she leapt off, landed painfully on a rocky outcrop. She got up just in time to see the immense gland burst, throwing searing, toxic fluids all over the slicer and the pit floor and a few of the fleeing insects and, to her horror, her brother.

"Artem, oh Jesus, Artem."

He hadn't been cowering. He'd been crawling closer, still fighting whatever the odds.

She stumbled to his side, glanced at the wound that slashed across his torso, neck, and around the side of his face. He was alive, but in so much agony that it was a curse as much as a blessing. Nearby, an acidic whorl rose off the seared tissue and corroded metal of what remained of the slicer. The gurgled scream that had greeted the monster's demise still echoed in her mind.

"You did good," Artem croaked, spittle flecking his lips. "You make sure that newsman knows you're a hero."

"Shh, shh."

She used all the elements of her limited med-kit: painkillers, salve strips, gauze pads. Still he cried in pain. She lifted him to lean on her shoulder, felt a sticky warmth against her arm. His pain hurt her deep.

What hurt her more though was his betrayal of her trust.

Their space-raft looped in a high eccentricity—five hundred klicks at furthest, two at closest—orbit around Vesta. Nik had switched on the emergency distress beacon as soon as his and Ana's space-raft had launched, and help was on its way from Pallas. He'd also had the smarts to inform the United Interplanetary Space Authority that he'd sighted outer system pirates—another remnant of the Fringe Wars— in the vicinity. Military vessels, bound by standard protocol, would be vectoring in to secure the local volume. There'd be no more slicers.

The colony was safe.

They were safe.

Lena set Artem up in a loose mesh-cradle, pumped him full of meds. The weightlessness helped him deal with his blistered skin and corroded flesh, but he still moaned in pain. He'd make it though.

"What will you write?" she asked Nik when their space-rafts had line-of-sight comm as they shot close over Vesta's plains.

"What I always do."

Below, Lena spied movement. A flinger stood on its hind legs, antennae twitching at the stars. It circled about, drew back its muscular tail. A whiplike blur later, a glittering speck raced into the heavens. "What's that?"

"The truth."

The truth meant revealing the unlicensed second colony. The truth meant Genotech prosecuted, Artem incarcerated. Even though ore was leaving Vesta again, even though the experiment was a success, with the truth, the corps would sink the technology in a legal mire as dangerous as quicksand. Nobody would touch it. Belt mining would remain trapped in the dark ages.

"What about the bigger picture?"

"The bigger picture? Not my concern. I just write what happened."

"What happened? What happened?" she stuttered. Everything was slipping away. Was it all going to be for nothing? She had to try. "What happened is that my brother saved your fucking life. If he hadn't tracked that monster, if he hadn't killed it, where'd you think you'd be now? I'll tell you where: blasted to slag. All of us would be."

Artem moaned softly.

"He killed it?" Nik asked.

Lena gripped her brother's hand. "Rode one of those suicide bugs straight into its ugly cybernetic side," she lied. "Nearly killed himself for his efforts." Artem's eyes opened wide. Lena pressed her index finger over his lips. "My brother's a hero and you want to write a story that'll see him locked up, see his work abandoned, and see the corps carry on, business as usual, all because you have some misplaced allegiance to a code. Tell me, how many miners' deaths could you live with? Ten? A hundred? A thousand?"

"Not my concern," Nik said again, although this time there was less conviction in his words.

"Ten thousand?"

"Not my concern." Barely a whisper.

"A hundred thousand?"

Vesta receded, plains and prominences merging into a grainy wash. "I'll think about it," he said eventually, but the subtext was clear.

Lena severed the connection. He'd write the story they wanted. There'd be no mention of the second colony. Only his pride stopped him saying as much now. She should've felt happy, but where the feeling should've been there was only hollowness.

"You lied for me," Artem whispered.

"Not for you." Lena peeled off a dressing-salve from her brother's shoulder, inspected the salmon-pink tissue.

The space-raft carried on into the darkness, silent as the vacuum.

STEALING ARTURO

★

by William Ledbetter

In the no man's land of the asteroid belt, free from the laws governing both Earth and Mars, workers on board the space station Arturo *are little more than slave labor. Kept docile with a drug called Canker, generations are born and die without hope of escape. But ice miner Clarke Kooper has a plan—and the engineering know-how to make a break for it.*

I TRIED TO STAY AWAKE and upright as the elevator bucked and jerked its way down the spoke into the Earth-normal gravity of Ring One's sleeping level. The lights flickered as the weight settled over me, pushing my exhaustion deep into every cell. I didn't know how much longer I could take it. If the power failed and left me stuck in the elevator again, I might turn into a raving madman. Would I really ever escape this station? Were the months of covert effort wasted?

Felicia spoke, but her voice was there and not there, a feathery touch that revived memories of her fingers brushing back my hair. "You can do this. I believe in you, but you need sleep. And a shower."

I snorted and hugged her canister to my chest with one hand and scratched my two-day-old beard with the other. She was right. It had been nearly as long since I'd showered or slept. Extended periods working in the hub's microgravity always did this to me, but I had little choice, time was running out.

A hand appeared before the lift door had even opened halfway, grabbed the front of my shirt and yanked me out into the corridor. Since I didn't have my gravity legs yet, I fell directly to my knees. The two Security "officers" laughed, and the one with red hair—whom I had long ago assigned the name Meathead—gave me a little shove with a highly polished boot and I further lost my balance. I had enough warning to at least tuck Felicia's canister against my chest before I toppled over like a crippled old grandpa.

A foot pressed on the back of my head, trying to shove my face into the thick grime that had accumulated in the corner over the decades. Dust and debris were sucked into the air filtration system on low gravity levels, but down here, where the poor people lived, filth collected like it had throughout human history. Bits of plastic and a rusted screw decorated the black gunk only inches from my mouth, but I pushed back and rolled over quickly, causing Meathead to lose his balance and stumble backward.

I fought the centrifugal gravity and struggled to my feet, ready to kill the crisply uniformed bastard. As I braced to head-butt him, before he regained his balance, I heard Felicia's voice in my head.

"Don't be stupid, Clarke. You're only weeks away from your escape. You can't to be arrested now."

She was right, but I had to at least put up a token fight or they'd get suspicious. I gave the two goons a withering glare, tucked Felicia under my arm and tried to push past them. They grabbed my arms and shoved me against a bulkhead.

"Lieutenant Eisenhower sent us to ask about your ice production quota. He thinks you're holding out."

"I don't give a shit what Eisenhower thinks. I don't answer to him. I was hired by the station management."

The goon shoved me again, making my head bang against the wall.

"That's *Lieutenant* Eisenhower. You need to show some respect."

"Lieutenant is a rank that implies either training or experience, and he has neither. He's just the head guard dog and that doesn't demand respect in my book."

The second goon—the one with dark hair and beady eyes—took a swing at me, intending to pin my face between his fist and the bulkhead. I dodged, but not quite fast enough, and his punch glanced hard off of my cheekbone, then scraped my cheek with his wrist comm as it continued into the wall.

He cursed, and punches from both assailants rained down on me in a flurry. I bent low, intending to take a few hits and then try to dart between them, when someone yelled.

"Stop hitting him, you big turds!"

Everyone stopped and turned to see a scruffy young girl in patched clothes standing just behind Meathead. She looked to be around eight or nine, and I recognized her as the girl who lived with her mother two doors down from my cabin.

"Get lost, kid!" the dark-haired guy said and made a half-hearted swipe at her.

She didn't budge, just glared back at the man.

Both officers laughed, but threw no more punches. Instead, in an unexpected snatch, Meathead grabbed Felicia's canister from my grasp.

I straightened abruptly, shoved them both backward and grabbed for her can, but missed.

Meathead hefted it like a school yard bully playing keep away. "I think we'll have to confiscate this."

"No, you won't," I said.

They glanced at each other and grinned. "We already have, Kooper."

I shook my head slowly. "I don't think you understand. If you decide to keep my property, then you'll have to kill me or imprison me. And in either of those cases, you and everyone on this station will die within a couple of weeks after the water runs out. As your boss already mentioned, my production level is way down. We have about a week's worth of water in reserve. My predecessor already picked the local area clean of icy rocks and they're getting tough to find. Without me, you won't find any ice. Nor will you be able to bring a new ice miner in from Mars or Earth quick enough to stave off that rather ugly death. Of course the managers and your boss will probably hoard plenty for themselves, but do you think *you'll* get any?"

Meathead shifted his stance and glanced at his partner.

"And if you let me go, but still keep my property, then I have at my disposal forty-nine mining robots, each with a laser capable of burning right through the hull of this station. I wouldn't have a bit of trouble finding your cabin and I don't even have to hit you with the beam. I'd just wait until you were asleep and open a hole in the hull. Then *pffffttttt,* you'd squirt into vacuum like a long string of goober paste."

The kid laughed and Meathead's face flushed red.

"Or you can give that back to me and we'll pretend this never happened."

"Give it back to him!" the little girl said. "Are you morons trying to get us all killed?"

Meathead's buddy poked him in the arm. "Just give him the damned can and let's go get some grub. Eisenhower didn't tell you to take his stuff anyway."

I smiled and nodded, then winced at the pain in my jaw.

Meathead tossed Felicia's canister in my direction. It tumbled and I did some silly juggling to keep it from hitting the floor. The goons laughed, and by the time I had it tucked it safely under my arm, they were strutting down the corridor with their backs to the girl and me.

I took a deep breath and dabbed at the blood trickling down my cheek.

"You're a dumbass," she said.

I shrugged and slipped past her. "And you have a foul mouth. Go home before you get into trouble."

She followed me. "Me get into trouble? I saved your ass! If I hadn't come along they would have beat you into pudding."

"I guess I do owe you some thanks, but you shouldn't have done that. Those guys wouldn't hesitate to hit a kid."

I palmed the lock plate on my door. It slid open and I nearly dropped Felicia as the kid slipped past me into my dark cabin.

"What the f—" I growled then heard Felicia again.

"Don't yell at her, Clarke."

I took a deep breath and paused just inside the door. "Let's have some lights, Calvin."

The cabin computer turned on the lights and I could see her sitting in my only chair, legs dangling as she examined a power regulator module from one of my mining robots.

"You have an AI!"

"Just a smart computer," I said. "I spliced it into the cabin electronics. I do a lot of stuff like that. Now go home."

"My mom says you're crazy."

I glowered at her. "Does she also say that you're rude?"

The girl laughed. "All the time."

"Look, kid, you can't be in here. I could get in a lot of trouble." The door started to close, but I grabbed it and held it open. "Go home."

"Why would *you* get in trouble?"

"I'm sure your mom has warned you about being alone with strange men."

She reached for a paper book I had laying on the table, then stopped and looked at me with a perplexed expression. "You talk funny. You weren't born on the station?"

"No. I was born on Earth. In Chicago. Now, you really need to leave."

With a slow shake of her head, she crossed her arms and grinned. "You'll have to throw me out and if you do, I'll start screaming that you touched me in the naughty place."

Anger flared and I activated my wrist unit—ready to call security to come remove her—then stopped. Had I really just considered calling Security?

"Calvin? Lock the door open and keep a video record until this kid leaves."

"Understood," Calvin said.

The kid shrugged. "My name is Nora, not kid."

I leaned against the wall next to the door and hoped I hadn't already attracted more attention from Security. The girl twisted her mouth into an odd slant as she looked around again. She had a squarish face and the same dark hair with pale skin that seemed to dominate the station's worker population, but her eyes were bright and inquisitive, which made her stand out from most of the drug addled adults.

"So how old are you? And why does your mother let you run around alone?"

"I'm nine. And my mom has to do double shifts until I'm old enough to work in the factory. Food and space for two she always says."

I nodded, but hadn't ever thought about how people managed to raise kids on the station.

"Mom won't let go to the factory yet, but I used to help out when I got paid for scrubbing air ducts. I used to be small enough to crawl inside, but I think they found a smaller kid."

My stomach tightened and I suddenly felt very ignorant about the people surrounding me.

"Would you like a food bar?"

"Sure," she said, and her face brightened.

I pulled one from my pants pocket and tossed it to her. She opened it and gobbled it down in three bites.

"It's a good thing that security guy is stupid," she said as she chewed.

I blinked at the sudden change of subject. "Why do you say that?"

"Because Mars will be at its closest point in a few weeks. They'd have plenty of time to kill you and get a replacement from Mars."

I couldn't help but laugh. "Holy crap, kid. You're a real piece of work."

"Stop calling me 'kid.' My name's Nora. By the way, you're a terrible liar. Decompression wouldn't squirt that guy through a small hole. His body would just block it. You'd need a big hole."

"I never said a *small* hole, but I think he got the point."

She shrugged and looked at me through squinted eyes. "You need to clean up. When's the last time you changed clothes?"

I looked down to see fresh blood droplets added to the food and sweat stains on my dingy island shirt.

"Sorry. Hey, this has been nice . . . Nora, but it's time for you to go."

She ignored my comment and nodded toward Felicia's canister. "What's in the can that you were ready to kill for?"

My initial reaction was to tell her it was none of her business, but then I decided maybe the truth would shock her into leaving. I stroked the cool black metal canister and then held it up. "This is my wife, Felicia."

The kid blinked then frowned. "Um, right. Is it some kind of computer? Or a game machine?"

"When my wife died, she was cremated and her ashes were sealed in this container."

That got her attention. She had a horrified look on her face and leaned forward on the chair. "Ashes? She wasn't recycled?"

I shook my head. "They . . . sometimes do things differently on Earth and Mars."

"That's kinda creepy," she said.

I shrugged.

"Then why do you talk to it? That's why my mom thinks you're nuts."

"Nora!"

The yell came from just behind my right ear and made me flinch. Nora's mother rushed into the cabin, grabbed her daughter by the arm and pulled her upright. "What are you doing here?"

"Just talking," Nora said, then grinned at me. "He tried to make me leave, but I was having fun. Did you know that his dead wife is in that can?"

"Oh, Nora," the woman said and ran a hand through limp, messy hair that was dark like her daughter's. She also had the same squarish face, but hers had sharp angles from being much too thin. Her eyes were dull with exhaustion and she seemed on the brink of tears.

"I'm so sorry, Mr. . . . ?"

"Clarke Kooper," I said and extended my hand.

She edged past me out the door, dragging the girl with her, and once safely in the hall, turned back and glanced at my bloody cheek and wild hair, half of which had come out of my ponytail during the fight. She took my still-extended hand. "I'm Wendy and I don't think you're crazy. Nora just . . . has a rather vivid imagination."

"She's been quite," I struggled for a word that wouldn't sound rude, "entertaining."

"I'm sure she has," Wendy said with a sigh then turned to Nora. "C'mon, you little monster, let's go eat some dinner."

As I watched them go down the hall I thought about inviting them to eat dinner with me, then reconsidered. I didn't need to form any new attachments. I'd either be gone or dead within a few weeks.

The next day in my hub-based control center, I kicked off from the interface station and floated to the wall hiding my salvation. I resisted the urge to run my hand along the section where the door would appear. On the other side, exposed to the bitter cold asteroid belt, was a four-by-three-meter external equipment blister I'd quietly and secretly converted into an escape pod.

I moved on to the robot launch tube, cycled it and opened the hatch. Burnt smelling air poofed into the cabin as I pulled out the basketball-sized mining drone called a Mining Operations Manager, or MOM. Once I locked it into the fixture on my test bench, I changed its status to inactive then opened the main access cover. I slipped my hand inside and removed the mostly empty nano replicator bladder.

The "mostly empty" designation could get me killed if station security found out. Nano-device manufacture was strictly controlled and each tiny robot made for a MOM had to be loaded into the MOM. But nothing could count the replicators that left the MOM out on an ice ball, the number of times they reproduced or the number that returned with it. This bladder was still a quarter full.

With a series of coded taps against the MOM's inner shell, I directed the remaining replicators into a hidden conduit that allowed them to flow into the empty spaces in the station's hull structure, where they would hide until I needed them.

A loud beep announced the door opening and when I turned the breath caught in my throat. Bernard Eisenhower drifted into the room. He wore his trademark half smile that never reached his eyes. He could be beating a suspect or chatting up a pretty girl and the smile was always the same. I tried to force myself to relax. He probably wore augmentations that helped him read and record fluctuations in body heat, heart rate and eye movements.

"Hello, Clarke. How goes the dowsing? Your magic water stick still working?"

I smiled and pushed my feet into the cleats at my workbench. "Business is slow. But given time, I'm able to find enough ice to keep us going."

He worked his way around the room, looking into every open device, picking up and examining each scroll screen. He nodded repeatedly to himself.

"My boys told me about your little threat yesterday."

"They should leave me alone. I'm just trying to do my job."

"No, you aren't doing your job, Clarke. Instead, you're playing a dangerous game with *Arturo Station*'s water supply. That makes it a Security issue, which is why I sent my men to talk with you in the first place."

Eisenhower might be a bully and abusive with his power, but he wasn't totally stupid. After my first week on *Arturo Station*, when I realized the highly addictive productivity enhancement drug called Canker had been put into my food—and that of nearly every worker on board—I started planning how to get out of the situation. That had been nearly a year ago, and much of the ice I collected had been stored in secret tanks I'd hidden inside the hull, but the official ice I "found" for the station had dropped at a steady rate ever since. Making management and security think we had a limited supply was my only insurance if my escape plot were ever discovered.

"My predecessor used up all the close ice balls. I have to send my bots further and further out. It takes time. Maybe management should move the station to richer hunting grounds or better yet, tighten up their water reclamation system."

"Bullshit, Clarke. There's ice out there close. Our scanners see it."

"In small amounts. It would take twice as long if I tried to mine every little grapefruit-sized nugget out there."

Eisenhower glared at me. "Your replacement is on the way. I'm sure he'll have better luck."

I snorted and shrugged.

"You don't believe that?"

"Hell no. If my replacement were on the way you wouldn't be wasting your time talking to me. My corpsicle would already be tumbling out toward Jupiter."

His smile almost broadened and he started toward the hatch. "Don't push it, Clarke. We have backups you don't know about and we *will* send you spinning to Jupiter if that ice tonnage doesn't come up a lot and very quickly."

I exited at my level and Nora was waiting again, this time just outside the lift. Her face lit up and she started chattering.

"You're really from Earth?"

"Yep."

"I was born here," she said. "Momma too. She was in the first generation born on the station."

"So she's never been off of *Arturo*?"

Nora shook her head as we approached my door. "No. Momma said they'll never let us leave."

Many of the workers would be afraid to leave. Canker was an ugly thing. It was named for the sores that formed around a user's mouth during the long and nasty withdrawal period. It left scars on most and even killed some. *Arturo Station* was just one of dozens that operated outside the Earth and Mars protective zones, so unless those governments had overwhelming evidence these atrocities were going on—something that would get a lot of press attention—then they would ignore the rumors. They had too many of their own problems to go looking for more.

Nora and her mother would likely spend their entire lives as slaves in this illicit bioware factory.

"So why aren't you in school?" I said as I opened my door.

She shrugged. "I've learned everything they have to teach me."

I snorted. "Sure you have. So you're an expert on Mars history, European literature and calculus?"

"They don't teach us that stuff. But I know how to clean bio-vats and assemble crystal matrices."

I just stared at her as she slipped past me and into my cabin. She looked around, then turned back to me.

"I'll clean your cabin for five credits!"

"Huh?"

"Or I can mend clothes? Anything like that. I need to earn some money. Seth has been coming a lot more since I lost my duct cleaning job. I hate Seth."

I scratched my beard. "Sure."

I locked the door open again and started giving her instructions on what to clean. She worked fast, folding clothes, shelving books, separating my trash into the proper recycling bags.

I hated this station and its criminal overlords since I first realized I'd been tricked, but had always kind of blamed myself for my own stupidity in coming. That wasn't the case for these people. They had no choice. They were born on the station and probably didn't even exist in any citizen records outside this place, but were still made to pay for food and a sleeping berth. It wasn't mean or even greedy, it was evil.

"Well?" she said. "What now?"

"That's enough cleaning for now. Calvin? Please transfer fifty credits to Nora's account."

Her eyes widened a bit and she shook her head. "That amount of work wasn't even worth five."

"It was to me."

She bit her lip and stared at me for a second before darting down the hall.

"This is fantastic," Nora said in a whisper.

I could barely see her mouth below the interface goggles, but it was stretched into a wide smile. I glanced down at the scroll screen echoing what she saw. The MOM's work lights swept along one of *Arturo Station*'s four rotation rings, revealing a complex field of conduits, access hatches, antennae and stenciled identification labels.

"Could you really find that jerk's cabin from the outside?" she said, as she tapped and spun the thumb controls on the tele-operation yoke like an expert.

"If I knew his cabin address," I said, then briefly took the controls to zoom the MOM's camera down to read some of the hull identifier text. It read R1S4-43. "These station habitat rings are assembled from hundreds of identical wedge-shaped sections. One for each cabin. So it's just easier to keep the construction identification tags as a cabin address."

"Cool!" she said and took the controls yoke away from me again. "How did you use that camera zoom?"

I showed her and suddenly the view slaved to my scroll screen started zooming all over the station.

"I bet you spy on people all the time!"

"I do not," I said and took the yoke from her again. "And I think this lesson is over."

"Noooo!"

"We can do it again later."

I helped her remove the interface goggles. Her hair floated nearly straight up and she wore a wicked grin.

"You have a great job."

"You didn't think so until I let you drive a robot."

Nora's mother refused to let her come with me at first. After nearly an hour of Nora's begging, her mother finally allowed her to accompany me to my hub control center for the day instead of staying in her cabin alone. I thought she might like to watch me launch and retrieve some robots. She'd been fascinated for a while by the video feeds coming back from some of the MOMs as they shepherded their flock of nano-disassemblers through the process of stripping the rock and minerals away, leaving the remaining ice in strange, twisted, lacy sculptures that were returned to the station by the MOM.

But she eventually got bored with the video feed, and started playing in the microgravity. My control center was really too small of a space for her to be flailing and bumping around, so I had to do something.

"I like having you for a friend," she said and then glanced away as if embarrassed that she said it aloud.

"I like you too," I said and then felt suddenly and horribly guilty again. My makeshift escape pod was finished. Using nothing but nano-scale robots, I'd bypassed critical systems without sounding alarms and had slowly separated the equipment blister from the station hub. The little ship contained a minimalist acceleration sling and enough air and water for the two-week trip to Mars.

So why did I feel so damned guilty? She wasn't my kid, but when my hands started shaking I knew I couldn't leave her here. I started rearranging the computer model of my escape pod, adding a second acceleration sling, trying to find places to attach more tanks. I'd need near twice as much water and air. I'd also need more fuel to get that extra mass to Mars. Food? Should I take more food or let her suffer the same excruciating withdrawal I would?

Felicia's voice echoed in my head, telling me no, that I couldn't take Nora. I looked up at her canister locked in its special mount, but ignored her and kept working.

"What are you doing now?" Nora said from right beside me.

I flinched and closed the scroll screen. "Just some work."

She reached out and touched Felicia's canister. "What was she like?"

I tensed up. I hadn't talked to anyone about Felicia since her death and sure never expected to start with a nine-year-old kid, but as I stared at Nora's open and curious face, I realized I actually did want to talk about her.

"She was very brave and smart. She laughed a lot and loved jokes. And singing. I think she would have liked you."

"You loved her a lot?"

I nodded, the lump in my throat preventing me from saying more.

"And you still talk to her?"

"Yeah," I croaked.

Then she looked at me and squinted. "Does she ever talk back?"

"Sort of," I said. "I can still hear her in my mind sometimes."

"How did she die?"

I swallowed hard. I'd never had to say the truth out loud, in my own words. The helmet-cam video of the incident had told the story back on Phobos, so the was never an investigation. I was reprimanded and reassigned, but never once had to talk about it.

My stomach clenched tight and my pulse raced. I'd always hated the cold vacuum, but after Felicia's death, I went to great extremes to avoid it. Herding robots from a warm, safe workstation had been as close to cold space as I intended to get. Until I formed my escape plan.

I blinked at Nora and took a deep breath.

"We lived on Phobos station. We were both surface equipment technicians. One day while we were outside I started goofing around. I jumped up on a big rock that gave way and rolled out from under me. I knew better. I knew to not step on boulders and still . . . Anyway, the big rock rolled down a slope and on top of Felicia. The gravity was low, but the rock had mass and momentum. It tore her suit and pinned her down. By the time I got the rock off of her and fixed her suit, it was too late."

She touched the canister again.

"It was an accident," she whispered. "But that didn't stop you from feeling it was your fault?"

I nodded. How could a freaking nine-year-old kid understand those kinds of feelings?

Felicia was right. I couldn't take Nora with me. It would be wrong to separate her from her mother, even for her own good. And of course I'd be instantly arrested at Mars for being a child abductor. I'd have to find a way to take them both.

"I think my mom would like you," she said with an impish grin. "I asked her to invite you to our cabin for dinner, but she said that probably wasn't a good idea. It might make Seth mad."

"Is he your dad?"

"I think so, but my mom won't admit it. He spends the night with mom sometimes and she says I have to be nice to him since he's her boss."

I swallowed and felt the panic rising in me again. I had to do something.

When her shift ended, Wendy came to collect Nora.

She hesitated, looking uncomfortable at first, then her gaze hardened. "You sent two payments of fifty credits each to Nora's account. She cleaned for you?"

"Yeah, my cabin and then she cleaned up in here," I said and motioned around my still cluttered work bay.

Nora looked momentarily surprised, then immediately hid it.

"If she wants to come back, I can teach her how to scrub down the robots. They have to be cleaned after every trip out and I hate doing it."

Wendy stared at me, as if trying to read my mind, read my true motivations for being with her daughter.

"There are video recordings of each time she's come to see me. I'll give you access to them."

Then her hard expression collapsed and she looked twice as tired as before. "Sorry, I just . . ."

"No need."

After they left I floated in the middle of my suddenly very quiet and lonely work bay. I had made no friends and had no lovers since arriving on *Arturo Station*. It had made my planning easy. But not now.

I pulled Felicia's canister from its mount and held it to my chest.

"I wasn't really brave," she said. "That was just an act to impress you."

"Shut up. You're the most amazing person I know."

"Knew," she said.

I shrugged. "I miss you."

She didn't answer and I floated around the bay for a long time, holding her and remembering. Finally I bumped against the wall that hid my escape pod and new I had to do something. There are the mistakes of our actions, like my stupidity that killed Felicia, but also mistakes of our inactions.

"How can I do this?" I whispered to the can.

"You already know," she said. "You've already decided."

She was right, as always, and the answer was quite simple.

But the execution would be a cast iron bitch.

I'd done it again. The gradual increase in gravity from nothing to Earth normal felt as if it would crush me and I could barely stay on my feet. I'd worked more than twenty hours getting everything ready and had almost finished, but with just a few small tasks left, I had to stop and sleep. Even with help from Canker, if I continued on this path I would forget something critical and it would all be wasted.

When the lift door opened I was nearly knocked down by a scowling man who actually growled at me before the door closed. I staggered down the corridor to my cabin, glad for once that it was late in the evening shift and Nora hadn't been there to greet me. Before I could even cross the room to my bed, I heard a pounding on the door and the cabin computer announced Nora.

"Damn." I couldn't. Not now. I ignored her and lay down, but the pounding was insistent and the computer eventually informed me that she claimed it was an emergency.

I opened the door and my fatigue instantly vanished. Tears streaked Nora's face and her hands were covered with dried blood. She grabbed my arm and dragged me down the hall.

"You have to help my mom! Seth beat her up. She's hurt bad."

I ran the last few steps to the still open door.

Her mother lay curled into a fetal ball on the bed. Wet bloody towels lay on the floor beside her, but they hadn't stopped any of the bleeding. Her face was still a bloody mess.

I knelt next to her. Fury and frustration pushed me to the edge of yelling, but I made my voice soft. "Wendy? This is Clarke. Can you hear me?"

She groaned and said something I couldn't make out.

"Before you came, she said her stomach hurts and she can't breathe."

My fury turned to fear as I realized that probably meant internal injuries. "Did you call Security?"

"Twice. The first time while he was still hitting her. They still haven't come."

Security officers were supposed to respond immediately to all injuries and provide transport if needed. Bastards were probably trying to protect Seth since he was a manager.

"We're going to have to take her to the Medical Unit ourselves," I said. "But we'll need some help. Stay with her and I'll be right back."

A minute later, with Nora's help, we slid Wendy and her mattress onto the collapsible equipment dolly I had grabbed from my cabin. It wasn't a good fit, but by positioning Wendy's weight over the wheels and letting half of the mattress drag behind, we managed to roll her through the mostly abandoned corridors, halfway around the ring to the Medical Unit.

★ ★ ★

The soft yet insistent chiming from my wrist unit eventually made me open my eyes. At first confused by my surroundings, I then spotted Nora standing next to her mother's regrowth tank and it all came back in a rush. If my alarm was sounding, it meant I had an hour before my automated units went active, and I wasn't ready yet.

I stepped up beside Nora and looked down at her mom. Wendy floated in a tank filled with blue-tinted gel. A tube came from her mouth and tiny blinking monitoring units were attached to her in various locations. She was awake, and even though buried in medical artifacts, already looked much better.

"How is she?"

"The medtechs say she'll be okay, but she'll have to stay here in the tank for a few days."

The letters "TNK YU" appeared on a screen attached to the tank, and I realized Wendy had a small keypad attached to one hand.

I smiled, wishing I could say something cheerful and positive, but the Security officer who came to get statements from Nora and Wendy after we arrived just said they would "talk to" Seth. He was a manager. He was effectively immune to punishment. Of course, if my plan worked, things would get better soon enough, but I had to get to my hub workstation and prepare.

"I'm going to have to go," I said. "I have something important to take care of, but I'll be back later."

I wasn't sure if that last statement was true or not, but I would try.

"PPLS TAK CAR OF NORA."

I stared at the message, wondering how to answer. I couldn't take her. If my crazy attempt at seizing control of the station didn't work, then I'd be in a lot of trouble. I didn't want Nora with me if that happened. I'd assumed Nora would want to stay with her mom.

"Nora, would you rather stay here or come with me?"

She looked at me and screwed up her face. I could tell she didn't know what to do and was on the verge of tears.

"GO," appeared on the screen. "I NED SLEEEP. PLS TAK HER."

I swallowed and nodded. "Okay, kiddo. Let's go. We have a lot to do in the next hour."

Everything was ready, with five minutes left on the clock. I looked up from my screen and saw Nora floating in the corner of my little workshop, quietly spinning a screwdriver in the air before her face. Her expression held not even a flicker of hope.

"Be careful with that screwdriver," I said.

"I'd punch it through Seth's head if I could," she said with enough venom that it made me wince. "I hate him!"

"Things are going to get better," I said.

She glanced at me, then away. "I don't see how. He'll keep beating my mom and Security won't stop him."

"Look at me."

She looked up, a little startled at my tone. I wanted to tell her what was about to happen, but didn't dare risk saying anything that could tip off Eisenhower's watchers.

"This is a dangerous room. If anything unexpected happens, you have to do exactly as I say. Do you understand?"

Her eyes locked on mine and squinted slightly. She knew there was something unusual in my statement.

"Um . . . okay," she said.

I nodded slowly, then picked up Felicia's canister and held it tight as I watched the screen.

While building my escape pod, I'd already learned how to find and bypass control systems without alerting Security, but that had been on a very small scale and in a localized area. So I spent the majority of the previous day interrogating *Arturo Station*'s control and security systems. They had not only the standard triple-redundant, hard-wired arrangement, but also a fourth and fifth version running along the outside skin in armored cable troughs.

Using my unique method of programming that involved combinations of verbal code words, eye movements, keyboard entries and finger taps, I instructed my robotic accomplices to build fifteen wireless bypasses, inside and outside the hull. Then, when I seized control, my nano-robots would proceed to destroy the original lines. They would send their robots and technicians out to find the problem, but find only empty troughs.

When the timer hit zero, our world changed with a simple message. EMERGENCY CONTROL CENTER ESTABLISHED.

A virtual control panel appeared on the screen and I started selecting options. The first thing I did was call up a crew status screen.

In typical Eisenhower style, it showed the location of every person on the station. I applied a filter to just see managers, security officers, and control room employees. Once I had a good feel for their locations, I sent the emergency de-spin command.

"EMERGENCY DE-SPIN WILL COMMENCE IN TEN MINUTES. THE STATION WILL THEN BE IN A ZERO-GRAVITY SITUATION. PLEASE FIND A SECURE LOCATION."

"Holy crap! What're you doing?" Nora said.

"Buckle in, kid," I said.

"Nora!" she said as she pulled her way along the wall and started to slip her arms into straps.

"Not there. On that wall over there," I said and pointed to the aft wall.

She did as told, then said, "This must be the unexpected situation you expected."

I smiled and nodded, but kept my gaze on the personnel screen. As I hoped, all of the control employees and managers were racing for their duty stations or secure cabins in Ring Four. Security, however, was a different matter. They were scattered around the station and seemed to be running in circles. Two were still in Ring One. I cursed under my breath.

"What the hell are you doing?" she whispered.

"Stop cursing," I said.

"Fine. But what are you doing?"

"I'm stealing the station. I'm going to fly it to Mars orbit."

She said nothing, and when I looked up, she was staring at me with her mouth hanging open.

"How? I mean your robots are cool, but they can't push this huge station!"

"Sure they can. It would just take a long time to build up speed. But there's no need. How do you think they got the station out here? The fusion reactor that gives us electricity can also power the engine they use to move the station. Luckily, we have enough fuel to accelerate up to speed and slow us down at Mars."

"Wow," she whispered. "But what about security? Even if you control the station, they'll come get you."

"I have a plan for that too," I said as the warning sounded the two-minute mark. Except for five security officers, all the station's key personnel, a total of ninety-seven, had scurried to Ring Four as I hoped.

The klaxon sounded and green lights appeared all over my screen's station diagram, indicating each section and ring had been sealed off. When the last hatch lock engaged, the station's hull shuddered and groaned.

"Nothing's happening!" Nora squealed.

"Sure it is. The station takes about ten minutes to stop spinning."

"But . . ." she stopped and looked around the workshop. Some stuff along the walls shifted around, but there was little change in the hub. "Oh right. We were already in zero gravity."

"Microgravity."

"Wait! What about my mom? Will she be okay?"

"She's suspended in a tank of gel. She'll be even safer than we are."

When the control status showed we had come to a complete halt, I engaged the drive at ten percent thrust. The station creaked and moaned again; this time anything not locked down started sliding aft. Felicia's canister rolled toward the edge of my bench, but I grabbed it in mid-air as it launched.

"I wonder what you would have thought of this," I muttered, but she didn't answer.

Just before I touched the icon to disengage Ring Four, the screen turned to static.

"Damn it!" I said and slapped the bench.

"Don't curse," Nora said, with a smug voice. I nearly yelled at her to shut up, but instead clenched my teeth. She had earlier hit on my plan's biggest weakness. The station was essentially four equally-sized rings attached to a tubular central core. Since the only way to travel between rings was to take elevators up the spokes to the core, sealing each ring in times of emergency was quite easy. But given enough time, Eisenhower and his goons would get out of their locked sections and come after me. To prevent that, I had planned to disconnect Ring Four from the rest of the station and leave it behind for the authorities to come and collect after we'd told our story on Mars. That now looked doubtful. I wondered briefly how I would hold up under torture.

"What happened?" Nora asked.

One glance at her and I realized they wouldn't need torture. They could make me do anything if they could get to Nora.

"I think they're jamming my wireless communications. I'm crippled without it."

"Damn," she muttered. I glared at her for a second, then grabbed a MOM unit from the rack and powered it up. Using her directional antenna, I confirmed my suspicion. The signal was strong from the aft direction, where Ring Four was located.

I closed my eyes and cradled the MOM in my lap for a few minutes. How had Eisenhower figured it out so fast? Felicia's voice answered the question.

"It doesn't matter. You know what you have to do now."

I took a deep breath and pulled along the wall to the emergency locker, where I yanked out two balloon suits.

"Put this on. It's an adult small, but may still be big on you, so cinch it up around the waist, wrists and neck. Just not tight enough to cut off the blood flow."

She took the clear plastic compressed suit. "I know how. We have emergency drills, remember?"

I struggled into mine as the dread continued to build. First the rapid breathing, then the shakes and vomit rising in my throat. I hadn't been in any kind of pressure suit or vacuum since Felicia's death. I didn't want to do this.

I started to explain the entire situation to Nora, then stopped. I didn't think Security could still hear me since I'd seized the control system, but I wasn't sure. I grabbed a piece of paper and quickly wrote it down.

I have a secret space pod attached to the other side of the outer wall. I have my nanobots programmed to automatically open and then close a hole in the hull to let me get to the pod. Just in case they are slow and some air leaks out, your suit will inflate automatically and protect you until you can get out through the hatch.

I handed the sheet of paper to her and and waited for her to read it.

"Understand?" I asked.

"You're leaving? No!"

"I have to. I'll be right back."

"Send a robot!"

"No radio communications. I have to keep my hands on the MOM to talk to it."

Her lip quivered, but she didn't cry.

I snatched Felicia from the bench and handed her to Nora. "Can you take care of her while I'm gone?"

She nodded, then sealed the suit's breathing mask over her face.

I sealed my suit, grabbed my tool harness and tucked a MOM under my arm, then used the tip of the screwdriver Nora had been playing with to tap a series of commands on the wall. A section of the wall started to fade, then turned into a hole that continued to grow until I could step through and into my pod. I then tapped the command to close the hatch and the hole.

I switched on the air circulation and heaters, then tapped the separation command against the wall. Within seconds, the pod floated free and I turned it toward the aft part of the station. There were only two antennas positioned on Ring Four that could beam directly at my small comm array, so I moved the pod to a point between them and instructed it to maintain position relative to the moving station.

Then came the part that terrified me. With shaking hands I attached my tether to an interior bracket, then opened the pod's little hatch and held on as the atmosphere vented. The suit inflated, but I immediately felt cold. The balloon suit heaters weren't meant for EVA or any kind of extended vacuum exposure, they were designed to give people a chance to survive a hull breach long enough to escape to a pressurized area. I had to work fast.

I gripped the MOM's carrying handle in one hand and pulled through the hatch with the other. I hadn't been in hard vacuum for many years and was immediately swept by gut-wrenching vertigo. The only lights on the station exterior were flashing navigation strobes and a few floods that illuminated airlocks and important maintenance panels. Since there were few soft shadows this deep in space, the starkly lit edges contrasted with total blackness and made depth perception difficult. After a few seconds my mind sorted through the individual islands of light and I was able to get my bearings. By tapping on the MOM's case with the screwdriver, I activated her flood lights and turned them toward Ring Four's hull.

I was shivering and my teeth were chattering by the time I located the first antenna. It looked much further away than I'd thought it would be, but I had little time and had to try. My shaking hands made tapped commands to the MOM very difficult, but after the third try, a tiny aiming screen flipped open on the MOM's side and I targeted the antenna, then triggered the heavy mining laser.

At first nothing appeared to happen. I could see the beam diagrammed on the tiny screen, but only occasional sparkles along its actual path as it vaporized some of the dust that orbited the station. Then parts of the antenna started to glow orange and the dish slumped backward against the station's forward momentum.

Tiny warning lights flashed along the upper edge of my breathing mask, informing me I had only twenty minutes of compressed air left and my temperature was dropping to dangerous levels. I didn't need warnings to tell me that. I could barely feel my fingers and my shaking hands were almost useless. I found it hard to think straight. I knew I probably couldn't control my instruction taps well enough to turn the laser off and back on again, so I swung it upward away from the station and then turned toward the other antenna.

I couldn't see the antenna. In order to use the MOM's flood lights, I'd have to turn off the laser or risk blowing a hole in the hull. As I tried to tap the off command for a third time, sound crackled through my ear piece. The MOM was sending me a message telling me she would overheat if she didn't stop the laser.

"I'm trying, damn it!" I said through chattering teeth. Then I realized she had contacted me via radio.

"Turn off laser, MOM."

"Laser off."

"I need you to acc . . . ess the EMERGENCY CONTROL CENTER screen back in the wor . . . kshop."

"Contact established."

"Ini . . . tiate the Ring Four sep . . . aration pro . . . proto . . . col."

"Initiated."

Without a sound, huge mechanical locks swung away from the ring struts. Clouds of chipped paint and ice crystals puffed into space and the ring separated into two C-shaped halves, each carrying three struts. Since the rest of *Arturo* was still under thrust, the two halves tumbled away slowly and fell behind. In the distance, near one of the Ring Four sections, I saw a wheeling, roughly star-shaped figure that resembled a human body. Then it passed out of the light and was gone.

Could I have breached the hull? It didn't matter now. If I had it was too late and I was a murderer.

I could no longer feel my hands or feet, but using tiny puffs from the MOM's attitude thrusters and hooking my arms and wrists around the hatch frame, I pulled myself back into the pod. Using the MOM as an interface, I verbally commanded it to close the pod's hatch, pressurize the cabin and turn the heat on high.

I felt no elation as I left the pod and floated back into my little hub workshop, only exhaustion and a niggling worry about what could only have been a floating body. My hands and feet felt as if they were on fire, but I knew from my winters in Chicago that feeling the pain was a good sign.

I instructed the nanobots to seal the hull again and turned to Nora. She sat in the control seat with my interface goggles covering the upper half of her head. I immediately realized that her bubble suit hood was pulled down around her neck, but before I could yell at her I also saw that her quivering mouth and chin were covered with tears.

"Nora?"

She didn't answer.

I pulled myself over to the control station and looked at the scroll screen attached to the workspace next to her. It showed the same employee location diagram I had used to watch the Ring Four occupants scurry back to their cabins, only now it was separated into two large C-shaped sections. One of the cabin wedges was flashing red with a decompression tag. Blinking employee ID markers filled the corridor outside the ruptured cabin. So perhaps I really had killed someone.

Nora flinched when I gently pulled the goggles from her head. Tiny tear beads left a glittering trail between the goggles and her face, then started falling aft. She slapped them aside and ran wet hands through her rumpled hair.

"I'm sorry you had to see that, Nora. I'm not sure what happened. Nobody should have died. I don't know—I just . . ."

She cocked her head at me and squinted tear-clogged lashes together. "You didn't kill anyone. I did."

I blinked at her, totally confused.

She pointed at the employee location diagram. "You left that open.

I saw where Seth's cabin was and I remembered what you told that guy about burning a hole in his wall."

A cold chill crept down my back.

"And you'd already showed me how to control the MOMs."

I couldn't speak, but I grabbed her and pulled her into a tight hug. She broke down into great gulping sobs muffled against my chest. Then she spoke. In long unbroken strings.

"I saw it all! Through the camera. I'm not sorry he's dead, but . . . I didn't know you were going to leave them behind. Will I go to jail? He just clawed at . . . at nothing. I thought he'd die instantly, but . . ."

"Shhhh . . . It's all over."

"Will I go to jail?"

"No . . . I don't know. I don't think so. You were trying to protect your mother."

She cried again. I stroked her hair and there was nothing I could say that would make it better, but I might still be able to protect her. I'd gone to this much trouble to get Nora fee, I wasn't about to let her be incarcerated by the Martian state if I could help it.

Since the MOM systems are under my control, if I admitted to ordering the attack on Seth, the Martian investigators would probably not see any need to dig further. I decided to send the authorities a message admitting that I had stolen the station and killed Seth. Perhaps, under the circumstances, they would be lenient.

After a couple of minutes, I sat Nora back in the control seat and looked at the EMERGENCY CONTROL CENTER screen. Just over an hour had passed since I sent the de-spin command. I ordered the station to slowly spin up again, increased the thrust to sixty percent and triggered the automatic course corrections that would send us to Mars.

After the station's remaining three rings were once again spinning and providing Earth normal gravity, we entered the elevator for Ring One so that we could go see Nora's mother in the Medical Unit.

When the lift doors closed, Nora looked up and me and said, "I can't stop thinking about what I did."

"I know," I said and knelt down next to her. "Look, what you did is wrong and that will never change, but it's over. You can get past this and live your life. I didn't think I could go on after Felicia died, but I did. Does that make sense?"

She shook her head slowly. "It's not the same thing."

"No. It's not the same," I said and then stood up. I couldn't look her in the eye for my next statement. "When we get to Mars, it will be kind of crazy, but I need you to do something for me. I don't want you to lie to anyone, but I also don't want you to tell about Seth unless you're asked."

Her eyes squinted at me, immediately suspicious. "Why?"

Before I could answer, the door opened and a burner gun was thrust into my face, with Meathead attached to the other end.

"My last orders from Lieutenant Eisenhower were to arrest your sorry ass and that's what I'm going to do."

I sighed and gently pushed Nora behind me.

"No, you're not," I said, trying to sound calm and reasonable, "and I'll tell you why. We're on our way to Mars. It's all automated at this point and the controls are locked down. Nothing you do to me will change that. I've also already started broadcasting messages to the press about what has happened here, how we were all enslaved, but finally managed to take over the station and come seeking freedom and justice from the Martian people."

Meathead blinked and glanced at his equally confused partner. Most of that had been a lie. I wasn't really broadcasting to Mars yet, but still had the better part of two weeks to start that up.

"So? You're still under arrest."

"You don't want to be jailed for murdering me as soon as we get to Mars space, do you?"

"No one said anything about killing you," he muttered and lowered the gun.

"Good. If you don't beat anyone up during the next two weeks, we might actually be able to pass you two off as heroes who helped save all these poor people. Wouldn't you like to be a hero?"

Meathead chewed on his lip and glanced at his partner who just shrugged.

"It's not like he can go anywhere," Nora said. "You'll know where to find him if you decide you need to beat him up later."

"Gee, thanks," I muttered.

Meathead holstered his gun. "There will be a trial, you know."

"Yeah, but wouldn't it be better for the press to think you're a hero instead of a bully?"

"Girls love heroes," Nora said.

That made him smile, then he produced a stern face again. "Why should we trust you? What would stop you from making us out as the bad guys when the trial comes?"

"I just want to get this station to Mars. I don't really care what happens to you two after that. Besides, you know that with my robots I could have killed you any time I wanted, and yet you're still here."

He thought about that for a second, then shrugged. "C'mon, Ramon. Let's go get some grub."

Nora and I started down the corridor in the other direction, toward the Medical Unit.

"You did good, Clarke," Felicia said, and I stopped in the middle of the hall. I had forgotten Felicia's canister in my workshop. It was the first time since her death that I'd gone farther than the bathroom without her.

I wasn't really crazy, not totally. I knew that Felicia's voice was all in my head, but part of me had always believed that voice would go away if I didn't keep what was left of her near me. Now I knew that wasn't true.

"What's wrong?" Nora said.

I took a deep breath, shook my head and continued walking. "Nothing important. Let's go see your mom."

RULES OF ENGAGEMENT

★

by Matthew Johnson

Since the introduction of the Hybrid Warrior implant progam, violent crime by military personnel had dropped to almost nothing. The same cybernetic implants that ensured proceedures were followed on the battlefield kept soldiers on the right side of the law, stateside. So why was PFC Kevin Bishop awaiting a death sentence?

A REPORTER AT LARGE

IT WAS NOT MUCH of a fight, as bar fights go: not even enough to get Kevin Bishop, Tony Cervantes and Tom Hollis thrown out of the bar in which they had spent the afternoon and evening of July ninth. The three soldiers had been drinking at The Swiss Bar and Grill, a bar popular with college students on weeknights but largely taken over by military on weekends, when their implants relax the usual restrictions on alcohol. Bishop, Cervantes and Hollis had served together in the second Battalion of the twenty-third Infantry Division (more often referred to as the 2-23 IN), mostly in Somalia and Yemen, and two of them were still on active duty. Fire team Chinook had survived the worst that the war and al-Shabaab could throw at them, but before long two would be in prison and one would be dead.

The immediate cause of the fight was money. Bishop, who had ordered the last two rounds, had revealed that he was unable to pay his share of the night's tab. The entire 2-23 IN had been flush with back pay when they had come home from deployment in Yemen, bringing a welcome stream of money into the city's bars; it was not unusual during that period for John Pratt, The Swiss's owner, to make two or more bank runs per night, each time with a duffel bag full of money. (Soldiers in the 2-23 IN pay for almost everything in cash, due to a widely-held belief that their implants track direct payments.) Two months later the money was beginning to run out, and for Bishop—who was no longer receiving combat pay and was also making regular payments to the city's *ghat* dealers—it already had.

There are two common reasons why soldiers, especially regular infantry, enlist in the Army. One is self-improvement: though some join with an eye on pursuing a military career, many more do so for the neural implant that, after their tour, opens doors to otherwise unattainable jobs. That was why Hollis had joined, and why he now had a job with the city that paid well enough for Bishop to expect him to pick up the tab. When Hollis stood up and dropped a twenty on the table, just enough to cover his share of the bill, Bishop punched him in the side of the head.

"Get away from me," Hollis said. Bishop leaned forward and started swinging wildly with both arms. Hollis held his forearms up to ward off Bishop's punches until the buzz in Bishop's head got loud enough to make him stop. Tony Cervantes took Bishop by the arm, led him back to his chair and poured him a beer from a neighboring table's pitcher.

"What do you want from me?" Hollis asked, shouting to be heard over the dance remix of Julee Cruz's "Hipper Than Me," that summer's inescapable hit, playing on the Swiss's speakers.

Bishop drank his beer in one long pull, until the buzz quieted enough for him to talk. "I want you to have my back for a fucking change," he said.

Bishop had joined the infantry for the other common reason, because he—and his parents—feared that it was either the Army or jail. Though he had never had any major trouble with the law, when Bishop turned nineteen he was no nearer to finishing high school than he had been five years before, and his father had given him a choice: he could join the Army or go on the street, but he could no longer live at home.

There is surprisingly little connection between the reason why a soldier joins the military and his performance there. Though Bishop found basic training difficult, once he had passed that and been fitted with his implant he thrived. There was an appealing simplicity to Army life: if you followed orders and didn't make trouble, you were "squared away"; fail in any of those respects and you were a "shit bag"—the lowest of the low, and subject both to constant harassment from superiors and fellow soldiers and to buzz from your implant. Though he had occasional run-ins with superiors, when he was deployed in Yemen he found a way to make use of his natural rebelliousness as a "pit bull," someone willing to do things and take chances other soldiers wouldn't, and was promoted to Private First Class and recommended for an Army Achievement Medal. Now that he was back home, though, and unable to return to active duty until he had been declared medically fit, he was falling back into old habits: he would later say that it was only the fact that Cervantes, his team leader, was in the same situation that had kept him from getting into serious trouble.

If Bishop was fire team Chinook's "bad cop," Tony Cervantes was the good cop. He had not needed the army to provide either money or stability: his parents, Daniel and Anita, started an implant fund for him when he was in middle school. If he had wanted for anything, his father told me, it was focus. After his high-school football career failed to lead any further he had spent a year doing little but sleeping and playing video games before settling on the Army.

"I was against it at first," Daniel Cervantes told me. He and Anita still live in the home where Tony was raised, in the solidly middle-class Albuquerque neighborhood of North Valley. "I served a tour in Iraq when I was his age, and I saw what it did to a lot of kids. But he told me that he needed something like this, something that would give him a purpose like football had, and once I saw what the idea of it did to him I changed my mind." Between enlistment and basic training Cervantes began to train on his own, lifting weights and hiking the Sandia mountains with a full backpack. His size and his attitude made him stand out during training and, once deployed, he was promoted to Sergeant and put in charge of a fire team that consisted of Kevin Bishop, Tom Hollis and himself.

The incident that had left Bishop and Cervantes in medical limbo had taken place more than a year before. The 2-23 IN's base, FOB Gambit, is in Ta'izz, or "Brooklyn"—soldiers have nicknamed all of Yemen's cities after New York boroughs, due to the mud-brick high-rises that make them look like a sandcastle version of Manhattan. Their main duty in Yemen is counterinsurgency: as part of the mission to root the al-Shabaab out of Yemen and Somalia and make the Gulf of Aden safe for shipping again, the Cervantes' team conducted daily "block parties" in which they would cordon off an area and go door-to-door, taking a census of the population and comparing it to intelligence. Mostly these would follow a schedule, moving in a grid around the city to keep tabs on as much of the population as possible, but at other times the mission would be a follow-up on some fresh intelligence. On that day fire team Chinook was one of three fire teams dispatched in a Stryker personnel carrier to a neighborhood centered around the Abu Walad stadium, following a tip from one of the interpreters, or "terps," who worked for the Battalion that a high-value Shabaab figure was hiding out in a house there. (Though implants provide near-simultaneous translation, the Army still relies on interpreters to provide a friendlier face and to catch subtle cues, such as a speaker's tone of voice or body language, that might be missed by a non-native speaker.) Now the terp, a Somali man in a black-and-white keffiyeh and a borrowed ballistic vest, was whispering directions to the driver as the Stryker crawled along the narrow road. Though there was no other traffic the vehicle moved in fits and starts, stopping periodically when one of its slaved drones detected signs of an EFP. Bishop began bouncing in his seat.

"Keep your shit together," Cervantes told him.

Bishop tucked a wad of *ghat* between his teeth and lower lip and started working it around his mouth. "Sorry," he said. "I'm just buzzing."

I first met Kevin Bishop in the visiting room at Washington State Penitentiary, where he is currently serving a death sentence and awaiting execution. His trial received some attention in the media, but the local papers had covered it as a straightforward crime story: I only became interested when I learned, through a friend in the military, about Bishop's experiences in Yemen, and found out just how remarkable it was that he was in prison at all.

A decade ago, servicemen were not an unusual sight in the Penitentiary. Since the introduction of the Hybrid Warrior implant progam, though, violent crime by military personnel in Tacoma—as well as everywhere else that the 2-23 IN has been posted—has dropped to almost nothing. When I asked Bishop why he thought it had failed in his case, he explained that there were three ways around the negative reinforcement the implant uses to control behaviour, which soldiers call "the buzz."

"The easiest way is to drown out the buzz with drugs, booze, or both at once," he told me. Though he says he no longer chews ghat, his gums and teeth are permanently stained green. His fingers twitch constantly, seeking out any object—a pen, my notebook, a cigarette—that they can use to beat out their rhythm. "That's why so many guys started chewing ghat, so if you have to violate the rules of engagement—like maybe shooting somebody you know is a Shabaab, but they haven't shot at you yet—you can ignore the buzz long enough to do it." The other method was to trick your implant: "If you can make yourself believe, I mean really believe, that the Shabaab had fired on you even though you hadn't heard it, or that a girl wasn't a whore even though you were paying her for sex, sometimes your implant will let it go." The problem with that method was that to trick the implant you had to trick yourself, and you might wind up married to a Ukrainian bar girl, as Tom Hollis had.

And then there was Dirty.

"Dirty" Dunn, known as Daniel to his mother if no one else, was a legend in the 2-23 IN as the man who had, supposedly, hacked the buzz. "Hacked" is something of a misleading word, because he had done nothing to modify his implant's hardware or software. Dirty's method, instead, was to start the week leading up to a leave with a series of small but increasingly frequent violations of the Code of Conduct. "He'd stop polishing his boots, stop making his bed, even stop showering, just put up with the shit his CO gave him—and the buzz, which would get worse and worse," Bishop explained. "As soon as his leave started he'd go to a drinky bar and get pissed, do whatever drugs he could find, get in a fight, and have a whore do things to him 'til it hurt—and when he got that far he didn't just feel the buzz, it hurt like hell. Then, when he'd broken every rule that he could without being put in stockade, he'd go back to base, shower, make his bed, shine his shoes, and then he'd have the greatest fucking orgasm of his life."

Kevin Bishop never tried Dirty's method, but he told me he had no doubt that it worked: like every soldier, he knew how much of a relief it was after he had heard an AK-47 fire, or an EFG go off, when the implant allowed him to fire his weapon. Being in a situation where he was anticipating something like that—such as riding in a Stryker on the way to a block party—could bring on the buzz even if he wasn't doing anything wrong.

The mud-brick skyscrapers in a traditional Yemeni city are built without any space between them, making literal "blocks": as the Stryker neared its target the streets between became too narrow for driving, so it slowed and turned ninety degrees to bar the way in and out. While one of its drones turned in a tight circle overhead, watching for an ambush, the others set up a perimeter around the area that was to be searched that day.

"Bella Bella will stay by the Stryker and handle any PUCs," Staff-Sergeant Brenda Hamm said to Cervantes and the leaders of the other two fire teams. "Aleut takes the left side and Chinook the right." So long as the Stryker was rolling, Hamm, the squad leader, was in command of all three fire teams: once they were on the ground Cervantes was expected to lead his team on his own unless he got direct orders from Hamm. "Have fun."

Cervantes saluted and then turned to Hollis and Bishop. "Bishop, keep your drone heeled and stay on me. Hollis, get your Raptor up— I want a map of that building before we set foot inside."

Hollis nodded and shut one eye, making mental room for the feed from his drones. Each fire team in 2-23 IN is made up of two regular infantry and one drone operator, who has an upgraded implant that lets him multitask between multiple drones as well as what they're doing on the ground. "Vehicle's clear," he said a few moments later.

"All right," Cervantes said. "Let's see what Brooklyn has to throw at us today."

Even after he had left Yemen, Bishop had little trouble maintaining his ghat habit. Both Tacoma, the nearest city to Fort Lewis, and Seattle, which is not much farther, have large Somali communities, and while ghat is technically illegal it is not a high priority for the DEA. After he and Cervantes were moved out of the 2-23 IN and reassigned to the

Warrior Transition Battalion, Bishop began to chew ghat nearly all the time. "I was always buzzing," he told me. "Every day we'd get our tests and our scans and wait, just kill time all day, and every day it got worse."

The purpose of the Warrior Transition Battalion, or WTB, is to provide specialized medical care for soldiers well enough to be out of the hospital but not currently able to return to active duty, as well as education and training for those granted medical discharges. Some critics, however, say that the main focus of the Battalion's staff is looking for reasons for soldiers to be "chaptered out," or discharged without benefits. The more common name for the Battalion within the Army, the "shitbag brigade," suggests that little sympathy is felt for the soldiers there.

Bishop and Cervantes were constant companions during their time in the WTB, amusing themselves as best they could with ping-pong and video games at the base's rec center during the day and drinking at The Swiss in the evenings. In the first few weeks, when it seemed like they would soon be returning to active duty, their conversation was focused mostly on stories and events from their time in Yemen. Later, when that prospect became less likely, they would discuss what they would do when they were discharged. Bishop's plans grew more grandiose as the time passed, from joining the police force to robbing drug smugglers near the Canadian border. Finally, when even being chaptered out began to seem impossibly remote, Bishop became focused on finding more immediate sources of both action and income.

This, it emerged, was the real reason behind the fight at The Swiss. Hollis often joined Bishop and Cervantes there on Friday evenings, when his wife Bohdanna took English classes at the Tacoma Community House. Earlier that afternoon, Bishop had tried to enlist Hollis and Cervantes into a plan to rob John Pratt when he made the last bank run of the night. Neither of the others took him seriously, by now used to Bishop's grandiose plans, but on this night he refused to let it drop: finally Hollis had called for the bill—at which point Bishop revealed that he was out of money, and the fight began.

Later, once Hollis had gone and Bishop had recovered from the buzz, he said to Cervantes, "I guess we'll have to do it next Friday. We'll need to get someone else, too."

Cervantes shook his head. "Let it go," he said. "And why would we need three people, anyway? How heavy do you think a bag of money is?"

"No, listen," Bishop said, leaning in close. "It'll be just like when we'd PUC a Shabaab in Brooklyn." (PUC—"person under control"— is Army slang for detaining a captive.) "First we rent a white van with plenty of room in the back. We need one guy with a quad to keep a tail on Pratt—all that money in a bag, he probably takes a different route each time, just like the top Shabaab guys. So when we know which way he's going, we get the van in front of him to make him stop, pull him in the back and bag him, keep him a few hours. When we let him go he'll be so glad to be alive he won't care about the money."

Cervantes brought his glass to his lips and took a long swallow. "That," he said, "is the stupidest plan I have ever heard. What if he calls 911? What if the van gets too banged up to drive when he hits it?"

"What if, what fucking if?" Bishop said. "When did you get to be such a bitch, *sir*?"

Ignoring him, Cervantes took another drink. "Here's how you do it," he said after a few moments. He tipped the napkin dispenser on its side on the table and put the salt and pepper shakers on either side of it. "Send the quad, like you said, but use it to figure out which bank he's going to. Keep the van the next street over, then once you know where he's going you get ahead of him, take out the ATM camera with a spray can or something. Then we just wait for him to roll down the window to deposit the money and we get a gun on him."

"Fuck, man, that's awesome," Bishop said. "Let's do it tonight!"

"I'm just *saying*," Cervantes said. He raised his glass and drained it.

The soldiers began to come out of the Stryker once the drones were done sweeping the street. The air was full of the yeasty smell of canjeero, the Somali flatbread that is a staple breakfast food in Yemen. "I'm going to watch out for a kitchen, okay?" Bishop asked Cervantes. "Somebody around here has to be cooking something."

The terp was the last to emerge, his keffiyeh pulled down almost over his eyes. Life can be very dangerous for terps: some will only work wearing masks, to protect themselves and their families.

"You're sure Guleed is here?" Hamm asked.

"In one of the houses in this block, I hear," the terp said. "I don't know which one. Maybe the owner, even, doesn't know."

Hamm nodded. "Cervantes, take him up with you. We'll watch the road."

Cervantes led Bishop, Hollis and the terp to the furthest doorway. "Hollis, find us something to shoot."

Bishop chewed his wad of ghat, spat green goo onto the doorframe as they went in. A map of the building, made during the last block party, appeared on his retinal display along with a list of the known occupants: his Earworm, reading his mood, was playing "Blood and Snow" by the Icelandic death metal band Galdramenn. He and Cervantes heeled their quadrotor drones, trying to maintain a 360-degree field of vision while Hollis kept his Raptor circling the block and sent his two quadrotors ahead, mapping the inside of the building.

If you ask people who have known Tom Hollis to name one thing that defined him, they will tell you this: he is a hunter. He grew up in a semirural part of Bradfordsville, Kentucky, where he and his father had hunted rabbits, wild turkeys and deer at every opportunity. By the time he finished school, though, it was clear that the hard times that had hit the area since the Louisville Ford plant had closed were not going to go away any time soon, and Hollis enlisted in the Army. He excelled in marksmanship and drone operation and, after a successful first tour and promotion to Specialist, was fitted with an upgraded implant and assigned as fire team Chinook's Raptor operator (the Army does not use the term "pilot.") During block parties, his job was to map out the interior of a building with his quadrotors and compare what they found with the layout observed by the Raptor, as well as looking for anything that might seem suspicious, such as fresh plaster or recent infrared traces in empty rooms.

Because of the ease with which their mud brick walls can be taken down and rearranged, Yemeni houses are particularly challenging to search. Cervantes, Bishop and Hollis cleared each floor of the building methodically, starting with the animal pen at the ground floor and moving up through the bedrooms, kitchen and finally the *mafraj* on the top floor, where the man of the house would entertain guests in the evening.

"This room should be bigger," Hollis said once his quadrotors had cleared the room. He pointed at one of the walls. "Last time that wall was about three feet south."

Cervantes trained his quadrotor's infrared sensors on the wall, but no heat traces appeared. "What do you think?"

"Don't know," Hollis said. "I'm not getting any heat traces, but it's pretty hot already—might be body temp in there."

"You see anything from the outside?"

Hollis shook his head. "Roof's all covered with old car parts—mufflers and shit. Bounces the radar. Mud brick's easy to take down and put up, though. Could just be the neighbors wanted a bigger living room."

"Check out the wall from in here, then. Bishop, take a look around the room. Both of you, keep a quad watching your tail." Cervantes turned to the terp. "You, come with me."

More than a dozen people had clustered in the mafraj when they heard the soldiers entering: children, brothers, brothers-in-law, veiled women only distinguishable by the color of their chadors, and the head of the household, a man whom Cervantes' implant identified as Murad Sharar. Cervantes asked him to name all of the adult men and women there, so he could check them against the census from the last block party, and to have the men present themselves to the drone camera for facial recognition and the women for voiceprints. In a normal block party anyone new to the household would be recorded or photographed, but today anyone who wasn't already in the census was to be zip-tied and held at the Stryker. As the terp spoke to Sharar, a translation scrolled down Cervantes' retinal display.

"We're looking for Mohammed Guleed," Cervantes said once the census had checked out. "We have money for anyone who helps us find him. He is a dangerous man."

"I don't know any *Guleed*," Sharar said, looking sideways at the terp.

"Hey, hey—talk to me," Cervantes said. "Have you heard the name?" Cervantes asked. "From a neighbor? On the street? We have money for anyone who helps us find him."

Bishop spoke quietly to Cervantes while the terp was translating. "Look at this," Bishop said, holding an AK-47 assault rifle. "Under the couch."

"Okay, get it out of here," Cervantes said.

"Get it out of here?" Bishop asked. "They were hiding a fucking gun from us." He spat another wad of green goo onto the white plaster wall.

Sharar was talking more quickly now, making the terp struggle to keep up. "He says the rifle is just for protection. There have been many robberies in this neighborhood."

"You know this is bullshit," Bishop said. "They've got a secret room here. Guleed's probably in there laughing at us."

Cervantes looked over at Hollis, who shrugged. He held a hand up to Bishop. "Just get it out of here. Take it downstairs, okay?"

"Yes *sir*," Bishop said. He took the AK-47 and headed for the stairway. "Is it all right if I get a goat grab? I saw some stuff cooking in the kitchen, it'll probably just burn if we leave it."

"Fine. Get me a falafel." Cervantes turned back to Sharar. "Now, I want you to tell me. If you help lead us to Guleed, there will be money, and we can protect you —"

There was a hollow bang as Hollis hit the wall with the butt of his rifle. Sharar put up his hands and began to talk quickly; suddenly all the women, brothers and brothers-in-law in the room started talking as well, making it hard for Cervantes' implant to isolate and translate what he was saying. "Tell him to slow down," he told the terp. "Did he say Guleed?"

"He says he has heard Guleed is in another building in this block. He wants to know how much you will pay him to find out which one."

"Why didn't he say that before?" Cervantes asked. He paused as his implant's translator caught up with the conversation, text scrolling up on his retinal display. He let his hand drop to his rifle. "Hold up. My feed says *Is Guleed still there?*"

The terp shook his head. "It is mixed up. Too many voices."

Cervantes turned back to Sharar and pointed to the corner of the room. "Okay, everybody but this guy, get over there and shut up." He took a pull from his camelbak and then turned to the terp. "And you, I want you to think really carefully about exactly what —"

A burst of gunfire came from downstairs, one Cervantes and Hollis—and, more importantly, their implants—recognized as coming from an AK-47. An indicator on their retinal displays changed from red to green, and the triggers on their SR-11 rifles unlocked. According to the rules of engagement, anyone in the area was now considered hostile.

★ ★ ★

Cervantes and Bishop went back to The Swiss on the Saturday after the fight, but they did not go inside: instead they sat in the back of a white van parked up the street, waiting for John Pratt to do his last bank run. They spent the evening playing shooter games on their retinal displays, drinking cans of beer and chewing ghat, aiming for the point where they'd be able to pull a gun on Pratt despite the buzz. Bishop was surprised, though, at how little resistance he had felt so far. "The fact is," he later told me, "when we did that op was the first time since coming home that I *didn't* feel the buzz."

Shortly before 1:30 Pratt came out the back door of The Swiss, wearing a heavy coat over a ballistic vest and carrying a locked suitcase full of the night's receipts. Once Pratt had driven out of the parking lot, Bishop launched the Kestrel Hi-Fli quadrotor they had bought the day before. Unlike the drones they had used in the army, which can fly mostly independently of their operators—military drones only transmit their feed, and implants only accept transmission, during algorithmically-determined microsecond windows, to prevent either from being compromised—FAA regulations require civilian drones to be under constant operator control, so Bishop had to close one eye to focus on the video feed it was sending him. The guns they were carrying were Shouqiang T-5s, a model which doesn't have the implant-linked trigger locks their service weapons had. Both Cervantes and Bishop, though, assumed that their implants alone would prevent them from firing. (When I asked Roy Healy, Bishop's court-appointed lawyer, why this point had not been raised at his trial, he said he hadn't thought it would make a difference: if anything, he said, Bishop's ability to overcome the implant might be taken as an aggravating factor.)

Cervantes waited a few minutes, until Pratt's car was out of sight, and then started the van moving. Bishop told him that Pratt was headed down Pacific Avenue, then called up a map that showed all of the ATMs in the area.

"Where's he going?" Cervantes asked.

"I don't know yet," Bishop said. "Either to Sound Credit Union or Umpqua Bank."

Cervantes turned onto Market Street and sped up. "Well?"

Bishop watched Pratt turn onto Commerce Street. "Sound Credit."

"Are you sure?"

"Yeah." Bishop looked down at the Kestrel's feed on his tablet, then back to Cervantes. "Yeah. I'm sure."

Cervantes sped up, rushing towards a yellow light on 17th Street. It turned red when he was a car-length away from the stop line; he rushed through the intersection without slowing, his eyes closed. After a few seconds he opened them again and glanced at the feed on Bishop's tablet. "Are we ahead?"

"Yeah, we've got about two blocks on him. Take the next left."

Cervantes slowed just enough to make the turn and after another block the ATM came into view. It was a drive-through machine set back from the street, with a plexiglas canopy spanning the driveway to shelter it from the rain. A heavily weatherbeaten brown Toyota Allegra was idling next to the ATM.

"Fuck," Cervantes said. He slowed the van and moved it into the driveway behind the other car. "How much time do we have?"

Bishop looked down at the drone feed and then over his shoulder. "Couple minutes—he hit another red light."

Cervantes worked his wad of ghat around in his mouth, rolled down his window and spat it out onto the sidewalk. "This is it," he said.

"We could do it next Saturday," Bishop said, but Cervantes was already out the door. Bishop saw him draw his pistol as he neared the other car, keeping it low and just hidden behind his right hip, and then swing it in a smooth arc so that it was inside the Allegra's passenger-side window before the people in that car could do anything. He heard shouting from inside the car, and Cervantes shouting, and then saw on the drone feed that Pratt's car was crossing 15th Street, a block away. He reached over to the steering wheel, his hand hovering over the horn; before he could honk it the Allegra sped away, bumping over the sidewalk and then peeling away down the road. Cervantes tracked the departing car with his pistol until it was out of sight and then froze, his arm pointed the way it had gone.

Bishop saw the back end of the van come into view in the Kestrel's feed and realized that Pratt's car was nearly there. He blew a sharp honk on the horn: Cervantes dropped his arm to his side and ran back to the van's driver-side door. Pratt, apparently unnerved by the other car's sudden move, drove on instead of pulling into the ATM's driveway.

After Pratt's car had gone by, Cervantes got back into the van. Bishop kept his eyes on his tablet, guiding the Kestrel to rest on the roof, then got out and stowed it in the back. Before he could close the rear door the van was moving, and he had to crabwalk to the front and squeeze between the seats to sit down.

"That guy," Cervantes said. He was staring out the windshield, his foot heavy on the accelerator as they sped down Pacific Avenue. "That fucking guy."

Bishop shook his head. "I know. If he hadn't been there —"

"No, *that guy*," Cervantes said. "That was the terp. That guy was the terp who set us up."

Though there was no outward sign that Cervantes and Hollis could now fire their weapons, everyone in the room knew it. Bishop has described that moment, when the rules of engagement allow them to defend themselves, as a feeling of release: "You can breathe again, like you just took off a belt that's too small for you," he told me. "The locals can see it, too, 'cause now you fucking feel like you're Superman. That's when you really know if they really are Shabaab or not, 'cause if they are, this is when they shit themselves."

Hollis backed into the corner nearest the door, bringing his rifle up to cover both the people in the room and anyone who might come in; at the same time his quadrotors buzzed through the lower floors, trying to find the source of the AK-47 fire, and he put the Raptor into a tight spiral over the building's roof. Cervantes took a step back and pointed his rifle at both Sharar and the terp, waving them over to the corner where the others were huddled. Both men raised their hands and started talking quickly, one in English and the other in Arabic. Cervantes ignored the garbled translation feed running down his retinal display and sent a message to Bishop: *Where are you?*

I'm in the kitchen, the reply came a few moments later. *What's going on?*

Hoping you could tell me, Cervantes sent. *Shots didn't come from up here.*

"Movement on the roof," Hollis said. "Trap door—missed it, sorry."

Cervantes shook his head. "Don't sweat it. You got a visual?"

"Six Shabaab—man, they were packed like sardines in there."

"Guleed?"

"I'm just seeing the backs of their heads right now. They're climbing onto the roof and running for the next building."

"Ping the other teams with our status, then send one of your quads up there to get me an identification. For now, paint them all—" Cervantes' voice caught as he was hit by the buzz from his implant. Guleed was a high-value target, which meant that he was to be captured alive unless he was certain to escape or about to harm military personnel. "Paint them green for now."

"Got it."

A message from staff sergeant Hamm popped up on Cervantes' display: *Detain hostiles until further orders. Fire teams Aleut and Bella Bella will pursue target.* Cervantes started to compose a reply, then wiped it. "Keep an eye on them," he said to Hollis, then sent a message to Bishop: *Meet me at the front door.* He sent his quadrotor out the window and started down the stairs.

The buzz was deafening by the time he reached Bishop. He held out a hand: "Give me some."

Bishop frowned as he followed Cervantes out onto the street. Cervantes rarely chewed ghat, and never on missions. "Sir?"

"Fucking give me some."

Keeping a one-handed grip on his rifle, Bishop reached into his pants pocket and pulled out a baggie full of glossy, red-brown leaves. He opened it, releasing a pungent smell like mint mixed with sumac, then held it out to Cervantes, who took out a large handful of the leaves and put them in his mouth. Cervantes' cheeks bulged as he broke into a run, dodging the garbage being thrown from windows above while trying to catch up with the green dots going from rooftop to rooftop on his GPS map.

A message from Hollis flashed on Cervantes' display: *Got a visual. Guleed confirmed.* All but one of the dots changed from green to red, and a moment later two winked out as the muffled roar of the Raptor's 8-ball missiles filled the air.

Bishop laughed. "Looks like Hollis got another couple heads for his wall."

A visual from his quadrotor showed that Guleed and the other remaining Shabaab had reached the edge of the roof they were on, past which the next roof was more than ten feet away.

"Think he'll try to jump?" Bishop asked.

Cervantes spat thick green liquid onto the ground, his mouth too full of leaves to talk. *Get your quad in front of him,* he sent. *We'll box him in.* He took direct control of his quadrotor and made it hover a few feet behind Guleed and the others, broadcasting in Arabic, Somali and then English: "THIS IS THE UNITED STATES ARMY. YOU ARE BEING DETAINED UNDER THE AUTHORITY OF THE GOVERNMENT OF THE REPUBLIC OF YEMEN. LAY DOWN YOUR WEAPONS AND SURRENDER AND YOU WILL NOT BE HARMED."

Through the now-constant feed Cervantes saw a green-tinted Guleed turn back to see Bishop's quadrotor rising up in front of him. The whine of the Raptor's engine showed that it was turning and targeting the three flashing-red Shabaab around him. They held up their hands and clustered around Guleed, obscuring him: Cervantes could just see him reaching into the pocket of his shalwar kameez and taking out something shiny.

Cell phone? Bishop sent. Cervantes moved his quadrotor to get a better look and started composing a warning for it to broadcast. Guleed jabbed at the phone with his thumb, three quick jabs. The feed from the quadrotors went dark, and a moment later the world went dark as well.

"How could it be the same guy?" Bishop asked. "What would he be doing here?"

"Good question," Cervantes said. He was quiet as he drove north on Pacific Avenue, looking for the Toyota that had sped away. "I think I lost him."

Bishop chewed his wad of ghat for a minute, then rolled down the window and spat onto the street. "You sure it was the same guy?"

"I saw his eyes." Ahead of them a traffic light had turned red, and with a sigh Cervantes slowed the car as he approached it.

"Okay, so it was the guy. So what? Half of Seattle's Somali now, and it makes sense he'd get out—they bring the terps over here after their tour so the Shabaab won't kill them for helping us."

"He *is* a Shabaab." Cervantes was looking straight ahead, his eyes locked on the traffic light. "He lied to me. He knew what was happening and he helped Guleed get away. So what is he doing here?"

Bishop said nothing.

The light changed and Cervantes accelerated quickly. "Do you think you could find him with the quad?"

"Now? We'd have to stop to launch it, and we don't even know where he went."

Cervantes lifted his foot from the gas pedal, letting the car slow down before the merge with Schuster Parkway. He turned right on 8th and pulled over. "The Shabaab's never touched us on American soil. Hitting a target here is their fucking wet dream."

Bishop opened his mouth and then closed it another moment, unable to find the words for what he wanted to say. "So you want to PUC him?" he asked finally.

"He's not here alone," Cervantes said. "We need to track him—find out where he's going, who he's talking to."

"But—" Bishop winced and rubbed his eyes. "We can't do that with a quad we bought at Best Buy."

Cervantes shrugged. "So we get Hollis to help."

The Pentagon has not yet declassified whatever information it has on the device that disabled Cervantes, Bishop and their quadrotors, but that has not stopped people from speculating. Much of that speculation has focused on the fact that it wasn't used until Bishop and Cervantes had assumed direct control of their drones, though it is also true that Guleed was essentially cornered as well. Hollis' Raptor was not affected, but it's not known whether it recorded any unusual electromagnetic activity at the time. While al-Shabaab has been surprisingly successful at downing drones, their methods, such as using kites to tangle a quad's rotors, have always been low-tech. The most popular theory is that the device was provided, willingly or unwillingly, by Iran, which has a robust and long-running anti-drone program. Army personnel other than Raptor operators are now forbidden from taking direct control of their drones while in the field, and perhaps because of this no similar incidents have been reported.

Cervantes and Bishop awoke several hours later, apparently unharmed, and after being held for observation and implant servicing at the Army hospital in Sana'a, they were given "three hots and a cot"— a one-day leave outside of the combat zone—and then returned to active duty. Though he had disobeyed orders by chasing after Guleed,

Cervantes did not receive any reprimand. Staff Sergeant Hamm, who is still serving with the 2-23 IN in Yemen, declined to speak with me, sending this message instead: "Whatever they did, it had nothing to do with what happened in Ta'izz. All three soldiers went on to serve with distinction for the rest of their tours, and none of them showed any signs of anything being wrong." When I asked if the failure to catch Guleed, and Cervantes' belief that the interpreter had betrayed them, might have had an effect on him later, Hamm wrote back, "We caught Guleed two blocks away. So far as I know Tony put all that behind him."

Tom Hollis agreed to meet with Bishop and Cervantes at the Sonic Drive-in two blocks from the two-bedroom bungalow he shared with his wife Bohdanna in Tacoma's quiet North End neighborhood. He had stopped going to The Swiss since the fight with Bishop, and did not want either of the men coming to his home.

Before they had even sat down, Cervantes began telling Hollis who he thought he had seen in the brown Allegra—though he left out why he and Bishop had been at the Sound Credit ATM that night. Hollis listened silently, sucking his milkshake through a straw and occasionally turning his gaze from Cervantes to Bishop and back again, until Cervantes had finished his story.

Hollis put down his milkshake. "You're sure it's him?"

"Yeah," Cervantes said. "We don't have anything on him yet, not even a name. But you've got red-light cameras, drones flying all over town—all I have to do is give you his face and his license plate and we can figure out who he is and what he's up to."

Hollis raised his milkshake and took another sip. He turned to Bishop. "What do you think?" he asked.

"Yeah," Bishop said. He had not wanted to come to the meeting, worried that Hollis would bear a grudge over their fight, and had kept his attention focused on his chili cheese fries, tapping his feet as Heaven Sent's "Shalimar" played on the restaurant's speakers. "I mean, yeah. I agree."

"So you saw him?"

"Yeah. No. I mean, Tony did, but he *saw* him."

Hollis was silent for a moment, then frowned. "It ain't that I don't believe you, but what you're talking about could get me fired, or even arrested maybe," he said. "I got a mortgage to pay, and if anything happens to me Bohdanna's got nothing."

"Are you kidding me?" Bishop asked. He pointed a fry at Cervantes, his hand trembling. "This guy is, he is not asking you, he is giving you an order."

Hollis stood up, his posture stiffening. He turned back to Cervantes. "Is this an order, sir?" he asked.

Bishop smiled. "Hell yes it is."

"I'm asking him."

The speakers played the first bars of "Hipper Than Me" as Cervantes sat silently. Finally he shook his head. "We really could use you," he said.

"Call the cops," Hollis said as he turned to leave. "Or the FBI, whoever. Tell them what you know and keep out of it."

"Yeah, go. Get out of here," Bishop called after him. "Go back to your Russian whore."

Hollis froze in his tracks, then craned his head around to look at Bishop. He closed one eye partway, as though he were looking down a gunsight. "She's Ukrainian," he said, then stepped out the door.

Bishop saw one of the restaurant's employees walking over to their table and stood up, waving her away. "Don't bother," he said. "We're going."

By the time the 2-23 IN was rotated back to Fort Lewis all three soldiers had been given commendations for actions before and after the incident, with Hollis also earning Sharpshooter badges in both the Rifle and Raptor categories. There is no record of any of them being offered or seeking out counseling during that period, and they received no special attention or screening during the Post-Deployment Health Assessment meant to identify potential problems that might occur when soldiers return to civilian life. Hollis received an honorable discharge and, thanks to his implant and an Army employment program, quickly found a job with the city of Seattle, using drones to predict and shape traffic patterns. Cervantes and Bishop decided to accept the three-week vacation offered and then go back to active duty. After the three weeks were up, though, the two soldiers were transferred to the Warrior Transition Battalion, and the 2-23 IN went back to Yemen without them.

The assignment to the WTB came as a surprise to Cervantes and

Bishop, since neither had received any serious injuries and had been serving in the field up to the end of their tour. As well, it raised the possibility that they would be either discharged or chaptered out, neither of which were attractive options for the two. Though he has no doubt that whatever had happened to their drones was the reason he and Cervantes were assigned there, Bishop says they were never asked any questions about it and did not receive any specialized treatment, only a daily MRI and system scan.

I got no answer when I asked the medical records department at the Battalion to let me see copies of Bishop and Cervantes' scans. Major William Jameson, who has been the chief technical officer for the Army's Hybrid Warrior program since its inception, contacted me a week after I sent my second request, and invited me to meet with him at his office at Fort Lewis. Jameson, a tall, affable New Englander whose John Lennon-style granny glasses make an impression at odds with his crew cut and uniform, supervised the 2-23 IN's deployment in Yemen. When I asked him about the case, Major Jameson said that he had been aware of it but had not handled it personally. "If they were in the WTB it was for a medical reason," he told me. "I can tell you that there was nothing wrong with those implants. If there had been, we wouldn't have let those soldiers off the base."

When I told him what Bishop had said, about the buzz going away when he was planning and carrying out the robbery plan, Jameson sighed. "There's a reason why we forbid soldiers from using drugs, and it's not just the law. The implant is designed to influence the brain on a very subtle level, chemically and electrically, and drugs can interfere with that." Ghat and other drugs, he told me, are the reason why the soldiers' later behavior and actions are so much at odds with how they performed on deployment: "Drugs won't affect the implant, but over time they can affect the brain in ways that are past the implant's ability to correct."

He also denies that the implant's reinforcement systems can be hacked to give pleasure the way Bishop described. "It's just like the old joke about hitting yourself with a hammer," he told me. "It feels so good when it stops."

Six days later, Bishop got a message from Cervantes: *Found him. Tacoma Mall food court.*

Without access to Hollis' drones, Bishop and Cervantes had been forced to look for the terp on foot. Cervantes used an app called SketchArtist to make a picture of the man he had seen in the Allegra and he and Bishop had spent the week on a search-and-detain mission around the parts of Tacoma and Seattle with the largest Somali populations.

Bishop, who had been searching the Hilltop neighborhood a few miles northeast of Tacoma Mall, drove as quickly as he could without speeding, conscious both of the gun and of a large freezer bag of ghat that he had in the car. He took a leaf from the bag and started to chew it as he locked the car and went into the mall. The food court was full of Korean and Somali teenagers, as it usually is on Friday evenings, snacking on short ribs and sambusas. The smell of canjeero coming from the Casho Cambuulo stall summoned memories of Yemen as Bishop scanned the court for Cervantes' face.

Another message from Cervantes arrived, containing a map of the mall with a location pin on one of the bathrooms. Bishop broke into a run, keeping his right hand on the pistol in his jacket pocket to keep it from falling out, and turned off the mall's main corridor to an open area with an information panel, two benches and a small play structure. The sign on the bathroom door was a stick-figure picture of a man and woman with a child between them, holding their hands, and inside the small empty room was a Koala Kare diaper station along with two stalls and a sink. Bishop turned sideways and stood edge-on to the door, so he wouldn't be in the way when he needed to open it. Through the thick door he could just hear Cervantes' voice over the mall noise.

Bishop pulled the handle and the door swung inward. A frightened-looking Somali man was on the other side, trying to get away from Cervantes. Bishop grabbed the man's wrist and pulled him inside; Cervantes followed, closed the door behind him and leaned back against it.

Kahin Jama, a twenty-four-year-old Somali man, was a recently-settled refugee from Yemen. When he found himself trapped between Bishop and Cervantes he pulled out his wallet and dropped it on the floor. "Please don't hurt me," he said.

Bishop took off Jama's belt and drew it tight around Jama's wrists, like a zip-tie. Then he drew his gun from his jacket pocket and trained it on Jama.

"Why are you here?" Cervantes asked.

"Don't hurt me," Jama said to Bishop.

Cervantes brought a fist down between Jama's shoulders, knocking him to his knees. "Talk to *me*," he said. "I bet you thought we'd never find you, huh?"

"Please," Jama said, sobbing. He held his hands up on either side of his eyes, like a horse's blinders. "I didn't see your face. Let me go, I won't tell anyone, I promise."

Bishop sidled over to a sink and spat green goo into it. "Do you think . . ." he asked.

"He fooled us once," Cervantes said. He took a step forward, drew his gun from his cargo pants and pressed the barrel to the back of Jama's head. "What are you doing here? *Where is Guleed?*"

The door behind Cervantes pushed inward, knocking him briefly off balance. Jama threw himself at the now-open doorway, trying to get to his feet, and Bishop shot him in the back. Jama fell forward and landed at the feet of Emily Park, a thirty-two-year-old mother who was bringing her two-year-old son Levi to the washroom for a diaper change.

Bishop later said that he did not notice either Park or her son screaming. Instead, as he looked down at the gun in his hand, his only thought was *How did I do that?* A moment later he fired again, obeying his conditioning to do a "double tap"—two shots into a target's chest or back.

Jama's body kept the door from closing fully and they could see a crowd of people outside. Cervantes turned to face the crowd, and Bishop moved to stand beside him. Both held their guns in front of them, and the screaming got louder. Many of the people in the mall that day were refugees, and for them the sight of Bishop and Cervantes was not only frightening but triggered painful memories as well. Those nearest to the soldiers froze or fell to the floor, while some further away ran for safety.

Cervantes and Bishop turned partway away from each other, dividing the mall corridor into two arcs of fire. When soldiers in a counterinsurgency campaign are surrounded by hostile forces, they are trained to execute what soldiers call a "death blossom"—a constant barrage of fire in all directions until the enemy is killed or forced to retreat. Bishop and Cervantes had participated in three of these while serving in Yemen, two of them while assigned to Abyan province following the incident that downed their drones.

"Looks like we're boxed in," Cervantes said. "I don't think we're getting any backup."

Bishop nodded and began to scan the crowd, picking targets. Emily Park's cell phone began to ring, playing a tinny version of "Hipper Than Me," and suddenly, Bishop says, he was aware of where he was, tasting the ghat in his mouth and hearing the screams of the terrified mall customers.

He turned to Cervantes. "Tony. Hey, Tony," he said.

"What is it?"

"This is—this isn't right," Bishop said. His jaw was working furiously and he had to spit out ghat juice before he could keep talking. "These people, they aren't Shabaab, man. You need to put down the gun."

Cervantes shook his head. "They're lying," he said.

Levi Park began to cry, a single, rising note. Cervantes aimed his gun at him and Bishop fired, two quick shots into Cervantes' back.

"The crazy thing is," Bishop told me later, "all that stuff, everything we did, I never felt like anything was wrong. The only time I felt the buzz was when I shot Tony."

Daniel Perez, a professor of neurocybernetics at the Medical College of Georgia, first heard about the case when I contacted him after meeting Bishop. Though he was too late to give testimony in Bishop's defense, he has met with Bishop several times since then. "The reason the Army hasn't found anything may be because it's not just something the implant is doing, but an interaction between the implant and the brain," Perez told me. He has studied the effects of cognitive implants since they were first introduced, and he describes them as an interaction of two chaotic systems. "In order to work with a human brain, the implants have to be able to rewrite their programming, even while they're running. But our brains do this too, and the studies we've done don't shed much light on how they might interact in highly stressful, emotionally charged situations."

Though the Army denies that the soldiers' implants had anything to do with their crimes, Perez has joined the effort to apply for a stay of execution for Bishop, and has also called for a freeze on military implants until more long-term studies can be done. He told me about experiments he's done in which similar implants were used to help teach rats how to get food from a machine, and the rats were then made to switch to another method. "Even when they learned the new way to get the cheese, the implant punished them for it," he said. "And when we switched back they got a huge dopamine rush." He feels that Bishop's lawyers should have raised the possibility that the implants, alone or in conjunction with other factors, predisposed the soldiers to violence in a way they might not have been before.

I asked Perez how he could square this with Major Jameson's claim that the implants were undamaged, as well as the fact that other soldiers from the 2-23 IN had not been involved in any similar incidents. "Their implants weren't damaged, just reset," Perez said. "It's a learning device: whatever it takes as normal, it reinforces. What happened to Bishop and Cervantes may just have happened *sooner.*"

On the morning of November third, two months after I met with Perez, Tom Hollis arrived at the Seattle Municipal Tower trailed by two Cormorant drones and carrying a Swiss Arms K91 rifle over his shoulder. Witnesses say he looked like he was going hunting.

TEN RULES FOR BEING AN INTERGALACTIC SMUGGLER
(the Successful Kind)

★

by Holly Black

Growing up on Mars, you dreamed of a life full of adventure in space. Your parents loved to tell you how bad things could get out there in the void. You're about to discover for yourself how right they were, and that if you want to make it in an uncaring universe, there are rules that have to be followed.

1. *There are no rules.*

THAT'S WHAT YOUR UNCLE TELLS YOU, after he finds you stowing away in his transport ship, the *Celeris,* which you used to call the *Celery* when you were growing up, back when you only dreamed of getting off the crappy planet your parents brought you to as a baby. No matter how many times you told them their dumb dream of being homesteaders and digging in the red dirt wasn't yours, no matter how many times you begged your uncle to take you with him, even though your parents swore that he was a smuggler and bad news besides, it wasn't until you climbed out of your hidey-hole with the vastness of

309

space in the transparent alumina windows behind you that anyone really believed you'd meant any of it.

Once you're caught, he gives you a long lecture about how there are laws and there's right and wrong, but those aren't *rules*. And, he says, there are especially no rules for situations like this. Which turns out to be to your advantage, because he's pissed but not that pissed. His basic philosophy is to laugh in the face of danger and also in the face of annoyance. And since he thinks his brother is a bit of a damp rag and likes the idea of being a hero to his niece, it turns out that *no rules* means not turning around and dumping you back on Mars.

He also turns out to be a smuggler. Grudgingly, you have to admit that your parents might not be wrong about everything.

2. *Spaceports are dangerous.*

YOUR UNCLE TELLS YOU this several times as you dock in the Zvezda-9 Spaceport, but it's not like you don't know it already. Your parents have told you a million stories about how alien races like the spidery and psychopathic Charkazaks—fugitives after their world was destroyed by InterPlanetary forces—take girls like you hostage and force you to do things so bad, they won't even describe them. From all your parents' warnings about spaceports, when you step off of *Celeris,* you expect a dozen shady aliens to jump out of the shadows, offering you morality-disrupting powders, fear inhibitors, and *nucleus accumbens* stimulators.

Except it turns out that spaceports aren't that interesting. Zvezda-9 is a big stretch of cement tunnels, vast microgravity farms, hotel pods, and general stores with overpriced food that's either dehydrated or in a tube. There are also InterPlanetary offices, where greasy-looking people from a variety of worlds wait in long lines for licenses. They all stare at your homespun clothes. You want to grab your uncle's hand, but you already feel like enough of a backworld yokel, so you curl your fingers into a fist instead.

There are aliens—it wasn't like your parents were wrong about that. Most of them look human and simultaneously inhuman, and the juxtaposition is so odd that you can't keep from staring. You spot a woman whose whole lower face is a jagged-toothed mouth. A man with gray-skinned cheeks that grow from his face like gills or possibly just really strange ears loads up a hovercart nearby, the stripes on his body smeared so you know they are paint and not pigmentation. Someone passes you in a heavy, hairy cloak, and you get the impression of thousands of eyes inside of the hood. It's creepy as hell.

You do not, however, see a single Charkazak. No one offers you any drugs.

"Stop acting stupid," your uncle growls, and you *try* to act less stupid and keep from staring. You try to act like you stroll around spaceports all the time, like you know how to use the gun you swiped from your mother and strapped to your thigh under your skirt, like the tough expression you plaster on your face actually *makes* you tough. You try to roll your hips and swagger, like you're a grown lady, but not too much of a lady.

Your uncle laughs at you, but it's a good kind of laughter, like at least you're sort of maybe pulling it off.

Later that night, he buys you some kind of vat-meat tacos, and he and some of his human "transporter" buddies get to drinking and telling stories. They tell you about run-ins with space pirates and times when the InterPlanetary Centurions stopped their ships, looking for illicit cargo. Your uncle has a million stories about narrow getaways and hidey-holes, in addition to a large cast of seedy accomplices able to forge passable paperwork, but who apparently excel at getting him into dangerous yet hilarious situations. You laugh your way into the night.

The next day your uncle buys you a pair of black pants and a shirt like his, made from a self-cleaning material that's both hydrophobic and insulating, plus a shiny chromium steel clip for your hair. You can't stop smiling. And although you don't say it out loud to him, in that moment you're sure that the two of you are going to be the greatest smuggling duo of all time.

3. *When someone says they'll pay double your normal rate, they're offering to pay at least half what you'd charge them if you knew the whole story.*

THE *CELERIS* stays docked in the spaceport for a couple of weeks while your uncle buys some used parts to repair the worst of wear and tear to her systems and looks for the right official job—and then an unofficial job to make the most of that InterPlanetary transport license.

You try to keep out of your uncle's way so he doesn't start thinking of you as some kid who's always underfoot. You don't want to get sent back home. Instead, you hang around the spaceport, trying to make yourself less ignorant. You go into the store that sells navigational charts and stare at the shifting patterns of stars. You go into the pawnshop and look at the fancy laser pistols and the odd alien gadgets, until the guy behind the counter gets tired of your face and orders you to buy something or get out.

After a while the spaceport seems less scary. Some of your uncle's friends pay you pocket money to run errands, money that you use to buy caff bars and extra batteries for your mother's gun and holographic hoop earrings that you think make you look like a pirate. Just when you start to feel a little bit cocky and comfortable, your uncle informs you that it's time to leave.

He's lined up the jobs. He's found a client.

A little man with a red face and red hair sits in their eating area on the ship, sipping archer ethanol, booze culled from the Sagittarius B2 cloud, out of a coffee can. The man tells your uncle that he supplies alien tissue to a scientist who has his laboratory on one of the outer worlds, where the rules about gene splicing and cloning are more lax. The little man has come across a particularly valuable shipment of frozen alien corpses and needs for it to get where it's going fast, with few questions asked.

The assignment creeps you out, but you can tell that your uncle has been distracted by the ludicrously high offer the man is waving around. It's more money than you've ever imagined being paid for anything, and even with the cost of fuel and bribing Centurions, you're pretty sure there would be enough to refit the *Celeris* in style. No more used parts, no more stopgap repairs. He could have all new everything.

"Half now," the man says. "Half when the cargo arrives *intact*. And it better get there inside a month, or I will take the extra time out of your hide. I am paying for speed—and silence."

"Oh, it'll be there," your uncle says, and pours a little archer ethanol into a plastic cup for himself. Even the smell of it singes your nose hair. "This little ship has got hidden depths—*literally*." He grins while he's speaking, like the offer of so much money has made him drunker than all the booze in the sky. "Hidden depths. Like me."

The red-haired man doesn't seem all that impressed.

You have lots of questions about where the alien bodies came from and what exactly the scientist is going to do with them, but a quick glance from your uncle confirms that you're supposed to swallow those and keep pouring drinks. You have your guesses, though—you've heard stories about space pirates with alien parts grafted on instead of their own. New ears and eyes, new second stomachs tough enough to digest acid, second livers and new teeth and organs humans don't even have—like poison glands or hidden quills. And then there were worse stories: ones about cloned hybrids, pitiless and monstrous enough to fight the surviving Charkazak and win.

But you're a stupid kid from a backworld planet and you know it, so you quash your curiosity. After the client leaves, you clean up some and fold your stuff so it tucks away in the netting over your bunk back in your room. You go down to the cargo hold and move around boxes, so the way to the secret storage compartment is clear for when the redhead comes back with his alien parts in the morning. That night you look out through the transparent alumina windows at ships docking on Zvezda-9, and you get excited about leaving for your first mission in the morning.

But in the morning, the *Celeris* doesn't depart.

It turns out that it takes time to get ready for a run like this—it takes supplies and paperwork; it takes charting a course and new fuel and lots of batteries and a ton of water. The whole while you careen between sadness over leaving Zvezda-9 now that you've become familiar with it and wishing you were in space already. You visit your favorite spots mournfully, unsure if you'll ever see them again, and you pace the halls of the *Celeris* at night until your uncle orders you to your bunk. His temper is a short-sparking fuse. He sends you to buy supplies and then complains loudly about what you get, even though you're the one who'll be doing the reheating and reconstituting.

The client arrives in the middle of the night. You sit in the shadows above the cargo bay and watch what he loads—a long cylindrical casket, big enough for several human-size bodies. Smoke curls off of it when it's jostled, as though it is very, very cold inside.

An hour later you're back among the stars. There, your uncle starts to relax, as though space is his real home and being on a planet for too long was what was making him tense. Over the next week, he teaches you a few simple repairs he has to do regularly for the *Celeris,* shows you a few of his favorite smuggling hidey-holes, teaches you a card game and then how to cheat at that card game, and even lets you fly the ship for an hour with him hanging over your shoulder, nagging you about everything you're doing wrong.

Considering that he turns on autopilot while he sleeps, letting you put your hands on the controls while he watches isn't that big of a vote of confidence, but sitting in the cockpit, gazing out at the spray of stars, makes you feel important and wholly yourself, as though all your time laboring in that red dirt was worth something, because it brought you to this.

Mostly the trip is uneventful, except for an evening when your uncle comes up from the cargo hold and won't look at you. He downs a whole bottle of archer ethanol and then gets noisily sick while you watch the computer navigate and fiddle with your earrings. He never says what set him off, but the next day he's himself again and you both try to pretend that it never happened.

Then you wake up because the whole ship is shaking. At first you think you're passing through an asteroid field, but then you realize something bad is happening. There's the faint smell of fire and the sound of the ship venting it. Then the gravity starts going crazy— lurching on and off, bouncing you against the floor and the walls.

Once it stabilizes, you manage to crawl out into the corridor. Your heart is pounding like crazy, fear making you light-headed. You clutch your mother's gun to you like it's some kind of teddy bear. There's shouting—more voices than there should be on board. You think you hear your uncle calling your name and then something else. Something loud and anguished and final.

You head automatically for the cockpit when a man runs into the corridor, skidding to a stop at the sight of you. Based on the mismatched array of weapons and armor, you figure he's got to be a pirate—if he was a Centurion, he'd be in uniform. He reaches for his weapon, like he's just shaking off the shock of seeing a kid in her nightgown aboard a smuggling ship, but you've already swung your mother's gun up. You blast him in the head before you allow yourself to consider what you're doing.

When he drops, you start trembling all over. You think you're going to throw up, but you can hear more of them coming, so you try to concentrate on moving through the ship, on remembering all the hidey-holes your uncle pointed out to you.

The lights go out all of a sudden, so you have to feel your way in the dark, but soon you've found one big enough for you to fit yourself into and you're shut up inside.

Snug as a bug in a rug, your mom would say.

You start crying, thinking about her. You know your uncle is probably dead, but you don't want to admit that to yourself yet, so you pretend you're not thinking of him when you wipe away your tears.

4. ***If your ship gets raided by space pirates, don't hide in the cargo hold, because everybody wants what's in the cargo hold.***

THE *CELERIS* is a small enough ship that you can hear the pirates walking through it, talking to one another. You try to count different voices, but all you can figure out is that there's more than five and probably less than ten. Which doesn't mean that much, since they boarded from another ship and there could be any number of them back there.

Did you find it? you hear them say, over and over again. *We've got to find it before it finds us.*

Which doesn't mean anything to you. You wonder if they attacked the wrong ship. You wonder if your uncle got murdered for nothing, for less than nothing, since the credits he got paid are in his bank account and not anywhere aboard the ship.

You hear the acceleration of the engines and feel the odd sensation of forward momentum. Which means they're probably taking the whole ship, not just gutting it for parts and leaving it to spin endlessly in the void—which would have meant no life support for you. Maybe you'll survive this, you think. Maybe no one even knew you were aboard, maybe they thought the guy you shot was shot by your uncle. If they docked on a planet, even a terrible planet, maybe you could sneak off the ship and hide in the station.

To do that, you need to make sure you stay hydrated. You'll need food too, but not right away. A bathroom, ideally. You and your uncle usually ate in the little kitchen area—he called it the galley—off the main cockpit, where there's a small burner, lots of packages of freeze-dried food, tubes of paste, and a jar of nutrient powder. You're sure that some of the pirates have raided it by now, drinking through your uncle's supply of archer ethanol—you've heard them, rowdy and full of good cheer, like they'd done something heroic instead of something awful.

If they catch you, they'll most likely kill you. You're using up oxygen, just breathing. But you know all the other things pirates might do instead—sell you, use you, cook you, eat you. Your parents loved to tell you how bad things could get when you talked about wanting to have adventures in space.

There's food in the cargo hold, you know—those were the supplies that went on the official roster as his official shipment. Your uncle had the papers to sell that stuff to a homesteader planet. He'd been planning on sending you down to haggle with them—and had loaded you down with plenty of pieces of dubious bargaining wisdom in preparation.

Don't be afraid of silence, he'd told you. *Silence shows your strength. Have a bottom line,* he'd told you. *Sometimes to make a deal, you've got to walk away from a deal.*

But it turned out that pirates didn't care about negotiating. Just like your uncle had told you in the beginning, there aren't any rules.

You doze impatiently waiting for your chance to slip down to the cargo hold. Your leg cramps from the position you've folded yourself into, and finally you decide that even though you can still hear voices, they're faint, and you're going to have to go for it.

You unfold yourself and step into the hallway. The floor is cold against your feet, and you feel light-headed from being in one position so long, but you begin to pad your way toward the cargo bay. There's a steel ladder to a crow's nest above the cargo bay, and as you climb down it, you know that if there's a pirate patrolling beneath you, he's going to see you before you see him, your pale nightgown fluttering around you like a white flag of surrender. There's nothing you can do about it, though, so you just try to keep on going and stay quiet.

You're in luck. There's no one there. You climb all the way down and start to open up the shipping crates. You find luxuries that settlers love—caff bars, tins of coffee, jars of spicy peppers, fermented soy, and plenty of both salt and sugar. Ripping into one of the caff bars, you realize the stuff won't keep you fed until the pirates dock, unless they dock very soon. Worse, there's nothing to drink.

Despairing, you grab another caff bar and begin to look over the few remaining crates. You find some machinery—farming stuff—and what appears to be an array of tents suitable for a desert environment.

You're freaking out, sure that you're about to be caught, when you remember the secret hold, where the alien bodies are being stored. There might not be anything particularly useful there, but it's at least a little more spacious than your last hiding place, and if you keep to the corners, you'll have a great shot at picking off any pirates who discover the compartment before they can spot you.

It takes you a few tries to get the hatch open, but you manage it and slide down into the darkness. The only lights are the dim blinking green and blue and red buttons on the side of the cylindrical casket. You crawl over to it and look at the buttons. Maybe, you think, maybe it has life support built into it. Maybe you could dump out the contents and put yourself inside if things got really bad.

You squint at the control panel. There's a large button, clearly labeled: VIEW SCREEN.

You press it.

5. *If your ship gets raided by space pirates and you wind up hiding in the cargo hold, even though you know it's a bad idea, don't go poking through the secret cargo.*

A SQUARE of the shiny white case turns clear and the inside glows. The whole thing hums a little, as though expecting more instructions, a thin mechanical whine. You lean down, looking at what's inside, and then it's all you can do not to scream.

There's a Charkazak, its eight terrible black legs drawn up against the shiny black carapace of its chest. Its humanoid face, with black lips and red tattoos along its cheekbones. A chest that rises and falls with breath.

That thing is alive.

You stumble back, falling against the steel, more scared than you were when you faced down the pirate in the hallway, more scared than when you felt the blast hit the side of the ship and realized the *Celeris* was being raided.

You've heard horror stories about the Charkazaks all your life, on the news, whispered about at slumber parties of kids on the farm, and even on Zvezda-9. They were a race of warriors who worshipped death, becoming bodyguards for the most corrupt merchants and glorying in being soldiers on the front lines of the most awful wars just so they'd have more opportunities for bloodshed. They were so awful that they wouldn't follow InterPlanetary laws regarding who it was okay to kill and who it wasn't, nor did they believe in things like surrender or mercy. They invaded planets, brought down ships, and generally behaved like the monsters they appeared to be. When Centurions were dispatched to discipline the Charkazaks, they fought back with such viciousness that the only way to keep them from overrunning the galaxy was the obliteration of their planet and all the Charkazaks on it. Those that were off-planet when the Charkazaks, homeworld was destroyed became even more vicious than before. And as you look at the living one cocooned in metal, you feel like a child hearing those stories for the first time—more like a child than you've felt since you stowed away after that last stupid fight with your parents.

This—*this* must have been what the pirates meant when they worried about it finding them before they found it. You wonder how the redheaded dirtbag who hired your uncle acquired such a thing and where you'd really been transporting it. That Charkazak is the reason your uncle is dead.

The whine gets a little louder, and one of the red buttons on the side of the case begins to blink, like a throbbing pulse. Between that and the dim light from the screen, the secret cargo area feels too bright, but you wait and wait and finally all the lights switch themselves off.

You wouldn't think you could sleep with that thing near you, but you're so relieved to be able to stretch out your limbs that you sleep after all. You dream of someone calling your name from very far away. When you wake, your body is stiff with cold and everything is still dark. You realize that you're freezing and that if you don't get warmed up fast, you might be in serious trouble.

Tents, you remember. There are tents up in the regular cargo hold.

But as you feel around in the dark, you can't quite make out how to open up the hatch. Then you remember that the casket lit up—surely that would be enough for you to find the latch by—so you go over and press the green button again.

It lights up the case and you try not to look inside. You scuttle up instead and grab a couple of tents. You're dragging them back down when you hear the tramping of heavy footfalls. They speed up, like maybe they heard the thud of the material hitting the floor, and you swear under your breath. You move as quickly and quietly as you can, back under the floor, yanking the cover of the hidden compartment into place.

The light is still shining from the casket, and you're afraid that the glow will show through the seams and reveal your hiding spot. You press the green button again, hoping that will turn off the view screen, but it doesn't. The other light—the red one—starts blinking again, and you're panicking, because it's brighter and more obvious than the glow from the casket.

Push to open, the red button says. And as the footfalls come closer, as you hear the pirate feel around for the latch, a sudden strange calm comes over you. Since you're going to die—or worse—you figure, screw everything. Screw the pirates, screw yourself, screw every goddamn thing. You owe your uncle some final revenge. You're not going out like some dumb farmer kid. You're going to give those pirates exactly what they were looking for.

So you press the button. Twice. There is a horrible loud sound, like a giant exhalation of breath. The top of the casket slides open.

6. *And if you do go ahead and poke through the secret cargo, then for the love of all that is holy, watch out which buttons you push.*

FOR A MOMENT, you almost believe that you can take back the last five minutes. It seems so impossible that you could have done what you did. You were tired and freaked out, but you'd been pretty clever right up until then, clever and quiet and careful. Not crazy. No death wish. For a moment, you're just angry, so angry—at yourself, at the world. It feels so unfair that you're going to die because of one stupid decision, one bad moment.

"Hey," the pirate calls. "Kid, we know you're on board. We knew you'd show yourself eventually. Now come on out, and we'll go easy on you."

You snort, because it's a ridiculous thing to say. What does that mean—*go easy on you*—like surely he knows that implies nothing easy at all? Plus, it's too late. He's swaggering around, cocky, without realizing that you're both about to be dead. You're all about to be dead.

"Come out, come out, wherever you are," he calls, a laugh in his voice.

From the casket the Charkazak unfolds itself, bathed in the glow of the light from within. It rises, up and up and up. Eight legs, two sets of arms with six-jointed fingers on its shining onyx chest, and large luminous eyes. It might have human features, but you can't read its expression. It seems to shudder all over, then swings its head your way.

Fear makes you nearly pee your pants. You freeze so completely that you don't even draw in breath. It moves toward you—fast, its legs a blur—and leans down, all wide eyes and flaring nose slits.

Your mother's gun is lying beside you, but you don't grab for it. You released the Charkazak, after all. There's no point fighting it.

You whimper.

"Come on, girl," calls the pirate. "You think I've never been on a cheap old smuggling ship before? You think I can't find you? Come out or I'm going to make you sorry."

You close your eyes, but you can still hear the scratch of Charkazak feet against the floor, can smell the medicinal odor that clings to it from its containment, can hear its ragged breaths.

"I know you killed Richard," says the pirate, his voice falling into a false, honeyed tone. He's come closer to the grate that conceals the hidden cargo area. Maybe he knew where it was all along. Maybe you were a fool, thinking they didn't know where you were. He laughs. "You did me a favor there. I owed him money."

You hear the slide of metal on metal and open your eyes. The Charkazak is no longer in front of you. You let out your breath all at once, so fast that you feel dizzy.

"Hey, there, you—" the pirate says, then there's a gasp and a wet, liquid sound.

You sit in the cargo hold for a while—you don't know for how long—too scared to move. But then you force yourself numbly to your feet. You walk past the body of the pirate, with a massive bloody hole in his chest like that Charkazak thrust a clawed hand into his chest and pulled out his heart. The pirate's gurgling a little, but his eyes are shut, and you wouldn't know how to help him, even if you wanted to, which you don't.

You go straight to the galley, passing two more bodies. They are bent at odd angles, one missing the top of her head, her long red-blond hair in a cloud around her face. There is an odd spatter of red along one wall, and laser blasts have blackened the corridor.

In the galley, you wash your hands and then make yourself a cup of tea. You eat an entire sleeve of sugar cookies and then you heat up a freeze-dried package of salty, soy-drenched noodle soup and eat that, too. There's no point in dying on an empty stomach.

After that, you feel super sleepy, your eyes heavy, so you go back to your tiny room, climb under the covers, and close your eyes.

7. *On a spaceship, there really aren't that many places to hide.*

THE CHARKAZAK isn't like the pirates. It's a monster, and you can't hide from monsters. So you don't.

But it doesn't come for you.

You go into the bathroom and take a shower. You change your clothes and check your mother's gun for ammo.

Out in the hallway, the bodies are gone. You return to the galley and drink more tea, noting how the food has been picked over. You didn't count the night before, though, so you're not sure what was eaten by pirates and what was eaten by the alien.

You make some oatmeal with powdery reconstituted milk.

While you're eating, there's movement in the hallway. You duck down under the table, hoping that you're not worth the Charkazak's notice. Maybe you're like a rat to it, some kind of ship vermin. Maybe you don't matter. You wrap your arms around your legs and *hope* you don't matter.

It skitters into the room, and you can't help noticing that as large as it is, there is a certain gliding elegance to its movements.

Then the Charkazak's body crouches low, bending forward, two pairs of arms reaching to the floor to take its weight. Its head tilts under the table, looking straight at you.

It blinks. Twice.

"Um, hi," you say, because you don't know what else to do.

It keeps looking at you, tilting its head the other way this time. *Don't be afraid of silence,* your uncle told you, but you are afraid.

You don't have the upper hand in this situation. You don't have anything to bargain with in trade for your life.

8. *You'll catch more Charkazaks with salt than with sugar.*

"I could make you something," you say, "if you don't know how to cook."

"I know how," it says after a long moment, and you're completely startled by its voice, which has a little hiss behind it and an accent you're not used to but that you understand easily enough. It's a young voice, a not-much-older-than-you voice, and you have no idea what to make of that.

Of course some part of you knew that Charkazaks could talk—or at least understand commands. They couldn't have betrayed any treaties if they didn't talk, couldn't have committed treason if they hadn't sworn fealty to the InterPlanetary government, but you're still surprised. Monsters aren't supposed to sound like everybody else.

It—*he*—leans up and begins to move things on the counter, turning on the water heater and setting out two tin cups. His many legs move, swift as a centipede's, and equally disturbing.

"I am going to make some of this red fern tea," he says, opening one of the tins of leaves. "You will drink it."

You listen to the crinkle of paper, the whine of the steam, and the sound of water splashing into the cup. Tea making is confusing, because you associate it with comfortably curling up with your holo-reader and sleeping off a minor illness. Monsters aren't supposed to be able to make tea. If monsters can make tea, then nothing's safe.

"What happened to their ship?" you ask, because he *hasn't* killed you so maybe he'll *keep on* not killing you.

You heard the metal spoon clank against the sides of the cup. "Their ship is unharmed."

Which meant that everyone who'd once been inside of it was dead.

The Charkazak leans down again and passes you a cup with his delicate, multi-jointed fingers. It's warm in your hands.

"Th-thank you," you manage, and take a sip. Then you start to cough. It's *salty*, like your mother described the seas of old earth.

"Is there something wrong with it?" the Charkazak asks, folding his limbs under him, so he can look at you.

You shake your head, terrified. You force yourself to take another swig and try not to choke. You don't think you quite pull it off, though, because he looks oddly stricken, studying you with those large, pale eyes.

"Was this your parents' ship?" he asks, taking the cup from you and drinking deeply, as though he's not afraid of tasting your spit or getting your germs. As though he really, really likes salt.

"How do you know the *Celeris* isn't mine?" you ask. Then you remember that you're trying to get him to think of you as some kind of ship vermin, entirely unimportant, and wish you could take back those words.

"*Is* it yours?" he asks, not seeming unwilling to believe it, just confused.

"No," you admit. "The ship belonged to my uncle, but I'm pretty sure he's dead."

He tilts his head and narrows his eyes, studying you. "You freed me," he accuses softly. "By accident?"

You don't want to tell him that you thought of him as a bullet to the head. Your big murder-suicide plan, now staring at you with that implacable gaze. "I—" you begin, but you can't think of a lie fast enough.

He nods and picks up something from the counter. Then he leaves, the sharpness of his many steps across the floor a reminder of just how fast and lethal the Charkazaks are.

Once he's gone, you draw up your legs, wrap your arms around them, and feel smaller and stupider than ever.

You no longer believe that he'll just kill you outright, but that makes you realize how bleak your future has become. Even if the Charkazak dumps you off at some space station, even if you drain your uncle's bank account of all his credits, the only place you have to go is home. You didn't learn enough from your uncle to fly the *Celeris* yourself. You've got no way to make any money back on Zvezda-9. You're just a farming kid with delusions of grandeur.

Of course, you're not sure that the Charkazak will let you off the ship. He's from a fugitive race, hunted by InterPlanetary Centurions—he might want to keep you around so he could shove your face in front of any call screens until he moved outside regulated space. Then you'd be in the same situation you were in with the pirates; he could sell you or eat you or . . . well, you've heard stories about Charkazaks ripping humans apart in a sexual frenzy, but you're trying not to think about that.

You decide you're going to make dinner for him. You break out more rehydratable noodles and start in on making a vat-meat goulash. There's a tube of apple-quince jelly and some cheese that you figure you can either make into a dessert or some kind of first course.

Halfway through, you think about cooking for your uncle, and tears come to your eyes. You have to sit down and sob for a little while, but it passes.

Once the food's done, you pad through the halls of the ship to find the Charkazak. A smear of blood still marks one of the walls, wiped by something but not wiped clean.

9. *The dead are a lot less trouble than the living.*

YOU LOOK FOR the Charkazak in the cargo area, but you find dead bodies instead. They're lined up on the floor, the cold keeping them from decaying quickly, but they're still a mess. Eleven pirates, men and women, scarred and tough-looking, and your uncle, all with their eyes open, staring at a nothing that's even bigger than space. Your uncle's shirt is blackened from blaster fire. They must have shot him soon after boarding. You lean down and take out his identification card from his pocket, running your finger over the holo-picture of him, the one where he's not horribly pale, the one where his lips aren't blue and his eyes aren't cloudy. The one where he isn't dead.

You wanted to be just like him—you wanted to have adventures and see the universe. You didn't want to believe there were rules.

See where it got him, your mother would say. *See where it got you.*

Leaning over his body, you close his eyes. "I love you," you tell him, brushing his hair back from his face. "I love you and all your hidden depths."

On your way out, you can't help but notice how nine of those eleven pirates died, though. They were sliced open or stabbed through. One was missing a limb as though it had been pulled clean off her.

You find the Charkazak in the cockpit, pressing buttons with those long, delicate fingers, his dagger-like feet balanced easily against the floor. He turns toward you swiftly, a blur of gray skin and gleaming black carapace, his body hunched, as if braced for flight.

"I made dinner," you say lamely, heart pounding.

He doesn't immediately respond. You watch as he slowly relaxes and wonder if, for a moment, he'd thought you were stupid enough to attack him.

"It's ready, b-but I could j-just bring you a plate if you're b-busy." You're stammering.

He touches the screen again, twice, quickly, then begins to unfurl toward you. "I am honored by your hospitality," he says, and each time he speaks, you are startled anew that he sounds almost human. "We will eat together."

You go together through the hall, with you walking in front. You can hear him behind you, can hear the clattering sound of his many feet, and you steel yourself not to look, because you're afraid that if you do, despite everything, you'll run. You'll scream.

10. *Good food is universal. And it's universally true that you're not going to get any good food in space.*

IN THE GALLEY, he manages to perch on the bench while you plate the goulash. He waits, watching.

Finally, he says, "I'm called Reth."

Which is odd, because of course you knew he must have a name, but you'd never have asked him for it. "I'm Tera."

"Tera," he echoes, and then begins to eat, his long fingers making him seem like a mantis.

You wait until you've pulled out the cheese and apple-quince paste to ask him the question that's been haunting you. "What are you going to do with me?"

He tilts his head, studying you. "I know you're afraid. I even know why."

You are silent, because of course you're scared. And of course he knows why.

"They caught me off the salty sea of Callisto—and I heard them talking while they processed me. I am on my way to be harvested for experiments and organs, just like the rest of my race."

You study his strange face—those luminous eyes, the grayish color of his skin, those tattooed marks that remind you of the stripes on a tiger, his high cheekbones, and the sharp elegance of his features, which make him both almost human and very alien. You hear the anger in his voice, but he's got something to be angry about.

"I know what they say about my people. I know the rumors of savagery and horror. Not all of it is untrue, but the war—the reasons you have heard it was declared, those are *lies*. The InterPlanetary government wanted us to fight their wars, wanted our own government to sacrifice its children, and when the Charkazaks would not become a slave race, they decided to destroy us and engineer the army they desired from our flesh."

He could be lying, but he doesn't sound like he's lying.

He could be mistaken, but he doesn't sound like his knowledge is secondhand.

"I'm sorry," you say, because you can't imagine being hunted across the galaxy, whatever the reason.

Reth shakes his head. "No, don't say that. Because I have become like your legends about my people. I can kill quickly and surely now—and as for where I am taking this ship, I am completing the course that your uncle had set. I am planning on docking and destroying those scientists who would have cut me open and used my body for their experiments. I am going to destroy their laboratory, and I am going to free whatever creatures are being tormented there." He slams down two of his fists on the table and then seems startled by the action. He looks over at you with haunted, hunted eyes. He was trying to stop you from being scared, and he thinks he's scared you worse.

But he hasn't really. He's just startled you. You never heard of any Charkazaks saving anyone, and the anger in his voice is righteous fury, not the desire for bloodshed. He might not sell you to anyone, you realize. Might not rip you apart or eat you. Might not even mean you any harm at all, despite being the scariest thing you've ever seen.

You force yourself to reach across the table and touch his arm. His skin feels smooth, almost like patent leather. He tenses as your fingers brush up his arm and then goes entirely still.

"This dish you made is very good," he says suddenly, and you can hear in his voice a shy nervousness that fills you with a sudden giddy power. "I told you I knew how to work the cooking things—but all the food was unfamiliar. I ate one of the green packages and found it entirely strange. I feel sure I was supposed to do something more to it, but I wasn't sure what. . . ."

You keep your hand on his arm a moment more, fingers dragging over his skin, and his words gutter out. You wonder when the last time it was that someone touched him—or touched him without anger. You wonder how lonely it's possible to become out in the void of space.

The comm crackles at that moment, a voice booming from the speakers in the wall. "Centurion ship *Orion* hailing the *Celeris*. Are you there, Captain Lloyd?"

Reth's eyes narrow and he rises, looming above you on those long black legs.

"I know what you're thinking," he says softly. It makes you try to imagine what it would be like to grow up with all the world against you. "But if they know I'm here, they will destroy your ship. They won't face me—they've heard the same stories you have. They'll kill us both to avoid facing me."

Don't be afraid of silence, your uncle told you. *Silence shows your strength.*

You know it's not the nicest thing you've ever done, especially because you're pretty sure Reth's correct about the Centurions' likelihood of blowing up the ship rather than fighting him, but you make yourself stay quiet as the seconds tick by. Reth needs you to go to that comm, but you need things from him, too. Promises.

"Please," he says again.

"If you want my help, you have to agree to my terms," you say. "Agree that you'll teach me how to fly. That we will split the salvage profits from the pirate ship fifty-fifty. And that we'll be partners."

"Partners," he echoes, as though he's trying out the word, as though he doesn't know what to do with it. As though you're giving him something, instead of asking for something from him.

Have a bottom line, your uncle told you. *Sometimes to make a deal, you've got to walk away from a deal.*

But there isn't going to be any walking away this time. There was nowhere to walk to, not for either one of you.

"Agreed," he says, and the relief in his voice is enormous. You probably could have asked him for a *lot* more, and he would have agreed. You're even worse at this bargaining thing than you thought.

"And you have to agree that once we finish attacking the planet of the mad scientists, we'll take some actually profitable jobs," you amend, trying your best to sound tough. "Since I don't think we're going to get paid for the last one."

The comm crackles again. "Captain Lloyd, are you there? Please respond."

"Agreed, Tera," Reth says softly, like a vow.

11. *One more for the road. There really are no rules. There's laws and there's right and wrong, but those aren't rules. You make it up the best you can as you go along.*

You grin at Reth and go over to feed your uncle's ID into the comm. "This is Captain Tera Lloyd of the *Celeris,*" you say, once you get the right frequency. "Captain David Lloyd—my uncle—is dead, and I have taken control of the ship. We were in distress, but you're a little late to be of much help, *Orion.*"

Reth watches you speak, smiling a fierce alien smile as you tell the Centurions to buzz off, swearing up and down that they don't need to board and you don't need a tow. Finally, you agree to a small bribe, pull out your uncle's ID card, and wire the credits over.

The whole thing reminds you of one of your uncle's stories. You hope it would have made him laugh. You hope it would have made him proud.

You know you've been wrong a lot since you left home, but as you look out at the stars and the Charkazak begins to explain how the controls work, you begin to believe that you might still have a chance to become one-half of the best smuggling duo of all time.

WAR DOG

★

by Michael Barretta

The Dog was an Abomination. She was also his only companion.

HE SLOWED for a feathered corpse in the middle of the road. Up above, the local troop of macaques shrieked at a flock of gene-crafted micro-raptors. He rounded the blind curve and jerked the steering wheel back to avoid a washout from last night's thunderstorm. The truck bounced across broken asphalt, and the steering wheel twisted out of his hands. From the corner of his eye, he saw a man emerging from the woods. He jammed the brakes and his truck left the road, plowing to a stop into the soft red dirt undercut from the crumbling asphalt.

Not a man, but a shroom. The figure staggered, hands outstretched, and pressed its naked body against the side glass. He could see the delicate snowflake tracery of white rhizome fibers under its skin. The shroom's eyes glinted clear and blue. Its slack mouth drooled. The creature broke away, leaving a moist trail across the car. Its eyes turned skyward and fixed on a power pole draped with broken electrical lines and wild jasmine. It stepped away towards the pole, cast a look over its shoulder at him, almost as if it was still a person, and climbed.

He took his phone from his pocket and dialed 911.

"Gulf Breeze 911, where is your emergency?"

"Yes, this is Major William Jackson, 3rd Florida Infantry, Retired. I need to report a shroom on Soundside Drive."

331

"Okay," said the operator. "Are you sure it's a shroom?"

"Yes, it's a shroom. I know what one looks like."

"Of course, Major. Has it fruited yet?"

"No, not yet. It just started climbing." The former human, infected with a weaponized version of *Ophiocordyceps unilateralis*, clawed its way up the pole with fierce resolve.

"Can you show it to me?"

"Yes, hold on." He tabbed on the camera feature of the phone and spun it to face the shroom.

"We have your location. Can you vacate the area?"

"I ran off the road. I thought I was avoiding a person, and my truck is stuck."

"Do you have personal protective equipment?" Her voice took on a new urgency.

"Yes, I do. I think." He opened up the glove compartment and took out a government-supplied filtered hood. Three of them crowded the glove box.

"Major, we have a hazmat team on the way. We would like you to stay in your car and put on your personal protective gear. I've sent out a cellular warning to all citizens in the area. We want you to stay connected and keep us informed of the shroom's status."

"I think I can get upwind."

"Are you sure it's the only one?"

"No." It was a good question of the 911 operator to ask. There was rarely just one shroom. Infections typically occurred in clusters.

"Best if you stay in the car."

"Okay, I can do that." He leaned forward to get a better view. The shroom had climbed three quarters of the way up the pole. He propped his phone on the dashboard. "Can you still see it?"

"Yes, we can. We don't want you to worry. The hazmat team will decontaminate your vehicle should the shroom fruit before we get there, but if you have any powered ventilation we would like you to turn it off. Would you like me to pray with you?"

"No, I've already prayed, but you could pray for me; I don't mind listening," he lied. He behaved with enough piety to not arouse suspicion and used his combat-wounded veteran status to excuse the acts of contempt that he could not hide.

He opened one of the filter hood packages and pulled the battery lanyard. The filter pack hummed. He put it over his head and cinched it down around his neck. The hood fogged around his mouth and nose with every exhalation, but it wasn't too uncomfortable.

The shroom reached the top of the pole and checked its grip, tightening and loosening its limbs. A mockingbird, unaware of the danger, harried the creature. The shroom shuddered, going through the terminal phase of its design.

Then he remembered his only neighbor, the Dog.

The wind was blowing from the west. If the shroom fruited, its spores would drift over the Dog's homestead. Even if they didn't, the decontamination team would fog the area with caustic chemicals.

He decided.

He stepped out of his truck, abandoning its relative safety, and ran farther up the road. He took off his hood to breathe more easily and turned up the narrow dirt path that led to the Dog's home. Branches whipped at his face, and twice he ducked under immense dewy spans of banana-spider webs. He broke out into a clearing and slowed to catch his breath. It had been a long time since he had run. The emergency hood hummed in his hand.

He had seen the Dog twice before, and they had acknowledged each other at a careful distance. As veterans, they shared the bond of war, but whereas he had emerged from conflict a respected soldier, she had come out as an illegal gene splice, a piece of dangerous biological equipment.

A neat, wood-shingled house sat in the clearing. The Dog stood up in the midst of her garden with a small hand shovel held like a weapon. Leaf mold flecked the velvet gray fur of her arms.

He felt her fear, surprise, and anger. Dogs were focused telepaths by design and imprinted on their handlers at an intense and intimate level, but an unbonded person in close proximity could still feel strong emotional bleed-over. He imagined the Dog deciding whether to kill him or not. In the CSA, the Christian States of America, she was an abomination and regarded as military property to be neutralized by an ordnance disposal team, but he had known about her presence for almost a year and had not reported her. He hoped that that would work in his favor. He could see her muscles tense as she decided the best course of action.

"Shroom," he said. "You are in the dispersal range."

<Immune> he felt. The word filled his head and popped like a soap bubble. Her voice was soft and feminine and un-doglike. Her design was mostly human, so much so that she was inter-fertile with baseline humans, but that held little weight in the CSA. "Still, they'll decontaminate the whole area. You know what that means."

<Despair and sadness>, he felt. Hard work had built her hidden homestead in the middle of a blight zone.

"The hazmat team will arrive in a few minutes. Once they secure the scene, they'll disinfect with an aerial attack."

She bolted for her house and retrieved a military pack designed for her body. Like a good soldier, she was ready to bug out at a moment's notice. She surveyed all that she would lose, came to him, and hugged him. Her body, taut and muscular, smelled like warm sun. He could not remember the last time he'd been hugged.

She stepped back.

<Thank you>

"Be safe," he said.

She ran towards the edge of the woods, and, just before reaching it, dropped to all fours and moved with the grace and power of a cheetah, her spine curling and springing open, covering ground in twelve-foot leaps. She vanished into the brush.

He returned to his truck, winded from the exertion and wet with sweat. He put his hood back on. Military vehicles circled the shroom's pole. Amber strobes flashed, and men in hazmat suits set up decontamination gear. He looked up in time to see the shroom convulse. Ropey pink antlers burst out of its skull. The shroom swung its head, rattling the antlers and releasing a pink mist of spores that caught the wind and drifted. The shroom shuddered again, and more thick antlers erupted from its back, growing and branching with astonishing fungal speed. The yellow-suited hazmat team finished their setup, and a jet of flame erupted from the fire gun's nozzle to engulf the shroom. The antlers crisped, turned black, and broke away.

"Did you call this in?" asked the supervising officer.

"Yeah."

"Good job. Is your hood cinched down tight?"

"Yeah, I'm good."

"Okay, as soon as we clean up the scene we are decontaminating the area. You know what that means."

"I do."

The shroom fell from the pole, hitting the ground with a wet, hissing splat. Broken pieces rolled away, and the team hosed it down with more fire until the thing turned into a pile of ash. They worked the surrounding area with chemicals. Leaves dissolved and dripped under the chemical attack.

"Fruiting bodies visible upon arrival," said the supervising officer into his radio. "High concentration of spore release. Wind speed is light and variable. I'm recommending immediate chemical decontamination."

"Roger that," squawked the radio. "Chopper is on the way."

"This is going to be inconvenient," said the major to himself.

In the hospital isolation ward, he breathed the acrid chemical mist to purge his lungs of any shroom spores that might have infiltrated his lungs. Ventilation fans whirred for a few minutes. He dried himself as best as he could with the paper towels. The sealed door opened.

"Major," said a nurse. She handed him a paper hospital smock and watched as he dressed. "Would you follow me?"

He followed her, and she drew back a curtain.

"In here, please," she said.

He sat at the edge of the examining table. The curtain was pulled aside, and the Sisters of Eternal Grace stepped in to pray over him. One of the crones put her bony, knuckled hand on his forehead and tapped him. They rattled their donation can in front of him when they finished. He looked down at the hospital smock.

"I don't have any pockets."

The lead sister frowned at him and rattled the can again.

"I don't . . ."

Her face twisted into an uncharitable grimace of disgust.

The doctor entered. "Get out, hags."

The sisters scowled in unison but turned on their heels and left in a whirl of gray skirts and sensible shoes.

"You know they are going to bill you for that prayer. The VA will cover their costs, but you should be nice to them; they're connected like the mob," said the doctor. "Are you feeling okay? You look like shit."

He coughed. "I'm okay. Does that stuff work?"

"The shower washes off any spores on your skin, but the mist? No, it just scorches your lungs. The spores are encysted. The prayer is the best treatment."

"Great."

"I've got something for you." He reached into his lab coat pocket and took out a bottle of pills, migraine medicine.

"Where did you get them?"

"There are ways, and then there are ways. People need things, and I can get them. How do you think I can help so many?"

"I can't pay for them."

"I still owe you."

"That debt was paid a long time ago."

"That debt can never be paid, but let me try. You need to be careful."

"About what?"

"The sampler found chimera hair and skin cells on your clothes."

"I was wearing old clothes from the war."

"Yeah, you can try that excuse, but the sampler is more sophisticated than that. It's the best piece of equipment we have in this hospital, and it is hotwired to the DOFF. They'll be watching you. You know how they love rooting out heretics and atheists."

"Yes, and Zionists and Papists and Colored." Every society needed an underclass to absorb injustice and excess force.

"Do you need a ride home?"

"No, I'll walk. I need the exercise."

"You also need some clothes. It's a long walk."

"We've walked farther on less."

"Yes, we have. You're good to go. I'll have the nurse bring you some clothes. The reverend-director of the hospital will want to stop by and pad your bill with another prayer or two."

"Prayer is the best medicine."

"I thought that was laughter."

"Not anymore."

Raindrops pummeled the road. He walked into a nightmare landscape of dripping, gray-green slime that coagulated in puddles and ran across the road in sticky, mucosal sheets. The aerial decontamination spray had turned the surrounding woods into a melted, Dalí-esque landscape. The larger trees resembled wilted saguaro, bent and sagging in graceful, bone-less curves. Whip-thin branches of heartwood dripped to the ground. The delicate gray bones of small creatures caught in the dissolving spray littered the sticky ground. His truck remained in the washout. With a jack and boards pulled from the bed of the truck, he managed to extricate it from the ditch and drive home.

Inside his home, he wedged a two-by-four into the cleats to bar the door shut. He showered off the slime of the melted forest. As he dressed, the wind shifted with frontal passage, and the house rocked in another direction. The temperature dropped as the cold front engulfed the house. Bizarre weather typified the new normal. He started a fire in the stone fireplace and hung a battered teakettle over it. Thunder boomed. Hailstones pummeled the roof. The ghosts of his family, trapped and framed above the fireplace, regarded him from a world before the I-War and the Second Civil War.

Another roll of thunder shook the house, and he popped two of the doctor's pain pills to break up the loci of pain that accreted around the piece of Yankee shrapnel lodged in his head. After a few moments, the white-hot dots of agony abated. He closed his eyes and listened to the crackle of the wood fire and the hiss of boiling water from his kettle.

Someone knocked on the front door. He roused to awareness and fetched his shotgun. He chambered a shell and peered through the glass peephole.

The Dog.

He unbarred the door and held it open. She was soaking wet, shivered in the unseasonal cold.

<Nowhere to go>

Desperate and intimate and voiceless thoughts flowed through his mind like sound. Her camouflage T-shirt clung to her shoulders. Blood oozed from a hailstone cut above her left eye. She wiped rain from her face, and he caught sight of the razor-sharp dew claw on her forearm. If she wanted the house, she could take it from him. He stepped back, swinging the door wider.

"I'll get you some dry clothes." He put the gun down and went into a backroom.

<Thank you>

He felt her gratitude and uncertainty follow him.

The Dog knelt in front of the fireplace and held her hands spread-fingered toward the fire. She turned to look over her shoulder. He handed her some old clothes that had belonged to his wife, and a towel. She stripped in front of the fireplace with immodest military efficiency. Soft velvet fur thinned on her breasts and thickened somewhat at the swell of her vulva. She dried herself with the towel and dressed. The remains of her home stained her feet milky green.

<Nothing left>

"I'm sorry. Are you hungry?'

<Yes>

He opened a packet of dehydrated chicken soup and dumped it into the tea kettle.

"It will take a few minutes"

<Smells good>

He added another log to the fire and stirred the soup mix. Ants boiled from the log and stepped into a miniature hell. They crisped in the embers. The Dog sat on the threadbare couch and curled her legs under her and tucked her hands between her thighs. He was not afraid even though there were strong reasons for baseline humans to fear Dogs. They were stronger and smarter, exotic and dangerous, beautiful, and, above all else, different. She was typical of her kind.

<You have mods?> she asked.

"Yes, I was a soldier once." Most soldiers of the old USA featured some viral-delivered enhancements. He saw pretty well in low-light conditions, couldn't run to fat even if he wanted to, and healed a bit faster than before. The processes that modified him had created her from scratch.

<Maybe you're a Dog>

"Maybe you're a woman."

She smiled against the exhaustion that threatened to overwhelm her. Her canines protruded a bit from her lips. He served the soup.

"You're safe here."

<I know>

She finished the soup and set the bowl down on the end table.

"What's your name?" he asked.

<M'ling> She slouched down on the couch and closed her eyes to sleep.

He waited for the fire to burn down to a safe level. He pulled down a comforter from the back of the couch and covered her. He curled on the adjacent sofa and fell asleep.

Under M'ling's ministrations, the backyard bloomed with fruit and vegetable and flower. Low-level agents of the Department of Faith Formation intruded several times, but each time she sensed their presence and vanished. At night, when the air cooled, they talked. She told him how a sniper killed her handler in Venezuela, and how she ripped the sniper's throat out with her teeth. She told him how she battled back from the psychic shock of his loss, her inability to accept another handler, and her escape from the decommissioning facility. In turn, he told her about fighting in Taiwan during the I-War with China, and later in Virginia, during the Second Civil War. They slept together, at first for companionship, and then for something more. At night he stroked the length of her body, soft velvet over hard muscle.

Stories of handlers that slept with their Dogs were ubiquitous in rocket-shattered Taiwanese cities. Contemplating bestiality with manufactured creatures of ethereal beauty was the least of sins in that brief and violent war. Handlers and their Dogs returning from long-range patrols self-segregated at the firebase, and it only added to the mystery and speculation. Once, on a mission, his fire team found a handler carrying the long, lithe frame of his Dog, not over his shoulder, but in his arms like a bridegroom carrying his bride. The handler, agonized with fatigue, refused to let anyone else touch her. He fell to his knees and then collapsed from exhaustion over her body. They convinced him to bury her. Over the grave, the handler cried and murmured gentle words, and when he had finished he said, "I can't."

"Can't what?"

"I can't. Do you understand?"

"I do."

"You can't."

When they looked away the handler shot himself in the head and they dug another grave.

At the time he could not understand the connection, the powerful bond between Dog and handler, each devoted to the other so intimately that the descriptive terms ascribed to the connection were meaningless. It was what made them such a terrifyingly effective weapon system.

Now he thought they worked well together, in a way in which he never expected to do again.

She stood and looked to him. <They're here again>

He heard a vehicle pull into his drive. He walked to the front door and waited. A man wearing a modified Roman collar, a badge, and a sidearm walked towards his porch. Two other men scanned the area. He opened the door before the man knocked.

"Major Jackson, I am Reverend-Inspector Carlyle."

"In what capacity are you here today?"

The man looked perplexed. "What do you mean?"

"Are you here as a reverend or as an inspector?"

"Both. Always."

"What can I do for you?"

"I have traces unexplained by your statements. Where is the abomination?"

"On my front step."

The reverend-inspector grinned with professional malice and indignation.

"Right. Harboring an abomination is a capital offense."

"Every offense is a capital offense these days."

"The purest metal comes from the hottest fires."

"Clever."

The reverend-inspector was the worst kind, a thick layer of true believer over a core of bully, the type to shout damnation on the street corners yet never lift a finger in a poorhouse or soup kitchen.

"May I come in?"

He stepped forward and was pushed back.

He moved his hand to draw his sidearm.

"Do you think that you can draw that weapon before I do something about it?"

The reverend-inspector moved his hand away from the weapon. Confusion and genuine fear crossed his face. He was unaccustomed to resistance.

"I have full authority . . ."

"Major."

"What?"

"Major. What you want to say is: *Major, I have full authority.* You will address me by my military rank. I've earned it, and you are not coming in my house without a warrant. This isn't the United States. Are you a Yankee?"

The reverend-inspector's face darkened at the insult. "Major, your story to my associates was unconvincing. There were no squatters in the woods. And I found these." He held up silver dog tags that flashed in the sun. "When I come back it will be with a warrant."

He stepped onto his porch, and the reverend-inspector stumbled backwards down the two steps.

"If you come back, we will duel over any further insult. Do you accept? I'll register our intent with the county."

The inspector flushed red, unprepared for the personal challenge. Duels were rare, but permitted between CSA landowners and military officers.

"I, I . . ."

"I thought not. Get off my property."

The reverend-inspector turned, stalked to his county car, and drove away.

M'ling emerged from the other room and pressed her body against his back. She wrapped her arms around him, and leaned her head on his shoulder.

"He will come back."

<They always come back>

He locked his desk drawer and stepped into the hangar. The helicopters inherited from the USA were slotted in their spaces but immobile for a lack of spare parts. All the mechanics he supervised had already left for Friday services, a euphemism for drinking moonshine in the back room of the local roadhouse.

He drove past a chain gang of un-saved and un-white conscripts supervised by mirror-shaded, shotgun-toting deputy-deacons. He stopped at the toll bridge and honked his horn for the attendant to lift the reflector-bedazzled log gate that blocked his way. The attendant came out of the booth and walked away from him.

"Hey, I need to get home," he yelled to the attendant, but the man entered the tollhouse and closed the door.

"Under new management, Major," said a voice from behind the driver's window. His door was wrenched open and a gun pressed against his temple.

He reached for his own gun in the glove box.

"No you don't, Major. No you don't. Please step out."

The pressure from the pistol barrel eased and he unfastened his seatbelt. He stepped out and recognized the highwaymen, a former military unit that did the unchristian work it took to enforce a Christian state. The man with the gun to his head pistol-whipped him, and he dropped to his knees. Two more heavy blows pounded on his head. Stars exploded, but he held to consciousness.

Rough hands grabbed him and dragged him into the surrounding woods. Twisted hemp rope secured him face-down over the hood of a car. They were strong and fast and, like him, ex-military.

"Major, what is good?"

He spit blood out of his mouth. Some of his teeth felt loose.

"I said, what is good?"

A fist punched him in the back of his head, bouncing his face against the hood of the car. '19 Mustang, he thought. The last year they made them.

"I'll tell you. Good is that which pleases God, and what pleases God is what I have to do. To the matter at hand: There is an abomination in our midst, and it needs to be purged. Fire has to be fought with fire, an abominable act for an abominable act."

A knife sliced open the back of his pants and eager hands jerked his trousers down. He breathed in fast, fearful pants.

"Where is the abomination?"

He remained silent.

"When we are done you know what you must do."

When they finished taking turns, they cut him free, and he fell to the ground. They left him alone and walked back to their camp behind the tollhouse. Darkness fell, and he pulled himself up and limped to his truck. Warm blood dressed his legs and back.

He drove home naked and broken.

He did not need to explain.

She knew.

He radiated humiliation and pain.

She reached for him, but he kept walking through the house to the backyard. He stepped into the small pool converted into a fishpond and sat in the water up to his neck. Carp and brim nibbled at him. In time, he went to bed, and she lay next to him, her hand on his chest. Between them, in the still of the night, thought and feeling ebbed and flowed in a gentle tide.

He awoke alone, his throat raw, his insides dirty. In the bathroom, he looked in the mirror and saw a small snowflake tracery of white on his cheek. He drank tepid water until he gagged. She was not in bed and he went in search. The backdoor to the living room lay open to the night. Dark clouds scudded across the full moon. M'ling stood on the steps in the pool that he sat in earlier. She glowed ghostly in the pre-dawn light, a specter worthy of darkest fear. The water lapped at her ankles. Naked and alien, she washed shadowed blood from her forearms and chest and mouth.

The highwaymen did not know what they had unleashed.

Predatory eyeshine regarded him with love. She stepped from the pool and embraced him. Retractable-clawed hands caressed the fibrous cluster at his cheek. Her dew claw rested across his throat. She would do it if he asked.

"No," he said. "I want every minute."

He made arrangements. The doctor visited him and injected him with an expensive antifungal that slowed the progression but could not stop it.

Long ago, the doctor, then a medic, paralyzed with fear over the onslaught of incoming artillery rounds, had curled into an exposed fetal ball in the open battlefield. The major, then a captain, had dragged the doctor into the shelter of the root ball crater of a fallen tree. Anti-personnel shells burst overhead, filling the air with white-hot blades of Yankee metal. They outlasted the fierce barrage and survived the night and spoke no more of it.

The doctor owed him.

"Do this for me and our debt is settled."

"I will."

The thirty-foot-long speedboat rolled under the topside weight of three big outboard engines and six fifty-five-gallon drums of fuel on the aft deck. Big men dressed in night camouflage unloaded alcohol, pornography, medicine, and other hard-to-find necessities. The run back to Cuba would take twenty hours, but in less than two they would be beyond the decrepit CSA Coast Guard.

By the light of the half moon, the fungal rhizomes luminesced. The fibers spread across his face and neck and reached for the thoughts in his head. The smuggler crew kept their distance. As she embraced him, his hand drifted to the swell of her belly. He pressed, feeling for a kick, but felt none. Maybe it was too soon.

<It's your daughter>

"Our daughter."

She kissed him one last time and boarded the boat.

As the boat receded into the night, sadness attenuated. His connection grew weaker and weaker until he could no longer feel her. He dropped to the wet ground, empty and hollow.

By unthinking instinct, he selected a dead pine that offered unobstructed access to the wind. Compulsion drove him to the topmost reaches, and he swayed in the amber morning light, rocking to-and-fro in the breeze. He thought his last thoughts of love and war before bizarre biological processes bundled his memories into microscopic spores that erupted from him in a pink haze to be scattered on the winds.

CONTRIBUTORS

Charlie Jane Anders writes about science fiction for io9.com, and she's hard at work on a fantasy novel. You can find her work in the *McSweeney's Joke Book of Book Jokes*, *Best Science Fiction Of The Year 2009*, *Sex for America*, and other anthologies. Anders has also contributed to *Mother Jones*, the *Wall Street Journal*, the *San Francisco Chronicle*, *ZYZZYVA*, *Pindeldyboz*, *Strange Horizons*, Tor.com, *The Magazine of Science Fiction and Fantasy*, *Asimov's Science Fiction Magazine*, *Lightspeed*, and many other publications. She organizes the Writers With Drinks reading series and with Annalee Newitz, she co-edited the anthology *She's Such a Geek* and published an indy magazine called *other* (a *"magazine of pop culture and politcs for the new outcasts"*). She wrote a novel called *Choir Boy*, which won a Lambda Literary Award and was a finalist for the Edmund White Award. As a contestant on *To Tell the Truth*, she wom $1,000. She has recently sold two novels to Tor, the first, *All the Birds in the Sky*, is scheduled for early 2016 publication, and has also completed a fantasy novel, and the only question I have is, how did she find time to write them?

Michael Barretta is a retired U.S. Navy Helicopter pilot with deployments around the world. He works for a major defense contractor. He holds a Master's degree in Strategic Planning and International Negotiation from the Naval Post-Graduate School and is nearing a completion of a Master's Degree in English from the University of West Florida. He has been published in *Jim Baen's Universe*, *New Scientist*, *Redstone*, and various anthologies. He resides in Gulf Breeze, Florida with his wife, Mary Jane, and five children.

★ ★ ★

Holly Black is the author of bestselling contemporary fantasy books for kids and teens. Some of her titles include The Spiderwick Chronicles (with Tony DiTerlizzi), The Modern Faerie Tale series, The Good Neighbors graphic novel trilogy (with Ted Naifeh), and her new Curse Workers series, which includes *White Cat* and *Red Glove*. She has been a finalist for the Mythopoeic Award, a finalist for an Eisner Award, and the recipient of the Andre Norton Award. She currently lives in New England with her husband, Theo, in a house with a secret door.

Robert R. Chase is Chief Counsel at an Army research laboratory. He has published more than two dozen stories in Analog and Asimov's as well as three novels, most notably *The Game of Fox and Lion*. The Army wants you to know that his opinions are his own and do not reflect those of the Army or the Federal Government. Really.

Eric Leif Davin, a science fiction historian, is the author of two books about science fiction—*Pioneers of Wonder: Conversations with the Founders of Science Fiction* and *Partners in Wonder: Women and the Birth of Science Fiction: 1926-1965*. In 2014 Damnation Books published his debut novel, *The Desperate and the Dead*, a work of historical horror. Its sequel, *The Scarlet Queen*, will appear in 2015.

Seth Dickinson is a lapsed doctoral student at NYU, where he studied social neuroscience, and both an alumnus of and an instructor at the Alpha Workshop for Young Writers. Since his 2012 debut, his fiction has appeared—or will soon appear—in *Lightspeed, Analog, Strange Horizons,* and *Beneath Ceaseless Skies*.

David Drake was attending Duke University Law School when he was drafted. He served the next two years in the Army, spending 1970 as an enlisted interrogator with the 11th armored Cavalry in Viet Nam and Cambodia. Upon return he completed his law degree at Duke and was for eight years Assistant Town Attorney for Chapel Hill, North Carolina. He has been a full-time freelance writer since 1981. His books include the genre-defining and bestselling Hammer's Slammers series, the RCN series including *What Distant Deeps, In the Stormy Red Sky, The Road of Danger,* and many more.

Stephen Gaskell is an author, games writer, and champion of science. His work has been published in numerous venues including *Writers of the Future, Interzone,* and *Clarkesworld.* He has imagined worlds for Ubisoft and Amplitude Studios, written treatments for Hollywood, and consulted for disruption technology think-tanks. Currently Lead Writer at Spiral Arm Studios, he is preparing the world for the coruscating vision of Maelstrom's Edge. In addition, he is currently seeking representation for his first novel, *The Unborn World,* a post-apocalyptic thriller set in Lagos, Nigeria. For news and freebies sign up for his newsletter at stephengaskell.com.

Matthew Johnson lives in Ottawa, Ontario with his wife Megan and their two sons. His novel *Fall From Earth,* a feminist Confucianist space opera, was published by Bundoran Press in 2009; a collection of his short fiction, *Irregular Verbs and Other Stories,* was published in 2014 by ChiZine Publications. In his other life he is Director of Education for MediaSmarts, a nonprofit media literacy organization, for which he writes blogs, lesson plans, articles, creates educational computer games and occasionally does pirate voices.

Derek Künsken writes science fiction, fantasy, and horror in Gatineau, Québec. His fiction has appeared in *Beneath Ceaseless Skies, On Spec, Black Gate,* and multiple times in *Asimov's.* "Persephone Descending" was his first appearance in both *Analog* and *StarShipSofa.* Derek has been short-listed for the Aurora and won the Asimov's Readers' Award, while his work has been podcast in all three Escape Artists podcasts, translated for several foreign sf magazines, and has appeared in the *Best Horror of the Year*. Derek blogs at www.blackgate.com and tweets at @DerekKunsken. "Persephone Descending" is part of a larger space opera universe he's been building recently.

★ ★ ★

William Ledbetter lives near Dallas with his family and too many animals. A Writers of the Future award winner, Bill is also a consulting editor at *Heroic Fantasy Quarterly*. Bill is the administrator of the annual Jim Baen Memorial Writing Contest for Baen Books. He can be found on the web at http://www.williamledbetter.com/.

★ ★ ★

David D. Levine is the author of *Arabella of Mars* (Tor 2016) and over fifty SF and fantasy stories. His story "Tk'Tk'Tk" won the Hugo Award, and he has been shortlisted for awards including the Hugo, Nebula, and Campbell. Stories have appeared in *Asimov's, Analog, F&SF*, five Year's Best anthologies, and his award-winning collection *Space Magic* from Wheatland Press. David is a contributor to George R. R. Martin's bestselling shared-world series Wild Cards. He is also a member of publishing cooperative Book View Cafe and nonprofit Oregon Science Fiction Conventions Inc. He has narrated podcasts for Escape Pod, PodCastle, and StarShipSofa, and his video "Dr. Talon's Letter to the Editor" was a finalist for the Parsec Award. In 2010 he spent two weeks at a simulated Mars base in the Utah desert. David lives in Portland, Oregon with his wife Kate Yule. His web site is www.daviddlevine.com.

★ ★ ★

Linda Nagata is a Nebula and Locus-award-winning author. Her more recent work includes short fiction "Nahiku West," runner up for the 2013 Theodore Sturgeon Memorial Award, and the novel *The Red: First Light,* a near-future military thriller that was a finalist for both the Nebula Award and the John W. Campbell Memorial Award.

Though best known for science fiction, she also writes fantasy, exemplified by her "scoundrel lit" series *Stories of the Puzzle Lands*. Linda has spent most of her life in Hawaii, where she's been a writer, a mom, and a programmer of database-driven websites. She lives with her husband in their long-time home on the island of Maui.

Brad R. Torgersen is the author of numerous stories, novelettes, and novellas which have appeared in the pages of *Analog Science Fiction and Fact* magazine, *Orson Scott Card's InterGalactic Medicine Show* webzine, Mike Resnick's *Galaxy's Edge* magazine, and beyond. He's a two-time winner of the *Analog* AnLab readers' choice award, a three-time Hugo award nominee, and a winner in the 26th annual Writers and Illustrators of the Future Contest. A full-time healthcare computer geek, Torgersen is a Chief Warrant Officer in the U.S. Army Reserve. He lives in Utah with his wife and daughter. His first novel, *The Chaplain's War* was released by Baen Books in 2014, preceded by his short fiction collections *Lights in the Deep* and *Racers of the Night*.

Michael Z. Williamson is retired military, having served twenty-five years in the U.S. Army and the U.S. Air Force. He was deployed for Operation Iraqi Freedom and Operation Desert Fox. Williamson is a state-ranked competitive shooter in combat rifle and combat pistol. He has consulted on military matters, weapons and disaster preparedness for Discovery Channel and Outdoor Channel productions and is Editor-at-Large for Survivalblog, with 300,000 weekly readers. In addition, Williamson tests and reviews firearms and gear for manufacturers. Williamson's books set in his Freehold Universe include *Freehold, Better to Beg Forgiveness . . .* , *Do Unto Others . . .*, and *When Diplomacy Fails . . .* He is also the author of *The Hero*—written in collaboration with *New York Times* bestselling author John Ringo. Williamson was born in England, raised in Liverpool and Toronto, Canada, and now lives in Indianapolis with his family.

Year's Best Military Science Fiction and Space Opera

You Decide Who Wins!

Other anthologies tell you which stories were the year's best—*we're letting you decide which of these you liked best*. Baen Books is pleased to announce the inaugural Year's Best Military Science Fiction and Space Opera Award. The award honors the best of the best in this grand storytelling tradition, and its winner will receive a plaque and an additional $500.00.

**To vote, go to
http://baen.com/yearsbestaward2014**

Registration with Baen Ebooks is required. You may also send a postcard or letter with the name of your favorite story from this volume and its author to Baen Books Year's Best Award, P.O. Box 1188, Wake Forest, NC 27587. Voting closes August 31, 2015. Entries received after voting closes will not be counted.

So hurry, hurry, hurry! The winner will be announced at Dragoncon in Atlanta, held over Labor Day Weekend 2015.